LOVE AT DAWN

A ROMANCE ANTHOLOGY

MEG NAPIER   J. T. BOCK   G. G. GABRIEL

JULIE HALPERSON   SKYE KNIGHT   J. KEELY THRALL

LAUREL WANROW

NAPIERPRESS

SECOND SUNRISE

MEG NAPIER

CHAPTER ONE

"Dad? Dad, where are you?"

Abbie stopped to catch her breath, scanning the beach in both directions and aware that her winded cry probably couldn't be heard by anyone, let alone her father.

The walk from their house took about fifteen minutes, but she had run the path in less than five, frantic with worry when she realized her father was gone yet again.

This wandering off had begun only recently. At first, her father had seemed to take her mother's death from cancer late last fall in stride, repeating frequently that he hoped she had found peace and freedom from pain. He had even protested that there was no need for Abbie to move back in with him. But she had answered with reassurances that her accounting job could be done from anywhere with Internet and that she needed a break from city life.

"Do you know how jealous my friends are that I get to live rent-free in a beautiful house just minutes from the ocean?" Her tone was playful, but the look her father gave her was not.

"Are you running away, Abigail Marie? Has that miscreant been messing with you again?"

They stared at each other in silence, and finally Abbie shrugged.

3

"Maybe? But I do want to be here, Dad. I'll never forgive myself for wasting so many of Mom's last few months trying to fix stupid mistakes instead of spending time with her."

She wasn't going to do anything similar with her father, that was for damn sure. When she moved down here two months ago, abandoning the fight with her cheating, rotten ex over the Brooklyn brownstone they had purchased together, her father had seemed fine. And most of the time, he still seemed fine. His conversations made perfect sense, he was keenly interested in current events, and he asked pertinent questions about the confusing-to-most-laymen SEC regulations Abbie maneuvered around and through in her daily auditing work. And he claimed to love the disorder and attention-demanding aromas that accompanied her part-time Etsy line of vegan cookies.

But this disappearing! And the odd stories he kept telling about the people he was encountering.

For all his seeming mental acuity, her father's gait had deteriorated sharply in recent years, the Vietnam War leg injuries he had managed over the decades with a fierce exercise regimen finally catching up to him. He needed a walker but grudgingly used a cane instead. Solitary walks on the beach were now definitely out of the question, a point both his doctor and his daughter frequently reiterated.

But on random days throughout the past two weeks, Abbie would take a bathroom break from her work and find him missing. She searched the house, modest though it was, certain he must be puttering around somewhere. A quick, frantic check of the garage—but no, thank goodness, he hadn't driven off—and then a frustrated run down the several blocks to the boardwalk.

There were always people on the beach, even on a blustery March morning like today, but Abbie couldn't see his now-diminished figure in either direction.

Where had he gone? It was probably ten days ago that he had first come back, his cheeks red and his eyes moist from fighting the cold ocean breeze.

"I was speaking to the most interesting young man and his little girl. They were building a sand castle, and we talked all about the changes to the coast in the last few years."

"Building a sand castle? Today? It's freezing out there."

"Is it? I didn't notice."

"Dad, your hands are like ice! Where are your gloves? And please tell me you weren't walking on the sand. You shouldn't be down there alone at all, but you have to stay on the boardwalk."

He had only smiled at her and told her not to be such a worrywart.

Worrywart. Who even used words like that anymore?

In the ensuing days they always talked over their morning coffee, and each day he assured her he was planning on reading the paper and working the crossword puzzle. But on this windy, damp morning, he seemed yet again to have changed his mind without telling her.

Which way to search? The path to the north took a curve out of sight not far in the distance, and at that point the boardwalk ended and her father would have to cross over to the sand or move back inland. Going south provided a longer stretch of boardwalk, but at this time of year there were inevitably bicyclists and skateboarders speeding along despite the posted prohibitions.

She peered southward one more time, and a jolt of relief shot through her. He was there, in the distance, heading towards her, slowly but steadily.

She ran and was almost knocked over by a rollerblader herself as the teenager shot her a defiant grin.

"Dad!" Her voice came out in a gasp as she struggled to hide her physical exertion and her distress. "I thought you said you'd tell me if you wanted to go out."

"Yes, sweetheart. But you were on a phone call and looked none too happy with whatever was going on. I wanted to get out and get some air. It's supposed to rain tomorrow, so I wanted to take advantage of this good weather. And I got to talk with Peter again and his lovely daughter, Samantha. She said I could call her Sam."

His eyes sparkled as he spoke, but an inexplicable sense of unease shot through her. Who was this guy and his daughter, and where were they? She peered in the direction her father had been walking but

5

didn't see anyone matching his description. Once more it struck her as odd that a father should be playing with his daughter on the beach on a cold March morning—a school morning, at that.

"Where are they, Dad?"

"Oh, just back there a ways." He gestured vaguely behind him, and Abbie looked again but still didn't see anyone.

"Let's get you home. You may call this good weather, but I think it's cold and damp. I can make you some hot chocolate or a cup of coffee or tea, if you'd like."

"Hot chocolate sounds wonderful, but I don't want to keep you from your work."

"Flexible hours. That's the new corporate mantra, remember? As long as I get my work done on time and show up for important meetings, my actual schedule is up to me."

"Peter was just telling me about his sometimes crazy schedule at the hospital."

"The hospital? What does he do there?"

"He's the head of the ED." Her father shook his head, a smile crinkling his beloved face. "Who knew? I thought that meant only the problem all the ads on tv talk about, and the thing in the hospital was called the ER, but apparently there, like everywhere else, I'm stuck in the last century."

A doctor. That was probably okay, right? An image flashed through her mind of a Venn diagram that included a crazy drifter looking to take advantage of a senior citizen and a responsible physician. The circles most likely never overlapped, thank goodness.

"He must work odd hours if he's free to play at the beach in the morning."

"Yes, he does. But he's anxious to spend as much free time as possible with his little girl. His wife and her parents were killed two years ago in a freak car accident, so his daughter's become his top priority."

"Oh my God. How horrible. It's just the two of them?"

"Yes. His parents live in New York, north of the city, and they come down frequently, or Sam goes to spend time with them. But Peter says it's important that they get through things together."

"Jeez, Dad, it sounds like you know his whole life story."

"I find him easy to talk to. I think you'd like him, sweetheart."

"Oh, no, you don't. No matchmaking. I'm done with men, at least for the foreseeable future."

"Abigail Marie, you're only twenty-five years old. That's a terrible attitude to have. Just because you're well rid of that skunk doesn't mean all men are bad."

Abbie closed her eyes and forced herself not to react. Almost everything in that last sentence rubbed her the wrong way, but the fact that he was losing time was particularly alarming. She was twenty-eight. But he still meant well. She knew he did. The worst disagreement they had ever had was when she told her parents she was engaged to John. They had both stared at her—no cries of joy, no hugs—and her father had finally said, "We were hoping you'd wait a bit, perhaps meet some other . . . get to know other people before settling down. You're still young and John's seen far more of the world than you have. You need to experience things on your own before tying yourself to one person for life."

She had glared at him, incredulous.

"You and Mom have been together since she was in high school. She probably never had time to meet anyone else, let alone get to know them. How can you talk to me about experiencing life on your own?"

"But that was different, darling." Her mom's voice had been gentle, placating. "Your dad was older, he'd been drafted, and we needed to make sure the rest of the world recognized our commitment to each other before he had to leave. And we did, in fact, end up experiencing many aspects of life on our own. Luckily for us, it strengthened our bond once we were finally together again."

Then, as now, Abbie had taken a deep breath and tried to react calmly. She was their only child. They loved her and wanted only the best for her.

"I love John, and I know he loves me. We're going to be happy together, and I want you to be happy for us."

They had been right and she so terribly wrong, but that didn't entitle her father to try and manipulate her now, seven years later.

"I'm sure he's a great guy, Dad, but I'm not looking to get involved with anyone right now." And she certainly wasn't going to admit what she was still chiding herself over: a growing fascination with an unembodied email correspondent, Islandersboy89, with whom she now traded short messages several times a week.

Abbie and her dad began the slow walk back to the house. Her father was leaning heavily on his cane, and Abbie bit her lip.

"I know you were only being polite this morning by not interrupting my phone call, but I'd still rather you tell me instead of going out alone, okay, Dad? Please?"

He stopped and smiled at her.

"I'm an old man, Abbie, darling, not a little child. I've lived here for more than forty years. I think I'll know when it's time to abandon my beloved ocean."

What could she say? What else did he have left? His wife was gone, most of his friends had either died or moved to nursing homes, and she, his only child, had failed to provide him grandchildren. Her parents had never hidden their surprise and abiding delight at her arrival late in their lives when they had thought their chances of conception long past. But it had perhaps been some unacknowledged doubt that had kept Abbie herself from trying to conceive after her headstrong marriage to John.

Thank God they hadn't had children together. She couldn't even imagine the mind games he might have employed with that kind of power over her.

Now she answered her dad's tired smile with a kiss. "I'm not trying to keep you from the sea, Dad. I'm just trying to keep you safe. You're all I have."

"Nonsense. You're young, smart, and beautiful. You shouldn't be wasting your time with a doddering old man like me."

"You're my doddering old man, Dad, and my time here is the

opposite of wasted. I'm working. I have a spectacular place to live, and I get to spend time with the person I love most in the world."

His slow shuffle stopped again as he studied her face once more.

"You've been the best daughter anyone could ever wish for, my darling girl. But we have to look ahead in life, not backward. Everything changes. Let all that heartache you've gone through wash away like a poorly constructed sandcastle too close to the water. Start imagining a better one, built further up on firmer ground."

"Oh, Dad." She squeezed his arm more tightly with her own, pressing it deep into her side. "How about I agree to visualizing that sandcastle if you agree to stop leaving the house on your own."

"You drive a hard bargain, little one. We'll take a walk together tomorrow morning, and if it rains, as my bones tell me it probably will, we'll go the next day. Deal?"

"Deal."

CHAPTER TWO

Peter's eyes widened and then closed for the briefest second. He had been out of the section for ten minutes. Ten minutes, and the list of names on the monitor now required scrolling to reach the bottom. The coffee in his hand had not even had time to cool, and today's "Wordle" stayed unsolved as he had only reached the second try. Today, like so many other days, he'd probably never have time to even lodge a third attempt.

"Dr. Layne, the guy in G says his pain's at a ten."

"Thanks . . . " He glanced at her ID card, but the way it was twisted he couldn't make out more than "Pri." The staff seemed to change so rapidly that it was hardly worth the few spare brain cells it would take to learn a name. But he still hated the impersonal feel of not even addressing fellow soldiers in the trenches by name.

"Sorry, but can you remind me your name?"

Perhaps she actually answered, but if so, her words were lost to the loud sounds of the commotion behind curtain M, and Peter was on the move, his attempt at courtesy another scrap of debris left on the emergency department's floor.

Three hours later, the coffee he had left on the workstation had turned from cool to gross. He should have skipped the indulgent cinnamon and nutmeg. They were good when the coffee was hot but didn't weather neglect.

Today's cases were numerous but not unusual: a forty-five-year-old man insisting his diverticulitis was appendicitis, a urinary tract infection that had been too long ignored necessitating catheterization, a broken wrist, and the afternoon's screamer insisting on the need for stronger pain meds. The list went on, and for an instant, his beloved dead wife's voice whispered in his head: "They're all unique human beings, aren't they? They're not only medical conditions."

She had been right, of course. He had to work harder to remember those words of wisdom more frequently. Better to think about them than focus on the endless pain he felt at the wrench life had thrown him and his little girl. How unfair it was that Marissa had stuck with him through the agonizing marathon of med school, internship, and residency, and now, when he had at least a decent income and somewhat regular hours, she was gone. How she had been the happiest of mothers, delighting in their little girl's every milestone, and in the weeks before she died, sending him texts reminding him to hurry home when she was ovulating, eager to add another child to their family.

He glanced at the wall clock. 6:42. The shift ended at seven, but he couldn't leave until his paperwork, all electronic, of course, was finished. Even if he started immediately—and God, please let the momentary lull in new patients last—he wouldn't get out 'til after 7:30. The sitter was tolerant, but she had made it clear over and over again that she wanted to be on her way home no later than eight.

He had been enormously lucky to find her—an empty-nested widow in her late fifties—and he couldn't risk losing her.

Getting home by eight was important to him, though, as well. He needed to be there for Sam, to read aloud her last story for the night, say prayers with her, and tuck her into bed.

They had a routine. He'd get home, Mrs. Barndt would chat for a few minutes, telling him about their afternoon and evening, and then Sam was allowed fifteen minutes of screen time while he quickly showered and changed. Then she'd sit on his lap in the rocker his wife had picked out when they first decided to try to get pregnant, now more than eight years ago. Sam was almost six, as she reminded him frequently, but she still happily snuggled into his lap for a nighttime story.

They were on to chapter books now. His mother sent books constantly, both classic titles and contemporaries, often with little Post-its attached about a particular choices's qualities.

"Language old, but the story still good."

"Skip the scary parts for now."

"Explain how some people used to be stupid and not understand that most girls are smarter than boys."

He had frowned at that one. He wanted his daughter—his *brilliant* daughter—to grow up confident and comfortable with her own abilities, but he didn't want her to automatically assume she was smarter than half the world's population. He'd have to skim that particular book on his own before reading it aloud to determine the best course of action.

They were coming to the end of *Charlotte's Web*, so tonight's quiet time would probably include shared tears. Next up was the first *Harry Potter*. Yes, she was too young, but some of her friends had already seen the movies. Sam had enthusiastically entered into their multi-generational pact that the book always had to come first, so they'd start the series, Peter editing when he thought necessary as he gauged her tolerance for some of the more mature themes.

How he adored his little monster. She was vivacious, argumentative, inquisitive, and caring—always wanting to take home squirrels she thought might be limping, or rabbits she feared might be too cold in the winter. If only he had more time to spend with her. Before and after school care four days a week was already a lot to ask of a six-year-old, and he hated that he was completely dependent on Mrs. Barnt's availability the rest of the time.

The last record completed, he logged out and headed for the locker room, steadfastly keeping his gaze averted from the monitor. Were he younger and single, he'd volunteer to stay late when things were crazy, but he had a little girl who needed him.

Three hours later, the dishwasher had been turned on, the laundry folded, Sam's lunch for tomorrow packed, and the breakfast cereal for both of them was on the counter, bananas that had gone soft but not yet too brown lying next to them. Once upon a time, his wife would have whisked those bananas aside to keep for banana bread, but those days were long gone.

He glanced at his phone and argued with himself. He was tired and should go to bed, but he hadn't checked his email since early morning. The little spark of hope that flickered was stupid. The conversations he'd been having with an unknown baker were silly. For all he knew, she could be older than his mother, or God forbid, a teenager. Or she might not even be a she.

He had first contacted Cookielady when his mother complained about porch bandits having apparently stolen her package. She had ordered Christmas cookies for Sam, and it seemed they had been swiped. Cookielady had responded quickly and agreed to send a second batch. His mother was perfectly capable of handling the issue herself, but she hadn't wanted to bother the vendor. Peter, far less patient, had insisted that enterprising business people wanted their customers happy.

His first email had been curt, but her answer was immediate and conciliatory. She'd send the replacement batch within two days and copied both him and his mother with the tracking info. She had wished him a Merry Christmas and said she hoped he'd enjoy the cookies.

He still didn't know what had compelled him to reply. He'd written that the cookies were for his mother to share with her grand-daughter, and that he would never taste them.

That was a shame, she had responded. Did he want an additional order shipped to him directly at a different address? She'd be happy to waive the shipping charges to help amend for the inconvenience over the lost package.

He actually hesitated for a moment. *Did* he want his own Christmas cookies? But no, of course he didn't. One thing hospital staff rooms were never short of during the holidays was cookies. And he rarely ate the things anyway. When he had time for food, he wanted something real. But for some inexplicable reason, he'd written more than just a polite, "no, thank you."

> Kind of you to offer, but no. I'm not into sweets, especially since I have little time to work out.

Her reply had been almost immediate.

> LOL. I know what that's like. Between my two jobs and my dad, I'm not sure I even remember when I last used my running shoes. Merry Christmas anyway!

Why hadn't he let it go at that?

> What's wrong with your dad? And Merry Christmas to you as well.

He shouldn't have asked. He kicked himself the second he hit send. Doctors, ALL doctors, knew better than to engage in idle chit-chat about other people's physical conditions. It was an invitation for disaster.

But her reply hadn't involved a litany of medical woes. She had told him a little about moving in with her grieving father and only touched on her worries about him growing frailer with age. And incomprehensibly, their correspondence had continued sporadically over the next several months. He, who seldom discussed personal matters with coworkers or casual acquaintances, had joked that his own mother was the antithesis of frail. She ordered cookies rather than bake them herself because her schedule as a Silver Sneakers teacher and counselor was so busy that she rarely spent time at home. But he had shared few other personal details and for some reason, hadn't mentioned Samantha.

One random comment had opened the door to shared political leanings, and it turned out they both were addicted to late night comedy monologues. More often than not, their emails would include a clip of one short joke or another, but last night she had mentioned being worried about her dad wandering off. He had no idea where she lived, and for reasons he couldn't quite explain, he still hadn't mentioned he was a doctor.

Their emails had become an escape valve of sorts—a tiny bit of his life that had nothing to do with his work, his worries over being a single dad, or his ongoing grief for his wife. But realistically speaking, she—and he was almost positive she really was a she—was probably in her fifties or perhaps even sixties herself, given her descriptions of the father. So he was carrying on a silly, flirtatious correspondence with someone his babysitter's age.

Which was probably fine in the long run. He had no time for a romantic relationship and even if he did, he never wanted Sam to feel like anything other than the number one priority in his life.

Still, Cookielady had somehow become a friend, of sorts. And friends looked out for each other. So he tapped the envelope icon on his phone and checked his email. Garbage, newsletters, reminders . . . and nothing new from her since last night. Calling himself ridiculous, he typed out a few words.

> Long day here. Hope yours was better and
> your dad's okay. Night.

Then he swiped the app shut and went to bed. Five AM was a relentless master.

CHAPTER THREE

Abbie stared at her phone. She should be asleep, but her father had already gotten up twice to visit the bathroom, and she was worried about him. Instead of confronting him or going back to sleep, she was handling her indecisiveness by checking email.

It looked like Islandersboy89 had been up late again, but he didn't seem to have had time to catch any tv. She'd had it on while she worked in the kitchen, but hadn't paid much attention. Orders for Easter cookies were inundating her, and work at her *real* job was busy, as well.

But he had taken the time to ask after her father, and she felt a wave of comfort sweep over her. Someone out there cared. He helped his mother and he checked up on her, someone who was essentially a stranger to him. For a second she allowed herself to fantasize: he was a tall, dark, handsome, and single prince, looking for a young-ish and okay-looking accountant and was eager to sweep her off her feet and . . . what? Carry her off to his kingdom while she left her father alone?

The bathroom door opened, and she got out of bed and slipped a sweatshirt over her pajamas. Opting for a non-worried, casual approach, she opened her door and affected a yawn, following it up with a look of surprise.

"Oh, Dad, you're up, too? I was having trouble sleeping and was going to make some milk with honey. Can I get you some?"

He smiled, but his features looked tired.

"No need, sweetheart. I don't think honey would do right now, anyway. I've had a touch of indigestion." He waved the hand not tightly gripping his cane in the air in the vague direction of his chest, and Abbie bit her lip. What had they had for dinner? It was hours—and several dozen cookies ago—but then she remembered.

She'd made a simple stir fry with tofu and frozen vegetables and served it over brown rice. Nothing that should have caused problems.

"Are you having chest pains, Dad?" She fought to keep her voice neutral and not reveal the cold fear creeping up her middle.

"No, sweetie. It's just indigestion. I hope I didn't wake you."

"No, no, of course you didn't. I told you, I was having trouble sleeping myself." She tried to assess him while not appearing to. Was he paler than usual? Breathing unevenly?

Nothing jumped out at her, but now she was committed to a trip to the kitchen with at least the pretense of making herself hot milk.

"Are you sure I can't get you anything?"

At his smiling shake of the head, she asked the question she knew would annoy him.

"You still have that bell I put next to your bed, right?" He was resistant to any type of tech assistance but had grudgingly consented to the old, hand-held pewter bell that had sat nestled on a high kitchen shelf for as long as Abbie could remember.

"Yes, dear. The bell is there. Now stop worrying and go take care of yourself. You're going to be exhausted in the morning."

She leaned over to kiss his wrinkled cheek. Even as an adult, she had had to reach up to kiss him, but now he was barely her own height. He turned and shuffled into his room, pushing the door mostly shut with only a thin sliver of space keeping it ajar.

Her parents had never closed doors all the way. As a child, she had always known she could go to them, regardless of the hour, and they would help her with whatever was bothering her or make room for her in their bed.

Abbie closed her eyes and tried to quell the tears that welled up. They had been the best of parents, and she had once dreamed of having her own children to love as much and as well as they had loved her.

The light in her father's room went out, and she hesitated a moment before returning to her own room. It wasn't like her father was going to check for a used cup in the sink, and she hated warm milk.

But back in bed she was too keyed up to sleep. She took up her phone and began to type a response to Islandersboy89.

> Sorry about your day. It was a long one here, too. Who'd have thought Easter cookies were such a big deal? Should I send some to your mom?

> My dad's okay, I guess. Every day he seems a little older, though, and a little less steady.

> Any big plans for the weekend? Are the Islanders playing? I assume that's what your name comes from. I don't follow hockey, but I have a friend who's totally into hockey romance. Again, who knew?! Dad's a Green Bay Packers fan, so from August to February it's football, football, football and nothing else. Come to think of it, I don't even know when the hockey season begins or ends, so I might sound like a complete idiot, and I'm probably boring you, anyway. Hope tomorrow—today, actually—is a better day.

She hesitated. Up 'til now, things had stayed mostly superficial and impersonal. But somehow Islandersboy89 had become important to her. If '89 was his birth year, they were close in age.

The uncomfortable idea that had struck her more than once returned. Was he married? Having been cheated on herself, she felt sick at the idea of a married man carrying on a relationship—even an innocuous email relationship—with another woman.

She stared at her screen, teeth gnawing at her bottom lip. It couldn't hurt to ask.

> Forgive me if I'm being nosy, but are you married?

The words sat there at the end of her rambling email. On the small phone screen, it looked like a ridiculously long message. She debated adding more of an apology or maybe even an excuse for her question, but exasperation won out. Either this was a decent, nice guy, or he was another cheating jerk, and neither possibility should matter to her, anyway. He probably lived on Long Island or more likely, north of the city near his mother, and sooner or later, he'd disappear from her screen forever.

She hit send and plugged in her phone. She needed to be on camera for a 9AM meeting, so it would help if she got a least a few hours sleep.

CHAPTER FOUR

Was he married?

It took him a few seconds to realize he'd stopped breathing, and the air left his lungs in a whoosh.

Was he married? A huge part of him instinctively insisted that of course, he was. Was it possible no one had asked him that question in the past two years?

Ten years ago, he and Marissa had been incredibly young, idealistic, and besotted with each other. They'd married against their respective parents' advice and blithely promised to love, honor, and cherish 'til death did them part. And then death had done just that. No matter how much he still loved her, or how much he loved the incredible creature they had made together, Marissa wasn't coming back. He had no wife. Which meant he wasn't married. Which meant the answer to Cookielady's question was "no."

But his fingers still hovered. She had asked, which meant . . . what? It probably meant she, too, was single. A shudder went through him at the thought that it could mean she was married and looking for a little extra-curricular fun, but nothing in the tone of any of her emails had conveyed that distasteful possibility.

Like you'd catch on even if that were true, he muttered to himself cynically.

Okay. Assuming she was single . . . she'd deduced his age and hockey team loyalty from the email name he'd picked out at age twelve—he shuddered again, this time in horror at how many years had passed—and hadn't been put off by his age. So she was either a contemporary or a cougar.

He tilted his head, considering. Young Benjamin Braddock had certainly had *some* fun with the-not-really-all-that-old Mrs. Robinson in "The Graduate," at least for a little while, hadn't he? And he, Peter, was far older and wiser than the young Dustin Hoffman character had been.

She'd said she had two jobs. One was creating cookies that his mother said were terrific. He wondered what the other one was. She cared for her aging father. And she was a friendly sounding board in his odd existence where he was both constantly surrounded by people and still very much alone.

Decision made, he typed his reply.

> Hockey season's just finishing up, but it wasn't a great year for the Islanders. Their season wasn't that different from what the poor Packers went through!

He stopped for a second and then continued.

> I've had some experience with aging seniors. Maybe a complete physical could rule out or identify any incipient issues.
>
> And no, I'm not married. You? Have to run.

And he did. Sam was taking longer than usual getting dressed, and if she didn't hurry, he'd be late.

"Come on, Samantha-bantha! Time to go!"

She bounded out of her room, and he caught her in a bear hug and spun her around.

"That's my girl. What do you say we get pizza tonight to celebrate reaching the end of the week?"

"With no yucky mushrooms?"

"I'll keep all the yucky stuff on my half. Deal?"

"Deal!"

CHAPTER FIVE

Not married.
    Thank God.

No, she corrected herself. There was no reason to thank any disinterested deity. It didn't matter whether he was married or not. It mattered that he was a decent human being. And he was probably right. Getting her dad to visit the doctor again was undoubtedly a good idea.

She had overslept, of course, and had to throw the top of herself together quickly for her morning meeting. End of quarter deadlines were always stressful, and her department, like so many others, was currently understaffed.

The meeting over, she took a minute to check her personal email while walking to the kitchen. She was starving. Maybe a 2AM snack would have been useful after all. She wondered what Islandersboy's morning had been like.

Her father's coffee cup by the sink grabbed her attention and cut short her musing.

Damn. He couldn't have done it again, could he? She had given him a quick peck on the cheek before logging in to her meeting, and he had headed to the living room with his coffee. He always kept it with

23

him while he did the crossword puzzle and by his side while he more often than not fell back asleep.

His mug in the kitchen meant he might have gone wandering yet again.

"Dad? Dad?!"

No answer.

The forecasted rain had held off, but it was dark and windy outside. Abbie grabbed her jacket, slipped into her sneakers, and took off.

This couldn't be happening a second day in a row. He had promised!

Her search this afternoon was shorter. She caught sight of his diminished figure leaning against a railing the moment she turned the last corner leading to the beach.

God, he looked so frail and hunched over. His back was towards her as he stared towards the sea, his heavy gray coat appearing too big for his small frame.

"Dad!"

He turned and gave her a wan smile as she ran up to him, raising his hand to forestall her scolding.

"No need to worry, sweetheart. I didn't go far, see? I'm right here."

"But Dad, you promised you wouldn't go at all without telling me."

"I heard that David or Jason or whatever his name is yammering on, and I didn't want to bother you. Besides, I knew I wasn't going to go far. Little Samantha was just telling me she was going to start reading Harry Potter."

Abbie looked around, confused.

"The doctor's little girl? Are they out here again?"

"Oh, yes. I see them almost every time I come down here. He's so good with her. But they both seem lonely."

Abbie's eyes widened in frustration. He was driving her crazy, this person she loved more than any other.

"Where are they, Dad? I'd like to maybe meet this doctor and give him my phone number so he can let me know where you are the next time you leave after promising me you won't."

Her father's face turned stern, and for a moment, he looked like his old self, and Abbie felt like a chastised little girl who had crossed a line.

"I'm not a child, Abigail Marie, as I keep telling you."

Don't say anything you'll regret. She turned her head to look out at the distant surf. When she was little, she had conflated the stories she heard from her family's sporadic church attendance with the sounds of the sea she loved so well and imagined the waves coming in and out were an earthly manifestation of God's heartbeat. The sounds, smells, and the very taste of the salty air were a part of her—she, who had been away from the coast for so long. How much more integral they must be to her father.

She turned back to him and forced a gentle smile. "I'm serious, Dad. I'd like to meet them. Are they still around?"

But where a second ago her father had appeared both younger and somewhat disappointed in her, an air of distracted confusion now seemed to have settled in.

He looked first north and then south and then gave a small shrug.

"They must have gone home."

Abbie, too, scanned the beach but saw no one fitting his earlier description. *Could he be imagining them?*

"Let's go home, Dad. I'm pretty hungry, and I bet you are, too. And I'd like to call Dr. Gladstone's office this afternoon and see if I can get us both in for a check-up."

Her father's eyes narrowed in concern. "Are you not feeling well, sweetheart?"

The lies fell quickly from her lips.

"They're going to have an all-staff, in-person meeting at the end of the month, and they're advising us to make sure our medical status is up to date. They're apparently considering a change in insurance providers."

All utter nonsense, and she felt a momentary twinge of guilt but continued on, anyway.

"I thought since it had been a while for both of us, we could get appointments together."

"I'm fine, darling, but if it will make you feel better, I'll be happy to go in with you. I'm just sorry your mother isn't here to take you, instead."

God help her. He thought she was afraid to go to the doctor's by herself. She exhaled slowly and attempted a grateful smile.

"I am too, Daddy, but I know she'd want us both to stay on top of things."

They made their way slowly back home, and her father fell asleep in his recliner almost the instant he settled there after eating only half a sandwich and drinking a little tea. Abbie nevertheless took her phone into her room before calling the doctor's office, not wanting to be overheard should he wake.

She explained to the receptionist that her father would think they both needed slots but that only he needed to be seen. An appointment was available on the following Wednesday, and Abbie gratefully took it. In the city, small independent practices had all but vanished, but here in the boonies, retiring physicians were sometimes able to find a brave, young idealist willing to take over their practice. Dr. Gladstone was just such a unicorn, and she'd been taking care of Abbie's father for going on five years, ever since the GP Abbie had grown up with had retired.

She spent the remainder of her afternoon working intently but setting an alarm to go off every thirty minutes. Each time it beeped, she moved quietly from the old guest bedroom that had first become her mother's sewing room and was now her office and checked on her father. He had obviously stirred, since the second time she checked he had a book open on his lap, and the time after that, the tv was on with the volume turned down. But each time she looked in on him, he was asleep. The long night and the morning's outing had evidently taken their toll.

Her work finally done, she logged off and considered. She had baking to do and hoped to get several orders ready for shipment first thing in the morning.

They usually had pizza on Friday night, but she hesitated. Heartburn had supposedly kept her father up the night before, so she didn't want to set him up for additional discomfort.

She walked into the living room, relieved to see him standing by the window peering out at the light rain.

"Did you have a good afternoon, Dad?"

"Oh, yes, sweetheart. And they said on the news that this rain will be clearing off and that we're in for a stretch of gorgeous spring weather."

"That will be a nice change, won't it? It seems like it's been gloomy for weeks."

"You don't mind going for the pizza, though, do you? It's just a light drizzle. Or we can wait for tomorrow night and have something else tonight."

His words were conciliatory, but Abbie could hear the hope in his voice. She smiled. Leave it to her Italian descendent father to remember it was pizza night.

Pizza it would be, then. She had a bottle of antacids you were supposed to take before eating that she used occasionally herself, so she'd give him one of those.

The neighborhood pizza place, opened when her parents were still young themselves, had somehow survived into the modern era, but the owners struggled to find help and had had to eliminate home delivery as soon as the pandemic restrictions had been lifted.

But Alonso knew her number and her order, and as soon as she said hello, he asked if she wanted their regular.

"Yes, please. But maybe go light on Dad's pepperoni, if you could. He's had a lot of heartburn lately."

"Not from my pizza, I trust. But I'll spread it out and throw on some extra olives so it doesn't look naked. And extra veggies with no cheese for you, right?"

"You know it, Alonso. Thanks. I'll be there in twenty minutes."

The rain had, indeed, stopped, but the slick roads must have caused problems anyway because as Abbie approached the pizzeria, police cars and an ambulance blocked the street in front of the restaurant.

She parked in back and walked around, looking at the people crouched around a figure lying on the ground. A motorcycle lay on its side in the middle of the road. Abbie stopped, shocked and fearful for the poor person in the street. She didn't normally put much stock in prayer, but she sent out a wish to whatever forces might be watching to help the unmoving figure.

The warm air from the pizza ovens hit her as she opened the door, and she inhaled the familiar, mouth-watering scent.

"Hey, Abbie. Be right with you." Alonso shot her a smile from the beverage dispenser where he was filling a paper cup. He brought it to a young girl who was sitting alone at one of the small tables.

"Here you go, princess. How about I bring you a plate of delicious breadsticks you can eat while you're waiting?"

Curious. It was odd to see a child alone like this, and as far as she knew, "Slice of Heaven" didn't make breadsticks.

The little girl seemed to give his question serious consideration, but after a moment, she nodded and said, "Yes, please. No mushrooms, though."

Alonso laughed. "There are no mushrooms on breadsticks, cara. It's only little pieces of leftover dough rolled up into sticks with a bit of sauce on the side to dip them in."

He turned to Abbie before going back to the counter.

"Sorry for the wait, but your pizzas will be ready soon. That accident outside managed to distract us all for a few minutes, so we got a little behind."

A strange and unfamiliar feeling of protective fear took hold. The little girl couldn't have been part of the accident, could she? That couldn't be her parent out there, lying on the ground, could it? She fervently hoped not.

As if sensing her distress, Alonso gestured toward the girl with a smile.

"Her dad saw it happen and went to see if he could help. They're regulars, too, aren't you, cara mia?" He smiled at the child, and she grinned broadly, revealing a gap where a front tooth was missing and nodding.

"But this little girl does not like mushrooms!"

Her nod changed to a vigorous shaking of her head, and Abbie laughed.

"Oh dear. You probably wouldn't like my pizza, then, 'cause it's all vegetables, including Alonso's wonderful mushrooms."

A look of distress came over the little girl's face. "They're so slimy."

Abbie tilted her head, wanting to show she took the criticism seriously.

"They are, but they're tasty, especially the way Alonso prepares them. He doesn't use the really slimy ones that come from a can, do you, Alonso?"

"Canned?" His face took on a comically theatrical look of horror. "Canned mushrooms? Never!"

They all laughed, and Alonso turned his attention back to his food prep.

"What do you like on your pizza?" Abbie asked the girl, who was sipping her drink and swinging her legs—too short to reach the floor —back and forth in some internal rhythm.

"I like cheese and olives. I don't really love broccoli, but Daddy likes me to have it, and it's not that bad."

"I like broccoli, too. I planted some in my garden just the other day because broccoli grows better in the springtime, before it gets too hot."

The girl's eyes grew wider.

"Are you a farmer?"

Abbie laughed.

"No, I'm a baker. But I like to grow vegetables like lettuce, broccoli, and tomatoes."

"What do you bake?"

"Mostly cookies."

Now the girl looked suspicious.

"Do you put vegetables in your cookies?"

Abbie made a thoughtful face.

"I never thought of that. Do you think I should?"

29

At the girl's look of horror and violent head shake, Abbie laughed again.

"I'm kidding! I sometimes make special cookies shaped like vegetables, but I'd never put vegetables in the cookies. I'm making cookies later tonight that will be decorated to look like carrots."

The girl still looked wary, but their conversation was interrupted.

"Here you are, Abbie. Light pepperoni for your dad, and even though it killed me to do so, I left off the garlic sauce as well. Let me know if he says anything."

"Thanks, Alonso. I will. Do they come in every week?" she asked quietly, looking towards the little girl.

"They're here on Fridays a couple times a month. Not every week like you and your dad, but pretty regularly."

Abbie turned back to the child.

"I'll bring some cookies for you next time I come and leave them with Alonso. That way you can decide for yourself if cookies can look like carrots and still taste good."

The girl nodded, excitedly. "Next week?"

"They'll be here next week. But they'll last if you don't make it next Friday. I'll bring a few extra for Alonso so he won't be tempted to eat yours."

They all smiled, and Abbie said good night and left, the warm boxes in her arms tantalizing her senses.

The ambulance was gone, but a group of people stood talking with the police officers. Abbie hoped the little girl's parents would be finished soon. The poor thing had looked so alone in there. But Abbie had liked her. She couldn't remember the last time she interacted directly with a small child, but this kid had been fun. Maybe she'd try to come up with something more creative than just a carrot design. A stalk of celery? Corn on the cob? It would be challenging, even if it didn't scream Easter.

CHAPTER SIX

"**W**as the man badly hurt?"

Peter had been dreading the question. It came the minute he started the car engine. The motorcyclist had, in fact, been badly injured and had still been unconscious when the ambulance pulled away.

Peter often saw gruesome injuries in the hospital, but seeing the guy come around the corner too fast, skid into the car parked in front of the pizzeria, and go flying over the handlebars, had been downright horrifying. He'd have to do whatever it took to make sure his daughter never hung around with motorcycle riders when she was older.

He was glad Samantha hadn't seen anything from her booster in the middle of the back seat. She had heard his gasp and his four-letter exclamation, though.

"Daddy, what happened?"

Peter found a spot to park, unbuckled Samantha, and ran with her into the pizza shop, depositing her on a chair at one of the small, white tables.

"Someone just fell off his motorcycle, and I'm going to go see if I can help. You stay right here, and I'll be back soon, okay little one?"

He strove to keep his tone even and calm while his eyes sought out the familiar face behind the counter.

The man nodded.

"We'll be fine here together, don't you worry. I called 911, and they're on their way."

Peter didn't know the guy's name, he realized with a brief wave of shame. They'd been getting pizza at the same place for years, and he was sure Marissa had probably known not only his name but his background and the names of all his family members. But Peter tended not to start conversations and usually kept things brief when people tried to engage him. He knew, though, that it was okay to leave Samantha with him, at least for a short while.

Now he had to answer his daughter truthfully while taking care not to upset her.

"The person took a pretty bad fall, but they'll do all they can to help him at the hospital."

"You couldn't make him better? Will you be able to fix him tomorrow, then?"

Her faith was touching. At six, she still saw him as both a superhero daddy and doctor. How many years of unquestioning love did he have left? Some of the altercations he witnessed in the hospital between parents and children filled him with horror and dread.

"I tried to help him, but he'll have to have special treatment. It's possible I'll see him in the morning, or perhaps one of the other doctors will be taking care of him." In truth, all he'd dared do tonight was check for vitals and cover the young man with his own jacket to try and keep him warm. Then he'd had to give a witness statement and all his contact info to the police.

"What did you do while you were waiting? Did you get to watch the pizza being made?"

"A little bit. And I talked to a nice lady who likes mushrooms like you do. And she bakes cookies that look like vegetables."

A lady who baked cookies. That was a crazy coincidence. But he was pretty sure his own cookie lady—and he had to stop picturing her now as Anne Bancroft—lived nowhere near the Jersey shore.

Although come to think of it, he had no idea where she lived. Probably Wisconsin, since her father liked the Packers.

"I'm not sure I'd want to eat cookies that look like vegetables. Would you?"

"She said they're good and that she'd make some for me and leave them with the pizza man."

"She did, did she? That would be interesting. We'll have to see next time we're there."

"She said next Friday. That nice man I dream about sometimes likes cookies, too."

Peter frowned. Samantha had spoken a few times of having a dream about an old man who liked to visit the beach. Was this one of those imaginary friends kids sometimes created? Did it indicate some problem he needed to worry about? He had no idea whether it was better to ignore her stories or encourage her to tell him more. He'd have to remember to ask his mom what she thought. For now he'd probe a little more and then try to change the subject.

"He likes cookies, does he? What else does he like?"

Sam was always either with him, at school, or with Mrs. Barndt. A thought struck him and alarm bells began ringing in his brain.

"Does Mrs. Barndt take you to see this man?"

He glanced in the rearview mirror and saw the look of genuine confusion on his daughter's face.

"What? Mrs. Barndt doesn't know him. I only see him at night when I'm sleeping. But he was really tired last time I saw him. He was talking about sandcastles. Can we go to the beach and build a sandcastle?"

That was at least one worry temporarily alleviated. Peter forced himself to lower his stress response and give her request serious consideration. Spring break was a week away, and he had put in for the days off to correspond with her time off from school. They were going to drive up to see his parents, but he could try to squeeze in a trip to the beach. Given how close they lived to the shore, he felt a momentary pang of shame that he had never taken Samantha to see the water or play in the sand.

"If the weather's good, we'll go to the beach when you're on spring vacation. That sound good to you?"

"Yes. Hurray! Maybe we'll see Grandpa Tony there."

"Grandpa Tony?"

"Yes. He said I could call him that."

Peter said nothing. Thanks to the accident, they were eating later than usual, and Samantha sometimes got ornery at bedtime when she was overtired.

He let the subject of her mysterious friend and the beach drop and asked her if she'd like to watch "The Little Mermaid" while they ate. That elicited another "hurray," and he marveled at her ability to bounce from one topic to another. But he'd have to ask his mother what she thought he should do about this imaginary man.

CHAPTER SEVEN

Cookies packed, everything else finally done, Abbie fell back against her pillows in utter exhaustion. An image of the solitary young figure from the pizza parlor came to mind. How on earth did people with young kids manage? She was totally wiped, and she only had herself and her father to worry about.

She should turn out the light. She reached out to do so but quickly changed her mind and picked up her phone instead. A quick peek. She had to check her Etsy account anyway, and then she'd take just a glance at her personal email.

Yes! He had written again, despite the fact that she hadn't answered his note from that morning.

> Hope your Friday was better than mine. I'd love to spend the weekend thinking about everything except work and the daily grind, but I have to clock in again tomorrow. How about you? And just checking—do you guys live in Wisconsin?

Wisconsin? What on earth had given him that idea? Oh, yes—she had mentioned the Packers, hadn't she? She smiled ruefully as her eyes zeroed in on the foam cheesehead her father had bought her when she was a child that still hung on a nail close to the ceiling.

She had never even been to Wisconsin. Her parents had once made a pilgrimage to Lambeau Field on their wedding anniversary, but she had already been in college, thank goodness.

Five minutes ago, she had been tired, but now she was suddenly energized. Maybe it had been talking to Alonso and that little girl, but for some reason she felt an unfamiliar but fierce desire to have connections of her own again. She had left many of her own friend-ships foolishly unattended when she married John, and then she intentionally tried to distance herself from the acquaintances—she couldn't call them friends—they had hung around with while they were together.

Work had gone virtual, she had moved in with her dad, and here she was, a twenty-eight-year-old recluse.

But there was a living, breathing, human being on the other end of this cyber connection: an unmarried male, presumably close to her own age, and he seemed to care.

She sat up straighter and began to key in her response.

> No. We're long-distance Packer backers. Or at least my dad is. I'm an East Coast girl through and through, and to be honest, I was only free to move back in with my father because I went through an ugly divorce and deserted the home I helped pay for in Brooklyn.

> And as for clocking in: my nine to five is a boring accounting job, and my baking business is strictly a side hustle I started when friends at my office started asking me to make them cookies after I had brought some to a party. It's been growing like crazy, though, and it seems like there's never a moment when I don't have something I'm supposed to be doing.

She hit send and was astonished to see a response come back almost immediately. She kept all notifications off on her phone so wouldn't even have seen it if the phone hadn't still been in her hand.

> What if you left your boring job behind and went full-time as Cookielady? It seems like that's where your heart lies.

> And since we're pulling back the curtain somewhat, I said I wasn't married because I'm a widower. It's been a while, but I've had a hard time thinking of myself as single. My job and my family take up all my energy, but it's nice to know you're out there, making the world a sweeter place. Sleep well.

Whoa. There was a lot in those two paragraphs.

Every once in a while she flirted with the idea of getting up and walking away from her two large work screens. But not often and not seriously. Yes, the time she spent in the kitchen filled her with creative enthusiasm, and she loved the little notes customers sometimes sent saying how happy her cookies made them. But Etsy didn't provide health insurance or retirement contributions.

But what if she doubled or tripled her current orders? She made a decent profit—not huge, but if it were compounded, could it be enough? Numbers were her forte, and she started to do mental calculations but then forced herself to stop. It was already past midnight. She might fantasize about making her cookies a full-time career, but tomorrow she had to actually do the work and fulfill four pending orders.

She put down her phone and turned out the light. Now she could think about the rest of his message. A widower. Maybe he was older and the 89 referred to a good hockey year. She had no clue, but she supposed she could check in the morning. He didn't write like an old person, though. Her father was a widower, and she couldn't imagine him typing out email messages late at night. Besides, this guy had a demanding job that kept him working long hours. But he had said she made the world a sweeter place. A pun, obviously, but it gave her a warm feeling anyway. She fell asleep on an unfamiliar cloud of contentment.

CHAPTER EIGHT

Peter worked Saturday and then had Sunday and Monday off. He felt guilty leaving Samantha with the sitter for so much of the weekend, but he also selfishly loved the peace and quiet of an empty apartment on Mondays. On this Monday, however, the fleeting idea of a presence in the kitchen, working away at her own passion while he puttered around, guiltily crossed his mind more than once.

His to-do list was usually long, and the six hour school day—he never left Sam in before or after-hours care when he wasn't working—was filled with laundry, grocery shopping, and every once in a while, a tiny chunk of unallocated time.

While he caught up on bills, Sam's words from the morning came back to him, and he frowned. She had told him that the old man had said good-bye to her at the beach, telling her he was moving to a place where there was sunshine every day but it never got too hot. But it was what she had said next that had truly shaken him.

"Grandpa Tony said that he hoped I'd have a new mama again sometime soon, but that my real mama still loves me and watches out for me. I asked him if he knew my mama, and he said he knew my real mama AND my new mama. Do you know her too, Daddy, the person who's going to be my new mama?"

Peter had been stupefied, his hands gripping the steering wheel as he struggled to come up with a response. He had once jokingly asked his mother if all important conversations took place in the car, and she had nodded calmly and only answered, "Of course, dear."

He desperately sought words, but Sam didn't seem concerned with his silence. "I hope she's pretty like the lady in the pizza shop. Did you see her, Daddy? And I hope she doesn't shout, 'One, two, three, eyes on me' all day the way Miss Miller does."

Peter's stupefaction grew, and his eyes focused fiercely on the car in front of him as he mentally composed first one, then another, response. At last he was able to offer a feeble comeback. "If you and I together—" he emphasized that last word "—ever meet anyone we want to be your new mama, I'm absolutely certain she won't shout, 'One, two, three, eyes on me.'"

"That's good. But I'll miss Grandpa Tony."

They were pulling into the drop-off circle, and Peter had never felt such relief at saying goodbye to his daughter. But guilt ate at him even as he wished her a good day and blew her a kiss. He'd have to find a way to deal with this bizarre fantasy. Or could he cross his fingers and hope that if this spectral grandfather had said goodbye, then maybe the whole thing would go away?

Now he stared at his screen, eyes bulging at the pages and pages of results that apparently addressed the topic of children's imaginary friends.

It was too much. He'd wait and see if she said any more and talk with his mother when they saw her next week. In the meantime, he'd send a quick note to the cookie lady.

Almost all the bays in the emergency department were already full when the ambulance brought in the 76-year-old male the next morning. His daughter was with him, saying she had been unable to rouse him when she checked on him after he failed to get up for breakfast.

The woman looked far too young to have a father so old looking. *Stop*, Peter chided himself. Such thoughts were unprofessional and unkind. But for some reason, his eyes kept returning to her stricken but beautiful face as she quietly confirmed that her father had been intellectually competent when he signed his DNR.

Anthony Curini was unresponsive, and his vitals were weak and growing weaker. They could perform an echocardiogram, but it would probably take several hours.

Peter was in the process of explaining the possible tests, treatments, and outcomes and about to suggest a Cat scan to check for brain activity, when the man flatlined. Alarms went off, and Peter shot the woman a questioning glance as he moved to the patient's side. But she put a hand on his arm and shook her head, tears sliding down her cheeks.

"Let him go. He's been waiting to see my mom again, and I don't want to drag him back for more unhappiness. Let him go, please?"

"Are you sure?" A PA and a nurse had both rushed over, and they confirmed the woman's identity as next of kin and her decision.

It had all taken only minutes, and as deaths went, it had been about as painless as one could hope for. But his heart still broke for the young woman who stood silent, her father's now lifeless hand in her own as she bent and kissed the gnarled fingers.

"My sympathies, Miss . . ." He hadn't been paying attention when the PA took down her information.

"Curini. I'm his . . ." She stopped and looked away. He watched as she bit her trembling bottom lip and felt a frisson of pain in his own heart. "I *was* his only child," she continued, "so I wasn't going to give up his name."

Without conscious thought, his eyes moved to her left hand which bore no ring. *Asshole,* his conscience screamed. *What's the matter with you today?*

"We can leave you alone for a few minutes, if you'd like. Someone from patient services will be here momentarily."

She nodded, and after watching her struggle to compose herself for a few seconds, he did something he'd never done before. He reached out and drew her to him, holding her slender figure against his for a moment and breathing in the sweet scent of her hair.

"I'm truly sorry about your father."

She sniffed and nodded against his chest before pulling away and giving him a tremulous smile.

"Thank you. But I know it's better this way. Better for him, and that's all that matters."

Life had come to a quiet stop in this tiny section of the large emergency wing, but all around him, patients were waiting, and he had to move on.

"Take care," he whispered and then turned and walked away.

Hospital bureaucracy would step in and take care of the formalities, but as he went about the rest of the day, her face and the absurdly improper feel of her body against his stayed with him.

After Sam was in bed that night, he opened up his email and sent a quick note to the cookie lady.

Another long day here. You doing okay?

He waited a while, but no response came. She'd mentioned her orders were up, so she was probably busy. He finally fell asleep, but his bed felt even colder and lonelier than usual.

CHAPTER NINE

Abbie walked along the beach, lifting her head every few minutes to gaze out at the sunrise. She wasn't sleeping well, but something was propelling her out of bed early in the morning even though she had taken time off from work. She wondered if the same magnetic force that had drawn her father to the shore so frequently in his last weeks was now working on her. But where his several final forays had been amongst misty gloom, sunshine now seemed determined to reclaim its rightful supremacy.

Ten days had passed since her father's death. Days of phone calls, forms, arrangements, and odd tokens of sympathy that she never would have anticipated. A woman who said she knew her father from the library had brought by a lasagna, and the dentist office had sent flowers. Abbie had posted nothing on social media, but news seemed to have spread around the town all by itself. Even the simple ceremony at the funeral parlor had drawn far more mourners than she ever would have anticipated.

Her coworkers, of course, had expressed sympathy and sent flowers, but Abbie had never grown particularly close to any of them.

She had continued baking and shipping off orders, not really sure what else to do. People had ordered cookies in good faith, and Easter and springtime weren't going to wait just because her father had died. And so she stood in the kitchen, creating chicks, bunny rabbits, miniature baskets, and carrots, with half her mind focussed on decorating and the other half wondering what in the world she was going to do with her life.

Now it was Friday, and as she was wrapping up an order and checking each cookie to make sure there were no cracks, she suddenly remembered the little girl from the pizza parlor. She had a few cookies shaped like carrots left, and not wanting to face any of the more unpleasant tasks that awaited her, Abbie quickly made another batch of dough and decided to go a little wild. Using the rim of one of her mixing bowls as a mold, she made four extra large cookies and put them in the oven. She then set to work assembling portions of colored frosting. Once the cookies were out and cool, Abbie created cookie pizzas, complete with "sauce," "olives," "broccoli," and coconut flakes as shredded cheese.

She placed three of the pizza cookies, along with the carrots, for the little girl and her family in a box, and wrapped the last "pizza" for Alonso. She wasn't hungry, but she drove to the restaurant to drop them off.

"Abbie! Where have you been? We missed you. You're early tonight, and you haven't ordered anything."

"I know, Alonso." She stopped and forced herself to breathe evenly. This wasn't getting easier, but it had to be done.

"My dad died last week."

"Oh, Abbie, I'm so sorry." He came out from behind the counter and wrapped her in a warm embrace. "He's with your mother now, and I'm sure they're looking out for you."

She gave a little nod. People had been telling her similar things for days, and she had said almost the same thing in the hospital. Had she done the right thing? Guilt nagged at her continually. Maybe he could have been saved and would have been home at this moment waiting for his pizza. Or maybe he really was with her mother, and they were both happy. She had no idea. But she couldn't change the fact that they were now both gone, and she was alone in the world.

Abbie reached down and pulled the box and wrapped cookie from the bag she had set down on the floor.

"Could you do me a favor, please, Alonso? I promised that little girl who was here last week that I'd bring her cookies. Could you keep these here and give them to her or her parents whenever they come in? And this one's for you."

He opened his cookie, and a look of astonished delight crossed his face.

"Abbie! This is outrageous. It looks exactly like a pizza. It's amazing." He broke a small piece off and tasted it. "Ahhh! *Delizioso. Squisito. Magnifico!* You are a genius. Maybe you can open a cookie shop next door, and we can become rich together!"

He shook his head in bemusement and continued. "You have your mother's heart. To make gifts for others during such a hard time is the mark of an angel. And little Samantha will be so happy. But she has only a father, poor thing. Her mother, too, is dead."

Abbie tilted her head, confused. The little girl's name was Samantha, and her mother was dead? Wasn't that the story her father had spoken about? How peculiar. But it didn't really matter. She'd made a promise, and she'd kept it.

"Well, tell her I hope she likes them when you see her. Good night, Alonso."

"Let me make you some pizza. I can do it quickly, with lots of extra veggies."

"No, thank you. I'm not really hungry. I'll be back again soon."

She turned and left, overcome yet again by a wave of sadness.

CHAPTER TEN

After sleeping fitfully, Abbie was out again early the next morning, walking the beach. The time would change the next weekend, making sunrise later again for a while, but for now, she could bask in both the early morning light and the relative calm of an almost empty shoreline.

Almost, but not quite. She stared at the huddled figures down close to the water, and as if being pulled by an unseen force, found herself walking towards them.

As she grew closer, she realized it was, indeed, a man with a young girl. It must be the father and daughter her dad had met. The girl stood up, and Abbie recognized her from the pizza shop.

"Cookie Lady!" The girl's cry was joyful, and she came running at Abbie, throwing her arms around her middle. "That pizza cookie was supercalifragilisticexpialidocious!"

Abbie laughed, totally astonished at finding her own arms wrapped around a jumping bundle of happy energy.

"Daddy, Daddy! This is the cookie lady."

The man had gotten to his feet and was walking towards them, the smile on his face turning to confusion.

Recognition hit Abbie at the same moment.

"You're the doctor."

"Your father—I'm sorry."

Their words overran each other, and they both stopped speaking, unsure of how to continue.

"I didn't know in the hospital that you already knew my father," Abbie said after a moment.

At his puzzled expression, Abbie hastened to explain.

"From here at the beach. He told me all about running into you and Samantha building sandcastles."

"We've never been to the beach before today. It's the end of Samantha's spring break, and she begged to be down here to see the sunrise."

Abbie stared at him. This made no sense. There couldn't be two young widower fathers with daughters named Samantha, could there?

"Forgive me for being rude, but is your name Peter?"

He nodded and then held out his hand. "Peter Layne. And I'm truly sorry for your loss."

Samantha had moved a few steps away, but now she was back, holding up a lovely, unblemished seashell.

"Grandpa Tony was sad he had to leave, but he told me that there would always be beautiful shells to remember him by. He said the shells used to have creatures living inside them that had to go away, too, so they leave their houses behind to remember them by."

Both adults stared at the little girl, speechless. Both opened their mouths to say something and then stopped. Finally, they spoke in unison once more.

"That's something my father used to tell me when I was little."

"This sounds crazy, but you're not by any chance actually called the cookie lady online, are you?"

They laughed as Abbie nodded, mouth open in shock. And then she gasped.

"Oh God, this isn't possible. You're not a hockey fan, are you?"

They stared at each other as Peter slowly nodded. "That would be me. Islandersboy89."

"I can't believe this. I thought my dad was imagining things when he talked about seeing you guys here at the beach."

"But he was. Or . . . I have no frigging clue. Samantha has never been down here, but she certainly seems to have known your dad. Was his name Tony?"

"Yes. Anthony."

They stared at each other, neither knowing what to say. Finally Peter reached out his hand and took her now icy fingers in his. He kissed them.

Abbie watched his head bent over her hand, and tears welled up in her eyes.

He lifted his head. "The cookies you left for Samantha were fabulous. I told you you made the world a sweeter place."

Abbie tried to keep her voice steady, but tears escaped her eyes and were rolling down her cheeks.

"My dad told me you were a wonderful father. How did he know that if you never met?"

Peter shrugged and reached a finger to wipe away a tear. "I missed talking with you this week by email, even though we were on vacation. Now I understand why you were quiet. It must have been a hard ten days."

"It was. And I spent a lot of it second guessing the decision I made at the hospital. But it looks like my dad knew he was leaving. And this sounds crazy, but I think he pushed me down here this morning in order to meet you."

Peter reached out and grasped her other hand. He now held both her cold, shaking hands in his warmer ones.

"At any other time, I'd say it sounded crazy, too. But there's something . . ." He searched for words and came up empty, shrugging his shoulders again. "Samantha's not crazy—a fact that's been driving *me* crazy with confusion. This Grandpa Tony's been a friend and a comfort to her, yet apparently he was both your father and a stranger she's never met. And my email correspondent, whom I've grown to care about, is a beautiful and kind woman who reached out to my daughter with love."

A strong breeze blew in from the water, and Abbie turned her head to look at the sea. The sun was rising brightly over the water, and more tears slipped out as she smiled. A new day had begun.

ABOUT THE AUTHOR

Meg Napier's books include:

SECOND ACT: a romantic suspense in the captivating world of ballet

SECOND SIGHT: a love story spanning centuries

SECOND STANZA: an intriguing mystery that will have you holding your breath until the final page

Meg wants you to get so caught up in her books that you convince yourself to keep reading just a second or two longer. All her titles include the word "Second" because almost nothing is perfect the first time around. Visit her website: **MegNapier.com** and sign up for her newsletter **https://www.megnapier.com/megs-mailing-list/** Once you've "confirmed," you'll receive a free copy of "Second Draft," a fun and magical tale about a feisty main character teaching her author a thing or two. Find Meg on social media platforms:

https://www.facebook.com/MegNapierAuthor
https://twitter.com/NapierMeg
https://instagram.com/megnapierauthor
https://bookbub.com/profile/meg-napier
https://www.goodreads.com/goodreadscommeg_napier

But most importantly: leave a review of something you've read and liked. Reviews are *the* key factor in helping a writer go from being an unknown nobody to being a writer readers look for. **YOU** are the one who can help make that possible. Thank you!

AN ARTIST'S TOUCH

J.T. BOCK

I sabelle fell in love with him before she had ever met him.

It was his painting that first captured her heart. The earthiness of its oil colors—golds, greens, and browns—and the sunlight playing across the subject's face as she bent over and craned her neck to look out an opened window. The painted sunlight was so rich and bright, it appeared to illuminate the dark city sidewalk where Isabelle stood in front of the gallery. On instinct, she withdrew into the shadows, afraid the light would burn her if she stood too close.

Yet, she remained transfixed. She continued to stare at the painting through the gallery's window, cleaned to a clear perfection. She marveled at the life the painter had breathed into the subject, and she wondered if he could breathe life into her as well. Merely gazing at the painting aroused feelings she'd considered as dead as the rest of her. She wondered what meeting the artist would be like.

She must've been standing in front of the window too long because a woman with burgundy hair and matching lips opened the door to the gallery and walked outside to stand next to her.

Isabelle sidled away.

"You've been staring at this painting for a time," the woman said to Isabelle while keeping her focus on the art. "He's a superb artist. Same style as the old masters: Vermeer, Caravaggio, Botticelli, da Vinci. You won't find another modern artist who can capture the Renaissance style with such authenticity."

The art dealer paused for Isabelle to comment. When she didn't reply, the woman took off her black horn-rimmed glasses and regarded her. "You must be a fan of the old masters."

"Yes." Isabelle hated speaking with dealers. Their chatter ruined the mood of the art. "How much for the painting?"

The woman appraised Isabelle's worn leather jacket, peasant-style dress, and the small gold rings encircling her fingers. "$35,000 for this piece. I have smaller ones inside that might interest you."

She opened the gallery's door and gestured for Isabelle to enter.

"My name is Anita." She held out her hand, and Isabelle shook it.

As quickly as she took Anita's hand, she dropped it. The mere touch of the dealer's heated flesh singed Isabelle's icy skin. She rubbed her burning hand along the folds of her dress to no avail. Her hand throbbed as if she'd touched real sunlight.

Inside the gallery, she could detect the sweet iron smell of Anita's blood mixing with her rose-scented perfume. She could hear Anita's heart beat out a steady rhythm, like the underlying bass in a song. Even the unmistakable smell of oil paint that filled the gallery wasn't enough to cover the delectable scent and alleviate Isabelle's sudden craving.

If Anita noticed Isabelle's unease, she kept it to herself. The woman flittered around the open space, eager to point out to her potential customer the rising artist's small pieces, priced in the low thousands.

As Anita chatted, Isabelle distanced herself with the pretense of studying the artwork. She was old, and with age came control. Why this woman caused her hunger to spike, her flesh to burn, Isabelle had no clue. Even the oil paint's mineral odor gave her a euphoric burst that made her lick her lips and long to lick the canvas.

Isabelle jolted back from the painting she'd been staring at. Her nose was inches from the canvas, as if trying to catch the scent of the cornflowers strewn about subject's feet. She clenched her hands in front of her and proceeded through the modest gallery to examine the other pieces—from a distance.

About a dozen more hung throughout. All were painted with the same richness as the one in the window but with varied themes. There were smaller pictures of flowers, larger pictures of landscapes, and pictures of women—young and old, soft and hard, nude and fully dressed. Some paintings were of their faces only, while others showed the women at a desk or lying on a chaise or looking out a window. There were no pictures with men as the focal point. They were in the background or along the sides or sitting at the women's feet.

They were used as props.

"Does he do portraits?" Isabelle asked. Maybe he could capture her in this light. Maybe in a painting she could appear alive.

"Nothing commissioned. He finds his own models." Anita put on her glasses to admire a portrait of a middle-aged woman's delicate face half-concealed by a mane of black hair.

"He doesn't like the models to find him." She gave a dismissive wave of her hand. "You know how artists are."

"I see."

"Do any interest you?" Anita asked in a tone that assumed Isabelle would answer no.

"All of them," Isabelle replied.

Anita choked back a laugh as if assuming she was joking. Then she took off her glasses, and her smile dropped away as her gaze drifted over Isabelle's face and her uncommon complexion.

Isabelle caught her reflection in a mirror behind Anita's desk. In the gallery's light, her skin appeared ivory, like the powdered face of a dandy from centuries ago, when she was alive.

Anita turned away to straighten folders strewn on top her desk. Isabelle assumed she did so to hide her shock and compose herself, because when she looked again at Isabelle, the art dealer wore a strained smile. "Yes, they are all wonderful pieces. I can give you pricing on—"

"I want them all. I can wire $100,000 as a down payment now. My finance manager can send the rest this week." Isabelle removed her phone from a pocket hidden in the folds of her dress. "Does that work for you?"

Anita's smile was no longer strained.

In the process of completing the sale and arranging delivery of the paintings, Isabelle found the artist's address. Anita had been so flustered at her large sale that she had left his folder open to his contact information.

Michael Cara.

He lived near the gallery in a warehouse converted into apartments for artists. Isabelle often passed it during her nighttime walks, though she had never considered peaking inside. In recent years, she hadn't been fond of company—dead or alive.

She made an exception that evening.

Perched on a ledge outside the window of his apartment, Isabelle watched him paint a woman sitting in a clearing. A checkered blanket was crumpled beneath the subject, with a large wicker basket set at her side. Trees and bushes surrounded her, creating a natural sanctum. Her face was turned to the side, head tilted up to the sunbeams peeking through the foliage. The sunlight gave the illusion of a halo around her head, its golden light reflected in her blonde hair.

Clothespins held several photographs of the model clamped to the canvas at varying angles. To Isabelle's eyes the painting was finished, but the artist kept fussing over the particulars—adding more yellow base, mixing more colors to dull the reds.

His large hands worked the brushes with a precision that her lean fingers lacked. She wondered how such strong hands, like those of a bricklayer, could be so delicate when adding the finishing details.

Isabelle admired painters. Over the centuries, she had mastered the flute, violin, and piano and seen her photographs printed in magazines and hung in galleries. But never could she paint a picture or sculpt an object. Her hands couldn't recreate the images in her mind, so she had turned to collecting works. Her failures taunted her, but they made her feel human. Imperfection was the only thing left of her humanity.

She stared at his broad back while he leaned forward to add minute highlights along the subject's hair. If anyone saw this man on the street, they might think he was a construction worker by his baggy, worn jeans and tank top flecked with paint. His wavy brown hair was pulled back into a faded baseball hat. Seeing the artist in the flesh made her desire him even more.

Pressing her cheek against the cold window, Isabelle splayed her hands over the glass to draw in his warmth, his mortality. She closed her eyes, pretending that she could feel his skin heating her fingertips. When she opened her eyes, Michael had turned on his stool and was looking in her direction. He squinted then stood and began walking toward her.

Isabelle leapt five stories from the ledge and ran home.

"Are any of these women his lover?" Isabelle asked when she finalized her purchases at the gallery three nights later.

"Oh, no, no." Anita shook her head and clucked her tongue.

She touched Isabelle's arm, leaned close to her, and whispered, though they were the only people in the gallery, "Just between you and me, I think he has a problem with relationships. I've never seen him with anyone, except when he's painting them. He never goes out. He never wants to leave his studio. I'm going to have to drag him to his own art opening next week. We still have a few more pieces left, even after you cleared out us out."

Anita nudged Isabelle with her elbow. She was her best friend after purchasing enough paintings to send her son to college.

"Keep my paintings for the opening," Isabelle said.

"You don't mind?"

"It will give me time to make space for him," she said, then clarified, "for his paintings, I mean."

"That's such a relief!" Anita clapped her hands, and Isabelle jumped at the sudden sound. "I didn't know what to do. You seemed intent on taking all his work right away, and I didn't want to deprive you."

"I'm used to deprivation."

"Aren't we all, darling." Anita winked and nudged her again.

Before leaving her house that night, Isabelle had fed on one of the blood bags she stored at home. So far, it had staved off her hunger and gave her skin a human glow, so she didn't appear so lifeless to the other woman.

"You will be at the opening, won't you?"

"I wouldn't miss it."

"But give others a chance to purchase his work," Anita teased. "Don't keep him all to yourself."

"That was my intention."

Anita laughed, and Isabelle found herself smiling for the first time in years. She thought she had forgotten how.

ISABELLE COULDN'T RECALL the last time her stomach had twisted in anxious knots, the way it did the night of Michael's art opening. She changed clothes more times than she'd care to admit before settling on a velvet burgundy dinner dress that she had worn to Frida Kahlo's New York debut. The long sleeves covered her arms. The front rose to the base of her neck, although the back plunged down, revealing her unearthly pale skin. She swept up the sides of her dull brown locks and allowed the waves to fall past her shoulders and over her exposed back. To her face, she applied foundation, blush, and lipstick and darkened her brows to blend with the living crowd.

It had been decades since she'd last mingled with people at a gathering like this one. In her early days she'd had many human friends, before she learned the trade-off of immortality. Friends and lovers grew old and died, leaving Isabelle alone to start again with new friends and lovers. Parts of her died with them decade after decade.

A handful of times, she'd given friends the immortal blood pumping through her veins, hoping to gain an eternal soulmate. But those relationships failed. Some grew depressed with a life relegated to darkness and despised her for what she'd made them into. A few became bored and left. Each time those undead friends abandoned her, the pain singed her soul, more unbearable than if she'd lost them to a natural, human death.

For the first two centuries of her immortal life, she had lived with undead communities on the fringes of society. They took up residences in large ancestral homes or on farms away from daily human life. Isabelle appreciated the solitude during her nights spent with them. They had offered her a chance to repair her heart when death or abandonment had severed her relationships.

The elders leading these communities had taught Isabelle how to navigate the shifting world from afar and invest in it to support her eternal life. They'd taught her how to blend with humans, whose changing speech and culture she wanted to understand, and how to adapt as sprawling cities replaced villages and a new government replaced the old.

Technology and beliefs evolved until the remnants of Isabelle's human life became part of her country's distant past, buried then dug up centuries later and placed under glass cases in museums. Her family's farm was rebuilt as a living history project.

Isabelle joked she was an un-living history project.

The elders didn't find this idea as amusing as she did. Maybe because the older they became, the more they removed themselves from the world and feelings like humor, happiness, love. Human affairs were too illogical, emotional. The elders had grown tired of humanity's repeated failures. No longer did they enjoy the wonder of human discoveries and advancements that would've been labeled sorcery in their day.

The elders simply stopped caring about life.

Isabelle thought she'd escape the emptiness plaguing her mentors, withdrawn into their rooms and tombs. If she surrounded herself with art and beauty and those who created it, she'd continue to feel human. She'd be too full for emptiness to take root. She hosted salons, became a patroness of the arts and sciences.

But these creators, inventors, and artists couldn't save her. As they left—from death or ennui—they took the humanity they'd shared with her, leaving a void where nothingness eventually rooted until it choked out any remaining passion for life.

So, twenty years ago, she withdrew from society—human and unhuman.

This last year had only grown worse for Isabelle. She'd passed her days in a dream-like haze. She'd feared this was her next evolution and refused to exist as a sleepwalker. Instead, she'd climb the highest building in the city and wait for the sunrise to turn her body to ash. The thought of this blistering pain didn't frighten her. In her final moments, she would feel something.

But on her way to meet her last dawn, she'd passed Michael's artwork hanging in the window and experienced a sensation so alien and confusing to her that she had to stop and backtrack to seek out its source.

Hope. The strange, euphoric feeling had been hope, and Michael's painting had been the source.

Now, as she left for the party, this hope fluttered within her chest. Its feathery light touch made her grin, and Isabelle reveled in this sensation like finding a long-lost family heirloom. One she swore to never lose again.

Tonight she'd meet Michael, and she'd make him an offer no artist would refuse.

PEOPLE CROWDED TOGETHER in the small gallery. Milling about the room, they nibbled on cheese and sipped wine while discussing each piece. Isabelle listened to their conversations and learned who were art students, browsers, and admirers and who were buyers with large collections seeking a hot, new investment.

Isabelle, however, sought to invest in a new life, and she believed this artist could help her achieve it.

Standing in an alcove set off from the main room, she caught sight of Michael propped against the wall with his hands in his jean pockets, refusing to budge. Anita flittered back and forth in front of him as she implored him to mingle with potential buyers.

"Michael, please," she said. "They are dying to meet you. It would be great PR for you to make an appearance." She motioned to the party with her empty champagne flute.

"What does it matter if I meet them or not? It's the paintings that mean something, not me." He glanced at the crowd in the adjoining room before diverting his gaze to the floor.

Isabelle moved to the edge of the alcove and pressed against the wall, out of sight.

"Just this once, please," Anita persisted. "People appreciate the painting more if they can meet the artist."

"I don't know what to say to them."

Isabelle leaned around the corner to see Michael shake his head. Dark waves of hair fell into his eyes. He pushed the strands back with his right hand, stained at the fingertips with traces of brown and yellow paint.

"You don't have to say anything. Just nod your head and look charming. It's not that hard for you to do, Michael." Anita touched his arm, then laughed.

He looked at Anita's hand before shifting out of her reach.

"Besides, there's one gal I really want you to meet," Anita said. "She bought all your paintings the other night. Cleaned us right out. Thankfully, she was willing to loan them to us for the opening, or else—"

"Is that her?" Michael asked. His gaze had shot over Anita's shoulder to land on Isabelle's face peeping around the corner.

Isabelle jerked back. If she had the power to phase through the wall, she would've. So ridiculous to react this way, since she came here to meet him.

"Where?" Anita's heels click-clacked against the floor as she approached, finding Isabelle flattened next to a sunrise painting.

The art dealer greeted her best client with a wide smile.

"Isabelle, why are you standing there by yourself? Come and meet Michael."

Anita grabbed Isabelle's elbow with her thin but strong hand and led her to Michael, slumped against the wall, thick arms crossed over his chest.

"Michael, this is Isabelle Carnier, your biggest fan."

He didn't reach out to shake her hand or even offer a greeting.

Anita huffed her disapproval. She let go of Isabelle's arm, then whispered in her ear, "See what you can do with him. I give up."

She toasted them with her empty glass before returning to the party.

Isabelle propped herself against the wall opposite Michael with her arms crossed to mirror his. His dark eyes bored into her face as if able to see her skin's true preternatural color under her thick foundation. Then his gaze dropped down her dress and to her combat boots, a leftover favorite from her punk era.

A hint of approval or intrigue or maybe interest flickered over his face before it fell back into a neutral expression.

But noting his possible interest was enough for her to clear her throat and say, "You have an amazing gift."

She cringed and almost wished she had said nothing. Such an ordinary thing to tell a talented artist, but it was the one sentence her brain could process.

"Thanks," he murmured. He uncrossed his arms and shoved his hands back into the pockets of his jeans.

"You should be proud of the turnout for your opening. There aren't many new artists who receive this kind of exposure."

"Yeah, I guess." Michael ran his right hand through his hair, leaving thick locks to stand at haphazard patterns. "But I don't like crowds."

Neither did Isabelle anymore, which gave her the courage to suggest, "What if I said you never have to do this again?"

"What do you mean?"

Isabelle pushed aside her unease and uncrossed her arms.

"I have a proposition for you." She took a breath, if only for effect. "Paint my portrait, and I will pay you enough so you won't have to do another gallery opening again. You will never have to suck up to any patrons. You can paint for creativity's sake and never worry about selling your paintings to survive."

Michael shook his head. "I can't do that. My models—"

"I know," Isabelle interrupted. "Your models don't find you."

He nodded as his gaze roamed over Isabelle's face. "And besides . . . "

"I'm not your typical model," Isabelle finished what he was tactful enough not to say.

His models were full of life and color, while Isabelle's skin was a dull alabaster, her eyes faded to a washed-out blue. Even the natural pink of her fingernails had lightened. Her lips had paled so much that she always wore lipstick to look as though she had lips. Her hair was the only part of her body that had retained its pigment, although it had dulled from auburn to a muddied brown.

"For many years, Michael, I was dead. I could feel nothing until I saw your paintings." A tear slid down her cheek. She wiped it away, then remembered, with a start, that it had been half a century since she had last cried.

"Here." She regained her composure and pressed into Michael's hand a white calling card with her number printed in a fine script. "Call me if you change your mind."

She left him standing against the wall staring at her card.

MICHAEL CALLED her the next week. "I'll give it a try. But I can't make any promises."

"That's fine," Isabelle replied. "I'm not looking for any."

He wanted to paint her in natural light, in sunlight. Perhaps he could better capture her in the dawn with its purple and pink hues at this time of year.

But Isabelle gave him a half lie, saying she had a skin disease that made her allergic to the sun's rays.

He sounded dismayed and hesitated over what he should do. Then he suggested a fire—the fireplace in his studio. He had never painted by firelight before. He sounded excited. Isabelle's heart pumped out a beat at the anticipation in his voice, and it startled her. It hadn't beaten since she was alive.

THE FOLLOWING NIGHT, Isabelle knocked on the door to Michael's apartment.

"It's unlocked. Come in," he called from inside, his voice muffled by the door and distance.

Isabelle obliged and entered a narrow, empty hallway. She

followed it into the same studio space where she'd spied on him from the window weeks ago.

"Hey," Michael said and walked in front of her carrying a light stand taller than him.

"Hello, Michael." She trailed after him and past a tripod with a camera situated next to an easel holding a blank canvas. Oil paints had been mixed onto a pallet and set on a stool atop a large sketch pad within easy reach of the artist's chair.

Isabelle sniffed as she walked by the paints, and her mouth watered. What had piqued her appetite, she couldn't tell. Not knowing how long she'd be in Michael's home, she'd drunk two blood bags to keep her hunger at bay. That was usually more than enough for someone her age.

She forced her focus from these odd hunger pains to Michael, who was setting the stand across from a light already brightening the scene. He turned it on, then adjusted a knob to change the light from white to a pastel pink to match the other one.

He caught her watching him and said, "I want to play with different lighting options in case the flames aren't enough or don't capture the feeling I need."

"You're the artist. I'm at your—" Isabelle lost her words when she finally took in the scene he'd set for her portrait.

"You don't like it," he said.

"No," she replied, softly at first, then louder with conviction so he wouldn't be offended. "No, I'm surprised. That's all."

"Do you want something else? We can look through my portfolio for ideas. I assumed you'd want a scene I hadn't done before."

"It's not that. This is perfect. Too perfect."

"Are you sure? Because I can change it."

"No." She nodded. "I mean yes, I'm sure. And, no, don't change it."

"Then what is it?"

Michael stood next to a velvet chaise longue set over a woven rug. With his hands on his hips, he looked from object to object as if he could uncover what was disturbing her.

"This reminds me of my family's farmhouse. Not the chaise

longue." She trailed her fingers over the velvet upholstery. "That would come later." When she hosted salons long into her immortal years.

"But this pewter pitcher with cornflowers in it." Isabelle brushed past him to the mantel. "My mother had a similar one, and this wooden bowel and cup are like those my family used."

Isabelle touched each one with reverence, as if Michael had plucked them from her past.

"I used the same type of blower to keep the fire going for my mother. This fireplace is nearly as large as the one in our kitchen." She stepped back onto the woven rug when the heat from the fire grew too hot against her shins. "Then there's this rug. My grandmother wove one similar to this. It was in my parents' bedroom."

"What made you choose these items?" she asked.

He shrugged. "It's what came to me after we talked."

"But why?"

He shrugged again. "It seemed like you. At the gallery, you were wearing a dress that reminded me of my mom's chaise." He pointed to where Isabelle had rested a hand on the soft, worn upholstery. "And your shoes contrasted with your dress. They were like work shoes, not exactly from a farm, but these props are from other shoots. I just put them together."

She nodded, although she remained unsettled by how a stranger could read her so well.

"What do you want me to do?" she asked, eager to get started.

"I want you to lie there," he pointed to the chaise, "and face the fire. And here." He handed Isabelle two large chenille throws. "Take off your clothes and wrap these blankets around yourself. You can change in the bathroom."

Isabelle returned from the bathroom, the gold and green throws wrapped around her body, and reclined across the chaise. Michael crouched in front of her and adjusted the blankets to drape just so. He then touched her face to tilt it this way, then that way. He moved her right arm to overlap the folds of the fabric to seem as if she were

67

deciding whether to reach out to the fire or stay on the couch wrapped in her blankets.

Michael posed and adjusted her without a word, his fingers and hands prodding her into various positions. Then he'd stand back, shake his head, and try again.

Isabelle lifted her arm to look at where he'd last grasped her. A red mark had formed, as if he had touched a hot blade to her skin.

"Don't move," Michael ordered and placed her hand to rest back on her hip.

"But I—"

"No talking."

Isabelle pressed her lips together so she wouldn't snap at him for his abrupt tone.

"I'm sorry." He squatted in front of her. He brought forward a handful of her hair to drape over her shoulder. "It's my process. I need silence at this stage."

"You want me to act like a mannequin. Be another prop, like this chaise or the flowers."

"Exactly."

She pressed her lips together again. Not from anger this time or disappointment at his response affirming she was indeed a prop to him, but because he was leaning close to her. His shoulder and neck were inches from her face as he adjusted her other arm over the back of the chaise. His breath caressed her cheek, his human warmth sliding over her cold skin. But it was his blood thudding louder and louder near her ears that overwhelmed Isabelle, forcing her to pull away.

"Don't move," he said once more.

To her relief—and the relief of her leg where she was digging in her nails—he stood and stepped back. His eyes trailed the length of her body from head to toe, as if he were studying a puzzle to determine the proper order of the pieces.

Grabbing the tripod and camera, Michael took it around the room, stopping to set it up at different angles and shoot the scene. He adjusted the throws around Isabelle's breasts and shifted her right leg to cross over her left, causing the blanket to barely cover her backside.

Michael tossed another log on the fire. Then he snapped two more pictures before he put away the camera and moved his easel catty-corner from Isabelle and sat behind it.

"Stay," he said, speaking for the first time in what seemed like an eternity.

Isabelle obliged and stared straight ahead into the fire. A frigid cold crept down her body despite the roaring fire and blankets. She considered moving to make Michael touch her again. His human heat would take away the chill, if only for a minute.

His pencil scratched along a page in the sketch pad that he rested on his lap. Out of the corner of her eye, she watched as he drew, then paused to study the scene, before shaking his head and returning to the pad to scratch out a new version. This process continued for another eternity until he tore the paper from the book and crumpled it.

"It's not working," he said with a heavy sigh. "You'll have to come back. I don't know when. It could be days, even weeks."

"I understand. These things take time, which I have plenty of."

So focused on not disturbing Michael's carefully set scene, she forgot about changing in the bathroom. Instead, she slithered out from under the blankets, trying not to flatten the folds he had created. When she looked over at him, his mouth had dropped open in shock as he gaped at her naked body.

When she glanced down, she noticed that her skin gleamed like unpolished marble under the pastel lights. Her pale and washed-out nipples blended with her bleached flesh.

Grabbing a blanket, she wrapped it around herself and sprinted to the bathroom. Next time she'd overfeed before her sitting, so she wouldn't appear so dead.

THE GALLERY HAD DELIVERED the paintings the day after her sitting with Michael. Isabelle hadn't hung them on the walls yet. She'd propped them around her living room against sofas, chairs, side tables. Every night while waiting for his call, she'd sit in the center of the room and imagine their painted light warming her skin. The paintings' serene subjects gave her hope that she could be content again even if Michael never finished her portrait.

Three weeks later, while Isabelle curled up amongst his paintings, assuming he had given up on her, Michael called.

"I started painting the scene without you in it. It seemed to help," he said.

"I'm glad you found your inspiration." *Without me.*

"Like I said, this is a new experience for me, painting by firelight and with—"

"A model so pale and lifeless." Isabelle rested her head against her hand, not believing what she'd just said.

When young and alive, she'd often spoke her mind. Her boldness had caught the attention of those who'd turned her. She'd taken her last human breath in front of the fireplace in her family's kitchen. That was another reason why the scene Michael had chosen for her portrait unsettled her.

"Yes, you are different from the others I've painted," Michael said after a long pause. "But I wouldn't put it like that."

"You didn't have to."

For several seconds, Michael didn't speak. Isabelle didn't even hear him breathing on the other end of the phone and was afraid he had hung up.

Her dead heart surprised her a second time as it pumped out a single beat when Michael spoke again.

"I know this is last minute, but can you sit for me tonight?"

"Give me five minutes," Isabelle replied.

She was there in four.

"YOUR EYES." Drawing close to her face, Michael cupped his hand under her chin and tilted her head up to the light.

His fresh breath sifted across Isabelle's mouth. She ran her tongue across her lips.

"What about them?" she asked.

"They're darker. Do you wear contacts?"

"No," Isabelle replied, worried she would repulse him again. She hadn't taken time to feed before she arrived; in fact, she hadn't been hungry lately.

"It's so odd." He tilted his head from side to side then rubbed his chin, darkened by stubble. "I could've sworn your eyes were a crystal blue, almost clear, but now they look darker, like an aqua-blue. There's green mixed in now."

Isabelle peered at the round mirror dangling by a wire on the wall near his easel. She studied her eyes and found that they were darker. Why hadn't she noticed that before?

Behind her, Michael remixed the paints on his palette. "I have to change the color I had picked for your eyes. Just don't change anything else."

Glancing up at her, he gave her shy smile. It was the first time he'd smiled at her.

"Is that blood I smell?" She shivered.

"I mix drops of my blood into the paint. It's a way for me to leave my mark on each piece." He looked up with another smile.

"That explains it," Isabelle replied.

She followed the same routine from the original sitting. She changed in the bathroom and wrapped the blankets around her body, covering up as much unearthly flesh as possible to avoid shocking Michael into cancelling this session.

After she draped herself over the chaise longue, he arranged her body. This time his touch didn't burn her skin or leave red blotches.

She inhaled a long breath to take in his clean scent as he leaned over her.

"Are you smelling me?" he asked in a teasing way that caused tingles across her belly.

"Yes," she said, smiling up at him.

"I showered."

"I can tell."

"I hadn't showered in a while. I was so focused on your portrait."

"I'm honored."

"That I was so focused that I didn't shower or that I finally showered before you got here?"

"Both."

He laughed. The tingling in her belly increased and felt as if fingers were tickling her flesh. This giddy sensation made her shift in her seat.

"Don't move."

"Whatever you want."

She grinned at the way his face flushed before he busied himself with grabbing his tablet computer from the mantel. Craning her neck, she watched him scroll through the photographs he'd taken last time.

After consulting the images, he arranged the chenille covers to fall over her body, creating a few folds by her breasts and smoothing others down by her stomach. She tried not to move as his fingers brushed her bare leg—his touch no longer a hot poker but as soft and comforting as the blankets.

"There." He scooted back to admire the fall of the fabric and the position of her body. "Now face the fire and don't move."

He cupped his hand under her jaw. Before he let go, he rubbed a circle along her jawline with his thumb. It was the most intimate touch she'd felt in years. She set her teeth to keep herself from crying and asking him to do it once more.

"Perfect," he murmured.

She pretended that he was talking about her personally, not as though he had positioned his still life in the perfect way.

Isabelle stared straight ahead. The swish, swish, swishing of his brush on the canvas, then the dab, dab, dabbing of it in the paint mingled with sound of the crackling fire. She fought the urge to turn her head and watch him paint. She wondered how he saw her.

"Hold that smile," he said.

"What smile?"

He sighed. "You lost it. What were you thinking about?"

"I'd rather not say."

Moments passed and he didn't say anything, didn't paint anything. She turned to see if he was watching her, but the canvas blocked him from view.

"I was wondering how you see me," she admitted.

She heard the paintbrush's bristles scratch against the canvas, then a patting sound as he stirred the paint.

"You'll see soon enough," he said.

She smiled.

"Hold that smile."

"I HAVE AN ITCH," Isabelle said the next night.

By her estimate, she'd been sitting still for almost two hours, and now her muscles ached. Her limbs pulsed with a nervous energy. She had to move.

She heard him put the brush down. He rose, then looked from the canvas, to her, then back to the canvas.

"Where is your itch?" Michael asked.

Isabelle grinned as a lewd thought crossed her mind.

"On my back," she admitted, thinking it best not to embarrass him. She wasn't sure if he would understand it as a joke. She wasn't sure if she would mean it as one.

"On my right shoulder blade," she explained further.

He padded across the wooden floor, barefoot. He said wearing shoes made him feel constricted at this stage in the process. His bare feet somehow made the sessions more casual, more intimate to Isabelle, like they were old friends hanging out in his loft. Session by session, he let down his guard around her.

He scratched her back with his short-cropped nails.

"Damn it, I'm sorry."

Isabelle didn't want to break her pose to see what he was apologizing for, so she continued to stare ahead as she asked, "What are you sorry about?"

He took off his paint-stained white t-shirt and dabbed her shoulder.

"I didn't realize I had paint on my fingers. I got color on you."

"It can only be an improvement," she laughed.

He tossed his shirt to the side.

She strained to look at him without moving her head. He had a small patch of curly hair on his chest and thinner brown hairs traveling lower past his stomach, leading underneath the loose-fitting jeans that hung at his waist.

Isabelle's cheeks warmed. The heat blossomed down her face to her neck and stopped at her chest above her breasts. Her hands twitched, but she held her position despite longing to touch her flesh and confirm the impossible—that she was blushing. The last time she'd felt herself blush, she'd been human.

"THIS IS the last night I'll need you." Michael stood behind the easel to give her privacy while she reclined on the chaise then placed the covers over her naked body.

"Oh." Isabelle tried not to show her disappointment. He didn't need her anymore, but she still needed him.

"When can I see it?" she asked.

"When it's finished. Maybe in a few weeks. It's hard to say when I'll know it's ready."

He didn't have a shirt on, and Isabelle wondered if, like being barefoot, this was part of his process. The closer he came to finishing, the more clothes he removed. And this thought sent another blush—and it was indeed a blush—down her face to her torso.

Once she was situated, Michael entered the scene to stoke the fire and adjust the lights. Then he stopped near Isabelle and leaned close enough for her to see the trail of dark hairs on his stomach more clearly, along with the matching soft tufts on his chest. Scents of his aftershave and soap teased her nose. The earthy, clean smells reminded her of walking through the forest surrounding her family's farm.

Images of pine needles, dewy leaves, and clear, blue skies came to mind. But what didn't come to mind, she realized, was his blood. Being so close to a human, especially one she desired, would fill her senses with the iron scent of their blood. Eating before human inter- action tamped down the urge, but the underlying temptation never went away, even at her age.

Staring into the fire while he moved around her, fussing with the scene, she wondered if she'd lost her craving for human blood. The idea of drinking it turned her stomach.

With a gasp, Isabelle realized that she hadn't fed since the second time she had posed for him.

"Are my fingers cold?"

"Pardon me?"

"You gasped and then jerked away. I thought my cold fingers shocked you."

"No." Isabelle settled herself underneath the blankets, finding it ironic that he considered his hands too cold for her. Although they did seem cooler than before. Or maybe her skin was warmer?

"Was it difficult?" Isabelle asked.

"To do what?" Michael knelt beside her to arrange the blankets.

"To paint me."

"No, it wasn't hard, although you seem to have changed. I know that can't be possible but . . ." He stared at the edge of the blanket where it fell at the crest of her breasts.

"May I?" He made a motion indicating he wanted to pull away the blanket.

"You may."

He slid it down to expose her breasts.

"Your skin color has changed. You *have* color."

She looked where he pointed and sucked in a breath. Her nipples were brown. Her skin held a rosy tint.

Michael was looking at her, too, and for the first time she felt like a human—a desired human being—rather than his prop to be posed.

"Those women in your paintings," she said. His dark eyes flicked back to her face. "Were you close to them?"

"Some were strangers. Some family and friends. Others, I dated."

Isabelle nodded.

Michael tugged up the blanket to cover her breasts. "All of them left after I painted them."

Isabelle watched as Michael sat back onto his heels and studied the folds of the blankets and the position of her arms and legs. She had become a prop again.

Then he lifted his gaze, and when their eyes met, her heart let out three quick thumps. As quickly as he caught her eye, he looked off to the side, leaving Isabelle with an empty space in her chest that made her dizzy. She didn't understand what was happening. What power did he have over her?

Michael clenched and unclenched his fists as if trying to stop himself from doing or saying something he might regret. Shaking his head, he rose to his feet.

"Do you know how hard it is to become close to someone, only to have them leave? Friends, family, girlfriends. I'd paint them, then they'd leave. It was as if they became too full of life after I painted them. They couldn't be confined to one place, to me, anymore. I was too dull for them. I know only how to interpret and paint life. It was hard for me to feel and enjoy it with them."

He strode to the fireplace and grabbed the poker. He jabbed at the logs with it until the flames grew, sending a blast of heat past him to Isabelle.

"Over the past year, I stopped having relationships with my models, with anyone. It's easier that way. If no one is in my life, then no one can leave."

"I understand that more than you'll ever know." Isabelle kicked off the blankets, then rose.

"I won't be abandoned again." He propped his arm on the mantel and stared into the fire as it consumed the log. "After your portrait is finished, you'll be gone. Already you look different, like the others."

She drew closer, and he lifted his head. Their eyes locked in understanding. He didn't draw back when her hand skimmed up his arm and over his shoulder. She let it trail down to the soft curls on his chest until it rested above his heart. He laid his hand over hers.

"Your skin has warmer tones mixed in." He brought her hand to his lips and kissed it.

He ran his fingers through her hair. "Your strands are a richer auburn with reddish highlights. I would think you'd dyed it, but I know you didn't."

"And your breasts." Michael took a small step back and let his eyes trail along her torso.

Isabelle grabbed his arms as he dropped his hands. She guided them back up to her breasts. "What about my breasts?"

Michael drew in a breath. He cupped her breasts as she wrapped her hands around his to hold them in place, letting him know how much she wanted his touch.

His thumbs made circles around her nipples. "These were almost as pale as the rest of you. But now they are darker, like . . ."

"Like they contain the color of life, like my body is full of life again."

He tensed and tried to withdraw, but Isabelle clutched his hands harder so he couldn't go.

"Michael, I won't leave you."

"They all say that."

"You don't understand. I haven't been alive for a long time. Whatever energy or life force you somehow conferred to the others, making them want to leave, has made me whole. It's made me feel human again."

She cupped his face in her hands, so he would know she spoke the truth when she said, "You see, I hadn't been alive for centuries before you painted me."

Isabelle kissed him, at first in appreciation for what he'd done for her. But when he wrapped his arms around her, the kiss deepened.

Her chest pressed against his. She could feel his heart beat in sync with her own. She nuzzled his neck. No scent of blood tempted her. His pulse didn't arouse her hunger but instead aroused her need to experience all of him.

Isabelle bent her knees and leaned back. He followed her unspoken request and laid her on her the rug in front of the fire, only pausing to unzip his jeans and slide them off.

They made love on the floor. Afterward, they slept entangled in front of the smoldering fire.

Isabelle hadn't realized she'd fallen asleep in Michael's arms until the first rays of the morning sun shone through the floor-to-ceiling windows of the loft. Isabelle peeled back the blankets that had covered them as they slept. She walked over to the large windows and hesitantly lifted her hand into a beam of light.

No burning sensation. No flaming red, blistering skin. Taking a deep breath, she walked forward and stood naked with her arms in the air, as if embracing the sun's rays.

Behind her, Michael stirred and woke up with a satisfied yawn.

"We should change your portrait," he said. "Use this light instead of the artificial ones. You are even more beautiful surrounded by the dawn."

"No." Isabelle glanced over her shoulder and said, "I think your painting is finished."

ABOUT THE AUTHOR

From a secret location outside of Washington, DC, J.T. Bock conjures tales to share with kindred readers looking for a fun escape. Her alternate identity enjoys spending time with her workaholic husband, traveling to interesting locales, and enjoying life to the fullest with an amazing group of family and friends and a good glass of wine. Check out J.T.'s latest adventures at **www.jtbock.com**. Follow her on Facebook (**J.T. Bock**) and Instagram (**jtbock_writer**) to learn about her superpowered UltraSecurity Series and her newest paranormal stories.

DELTA DAWN

G.G. GABRIEL

CHAPTER ONE

"First, you make the roux," the elegant Professor de Cuisine said, pointing to a burnished plaque on the wall to her right. Ainsley took a gulp of her champagne and peered around the culinary classroom. The high walls swept up what must have been at least twenty feet to an antique-looking tin panel ceiling. She stared at it instead of meeting the gazes of the others in the crowd who were already mingling.

"If you remember nothing else from this class, I promise you that you will remember that. In fact, I will make sure of it. My name is Professor Delphine Bergeron, and we are going to have some fun in this class."

The way people were talking, they all seemed to know each other, but Ainsley had made the trek from New York City all by herself. She'd been excited to get out of the city in February for a few days and could have killed her best friend, Deanna, for bailing at the last minute. But since this trip was courtesy of an incentive at work and still included the sunny days she'd been missing, she couldn't be too frustrated.

Ainsley prided herself on being a bit of a workaholic, and having Deanna here would have helped her focus on more than the frustration of "earning" this corporate-sponsored trip with someone else on the sales team whose numbers were "the same" as hers. That couldn't have been possible. She'd worked her ass off last year and knew there was no way that her final sales figures were exactly the same—to the penny—as someone else's in the company. One of them had made more, even if it was only by a few dollars, and the trip should have been offered only to that person. But no, instead she was *sharing* this incentive with another sales executive she'd never met.

The class was about to start, so she tried to shake off her tension. Cooking was something that she enjoyed. At least the idea of it was, and she was excited to learn more about Cajun and Creole cuisine. The best part about New York City was sometimes getting away from all the action, but the N'awlins vibe wasn't making her feel relaxed today. *Stay positive and professional, girl.*

She took a deep breath of Southern air and let the food, the carefree environment and the music charm her stress away. *Channel that charm.*

The professor clapped her hands once, sharply enough to put all eyes on her. "Everyone, you will notice that there are five cooking stations labeled by letter, and each is set up for four people. If you flip your name badge over, you will find your station. Please make your way to your cooking station now. Let's have some fun."

Ainsley checked her badge—C, right in the middle of the classroom that felt more like a cruise deck than a demonstration kitchen. The swirls inside her stomach worsened. She could have used some food before bubbles, but there hadn't been time on the plane once she had run and rerun her interview pitch for next week. Time was not something Ainsley had a lot of, and she really didn't need to be taking a vacation, much less a trip she earned for just doing her job.

All of her focus was pointed at getting this promotion. Only one other name had been mentioned as a possibility for Chief Sales Officer, so Ainsley had to stand out. CSO was the only job she'd wanted since she joined the company.

"Is everyone settled? Has everyone found your spot?" Professor Bergeron asked.

Yes. She was settled. And it looked like everyone else was as well. She studied the layout of her station. High-quality cookware, clean and shiny tools waiting on the counter, and four aprons…but just her. This must be her lucky day. No awkward coworker to talk to. She didn't mind cooking by herself either. She was used to doing everyone else's job anyway.

Hinges squealed as the door at the back of the room opened.

"I'm sorry I'm late. I'm so sorry, but my Über broke down, and I had to help fix the tire." A man in a tweed jacket and starched khakis burst into the room, suitcase and briefcase in hand.

"No problem, sweetie. And you are?" the professor asked.

He was loud, but he certainly wasn't hard on the eyes.

"Hunter Marsh."

No way. Ainsley stared daggers at him. *You have got to be kidding me.*

"I'm so sorry, ma'am," he continued. "I didn't even have time to drop my bags at the hotel, and it is hot out there." He wiped the sweat from his brow.

"Welcome to New Orleans." The professor met him in the middle of the room, reaching out and turning his badge over when she was close enough.

"You're at cooking station C. That's right over here." She directed him toward Ainsley.

This lug was the guy that tied with me for top sales? He didn't look like he had much upstairs, but that smile could sell underwear to a nudist. She smoothed out her expression and watched as he dragged his suitcase to their station.

"I'm Hunter. Pleased to meet you." He extended his hand.

"I'm Ainsley." His grip was surprisingly solid and warm. And not sweaty, considering his complaint about the heat.

"Ainsley? Ainsley Conners?"

"Yes."

"I've heard so much about you. Wow." He squeezed her hand gently.

"What? You have?"

"You're a legend. My mentor talked about you and how you

changed the sales program," Hunter explained. With a smile, he finally let go, and Ainsley was surprised that she kind of wanted to keep holding his hand.

"Really?" Unsure how to respond to his words or her reaction, she felt her cheeks heat.

"And sorry I'm late. My brother was supposed to come, but can you believe he backed out at the last minute? He had to stay in San Francisco for a bachelor party in Napa." Hunter turned to roll his matching Tumi bag and briefcase against the wall.

She traveled a lot and knew this type well. Million miler, always stayed at the same hotels to cash in on the upgrades and free drinks, and completely full of themselves.

"My best friend did the same thing to me. Put this on." She handed him a silly white apron that was decorated with brightly colored vegetables and the saying *First you make the roux.* The embroidery was clearly quality, but they could have just put a nice elegant fleur-de-lis on it, for goodness' sake.

Hunter tied the apron's top strings behind his neck with the reverence of someone competing on *Iron Chef* for a gold medal.

"Class, let's get started on learning about cookin' in New Orleans. Now what did I say was the most important thing you'll learn in this class?" Professor Bergeron asked and about half the class said limply, "First you make the roux."

"That ain't gonna work for me." She clapped and danced down the aisle between stations. "Let's say it together!"

The entire class erupted with the motto, and when Ainsley looked over, Hunter was all smiles.

CHAPTER TWO

"Corn and crab bisque, crawfish étouffée and chocolate pecan pie. Whoo-we, if we aren't full after this meal, we're in trouble," Hunter said as he pulled silk.

"I know. We may never need to eat again." Ainsley wiped her hands on a towel. "Are you almost finished shucking that corn?"

"No. She gave us a million ears." He looked down at a half full stockpot of whole ears of corn. It reminded him of snapping beans with his family on the porch when he was a kid.

"Give me some and I'll help." She moved toward him.

"Sure. But it's a messy job." He held up his hands, showing the juice from the sweet corn all over the cutting board.

He couldn't help sneaking a peek at Ainsley's smile every chance he got. Not only did she work at the same company, but they lived on opposite sides of the country. With the pandemic disrupting travel schedules, he hadn't ever met her in person, but rumors said to watch out. More than one person had told him that she might look sweet, but she was a shark at work.

"It's fine. I'm used to cleaning up after everyone else," she said.

"Hey now. We did win the same trip, didn't we?"

"Yes, but everyone knows that your region is the easiest with LA and San Francisco." Her movements were fast and efficient as she cleaned the cobs of corn.

"Is that so?" Hunter asked.

"It is so. And not only do you have Napa, Sonoma, and all of California wine country, you also have the entire state of Oregon."

"But you have the entire spirits division in your region," Hunter fired back.

"True," she said with a shrug.

"Let's not talk about work." He didn't want to get on the wrong side of anyone, but especially not her.

"Why? Are you afraid I'll know more about it?" she asked.

"No, but we came here to take a break from work. Not to fill our weekend with it." He was ready for a short break in a delicious city.

"Well, unlike you, I'm serious about my career. I can't just take a weekend off for fun like it's some part-time job."

"Hey now, I didn't mean it like that. I know this is still work. But it's forced fun." He offered her a grin.

"Forced fun. Maybe it isn't fun at all," she grumbled, though he caught her hiding a small smile.

Hunter clutched his chest and let his knees buckle a little. "That's a low blow." But she did reward his performance with a real smile this time. "Well, I already know that you're great at sales, and I can see that you at least have a tiny bit of fun cooking."

"That's true. I was excited about this trip."

"Yeah?"

"Then you showed up." Ainsley let her gaze linger on his for an extra second. "Just joking. You seem to be pretty good at this cooking gig too." She looked back at the corncob in her hand.

"How about this idea?" Hunter asked. "I'll chop the parsley and green onion for the chowder. And you finish the corn before we start prepping the ingredients for the étouffée. What do you think?"

"That sounds like a plan. Divide and conquer. You might not be so bad after all."

"I hope not," he said with another grin. She didn't look directly at him as she yanked the next cob clean, but her cheeks pinkened just a little.

"I probably would have met you before now if it hadn't been for the pandemic," she said after he'd stacked his parsley leaves and started chopping.

"Probably. These last couple years have been crazy with company travel restrictions. But we're here now, so we should enjoy it while we're in the Big Easy."

"I wish I could be so carefree." Her voice held a pinch of wistfulness.

"We've earned it. It was a hard year."

"It's not rocket science," she countered. "We do work for a wine and spirits company, and it was a pandemic. Everyone was drinking."

"True." But 2020 and into 2021 had been tough. Many of their brands were exclusive to restaurants, which were shut down and failing at unprecedented rates. It had been his idea, early on, to rebottle for residential use.

Hunter took a breath to explain the changes he'd implemented and just as quickly released it. He didn't need to impress her with bullet points from his annual review. Not that it seemed like much would impress this career-obsessed princess.

Besides, this was a mini vacation. For both of them, whether she wanted to accept that or not.

"How about this?" Was that a hint of concession he heard in her tone? "I'll enjoy the weekend, but don't pick on me when I do have to work some. I'm prepping for a big meeting next week."

If that was her compromise, he'd take it.

"I LOVE how they stress the importance of the roux. It just makes so much sense." Ainsley looked over at Hunter again. The lug had seemed like he was going to be an arrogant jerk, but he was softer than she expected. And she shouldn't judge someone just by his looks. Even though he did have a heck of a smile.

"It sure does. And delicious too," he agreed.

"I'm finished with this corn. What can I do to help with the étouffée?" She dropped the last cob into the stockpot.

"Well, I started it, but there are a lot of things to chop. How long is this recipe?"

"I'll help. Let me grab a knife." She slipped into the small space where the other cutting board was set up next to his. Their bodies couldn't help but touch, and although she was surprised to admit it to herself, she didn't really mind.

"If you take the knife like this," he said, showing her with his hands, "you can slice the onion this way and then turn it, and it makes for perfect diced onion."

"You're pretty good at this." She didn't love people showing her things, but his method made the chopping go faster. It was sweet of him to demonstrate.

"Well, cooking helps me relax. It's something about the chopping and precision and bringing everything together at the same time."

"Really? Work is the only thing that helps me relax."

"Wow. You're a barrel of fun." He gently bumped her hip as he teased. "Bring on the spreadsheets."

"Actually, it does. I love solving problems and usually have to pick up the pieces when someone drops the ball at work. That's what I'm good at, and I enjoy it."

"You mentioned that before, but what do you really do for fun?"

She paused to look at him. "Work is my fun." Was it really so odd that she enjoyed her career?

"How is that roux coming along?" the professor asked as she came to their station.

"I think it looks good, but it's pretty light," Ainsley said.

"Do we need something else in it?" Hunter asked.

"What you need, sugar, is just a little more time. We can fix this. A good rich roux only has a couple ingredients, so perfection just takes time and patience," Professor Bergeron said.

"I don't think she has much patience." He gave Ainsley a look.

"Hey now," she said.

"How long have you two been together?" the professor asked.

"Him?" Ainsley pointed at Hunter. "Oh, no. We're not together. We just met."

"With the way y'all were bantering back and forth, I thought you must be getting close to getting engaged. I see these things," the professor said with a wink.

"Uh-uh. Nope," Hunter said.

"Well, maybe I'm having an off day, but that doesn't happen very often," the woman said. "Who cut all this up?"

"That, actually, was a joint effort. I can't deny that he's good in the kitchen," Ainsley said.

"You too," he replied.

"You might not have cooked the roux long enough, but it looks like you two make a great team. Just remember, first you make the roux, and you'll be all right. Why don't you get that cookin', and I'll be back to check on you in a while."

"We kinda do," Ainsley grudgingly agreed.

"Keep stirring it, sweetheart," the professor told her. Then she nodded at Hunter. "And you too."

"What?" he asked when she'd walked away to another station.

"We make a good team," Ainsley said.

"I guess we do. What are you doing tonight for dinner?"

"Seriously? Look at all this food."

"I know, but all this cooking is making me hungry." He gave her a cheeky grin that was nearly swoon-worthy. "This is lunch, but we'll have to eat later too. And we're in a great food city. Have dinner with me tonight?"

"I HAVE TO ADMIT. It was a great suggestion to have dinner," Ainsley said as she and Hunter followed the maître d' to a table.

"Well, I'm a big guy and..." Hunter replied.

"I know. And all that cooking made you hungry. That's going to be the line I remember from this weekend. I barely want to eat after I cook."

"I saw you didn't finish everything. If I knew you better, I would have asked for your leftovers," he said with a laugh.

"So it turns out your dinner suggestion was good. I'm actually starving."

The soaring ceilings, beautiful floors and crisp white linens of Arnaud's always made Ainsley happy. It was definitely classic French Quarter elegance, but the food made the experience more special.

"Welcome to Arnaud's," a server said as he faced their table. "Can I start you off with an appetizer and something to drink?"

"Escargot," they said in unison.

Ainsley laughed. "Well, that makes that easy."

"Certainly. And to drink?" he asked, looking at her.

"Dirty Goose martini, three olives with just a whisper of vermouth."

"You read my mind," Hunter said. "Two, please."

"So, what were you thinking for dinner?" she asked after the server left.

"Anything as long as I have it with the soufflé potatoes."

"Uncanny. A dinner at Arnaud's without those potatoes isn't possible. And the béarnaise," she added. That béarnaise probably had poems written about it.

He held a hand over his heart and sighed dramatically. "Food is my first love."

"I can see that. Work is my first love."

"Really?" Hunter set his menu aside and gave her his full attention.

The impact of his clear gaze was more than she expected, and Ainsley looked down to adjust the napkin in her lap. "Why. Is that a surprise?"

"Definitely not. You have talked about it. A lot."

Well, that was direct. "I'm sorry."

"Don't be," Hunter said. "It's not bad to like your job."

"I can't help it. I just get so excited about my job. I love it and I love the team I've built since I've been here."

"I get it. It's a good place to work."

"I just want to show my parents that I am worth something," she admitted quietly.

"Well, I can tell you that you don't need this or any job to prove your worth. You are an incredibly accomplished person already."

It was kind of him to say that, but... "My parents wouldn't think so."

"From what I've seen and heard, it seems to me that you can do anything. And you are already pretty successful. You're a senior VP for a big company."

"So are you," she told him with an arch look. "It's never enough for them, though."

"Well, that's too bad. Don't let anyone let you feel less than you are. Even your parents." His confidence in her felt surprisingly good. Maybe because they were peers, and he knew exactly how much effort and dedication went into achieving what she had professionally.

"Can I just take you home with me and have you tell them that?" They'd believe it coming from this guy.

"You don't need my approval or anyone else's. From what I hear, you don't worry about what others think at the office. Why should they be different?"

"You haven't met my parents," she said, only half joking. But he did have a point.

"THANK YOU FOR A GREAT EVENING," Hunter said. "That was a dinner for the history books."

Ainsley had to admit that walking through the streets of New Orleans with someone was nice. And walking with Hunter Marsh might be even better than with just someone.

"It sure was," she agreed. "I'm certainly not hungry anymore."

"Speak for yourself. I could eat."

"I think I might have a drink before going up. I just love the

Carousel Bar." She peeked at his handsome profile as they walked. "You're welcome to join me."

Hunter turned to meet her gaze. "I don't want to impose," he said quietly.

"You aren't imposing. I'd like it." It felt nice to admit that out loud.

He pressed a warm hand to her lower back as the Hotel Monteleone doorman ushered them inside.

"Wow. And are there really two seats available in the back?" Hunter asked as they entered the bar.

They looked at each other. "Run."

"That's pretty good teamwork there," the bartender said as they settled in their seats. "What can I get you to drink?"

"Sazerac," Ainsley said.

"No way. That is what I was going to order," Hunter said.

The bartender gave them a look. "I hate to play devil's advocate, but you are in New Orleans. Ordering a Sazerac here is like a tourist ordering a piña colada in the Caribbean."

"He's right." She shrugged. "But I do like them."

"What I'd really like is his job," Hunter said under his breath.

"What?" She must not have heard him right.

"Don't you ever feel the corporate world is sucking the life out of you?"

"Not really. Every day, I wake up energized to try to do something new. To try to be a better person, a better manager and move the company forward."

"I bet you do. And I love it. Heck, I'm good at it. Just sometimes, I think how much I would love to work in a restaurant or bar." He nodded toward the bartender, who was pouring whiskey with one hand and dropping a straw into a drink with the other.

"Not work in. Run it. I could see you doing that. In fact..." She glanced across the bar. "Hey, bartender. I'm sorry, I don't know your name."

"It's Jack."

"Well, Jack, my friend here has a dream of being a bartender or owning a restaurant. Do you think he could make it out of the corporate world?"

"Corporate guy, huh? And you think you can make these cocktails?" Jack nodded at the drinks lined up in front of him.

"I'd like to try," Hunter replied with a grin.

"What's your name, boss?"

"It's Hunter," Ainsley called.

"Hey, all you characters here at the Carousel Bar. This here is Hunter, and he wants to try his hand at being a bartender. Should we give him a shot?" Jack asked in a booming voice.

"No. Really?" Hunter asked as the crowd roared in the affirmative.

"This is New Orleans. Anything can happen." The bartender held out his hand and Hunter popped quickly from the bar stool and over the counter.

"Who wants a cocktail?" Hunter yelled through a huge smile.

Ainsley could see his eyes sparkle, and he was good at it. He and Jack made a pretty great team, tossing bottles and mixers back and forth. This was clearly not his first time behind a bar.

"You take the martinis and I'll make the daiquiris," Jack said.

"Right on."

From dirty martinis to margaritas and frozen concoctions, Hunter rocked it. It seemed so natural for him, like it had when he was cooking in their culinary classes. Ainsley couldn't believe her eyes. It wasn't usual for executives to be seen slinging drinks in the Big Easy, but here he was. And it wasn't just mixing cocktails. Hunter was throwing the bottles up in the air and spinning them in his hands like he was Tom Cruise. At one point, he even had four different vodkas balanced between his fingers and was pouring them into separate chilled martini glasses at the same time. And that really seemed to impress the crowd.

"I learned that on a cruise," he told Ainsley with a wink.

And when he brought Ainsley the best Vieux Carré she had ever tasted, he bent over the bar and brushed his lips on her cheek, making her warm all over. The movement was so natural she wasn't sure he even realized he'd done it.

The next time he came over, she grabbed him by the tie, pulled him close, and planted a big one on him. Which, between the bartending and the kisses, caused the bar to erupt in raucous woo-hoos and applause.

What a night. She had gone from thinking he was an oaf when she first saw him at lunchtime to seeing something more in his current joy. Hunter was alive in the moment, and she'd bet he didn't get this excited about sales calls. This was what he was meant for.

CHAPTER THREE

"Hey, Hunter," Ainsley called from across the room with a wave. He might be mistaken, but there might actually have been a hint of excitement in her voice. Hunter couldn't stop his cheeks from pulling into a big grin.

"Hey there," he said. "I'm glad I didn't have to drag all my bags in with me today. I felt like such a goof yesterday."

"You would never know. I think the class, and certainly the professor, clearly couldn't resist your charm." Ainsley blushed a little as she said it. Maybe she found him charming too?

"Well, you know what they say about us Yankees. Full of charm." Then he burst out with a "Not."

She laughed with him, and it made Hunter feel like he was a teenager back in high school again. Why was this girl making him so tongue-tied? Normally he could string together words quite eloquently, but here he was calling himself a Yankee and acting like a child. In the boardroom or during a sales pitch, he was flawless. And getting hit on was never an issue. Back in San Francisco, he had been known to have to fight the girls—and the guys—away to escape a crowded bar. And it humored him. But with Ainsley, it felt different. It felt like something…bigger.

Inhaling deeply to find some composure, he asked, "What's on the menu?"

"Day two. Remember, Professor Bergeron said that today was going to really be challenging because we're making barbecue shrimp, gumbo and Bananas Foster."

"Good memory. I guess that would explain this giant bowl of shrimp in this colander," he replied.

"You'd think they could take the heads off." Ainsley grimaced.

"That's what gives the dish its flavor, honey," the professor said from behind them. "We're going to get the heads off, just like this"—she demonstrated the quick and efficient technique—"and cook them for a delicious sauce."

Ainsley picked up the little crustacean. "She makes it look easy."

"It isn't too tough. May I?" She could probably show him a thing or two in the boardroom or during a sales pitch, but he was happy to help her in the kitchen.

"Sure."

"Take your thumb and forefinger like this." He gently grasped the shrimp's head. "Then take the other hand and just twist."

"Like this?" Ainsley said before destroying the shrimp.

"Close. Can I see your hand?" Hunter asked. With a nod, she stepped closer, nearly close enough to embrace. He shaped the cool fingers of her right hand like she was saying *it's only this big.*

The next shrimp head popped right off.

"I got it!" She bounced up and down with excitement beside him.

Hunter smiled at her even as fireworks burst in his chest. He wanted nothing more than to wrap his arms around her. If they weren't in class, he might have asked for a kiss.

"You did," he said, laughing as she moved away. "It's not too hard, is it?" Was he sweating? He couldn't tell.

"That's a lot of shrimp to get through. Want to help me?" Ainsley swayed so her shoulder bumped his.

"Sure." Anything to stay close to her.

"You know," she started as they beheaded the cold shrimp, "I have been so stressed out about work, and this is really taking my mind off it."

"Why? You have nothing to worry about. You're at the top of your game." They were the two top sales personnel in the company.

"There's more to that than you think." Her tone was glum.

"What do you mean? What could you be worried about?"

"Hunter, please don't tell anyone this, but the Chief Sales Officer is leaving the company, and I am under consideration. I want it so bad, but I don't know if I will get it."

It took him a moment to find a reply. He hoped he sounded casual when he said, "Well, why not? You'd be great at it." It had never occurred to him that she might interview for the same job he was being tapped for.

"Thank you, but who knows. It sure would prove to my parents that I'm good at my job." The earnestness in her voice broke his heart.

"Ainsley." Setting down his shrimp, he faced her and waited for her to meet his gaze. "You are good at your job or you wouldn't be here."

"I know." But she didn't sound very confident for once.

"For now, let's just focus on lunch." Hopefully, that would give him a chance to process what she'd just revealed.

"Is everything okay?" she asked.

"Yes. We've just got to get through this and the other dishes before lunchtime." He offered what he hoped was a kind smile.

"You sure?"

But maybe not kind enough since she was still questioning it.

"Yeah. Hand me that towel. Actually, I'll be right back." Hunter said before running off to the men's room.

BY THE TIME HUNTER RETURNED, Ainsley had finished chopping and prepping the ingredients for the gumbo. She didn't understand what had happened. Hunter was acting strange. He loved cooking, and she knew he wouldn't want to miss twenty minutes of class for nothing.

"Is everything okay?" she asked.

"Yes. I'm just a little tired today, I guess."

"Sure." She tilted her head down and around to look up at Hunter.

"Oh my goodness. I can't help but smile when you do something like that."

She smiled back at him and bit her lip. "Okay. You could tell me if there was something wrong."

Maybe she shouldn't have told him that she was up for the CSO role. If she got the job, it would mean that she would be his boss. Even though he didn't seem like the kind of guy who would be bothered by that, something was wrong.

"Sorry I took a while. What's next?" he asked.

"I chopped the rest of the ingredients for the gumbo and cut up the chicken."

He might not be that type of guy, but if he was liking her as much as she was liking him, that could pose a problem. And it definitely seemed to Ainsley that she was liking him. A lot.

"Wow. It's a beautiful little mise en place," he said with a gesture toward her prepped ingredients.

"Someone's pulling out the big words," she joked. "And look at the roux."

"It's amazing."

"And it's going to be even more so when it finishes." Professor Bergeron appeared beside them again. This lady was like a ninja. "You won't believe the beautiful color it will become with the right amount of work. Something like this." She pulled a jar out of her apron that contained a dark, velvety sauce.

"It really will look like that?" Ainsley asked, amazed at the color.

"It sure will. If you keep stirring and stirring and slowly building it up, it will. Nurture your roux and give it time. It will turn out spectacular and make all your dishes taste great." The professor said, spinning the jar in her hands and examining the color at eye level.

"That is really cool," he said, reaching out to grab the roux.

"Yesterday's roux was a little lighter. Today's is the champion roux," the professor said.

"Incredible," Ainsley said.

"How are things going with the dishes? They are looking pretty good," Professor Bergeron asked.

"Thanks. They are," Ainsley said.

"Well, get that gumbo started, and I'll be back to help," Professor Bergeron said, pointing down into the mix.

"Thanks," Ainsley said.

"Yeah. Thanks," Hunter said. "Ainsley, that was good feedback. We are a good team."

"I think so. It all smells so good," he added, wafting the mist to his face.

"Have you ever cooked Cajun or Creole food before?" Ainsley asked.

"Actually, these are two cuisines I haven't tried a lot. I think I was intimidated to try," he answered, his shoulders going into a shrug.

"You look like you are an expert at it, though." She'd watched his every move, fascinated by his magic and competence in the kitchen. There were so many things she liked about him, which shocked her.

Forty-eight hours ago, Ainsley hadn't been looking. Now she was interested, but his standoffishness after she told him about the CSO job made her worry. Her parents' relationship had never been a good example, and she didn't have much trust left, but despite all of that, Hunter made her feel good.

―――――――

"Can I have two volunteers please?" Professor Bergeron asked, and the entire class raised their hands. Except Ainsley and Hunter. The professor squinted at them. "I'm just kidding. I already had these two in mind. Ainsley and Hunter, please come on down to the main stove."

They looked at each other. "Let's go," Ainsley said with a shrug.

The class applauded as they walked to the demonstration area.

A wall opened to reveal a space in front of their workstations. "This is our main kitchen," the professor said. Ainsley peered at the giant white marble counters and a gargantuan ten-burner built-in range gleaming with platinum fleur-de-lis.

101

"These two are going to help me make some bananas Foster for dessert. Yum," the professor said. "Have you had that before?"

"Yes," Ainsley and Hunter both said, smiling at each other.

"Let's get cooking! Just like we developed the roux, we are going to layer the flavors of this dessert. And then we are going to light it all on fire."

"Just for fun?" Hunter asked.

"For fun and flavor. We know what makes a difference down here. You'll see." The professor gestured them forward.

A half dozen ingredients were separated on either side of a beautiful recipe card in a red leather folder. Ainsley started grabbing the dry ingredients while Hunter went for the giant bowl of bananas.

"Would you look at that teamwork? These two know how to divide and conquer."

Hunter peeled and sliced the bananas as quickly as he could while still watching Ainsley. She carefully measured out the brown sugar, cinnamon and liquor, double-checking the recipe card at each step.

"I'll help with that," she said, sliding a cutting board and a bunch of bananas toward her.

The professor walked them through the rest of the dish as the class watched in silence. Finally, she pulled out a lighter, lit it near the sauté pan of liquor-soaked bananas, and flames shot a few feet in the air to everyone's delight.

"Bam!" the professor said, laughing as she threw something in that made it sparkle. "I think these two deserve a round of applause. Come on up here if you want some of this deliciousness."

Ainsley wrapped her arm around Hunter's waist and looked up. "If we can do this, we can work together too."

"Ainsley..." But Hunter wasn't sure what he wanted to say. Instead, he picked up his dish and headed to a table.

"What?" she asked as she followed him.

"Let's not talk about work. At least enjoy this amazing dessert."

"I'm sorry, but I just can't hold it in now that I told you. I'm so nervous. Please don't be mad at me," she said quietly.

"I'm not mad at you." And that was true. But he was certainly conflicted.

"What is it then? You have to admit that you have been acting weird since I told you. Are you worried that I would be your boss?"

"I'm not worried that you'd be my boss, Ainsley. I'm worried because they asked me to interview for the job too."

"What do you mean?"

"We're both being considered for the same job. And it sucks."

He needed to get out of there. Hunter gave her one last look, then left the kitchen.

HUNTER SPOTTED Ainsley as he entered the basement of Brennan's for their graduation from the New Orleans School of Cooking weekend seminar.

"Hello," she said as he stopped by her side.

"Hi." He took a deep breath. "I'm sorry that we are both being considered for this job. I don't want to bother you. I never meant for it to turn out this way. And I'm sorry for walking away this afternoon."

"I was worried about you. The professor asked where you went." Ainsley looked at him, but he was still a little ashamed of his behavior earlier and stared over her shoulder instead of meeting her eyes.

"Again. I'm sorry. I didn't know what to do, and class was over." He turned to walk away.

"Hunter, wait." She reached for his hand, and their fingers brushed before she clasped hers in front of her.

"Yes?"

"We could at least have a drink and some food. Couldn't we? After all, we are still colleagues."

"I would like that." And he realized it was true. He didn't want to feel like he was in competition with her. "I would like that very much."

"It was probably good that I found that out. I might have been in denial that anyone was in the running for the job."

"I wish I had your confidence, Ainsley. You would be amazing at that job."

"I wish." Now she was the one avoiding his gaze.

"No, you would," he assured her. "And think about the laugh they are going to have when they realize they sent two employees that are competing for the same job away for the weekend."

"I guess they were probably expecting us both to bring someone else."

"Look at this room, though. It's spectacular. How about we make a truce and enjoy the incredible evening they have planned."

"I agree. We deserve it. And may the best person—no, the right person—get the job." She held her arm out boldly to shake hands. Hunter took her hand, and instead of shaking, they got caught in each other's eyes. He let his thumb run over the soft skin on the back of her hand. As soon as he released his grip, he missed the warmth of her fingers around his.

"You know I love food, and I'm truly excited to see what they have prepared for us, but I don't feel like I can eat another thing. So much food," he said as they turned toward the front of the room.

"No way. I thought cooking makes you hungry," she teased.

"Yeah, but eating makes me full."

"Based on what they've done all weekend, I bet that this is going to blow us away." Ainsley grabbed his hand and pulled him into the dining room.

The New Orleans School of Cooking did not disappoint. And the wine cellar venue at Brennan's was spectacular. Each course was better than the next, and the wine pairings complemented each course effortlessly.

"I have to say yum at some point," Hunter said.

"I know. Wow," she agreed.

"We're doing pretty good for two people who weren't very hungry." He expected her to laugh with him, but her head was down as she stared at her phone.

"I just got an e-mail from corporate. Did you?" Ainsley asked.

"Why are you checking your phone here? It's such a perfect dinner."

"I'm always checking my phone. But really, just look."

"Okay." He pulled his iPhone from his pocket. "Oh, no. I'm assuming you have to be on the corporate jet tomorrow morning too, for an interview?"

"That's what my e-mail said. I wonder what the hurry is."

"I don't know. I wasn't supposed to be back until Wednesday."

She abruptly pushed back from their table and stood. "I have to go."

"Ainsley…" he started, but she was already walking away, so he jumped up to follow her.

"Professor Bergeron," she said, "thank you for an incredible weekend and such delicious food." She shook the instructor's hand but refused to look at Hunter.

"You are most welcome. We hope to see you both back here some-day," the professor said with a kind smile. Ainsley returned it wanly and turned toward the stairs to exit.

"Ainsley, please don't." He touched her shoulder.

She stopped, but didn't face him. "I can't, Hunter. I'm sorry. I have a tendency to make a mess of things in my personal life, and I've been working toward this opportunity for years. I can't jeopardize my career."

She disappeared up the stairs.

CHAPTER FOUR

The bright morning light that Hunter normally welcomed hit hard today. Something wasn't working in his mind . . . or maybe in his heart. The 5:30 a.m. run felt lackluster, and he couldn't muster the energy to enjoy breakfast even though the egg on the spellbinding crab Benedict was perfectly poached and the yolk drizzled effortlessly over a crisp, homemade English muffin. It truly was a symphony on his taste buds.

Despite that—and the perfectly steeped Italian coffee with luscious crema topping it—he couldn't shake this feeling that everything in the world was wrong. It wasn't just what had happened with Ainsley. No. This was an imbalance that was coming from something else, something deep down in him.

In a single weekend, Ainsley had reawakened his passion for cooking that he'd squashed for years trying to do something folks back in the Midwest would consider "successful." And she had done it all so easily. Like magic. She didn't have to pry it out of him because with her it was easy to talk about. When he talked to her about food, she looked at him like he was the one with the magic.

AINSLEY WANTED to slump into the corporate jet's sumptuous leather seat, but instead arched her back slightly and struck a power pose. Hunter would arrive soon, and she wasn't going to let him see her sweat.

"I'm Gregory, and I'll be assisting you today," the tall air host said. "Can I get you a drink before we depart?"

"Just a coffee."

"We have French press, espresso, or lattes."

"How about a nonfat sugar-free vanilla latte?"

"Coming right up," he said with a smile.

"Great."

And then Hunter appeared in the doorway. He looked sharp. He looked delicious. He looked like the thing that could get in the way of her career.

"What can I get for you to drink, sir?" the air host said, stopping him in the aisle.

"A bottled water and double espresso please," Hunter answered.

"Is this seat taken?" He gestured to the seat next to her.

"No. I think it's just us today on the plane," Ainsley said, putting her earbuds in before he could ask anything else. She had a right to be upset. Didn't she? After all, she didn't just work hard. She practically reinvented sales at the company. And she loved every minute of it.

"Ainsley, c'mon. We shouldn't be mad at each other."

She pointed to her earbud as though she couldn't hear him.

He arched an eyebrow at her. "We have to talk about this."

"Okay. Why?" She removed her earbuds but kept them in hand and plainly in sight.

"Well, first of all. We work together."

"We've managed to stay away from one another's work since you started."

"True. But there was a global pandemic that caused us to shut down most of our travel, and I was working closely with my customers to help supply them during that crazy time."

"Well, I think we should go back to that." Back to when she didn't have to choose between her heart and her head.

"You don't think we had a nice time this weekend?"

"That isn't important, Hunter. We can't pretend like we can have something, even a friendship, when we're competing for the most important job of our lives."

"How do you know it's the most important job of our lives?" he asked quietly.

She stared at him without a sound, her eyes set on his. Why didn't he understand?

He turned his gaze away and looked out the window. "Ainsley, I'd like to see you again. And I think you maybe want to see me again too."

"It is not possible. One of us is going to get this job, which would make one of us a direct line manager, and those relationships are against company policy. How could that work?"

"I don't know. I just don't want to give up on something that's been fun. I like you."

If only that were enough.

"I can't see any option for an 'us' to happen." Her tone was subdued. "Plus, you live on the other side of the country."

"We could try."

"Look, I wish you the best of luck in your interview," she lied. "Let's just agree to be colleagues and leave it at that."

"Ainsley . . ."

"That's all." She met his eyes one final time before moving to the seat farthest away in the back.

HUNTER WATCHED the foam dissipate from the center of the glass, then took a deep breath and slowly let it out. A week ago, his mind was so clear. Today was the day that he would march into the office after a superb breakfast and walk out as the Chief Sales Officer. He'd have his bragging rights back home, and he'd have the career success that he'd dreamed of.

But he didn't care about that anymore. Now, all he could think about was what color would define the dining room and if he'd buy All-Clad pots and pans or hire a poissonier. He could envision his restaurant so clearly in his mind.

It felt like all of this would be easier if Ainsley were around, but she'd barely even talked to him on the plane. How could a single weekend make such a difference?

Hunter pulled out his iPad and traced the lines of the dream restaurant design that his college friend Rob, who was studying architecture, had drafted for him many years ago. It had been years since he'd looked at the file, but the design would still work.

In fact, after a weekend focused on food and presentation, he could see it so vividly it was almost like he was there. A long shotgun space that was wider than others, exposed brick and wrought iron scrolled beams above big tufted banquets covered in olive green velvet and worn leather. A clear view of the expeditor's station so diners could watch the magic happen. Guests would come into the inviting space and leave amazed.

Hunter could hear the phone ringing now. A Michelin star? No two. Then three. And then he would expand and bring his love of food and wine to the world.

The screen of his iPad faded to dark, and he filled his lungs with Manhattan air. Life was short, and he had always loved the proverb, "Fortune favors the bold."

Hunter Marsh knew these were more than dreams, and he had a lot to think about.

———

A TINY BEAD of sweat traced the shape of Ainsley's face. She lightly brushed it away from her neck. Hopefully, they didn't see. It was like final exams.

"Thank you for giving us this time to chat, Ms. Conners. The CEO, CFO and the board are very happy to see you today and hear the vision you have if you were to become Chief Sales Officer. We understand that this has been a grueling process." Mr. Michaels, chairman of the board, said.

Grueling was an understatement.

"That being said, we want you to know that we asked these tough questions because we always believed you were the right candidate. As you know, the company is going through some challenging times, but we all believe we are ready to turn the corner."

"I know. I believe that too," Ainsley said with a decisive nod.

"You spoke of these challenges in a very compelling way. We love your vision and are even more excited about you as the CSO now than ever. We would like to offer you the position. However, there are some things we need to talk about before you accept."

"Of course, sir." She nearly gulped, but pushed the reaction away.

"We have unanimously agreed that you are the right fit for the Chief Sales Officer and that you would be a great addition to the C-suite."

"Thank you."

"And while it was a difficult decision, we cannot offer you everything at this moment. What we propose, though, given these difficult times, is that we promote you into the role now, but the increase in salary and title would need to be delayed for eighteen months until the company can manage it more easily. After you have implemented your changes."

Was he serious? Ainsley took a deep breath. They wanted her to do the work without the pay or even the recognition of a proper title.

"We would love to offer everything, but it's the current state of business. And you would have our full support. What are your thoughts on this?"

Did she believe that they'd actually give her the title and salary increase next year? After a moment of thought, she decided that she did trust it would happen, especially if she asked for an offer letter or executive contract.

She really wanted the job and wanted to say yes, but something felt different. Her heartbeat thrummed in her ears, drowning out the sound of the traffic on the street below.

"I appreciate everyone's comments and thoughts on this. I really would love the job and still feel like I am the right person to lead us forward as a company. But respectfully, I need twenty-four hours to think about whether or not I'm willing to do substantially more work without being given the title, the recognition and the pay. I work hard every day and would certainly admit if I didn't deliver, but I have every intention on delivering. I believe you reward people for their work, and you compensate them when you find them right for a promotion. I would appreciate a day to reflect on this."

Mr. Michaels looked at the other members of the team. "Can we reconvene on this tomorrow at the same time?"

After a few moments, the consensus was that they would make time to hear more tomorrow.

"I do appreciate your offer," Ainsley said. "I will see you tomorrow.

"We look forward to it," Mr. Michaels said.

"Thank you."

"And Ms. Conners?"

She gave Mr. Michaels her full attention.

"We want to be one hundred percent clear that you were always the top candidate in our minds. The fact that one of the other candidates declined the position had no bearing on our decision."

"Another candidate declined?" If her heart thumped any harder, it would escape from her chest.

"Yes. We didn't want to say anything, but in case you hear it, we want to be sure you know you were our first choice."

Lots of thoughts rushed through Ainsley's mind, and none of them were about the Chief Sales Officer position.

She needed a coffee, and she needed it now.

"AINSLEY, WHAT ARE YOU DOING HERE?" Hunter said, jumping up from his table.

"I'm here to see you, you big lug." She threw her arms around him.

He pulled her closer. No one had ever made him feel this way. One touch from her was like a warm fire on a wintry day.

Cupping her cheeks, he looked down at her. "I thought you would never talk to me again."

"Stop. Kiss me already," she demanded.

"I'm not gonna argue with that." He leaned down, pressing their lips together. He couldn't explain what it felt like to have her in his arms because he had never felt anything like it. He was erupting with joy, yet it was as natural as breathing.

"Wow," she whispered.

"Did you really say wow?"

"I did. And I'll say it again. Wow." She grinned at him.

"Yes. I agree. Wow," Hunter said and dropped another kiss on the corner of her mouth. "Would you like to join me for coffee?"

"Yes. Of course." She settled into the chair beside him.

"Wait. How did you find me? What is happening?"

"Duh. You told me about this place and that you came here every time you were in New York or the Hamptons. You said they have the best lattes in the world, and you don't even need sugar."

"You'll see." He motioned to the barista. "Two more, please."

"I believe you. I can't believe you did that," she accused.

"What did I do now?"

"Declining the job. I can't believe you did that for me."

"Ainsley, I really like you. A lot. But I didn't give up the Chief Sales Officer job for you. I gave it up for me." He reached across to pick up her hand, running his thumb over the soft skin of her wrist.

"Really?"

"Yes. You helped me see that even though I'm good at this job, my passion is in cooking. You showed me at the bar that I could be happy opening a restaurant. It made me think how crazy it sounds that I still worry about what my hometown and buddies would think. I'm going for it. I'm opening the restaurant. Look." He turned his iPad toward her so she could see the restaurant mock-ups and blueprints.

"Really. That is awesome. I'm so happy for you. Your restaurant is going to be so amazing." She gripped his hand in excitement. And support.

"And just so you know, when I declined the interview, it felt so good. It felt right. I was in there five minutes, explained that I was going to follow my dreams and start a restaurant and then I left. I don't think the board knew what to do with me."

"I'm proud of you for following your dream," Ainsley said.

She nodded her thanks when the barista put two lattes on the table in front of them.

"It felt incredible, but to be honest, I didn't exactly get the feeling that they were too disappointed. I'm pretty sure that they had their mind made up." He certainly knew she was the right person for the job. "Congratulations. You deserve it."

"What do you mean?" she asked as she lifted her cup.

"Well, I'm assuming that you're the CSO now, right?"

"Not exactly, but you are right. This latte is amazing. How have I never been to Sant Ambroeus before?" She took another sip of her drink.

"What do you mean? They had to choose you," he said. There had only ever been two candidates for the position.

"They did, but . . ." Ainsley looked down.

"But what?"

She took a deep breath. "I want to talk to you about it. I just don't know how." Her admission was quiet.

"Well, what happened? Did you say no?" he asked.

"I didn't say no, but I didn't exactly say yes either."

"I'm glad they were smart enough to recognize you. They should have done it a long time ago."

"They did, but they told me . . ." She put her head in her hands.

"What, Ainsley? Are you okay?"

"No. They did offer me the job. They told me that they wanted me out of all the candidates, but they also said that they couldn't give me the raise or the title."

"What? Why couldn't they? They are hiring for the Chief Sales Officer role, and you deserve everything that goes with it." He didn't understand why they would open the position but not truly offer a promotion.

"They are, but they said that they couldn't afford it right now."

"I get the pay thing, maybe," he conceded, "but why aren't they giving you the title? Not that you want the title and work without the pay."

"They didn't say." She stared into her latte and shook her head slightly.

"What was your answer?"

"I was so stupid. I told them that if they wanted me and thought that I was the right person that they should be giving me the title and the pay."

"That isn't stupid, Ainsley. That's right." He took the coffee cup from her, then clasped her hands between his. When she lifted her gaze to his, he said, "As long as you are doing this for you and not your parents."

"No. I'm doing it for myself. You helped me believe in my own worth. I'll probably never please my parents."

"You deserve the job, the title and the pay, but none of that is going to make you feel successful. You don't need anyone to tell you that. You already are. You just have to believe it."

"For the first time in my life, I truly believe that. We had some of the same struggles, and I think it is awesome that you are following your dreams. Maybe I should too."

"But, Ainsley, you helped me see what I needed. And this is your dream. You are great and deserving, but this job doesn't define you. You have a choice. Either you march back in there and demand what you want or believe in yourself and take it without the title and pay and prove that they were wrong. I think you should do the former, but I'll support you in either decision."

She frowned and looked down at their hands, his still holding hers. Supporting her.

"I don't know what to do," she said. "You are going off to your dream career and I'm stuck with this decision."

"What do you want to do? I feel like you already have your dream career."

"I do. I really do." Her voice held more confidence in those short words than he'd heard in the last few minutes.

"When are you meeting with them again?" Hunter asked.

"Tomorrow at noon. I asked them for twenty-four hours."

"Can I take you on a date after?"

"What?" Her head whipped up, and she stared at him.

"Whatever decision you make, I want to take you out to celebrate."

"Well, I wouldn't want to spend tomorrow evening with anyone else." Her hands flipped over, and her fingers wrapped around his. "Where are you taking me?"

"Well, that is a surprise." He winked.

"WELCOME BACK, MS. CONNERS," Mr. Michaels said politely as she settled in her chair.

"Thank you."

"We want to thank you for joining us again today. You gave us a lot to think about."

"I appreciate this opportunity. I really do." Ainsley was ready for this conversation. She sat tall and made sure her voice was clear and direct.

"We know that. We deliberated for a very long time after you left yesterday. We have talked, and we want to open the floor to you first."

"Well, thank you, Mr. Michaels. I have given it a lot of thought too. And I stand behind what I said yesterday. While I love my job and believe I am the best choice for Chief Sales Officer, I cannot accept this position without the title and the pay. I have proposed a plan that I think can be executed to reinvigorate sales at our company. If you believe in me based on my past performance, I'm here to execute that plan together."

"That is very honest."

"I should add that this was not an easy decision." Might as well be forthright with them.

"No explanations are necessary. We truly believe in your leadership and never doubted your ability to be the best at this job. We unanimously agreed that you were the sole choice for Chief Sales Officer and would like to offer this position to you."

"Not just the position," the CEO added. "The pay increase and title too."

Relief flooded her, but she maintained her composure. "Thank you."

"We all look forward to seeing you deliver results. You have led your teams to success time and time again."

"I'm excited for this challenge," Ainsley said proudly.

"One last thing, Ms. Conners. We have developed an additional incentive plan for you. In the case that you deliver, and we know you will, we think you'll be very happy."

"Thank you again to you and the entire board. We will do this together," she said.

AINSLEY CHECKED the address Hunter had given her and confirmed she was at the right place. The opaque door behind her swung open, and her handsome man stepped out onto the sidewalk next to her. Then he swept her into the most romantic kiss she'd ever had.

By the time he lifted his lips from hers, Ainsley's whole body tingled with excitement.

The world didn't even feel real today. She shivered as the cool New York air curled up her spine from the passing taxis on Fifth Avenue.

"Where are we?" she asked. "It's a beautiful building, but the windows are blocked out."

"You are standing in front of the future newest restaurant in New York City," Hunter explained with a bow.

"Woo! That is so exciting." She jumped into his arms. "I'm so excited for you, darling."

"I can't wait for you to see it. And I have something very special planned for you. Come see." He tugged her forward.

The doors opened to an old restaurant with a beautifully set table. Hunter gestured to the meal, then pulled a chair out for her. "A poached pear salad to start. And champagne to celebrate you."

"And you," she countered.

The building and layout looked perfect, and Ainsley knew that Hunter would make something iconic out of this space.

"But what happened?" he asked as he took the seat opposite her.

"I said yes."

"That's great. And?" He leaned across the table to kiss her cheek.

"And I held my ground," she boasted.

"They gave you the promotion and the raise?"

"They did. And they gave me a bonus incentive to deliver the plan I proposed."

"I think that is amazing. I knew we would be celebrating you today." He poured champagne into each of their glasses. "You deserve everything they gave you and more."

"Cheers to both of us for realizing our dreams," she said, and blew him a kiss.

"Cheers to us," Hunter said, raising his glass to hers.

ABOUT THE AUTHOR

G.G. Gabriel is a storyteller, who finds inspiration from life. Tales from adventures around the world pepper their stories from pen to paper. Writing is somewhere G.G. can be vulnerable and every story is hoped to inspire love, adventure and Happily Ever Afters. These things are what keep the words flowing from G.G.'s mind to paper.

G.G. adores traveling, loves to cook, enjoys stage productions and can't get enough books! Stay in touch!

Please visit my website and I'd love for you to leave a review on your favorite book-selling site or share on social media! Reading my story and your support is very much appreciated! You can follow G.G. on the following social media sites:

Website: **https://www.gggabriel.com**
Facebook: **https://www.facebook.com/ggwriter**
Twitter: **https://www.twitter.com/gggabrielwriter**

TO BRINK AND BACK

JULIE HALPERSON

The chaos of Brink's capital city swirled around the young woman as she waited at the start point of the tour. She would be known as Coda on this trip. It wasn't the first time she'd used a different name. The first time had been many years ago. When the pain had been different.

Now, the only thing she felt was a profound sense of emptiness. But Coda had an important decision to make, and she needed to find the mental peace in which to make it. A road trip to the locations where the society on the planet Brink had been founded seemed to answer both needs.

But perhaps most importantly of all, the trip would allow her to fulfill a promise to herself—to discretely scatter her father's ashes along the points where he'd made such a difference in so many lives. Yes, she knew the act was illegal without struggling through a painfully convoluted authorization process which she'd had neither time nor emotional energy to pursue. But this personal act of honoring her father and coming to grips with her past had to be a private pilgrimage, not a performance for a hero-worshipping public. The casting of his ashes had come to represent an act of finality that would enable her to set aside past wounds and take a step into her future.

And that's why her true identity needed to remain a secret.

It seemed that the tour had been created specifically for her. It would start here, at the end of her father's life. It would end at the beginning, where they had first landed. She had promised herself that she would not mourn. Not now. That could come later.

But there was also another potential aspect of the tour that caused her heart to beat faster in anticipation. Maybe *Her Bard* would be here.

HAD IT BEEN A MISTAKE, reaching out after such a long time, to let him know that she was taking this tour? Had she imagined a connection all those years ago, when she was so lonely, fearing to show her face to all but a select few? But those first poems, written by someone known only as the Bard, had hit her at her core. All the promises of new beginnings, being on the brink of a new life, had given her hope that something different was possible. It was a risk she'd decided she had to take with those first tentative comments, responding to what she'd felt from those words. She was safe and hidden behind an avatar and false name, communicating with someone she didn't know and who didn't know who *she* really was.

A shadow suddenly passed in front of her face and a bag landed on the depot floor with a thunk. She jumped, startled out of her musings of potential meetings.

"Here for the Scarlett Historical Tour?" The man next to her was grizzled, short, and dressed in well-worn traveling clothes.

She forced herself to smile and nodded. "Coda. Nice to meet you."

"John Smith." His grin revealed the even teeth of a Firster. "And, yes, that is my real name."

"John Smith" was the avatar name used as a default in everything from media adverts to professional papers as the quintessential every-man. "I guess people ask you that a lot," she said.

He nodded. "I'm looking forward to this tour. I was asked by Woodard—you've heard of him? The documentary specialist?—to be the historical expert."

Coda's stomach sank. She'd been ducking Woodard for the past week, not wanting any part of a documentary on Patric Damaker. Let the legend live and die with the man. She had nothing to add to the public record.

"You see, I was on that original flotilla. A true Firster." He waved his arm, encompassing the sky, the land, and all in between. "Not on his ship, of course."

A Firster. Those who had arrived in the original flotilla identified themselves as Firsters, claiming that title as point of pride. The story of the disaster and loss of life on Damaker's ship as it entered Brink's atmosphere was well known. His wife had perished. Others had suffered terrible injuries. She automatically reached up to rub her neck, her fingers searching out the rough vestiges of scars but finding only smooth skin. Her stay off-planet at a med center had removed all physical traces of the traumatizing landing. But there was no need to keep those scars hidden now. The time away from Brink had also brought her internal scars into perspective.

"Which ship were you on?" she asked. The first flotilla had consisted of three ships. Two had landed safely. The first ship had not.

Smith's response was swallowed by the roar of a transport pulling up to the depot, followed by a swoosh of the cabin door as it lifted, disgorging passengers. A tall man, wearing the robes of the Brotherhood, stepped out. A woman, almost hidden by the Brother's height, joined him. Were either of them her Bard? The anticipation of finally meeting him or her now collided with dismay at the thought of Woodard joining the group.

Two sleek land brovers, their shiny metal hulls emblazoned with the logo, "Scarlett Legendary Tours," coasted to a stop. Coda checked the time with her wrist minder's chrono function. Relief washed through her at the punctuality of the group. She was anxious to get on the road.

Mr. Scarlett himself, a youngish man wearing travelling clothes bearing the logo of an unrolled scroll with the word "Legend" printed across it, motioned for the group to gather closer together. He exuded excitement, tapping his forefinger along the edge of his tablet.

"Greetings, all. Welcome to the 'End to Beginning' tour." He took a deep breath. "With the passing of our world's Founder, Patric Damaker, this is a particularly auspicious time to make this journey. There's talk in the news of erecting a new monument to his governance here, in the capital city, where he formed the government that runs Brink. We're a smaller group than normal because of the national period of mourning. Let's introduce ourselves, and then we can get started. I'll go first. I'm Red Scarlett," he said, with a wave to his blazing hair. "Owner of Scarlett Legend Tours, always listed as one of the top tour companies in the categories of hospitality and efficiency." He gestured to a medium-sized, compactly built man standing nearby. "This is Fyfe, driver of our second land brover. I'll drive the first one. These vehicles are built for Brink and can handle pretty much everything this planet can throw at us."

Fyfe, leaning against his brover, gave a silent wave.

Red turned to Coda's first companion. "Mr. Smith here is a historian specializing in Brink's history. He was one of the original colonists, a true Firster, and has a unique perspective to provide on this tour."

She jerked up her head in alarm. This excursion hadn't been advertised as an educational tour.

"And over here, we have Micah Woodard. He signed up at the last minute, as he's working on a special project. A history of the Damaker family, commissioned by the Coalition. I'm sure you've seen him on the local vid-newscasts."

Coda felt the blood rush to her face. Her desired peaceful journey was threatened by Woodard's project. She couldn't bear to listen to rehashed histories that didn't tell the true story. Or the *full* story. Still...Coda stared thoughtfully at Woodard. Even though she had good reasons for avoiding the man, could he be her Bard? He was definitely a writer. But it could also be the historian Smith, the Brother Moncada, the driver Fyfe, even the herbalist Demi. She was fairly sure that it wasn't Demi— nothing in their correspondence years ago had indicated the Bard was female. Coda sighed. She was certainly spoiled for choice in who her secret correspondent might be.

"Completing the list of occupants of the first brover," Red said, "we have Ms. Coda. Would you like to introduce yourself to the group?"

Coda winced. She wasn't ready to share much of herself. It was hard enough to spend the entire trip in a brover surrounded by a so-called historian and someone writing a history on Brink's First Family. She must see if she could change this situation.

Fighting to control her voice and hide her discomfort, she scraped together a few words. "Nothing much to add. I'm looking forward to this trip as I'm taking the transport off-planet at Eos. The stops along the way sounded like a perfect way to spend the days before the transport leaves." Eos was still Brink's primary spaceport.

"Thank you," Red said as he turned to the remainder of the group. "Next, in the second brover, we have Ms. Demi Verdi, who is documenting Brink's flora as part of the Coalition Guardianship process."

Ms. Verdi waved, offering a soft hello.

"Standing next to Ms. Verdi is Brother Moncada." Red indicated the tall man dressed in the black, full-length robes of the traveling Brotherhood. The man acknowledged the introduction by gesturing with the clasped hand greeting of the Brothers. "Moncada is one of the few Speakers for the Brothers on Brink. He has requested we stop at a Speaker initiation ceremony along the way." Looking around, Red said, "I told him we could accommodate that request, as it's something that few of us would ever otherwise get to see."

Impressive, Coda thought. Speakership was a huge responsibility, having the trust to be the voice for such an important group.

He surveyed his small band of travelers. "I'm sure we'll get to know each other very well during the trip. I suspect this will be one of the most fascinating tours I've ever conducted, especially with the recent news about Brink's future." He went on to explain the daily schedule, meal breaks, accommodations and the main points of interest. Reaching into a box on the brover, he pulled out several bright red hats carrying the Scarlett logo. "Please keep these with you, they'll help me find you if we separate."

As the group shifted, sorting themselves into their respective brovers, Coda approached Red. "Can I suggest a rearrangement of the brover occupants? Let me travel with Fyfe and Moncada, and then Mr. Smith and Ms. Verdi could travel with Mr. Woodard and you? Maybe that would provide a fuller perspective of Brink to Mr. Woodard?"

Red looked thoughtful. "Excellent point, Ms. Coda." He strode off to make it happen. Coda relaxed slightly. She wasn't ready quite yet to listen about Brink's history and how it appeared to the outside world. The goal of this trip was to make her own peace with Brink.

But had she done the wrong thing to tell the Bard that she was going to be here?

WOODARD PUT two and two together as Red approached and suggested the rearrangement of the brovers. That way, the three of them could concentrate on discussing Brink's history. Perhaps they could make short detours from the published itinerary?

The arrangement sounded good. There was really no reason to complain.

But he was on hyper-alert, ears cocked for nuances in tone and an occasional sideways glance. Not only because he didn't want to miss one potential clue as to what the founding of Brink had truly been like, but more importantly, perhaps he'd discover if Damaker was the big hero that everyone claimed. Brink didn't breed saints. But then, he hadn't made it to where he was as a professional journalist by accepting common knowledge. He had fought for the commission for this documentary, and he wanted to deliver.

He tossed his kit into the back of the brover. The vehicle was clean and roomy, and Red seemed to know his business. Scarlett tours were well recommended and his client, the Coalition Media Group, was footing the bill. The CMG contract covered not just his time, but Smith's as well. And he'd been granted enough leeway to be creative if needed. This project could be his ticket to broader exposure within the Coalition, could help him get off-planet. Then he'd be able to better help his own family, provide a springboard to their future.

"You take the front seat," said Smith. "I can talk just as easily from the back." He pointed to the recharger port. "In case you need to recharge your equipment, you'll be closer."

"Smart idea." Woodard climbed into the brover's front passenger seat, stowing his equipment within easy reach.

Red maneuvered the brover to the track out of town, and they were on their way. Fyfe's voice came over the comm unit, reporting that they were also off and would be following the route to Point Decision.

"We will stop for a meal, right?" said Fyfe.

"Yep. Not sure where, we may diverge from the path a bit depending on what Mr. Woodard and Smith want to see." Red glanced at the chrono on the brover dashboard. "We should be able to decide close to zenith." His brow furrowed, peering up at the sky. Zenith was the local time when the sun was highest. "I'd say, maybe stop in a few hours. We should have enough water and such to keep us going until then. Just let your passengers know. And check in about an hour from now, ok?" He waved off the comm connection.

Raising his voice to carry to the back of the brover to include Smith and Demi, he said, "Woodard, why don't you fill me in on what you're looking for? I guess Smith already knows, but it would help me to know, too."

Woodard pulled his thoughts together, then said, "Basically, CMG commissioned a documentary of Brink's history to be included in the Coalition Guardian induction ceremonies. With Damaker's recent death, I wanted to also document what I can of his life and legacy."

The induction ceremonies were the first step in the process for Brink's entry into the Coalition of Inhabited Worlds. Coalition entry was huge for Brink and would open trade opportunities as well as give Brink representation to other worlds. The Coalition was the only central organization for inhabited planets. There were tiered levels of membership, starting with Coalition Guardianship. With time, Brink could move up to full membership. He'd heard that Coalition Guardianship also included an Ambassador. Damaker had been a shoo-in for that job. Who would take it now?

Red looked thoughtful. "Yeah, his death was a shocker. His only daughter had just come back planet-side a few days before." He paused a moment, merging into traffic. "Have you been in touch with her?"

"No, but not for lack of trying."

"Has anyone actually seen her?" Red asked, setting the autodrive controls.

Aurora Damaker was a mystery. The only child of Patric Damaker and his wife Mary, she had left Brink to complete her education on their home world. In the few media images of Aurora, her face was hidden. Rumor had it that she'd been disfigured in the same flotilla accident that killed her mother. Damaker himself had survived unscathed.

Scuttlebutt said his daughter had reconstructive surgery done off-planet. She could be anywhere now and no one might recognize her.

But why would she remain hidden? What was the mystery? Grief, certainly. But perhaps more than that. Damaker had never hidden himself from view, and Woodard wanted to know why Aurora seemed to be hiding now.

Smith asked, "What's our schedule for today?" He pointed to what appeared to be a pile of boulders over to the east. "I think that's Dirgix. Great place for a meal stop, bio breaks, etc."

Red considered this option and nodded in agreement. "Sure, let's head there. It fits the theme of the itinerary—Brink's history." He swiveled around. "You know it was originally named for Damaker's wife, Mary." He jerked the brover around a pothole in the road. "Later renamed by its citizens."

"What could Dirgix mean?" This came from the botanist, who had leaned forward, listening to the conversation.

Both Smith and Red shook their heads.

"No clue, but Lola's is still a great place for a meal," Smith suggested.

Red thumbed on the comm unit and relayed the route change to Fyfe.

Woodward stared out the window. He found the landscape a little boring. The road was well maintained, and this close to the capital city, there was a sameness in the architecture and the businesses. Thankfully, the weather was clear and forecasted to be fine for the next several days. It had been a while since he'd been in a yellow dust storm and he preferred to keep it that way.

Woodard had said this last part aloud and Demi nodded. "Yeah, the enclosures are helping to control the storms and regain the local ecology, but those yellow dust storms still happen." She pointed to a shimmer far off in the distance. "The yellow dust is part of the reason for the strong restrictions against adding any unapproved organic matter to Brink's ecology." She lifted her sample case. "Our research is just beginning to bear fruit in those areas. I think it's part of what we can offer the Coalition, help move us up the membership levels."

The agri-enclosures had been built to constrain the explosive growth of the Firster's terraforming program. Brink's ecology had reacted more quickly than expected once the new biologic elements had been introduced to the ecology. The Firsters had to move fast to limit further growth. The yellow dust storms had become more violent and torrential rains had flooded the new settlements. The enclosures held micro-climates for review and adjustments. Their shimmering bubble domes were dotted all over Brink's landscape.

Opening his scriber, Woodard planned to review the outline for his documentary series to prepare for the new stop at Dirgix. But when his screen winked to life, he was startled to find a fresh email from *her*. About this very tour—telling him she might actually be on it. A wave of emotions swept through him as he considered the impact of her words. Then he replied, *Are you here?*

A warm glow suffused his body. It had been pure luck that his old account was still actively rerouting notifications to his main feed—an echo-blast from the past. When he had first come to Brink as a stowie on a colony ship, he'd been lucky. He'd found a home with the colonists. And they'd provided him with schooling. This was years before Damaker had engineered the citizenship rules on Brink—that everyone had equal rights, with no distinction between those who'd first arrived or those who had come as colonists, or even those who'd arrived by stowing away. He knew how lucky he'd been to find his new family on Brink. He owed them everything.

He flicked open the conversation between old text-mates. One of the reasons he was on this particular tour.

Scrolling back to the beginning, he smiled. The woman had only been known as Dawn and sported a quirky avatar. He never knew her real name or face, and she had never known his. But she had made a difference in his life.

Because she'd said he had made a difference in hers.

Dawn was a Firster. But the trials of those early years had taken their toll. She'd told him she'd been under medical treatment because she'd lost her voice. But when doctors couldn't find anything wrong, everyone thought she was shamming.

But I'm not, she had texted. *I try to talk and nothing comes out. They make me practice with different sounds. But—nothing.*

How do you communicate? he'd asked. *With the teachers, your family?*

I only have my father. My mother is gone. An icon appeared, showing tears. *I use my tablet and text. Like with you.*

What would you say if you could talk?

Thank you for believing me.

And he did. Why would she lie? She didn't know him. He didn't know her.

And I would also say, she'd continued, *that I miss my old world, my mother. My father is so busy making a life here.*

He knew that feeling. He had lost his home world when he'd stowed away on the colonist ship. But since he had no family left there, stowing away had been his best option—his only true option—to escape a future on a planet that had treated his people like battle fodder.

I understand, he'd typed back. Then he sent her his offering for the next day, a poem about new beginnings and making peace with endings. *I post these on the Maker Site, if you want to see more of my offerings.*

Oh, I've seen those! They brighten my day.

Ha! So he had an audience of one, at least.

The chat continued. She commented on the Maker Site, entering discussions.

Maker Site was for a young crowd, and chat could range from love advice to deeply philosophical discussions. His readership grew and he was eventually offered syndication in a larger market.

Upon learning this news, she had asked, *Does this mean you'll no longer be on Maker Site?*

He could almost hear the wistfulness in her text. He hadn't considered that starting something new might mean leaving Maker Site. He realized he didn't want to leave that community; it had become like a family to him. Leaving it would be like leaving his home world again.

No, I'll still post on Maker Site. Some of it will be published elsewhere. They'll decide where, though.

So you lose control of your material?

He had to think about that. Expanding to a larger market was another way to increase the size of his online family. He decided to counter with a shrug icon. *I have no idea what people may do with my offerings once they are posted.*

There was no immediate response. Then she texted, *Good point. I guess it's not what we have control over. It's what we make of it.* A pause. *I mean, we can try to choose how we're impacted.*

He'd thought he felt a subtle shift of attitude in her. But that was impossible. He had never met her. He had no idea what she looked like beyond the stylized figure on Maker Site, and certainly no idea what she was thinking. But he had no reason to believe she was not revealing her true thoughts.

A few days later, she was back online, shouting in text. *I had a GREAT session with the speech therapist today!* Her excitement leaped through the words. *I realized I had no control over what happened when I came here. And neither did my father. You helped me find my voice. Find my words. Thank you!*

And in that moment, he had a realization of his own—he'd finally found his calling.

BAM! Woodard's world violently jerked sideways, and he dropped the tablet as he was forced to swing his arms forward to brace against the front of the brover.

"What the hell . . ."

The brover tilted crazily, and Red screamed in pain. From the back, Smith shouted, "Red, you ok?"

Red responded with a moan.

The world stopped moving and an eerie silence descended.

Woodard struggled to make sense of this alarming new development. Where was the strap latch so he could get out of the brover? A quick glance outside confirmed they were not on a cliff's edge or over a ravine, just tilted on the top of a dune.

"My shoulder. I don't think I can move it."

Smith jumped out of the back. The brover remained stable. "I think It's ok if you all come out. Looks like we're wedged pretty tight."

Demi was still in the rear seats and Smith called back to her, "How about you, Demi? Any aches or pains?"

Woodard could hear the sound of a strap unbuckling as she responded, "I'm fine." He felt the slight readjustment of the brover as she hoisted herself out.

Through gritted teeth, Red said, "We need to contact the other team. Would one of you hit the comm unit?"

Smith complied, and Red gave a quick update, then received confirmation from Fyfe that they would join up quickly.

Woodard found his strap latch and tugged at it in frustration. Where were they? When had they become separated? How long had he been daydreaming about his past?

The strap finally came loose, releasing him, and he moved to help Red unbuckle his own strap. "Why did we separate? I'm sorry, I was catching up on some work and wasn't paying attention to our surroundings. Obviously." He climbed out, then with Smith's help, assisted Red to a short distance away from the brover.

The smooth terrain had changed to large dunes. No trail in sight. He turned in a complete circle. Nothing. Not even birds, flying high above. The sky was clear, the air still.

"What happened?" Woodard had learned to completely block out his surroundings. It had been a necessary skill needed to work in crowded, noisy places. A trip down memory's path seemed to have had the same effect.

"I thought I remembered a shortcut to Dirgix." Smith jerked his head at the Direction Finder. "And it is a shortcut, as a bird flies. But the terraforming hasn't worked so well here." He paused, poking a finger under his cap to scratch his head. He said to Demi, "Maybe good for your research? Make some profit out of this?"

Woodard swore under his breath. The last thing he wanted to think about was Demi's study. "Let's not get distracted. Red, can you stand at all? Is there anything here that we can use to stabilize you?"

"Med kit in the cargo hold. Should be something for pain there." A grimace flashed across Red's face. "I think there are bandages. Maybe something we can use as a sling?" He gave a sickly grin. "I guess this is a good test of my emergency preparedness."

The comm unit crackled into life. "Red, we're closing in. How're you doing?"

Woodard gave a terse update. "I think the trouble is in getting over the dunes. Be careful. The grit crust has been broken, so traction is almost nonexistent."

"Ok, got it." A brief pause followed. Then Fyfe said, "Yeah, I think I see you. Appreciate the warning."

Woodard heard the approaching growl of the second brover. Fyfe slowed the vehicle to a crawl, found a level spot, and sprang out. Moncada followed, pulling out a small satchel and rushing over to Red. Coda approached more carefully over the uneven terrain.

Moncada, surprisingly, had some medical training, and quickly found what he needed in the available med kits. He gently assisted Red to the second brover, enlisting Smith's aid to stabilize him. Fyfe pulled the rest of the passengers together to shift the vehicle off the top of the dune.

"Red, what were you thinking? Going off road? In unknown territory?" Fyfe looked at Red like he was crazy.

Red winced. "Yeah, I know. It looked like a clear shortcut."

Smith interjected. "It's my fault. Terrain has changed since I was here before."

Fyfe looked over the brover, hands on hips, assessing the possibilities. "Man, this is Brink. We never know what this planet is going to throw at us." Careful of his footing, he went back to the other brover, and pulled out cables and hooks. He shook his head and said, "It's a good thing I'm a fixer and not a Finder." He waved for the rest of the group to come help. "We need to attach my brover to Red's. I may need you to help push."

Red laughed. "If you'd been a Finder, we'd have never been here."

Woodard wondered if there were any Finders in this group. Finders had a rare, almost unexplainable talent for Finding things that had been lost, sometimes for centuries. The universe was huge, civilizations came and went. A Finder could locate these old worlds. These Finds could then be auctioned to those hoping the Finds would have value by providing a Finder's Fee. The Coalition would track

Finds, record the auction. It was one of the reasons the Coalition had formed, although its purpose had expanded.

Enough about fixers and Finders. They needed to get moving. Fyfe pointed out which part of the brover needed steadying, then gestured to Smith and Coda. There was no other option. Calling for outside help would take too long.

Stop 1 - Dirgix/Maryville

ALTHOUGH DIRGIX WASN'T on their original itinerary, it was a good place for Coda to make a stop on her personal pilgrimage. While Red and Fyfe were checking the road worthiness of the brover link and the meal plans, she picked up her bag and went off on her own.

The air was calm and dry, the sky cloudless. If they had to have a road accident, at least they were lucky enough that the weather cooperated.

Dirgix was not that large, and she was able to catch a local bus on a route to the edge of town. She caught sight of some older buildings retaining the name Maryville, and it made her smile. She would continue to call it Maryville as well.

She had few memories of the tiny town. After the crash landing, Damaker had brought some of the Firsters to settle here. She'd been recovering from her burns and slowly coming out of the trauma of the landing. There was a small monument in the town's center commemorating Damaker's life partner, Mary, and her actions which had brought the flotilla to ground.

As other off-worlders had found Brink, the settlement had grown. The name had been changed at some point to Dirgix. Coda didn't know why and didn't care. The town would always be Maryville to her.

The bus came to the end of the route and she climbed out. Silence wrapped around her and she felt her tension drain away. This was the Brink she remembered.

The case she carried was heavy. Even hiking the short distance to the top of a small hill, her arm started to ache. She stumbled over a rock and nearly fell. Apparently her time off-world had impacted her sense of balance more than she'd expected.

Finally, she stopped. This was a good spot. A gentle breeze blew from behind her, which suited her task perfectly. Opening the sack, she filled her little cup with some of the bag's contents and carefully covered the brim with her other hand. Closing her eyes, she thought of her father and all he had meant to her. Then, just as she started to lift the cup high, a strident voice from behind startled her.

"What are you doing? Don't you know it's illegal to add non-native material to the local agriculture?"

She whirled, nearly dropping the precious cup.

Demi, from the tour group, stood there, glaring.

"Where did you come from?" Coda asked.

Demi gestured to the bus stop. "I was on the same bus as you. You were so wrapped up in your thoughts you didn't see or hear me get off the bus behind you." She held up her own pack. "I always collect samples when I stop. It helps track changes and conditions." Pointing with her clippers at Coda's cup, she said, "And that's why I stopped you."

Coda sagged, both physically and mentally. Her moment of connection with Brink was gone. She tried to think what to reveal. "The material is inert. Nothing that can impact Brink's ecostructure."

Still stern, Demi reached into her case. Pulling out a handheld scanner, she motioned Coda to hold out the cup. As she read the results, her face relaxed. Then she ran the same test on the contents of the case at Coda's feet.

Demi pressed something on the instrument. "Yes, the contents are inert. But you should have gotten approval to do this before we left. Did you?"

There was no way she could have done that. Coda shook her head. "I hadn't thought that far ahead." Taking a deep breath, she said, "These are my father's ashes. I wanted to scatter them throughout Brink." Fearful of being stopped so early in her mission, she said, "We're Firsters, and he gave his life for this planet." Letting out her breath, she continued. "I just want to give him back to Brink."

"The burner should have given you a certificate proving the remains were inert."

True, that would have been standard practice. But there was nothing standard about this cremation. Hedging, she said, "Yes, you're right. But by the time we reach Eos, they should all be gone. And until then, you can vouch for them, right?"

The internal battle within Demi was written on her face. What would Coda do if Demi stopped her from scattering the ashes? Or would she allow Coda her pilgrimage? It seemed pragmatism won. "I can see this is important to you. If you let me come with you when you scatter, I won't say anything to Red." She replaced her scanner in her pack. Then she pointed to the shimmering bubble in the distance. "But you can see why we have the law, right?"

Coda nodded, then turned again with the wind at her back. It had gone well when she had made her first contribution in Capital City. Taking a deep breath, she lifted her arms again, attempted to feel connected to the world beneath her feet, and then, remembering her father, she swung the contents high into the air. The ashes scattered, caught the sunlight turning golden, and were carried out over the plain.

Demi touched her shoulder. Fishing a cloth out of her bag, she gently wiped the tears off Coda's cheeks. Coda hadn't realized she'd been crying. She felt Demi slip an arm around her shoulders, turning her around, and they both headed back to the bus stop.

Demi stopped occasionally, squatting to take recordings of the plants and soil. She talked a little about her project. "The Coalition wants a baseline as part of the admittance package. Part of what Brink can bring to the table is what we're doing to control the rapid spread of non-native flora. The baseline and subsequent readings will prove what we're doing is working." Approaching the bus stop, she said, "Oh, look, there's Woodard and Smith."

Coda held firmly to her case. She had to trust Demi that the ash scattering would remain secret between them. She regarded the two men. How long had they been standing there? And had they seen anything?

WOODARD'S EARS were filled with Smith and Demi's chatter; Demi on her Coalition project and Smith providing historical context. Smith was going to be a good resource for the documentary. But he had seen the tear tracks on Coda's face and sensed an almost visible bond between the two women that hadn't been there when the travelers split apart after arriving.

"Any word on how Red is doing? And the vehicles?" Coda asked.

The accident had put a serious crimp in their schedule by diverting time from their expected itinerary, and that would probably mean less time spent on each site. He tried to shake off his disappointment. Showing his annoyance would just add another distraction. Roll with it, he told himself. Like always.

"Red's doing ok. The med center confirmed that Moncada's first aid was just what they would have done. Fyfe is discussing the situation with the vehicles." Remembering the look on Fyfe's face, a quick repair didn't seem hopeful.

Smith shook his head. "Seems we might have to double up. Use the second vehicle for storage and pile us all into the first one."

He heard Coda sigh and wondered if the accident would make some impact on her plans.

The bus arrived at the stop and they all stepped aboard.

Woodward's stomach grumbled. "Let's find that inn, Lola's, wasn't it? I'm hungry."

The trip back to the town center was silent. Even Demi and Smith seemed to have exhausted their conversation. Woodard didn't think that either one of them was his unseen friend from all those years ago. That left Fyfe, Moncada, Red, and Coda.

He hoped it was Coda.

She was all wrapped up in herself; she looked exhausted. She was still holding on to that plain brown case with a firm grip. Why would she carry it way out here, at the end of the bus line, he mused. There was a secret there. And he loved to unwrap secrets.

AT LOLA'S they found the rest of the group. Red was all smiles again, thanks to the pain blockers. "Luckily, I have Moncada with us to make sure I take the pills on time. When we reach Eos, I can have a follow-up with the med center there."

Lola's served traveler's fare, quick and easy to eat. But their specialty was a spiced fruit bread served with a nut butter. It was sold by the slice and by the loaf, and the nut butter by the jar, with an attached utensil for a spreader. "All Brink Goodness" was prominently emblazoned on the label.

"Ah, ha. This must be part of the new 'Brink First' initiative," said Demi. "It's a way to make sure that goods made on Brink are recognized."

"It's great," said Fyfe, spreading a thick smear of the nut butter on a slice of the bread. "Whoever thought of putting these two together was a genius." He handed the slice to Red. "Here, try it."

Red, mouth full, mumbled his thanks. After he swallowed, he said, "Perfect travel food. Let's take some with us. By the way, we'll need to replenish the water."

Woodard thought it was time for an update. "How are we going to go on, Red? What's happening with the vehicles?"

Red jerked his chin at Fyfe. "You want to take this one?"

Fyfe swallowed and nodded. "The mechanics here got Red's going again." He pointed his spreader at Red's arm. "But as you can see, we're down a driver."

He spread more butter on a new slice. "So, this is the plan. I continue to drive. We tow the second brover. Then," he gestured in the air with the knife, "we put the gear in the second vehicle, and we all find seats in the lead."

Red said, "Yup, that's the plan. We'll make up the time lost by the accident and still be at Eos on the agreed upon date."

Looking around the table, Woodard saw varying degrees of approval from most of his fellow travelers. But Ms. Coda looked like the famed nut bread didn't agree with her, as she'd placed a half-eaten slice back on her plate.

"What changes are you planning to the itinerary?" She toyed with her nut bread. "I mean, there were certain stops planned for Woodard's documentary, right? Are those still in the plan?"

Interesting, that she seemed to want all those stops. He had thought that she was more concerned with reaching Eos by the end date.

Coda continued, "I mean, all of us took this tour because it covered Brink's history, right?"

"Yes, part of my project is to sample the plant life, showing Brink's expansion," Demi said. "It's the reason I took this particular tour."

"I still want to make sure we stop at Whistling Winds. I'm committed to that Speaker Induction ceremony," Moncada said. "An Induction ceremony is an important event for the Speaker and the Community they represent." He smiled. "But you all know that."

"Ok by me," Smith said, "I get paid the same. I can talk in the brover as well as on the ground."

Everyone chuckled. Even Ms. Coda.

Red and Fyfe shared an assessing glance, then Fyfe shrugged. "Yeah, we're still planning all the stops."

Red continued, "There was some float in the schedule, so our personal time for exploration may be reduced." He carefully pushed himself to his feet. "Shall we go? The vehicles have been prepared."

Stop 2 – Point Decision

THE BROVER TRUNDLED TO A HALT. The extra mass of the linked vehicles lengthened the braking range, and they narrowly missed hitting the railing at Decision Inn, which was named after the town, Point Decision.

The tour group separated. Fyfe secured lodgings. Demi and Coda disappeared with that mysterious case in tow. Red went to check with the innkeeper to find a medical facility. Moncada offered to go with Red, in case there was a change in treatment plans.

"Hey Woodard, want to go to Point Decision?" Smith asked. "Maybe see if you want to record anything?"

That was the whole point of this trip, Woodward reminded himself. So far he hadn't been fulfilling the terms of his contract. "Yeah, let's go." Maybe he'd catch sight of Demi and Coda somewhere along the way.

CODA WAS glad that Demi was accompanying her. It was right that someone was present to bear witness. She had intended to do this alone, but found she was grateful for the company. And with her background as a naturalist, Demi understood the cycle of life and death.

The air was damp and the sky dark. Clearly there was a storm on the way.

The two women were alone on the top of the hill. Coda didn't want anyone besides Demi to see what she was doing, and it wasn't fair to involve anyone else in something that was technically illegal. It was such a little thing, not having the proper releases. But she hadn't wanted to explain why. And she didn't want to be stopped. This was the only way she could do this by herself in the way she that wanted to return him to Brink.

The hill was not large and was thankfully deserted. The breeze whipped around them. She gathered up her hair, tucking it into the Scarlett Tour cap.

"Which direction should I throw the ashes, do you think?"

Demi shook her head. "I think just up. Let the wind do what it will."

Grasping her small cup, Coda filled it to overflowing from the makeshift urn. Then, with her eyes shut, she tossed the contents up in the air. She had no words, no thoughts, just concentrated on the motion of releasing.

Rain drops splattered around them, forcing the ashes to the ground.

Demi grasped her hand, the sudden rain streaking her face. "Do you have any kind of rain gear?" She pulled out a collapsible poncho with a hood for herself, then withdrew a spare.

Coda reached for it gratefully. "Thanks. I wasn't as prepared as I should have been."

She stared down at the ground. The rain had quickly mixed the ashes with the soil on the hill. Her goal for Point Decision was now complete.

THE GROUP HAD GATHERED BACK at the inn for the midday meal and were sitting at a table littered with cleared plates and half-full glasses. Coda listened as Smith continued relating the history of Point Decision.

The town had been named after the Decision made by Damaker and his council to grant citizenship to all sentient beings on Brink: native born, the colonists that came in the later waves, and stowies. It was a hard-won decision and was considered one of Damaker's triumphs. There had been dissenting voices on all sides, but the cold hard fact was that all groups had put down stakes in Brink and deserved a say in its future. At least, this was the version recorded in historical records.

"What people forget," Smith said, "is that the original flotilla was filled with people literally escaping with their lives. Brink's first families, the Firsters, desperately wanted to have their own world where they could make their own rules. By the time the Firsters had migrated to this point, there were also representatives from all levels of Coalition society—First Families, Colonists, Techs, and Stowies." He looked over to Moncada. "And we can't forget the Brotherhood. The Brothers were instrumental in gluing the Firsters into, well, the Firsters."

Coda agreed. The Firsters had to pull together during the painful first years at Brink. Fighting the dust storms, the harsh weather, the plant life, while building the settlements to live in—the challenges of living on Brink took everyone working together.

The entire tour group was silent, keenly attentive to Smith's words. Even Fyfe, who was checking something on his tablet, had paused to listen.

"Here, at Point Decision," Smith continued, "Damaker convened representatives from each group. His idea was to equalize everyone. And to do that, all the groups were designated as full citizens of Brink. No class distinctions. All had the same rights and privileges. And responsibilities."

Woodard put in, "And he made himself leader."

Coda bristled at his words. She had to say something. "Not true. His name wasn't the only one put forward. But with each person having a vote, he won."

She fumed silently. What did Woodward know, anyway? He wasn't a Firster. He hadn't lived through those days, when no one knew what was going to come their way next.

Woodard wrapped his arms around his chest, looking smug. "I've heard that story and I've even seen the video record of the event." He shrugged. "It could be construed that Damaker stacked the votes."

Smith spread open his hands in a gesture of acceptance. "There have been such allegations almost since the beginning. But nothing can negate the fact that Damaker was the leader who brought us to Brink with the notion that everyone would have the same rights."

Demi abruptly changed the subject. "Have you all seen the CMG daily update for Brink? They're publishing a new essay offering, signed only as the Bard." She held up her tablet and looked at Red. "I wonder if one of us is the Bard? It's about Point Decision." She shrugged. "Or decision points."

Red looked mystified. "Not that I'm aware! Our itinerary is not exactly secret, but why would that influence the Bard? What is the offering?"

Demi read the first couple of lines aloud in her soft voice.

"Point Decision! Rerouting Brink to a level field.

Damaker credited with mighty feat . . ."

Coda hadn't read the CMG news reports since joining the tour. She hadn't even checked her personal accounts, so hearing there was a new regular essay from someone calling himself the Bard sent electricity spinning through her. Now she was almost positive that one of her companions was her friend. *He was here.* As Demi read the rest of the essay, none of the group showed any hint of familiarity with the content. Which one could he be?

"I wonder why he is only known as the Bard? Why doesn't he use his real name?" Demi wondered.

"Under the cover of darkness..." This came from Moncada. It sounded like a quote from the Brotherhood.

Fyfe hmphed. "I don't call that darkness. I call it bringing light. There's some reason he's not naming himself. Maybe there's more than one person calling themselves the Bard?"

"True." Red pushed himself away from the table. "Shall we go? Has everyone had their fill of Point Decision?"

Smith answered for everyone. "Yes, I believe so. Red, considering we're down a brover driver because of your wounded wing," he pointed at the man's sling, "I think we all agree it's time to shake off the dust of Decision and head on to Whistling Winds."

WOODARD HELD BACK as the others took their places in the brover. He watched Coda as she sat in the second tier of seats, carefully placing her ever-present case between her feet. All the others had tossed their carryalls in the back brover after the two groups had been combined.

But not Ms. Coda. What was so important that she apparently couldn't let out of her sight?

She and Demi had struck up some sort of friendship very quickly. Both of them had disappeared early in the morning. He had assumed Demi was picking flowers or other "agricultural samples" to support the research she was doing on the effects of terraforming on Brink's fauna. But what was Coda doing? There was a mystery there. What was she hiding?

He maneuvered himself to the seat behind her, letting Red take his place in the front row. It was better for Red, anyway. More space for him to rest his arm after the sprain yesterday. Who knew that Moncada had medical training? And that Fyfe could pull together materials to link the two brovers together? As the man had said, he was a definitely a born fixer.

Red had gripped Woodard's arm tightly while entering the brover, and apparently Moncada had noticed. He leaned forward. "You need any of those painkillers, Red? No need to be hurting, even though you decided to stay on the trip."

Turning to include them all, Red said, "I wouldn't miss this for the world."

Stop 3 – Whistling Winds

MONCADA DIRECTED Fyfe to the roadside inn, the Day Farer, on the outskirts of Whistling Winds. A line of moto bikes filled most of the parking area and people spilled out the open doors.

He said, "This is a nice size group for the induction. Interesting that there are so many bikers here. They usually stay away from road-side inns, keeping to their dwellings out on the plains." Getting out of the brover, he said, "Let's go in and join them, shall we?"

"Are you sure it's okay?" Red looked doubtful. "If it's a private ceremony..."

"I was invited before I left. I'm a Speaker for the Brotherhood, and I put out a call for other Speakers along the way." He walked up to the Day Farer's entrance and went inside.

The breeze caught at Coda's long brown hair and whipped it around. She caught it in one hand, twisted it, and tucked it under her hat. "Well, I need something to drink and to use the facilities, maybe get something to eat. Let's go see what's happening."

And with that, she walked inside, following Moncada.

Woodard had heard of Speaker Induction ceremonies but had never attended one. After stepping into the inn's common room, he found himself wishing he'd brought his video gear.

At the front of the room stood a large wooden altar, decorated with gaily colored flowers. A glass pitcher filled with an amber liquid perched on top. A group of four musicians sat nearby, holding instruments. The members of the tour group exchanged glances. Woodard wondered if it was really appropriate for all of them to be there, even if Moncada had been invited.

Coda went to a tall man standing beside the altar.

"We don't want to disrupt your ceremony," she said, "but is the inn open for other business?"

Another man standing nearby hurried over and introduced himself as the Way Farer's owner, Barnard. "Yes, indeed we are. This is a public ceremony, celebrating Eldred's induction as Speaker." He gestured to the young man by the altar, cloaked in robes of bright orange. "Our Speakers are always easy to find." Eldred seemed very quiet for a new Speaker. Maybe that wasn't so surprising, considering the size of the crowd.

The travelers settled at the edges of the room, where Barnard had directed them to the shared meal laid out near the bar. Woodard filled his plate with unusual tidbits. He'd heard someone say that this was a communal meal with many contributing to the feast. In a way, he felt honored to be here. This was truly something special that most people would never get to experience.

"Delicious," said Demi. As always, she started to separate the items on her plate. She had explained that there were always ingredients new to her, so Woodard wasn't surprised when she carried her plate over to the innkeeper and began to ask him about the various components. Demi appeared to be continually fascinated with Brink's agricultural diversity.

"I'm glad she's with us." Smith had found a good vantage point for the ceremony. "She shows me what Brink is capable of producing."

"What? You, a Firster, not already knowing that?"

Smith blushed. "Yeah, but she shows me the beauty in it. Not just all the slogging and hard work we had to do to expand from Eos to Capital City." He looked down at the inn's much trodden floor. "It's like I'm seeing Brink all over again, through new eyes." He swiveled his head to look at Woodard. "Thanks for hiring me."

Smith was right. Over the past few days, the passengers had bonded together and formed into a cohesive unit. Demi brought her assessing eye. Smith brought the past to life. Fyfe kept the wheels going. Moncada shared the insights of the Brotherhood. Red kept things sunny. And Coda contributed a fascinating mix of off-worldliness and mystery.

Woodard pondered for a moment. What did he, himself, bring to the group?

A hush fell over the room. A smiling Eldred stepped up to the altar, ablaze in his orange robes. An older pair moved to his side. Clearly, one was a parent—the resemblance was obvious. Barnard raised his arms to summon everyone's attention.

"We have gathered," he announced, "to celebrate Eldred's acceptance of the Speakerhood of Whistling Winds." The inn's proprietor dropped his arms. "We are a small community, yet we still follow Brink's leadership in appointing Speakers to represent us. Eldred has resided in Whistling Winds ever since he and his family arrived. When he showed interest in becoming a Speaker, he sought the training and successfully completed it. The community as a whole has come together and supported his taking on of this important role."

Reaching behind the altar, he pulled out a box, opened it and withdrew a glittering medallion, hung on a slender chain. Eldred tucked his head down and Barnard placed the medallion around his neck.

Moncada clapped his hands and called out. "Congratulations! It's wonderful to see such a strong community like this." He reached into his robes and pulled out his own medallion. "I'm also a Speaker. For the Brotherhood."

Coda had joined them at the edge of the gathering. Smith said, "Somehow, it's not surprising that Moncada is a Speaker. It's a wonderful thing for someone to show such commitment to their community." He took a sip from his drink. "With Damaker's passing, we have no Prime Speaker for our planet as a whole."

"Damaker wasn't a Speaker," said Coda.

"True. But he would have been the Speaker for all Brink as we join the Coalition, right?"

Surprise flitted across Coda's face. "I guess I hadn't thought about it that way."

Smith continued, "We will need to appoint a Prime Speaker for us all, someone who understands Brink's history…what Brink needs."

"Then, why don't you apply, Smith? You fit those requirements." Woodard made the suggestion mainly just to see what Smith's reaction would be.

Coda nodded. "Yeah, why not? You love Brink, you understand its history."

"Huh." Smith paused for a moment, then said, "As much as I would happily give service to Brink, I have no skills in diplomacy."

"Oh, so you think Brink's Speaker requires diplomacy?" Coda

continued. "I believe the Coalition is expecting Brink to provide an Ambassador. Wouldn't that be the same as a Speaker?"

Woodard considered her words. Ambassador. He'd heard rumors of a search to fill some sort of high-level position as Brink joined the Coalition. "But that wouldn't fill Damaker's place as head of Brink's government, right?"

Coda shrugged. "True, those are two different roles."

One of the moto team leaned in, joining the discussion. "Yeah, Brink needs to lead Brink. It would be better if someone from here took Damaker's place, instead of a Coalition puppet with no love of our planet."

There were murmurs of agreement around the bar. Smith said, "Something has to happen fast, though. Damaker was in the middle of negotiations with the Coalition when he died. Had he lived, he could have filled that position with someone who was right for Brink."

Woodard glanced at Coda. Was he imagining it, or were her eyes tear-filled? Her head was lowered, her face hidden. He might have imagined the tears, but didn't think so.

But suddenly, she straightened. "Damaker was only a man, like all of us. Do you think he is the only one that could be for Brink?" Her voice was challenging, the lengthening shadows making it difficult to see her face.

"No, of course not," the moto rider said. "But he had everyone's trust."

"Damaker laid the foundation." Fyfe lifted his mug. "I do think our initial Ambassadorship to the Coalition will have to be a Firster."

Transitioning to the Coalition would be tough enough for Brinkers, so a Firster would smooth the process. But who? The list of Firsters with any experience or recognition was slim. Woodard had no desire to fill that role, and said as much.

The newly recognized Speaker, Eldred, stuttered out, "I couldn't speak for Brink. It's hard enough to Speak for the Whistlers."

Moncada reached over and rubbed his head. "Young one, true enough. It's tough to be a fair Speaker. Being a Speaker means looking at the larger picture. Imagine what that means for Brink?"

Woodard wanted to move away from the buffet. He found a free table and grabbed it. Coda, Smith, and Demi joined him. Talk was slow, the music celebratory. Smith asked Demi to dance. Watching them match steps proved his suspicion; there was something happening there.

Coda had noticed, too. "It's nice, isn't it? That they seem to have found each other." She turned and caught his gaze. He smiled at her, but before he could respond, her next words surprised him. "Are you the Bard?"

Her voice was pitched low and a quick glance around the table revealed no interest in their conversation.

"Why do you say that?" He fumbled his glass as he set it down on the table, which rocked as if reflecting his emotions. "Are you Dawn?" How surreal. He took a steadying breath, feeling as though he were outside of his body, watching her watching him. She nodded, a smile playing over her mouth.

Her words had hit him like a thunderbolt. She had been here. All along.

He reached over and grasped her hand. Coda's soft, slender fingers wrapped around his. "Let's take a walk down by the river we spotted on the way in," she said in voice that suggested they had a lot to discuss.

Good idea.

As they walked out the inn's door, Woodard felt oddly disoriented. Cold reason told him he was still in Whistling Winds. Or at least, his body was. But the rest of him, heart, soul, and mind, was dizzily shifting between past and present.

"Catch me up," he said as they headed toward the river. "What happened to you in all these years?"

"Wait a moment," she said, leading them through tall trees to a row of cabins that were available for guests of the inn. Those in use had a small occupancy sign displayed. Although the inn was busy, most guests were still out celebrating the new Speaker. Coda found a vacant cabin and opened the door, flipping its sign to read "Occupied."

The room was not luxurious. But there were chairs, he noted, his detail-noticing journalist side automatically kicking in, plus a small hygiene unit, a bed and an inviting hearth. Nearby stood a well-stocked galley station.

They sat in the chairs at the hearth, facing each other. Somehow their hands had connected again. Woodard wanted answers. "Tell me. I feel like I know everything, but yet at the same time, I know nothing."

She chuckled. With her free hand, she touched the controls to activate the artificial heat. Flames leaped, crackling as they met the dust in the air.

"I went off-world, to my home world, Casilear." She reached up to pull her hair off her neck, where he could see the oh-so-faint traceries of healed scars. Woodard recognized the gesture as a nervous habit, that twisting of the hair off the base of her neck. He disengaged from their handclasp to gently touch her there. She stiffened and he immediately dropped his hand.

Coda gave him a shy smile. "Sorry. I'm not used to being touched there." She let her hair down and settled back into the chair. "You know the story, right? When the flotilla entered atmosphere, our ship was caught in a yellow dust storm. The engines stopped, caught fire. It was everything my mother could do to land us in one piece.

"My father had to make sure all the passengers got out. Our family was last. As he was reaching for me, a piece of the wreckage fell on my back. He pulled me out, got me to a safe distance." Her eyes filled with tears. "But Mom was gone."

Woodard had heard parts of this before—he'd been collecting Brinker stories for weeks.

"You're Aurora. Damaker's daughter."

She nodded.

"And that mysterious case you've been carrying?"

"His ashes."

"And your morning absences?" Finally, an answer to what she and Demi had been doing on their daily excursions.

She folded her hands in her lap. "Scattering them."

"You know that's illegal without special permission."

153

She looked at him, straight on. "I'm returning to Brink what it took from me. I don't want my father's body to lie in state and be worshiped." She sighed. "Besides, his remains are inert. The cremation process took every bit of Damaker out of it. My action is only symbolic."

"So, do you know who's been approached for the ambassadorship?" He instantly cursed his blunt journalistic instincts as he watched her draw back and consider her answer. The flames from the heating elements reflected on her somber face.

"Me. I owe them a response in three days."

At the end of the tour. Now he understood why she was so concerned about trip delays.

"I'm still not sure," she said. "I don't want this job only because I'm Patric Damaker's daughter. I need to be able to fight for Brink." She stood up and began to pace the room. "This trip has helped me. It reminded me how diverse Brink is. But today was the key to my decision."

The Speaker ceremony, he realized.

"I saw the people's pride in Brink," she continued. "And in their communities. For Eldred to be able to stand up and say he's a Speaker for Whistling Winds…" She returned to her seat and slumped. "And I felt the same. Pride in what Brink has accomplished, and pride in the willingness to work for it."

"So your answer is yes."

Her hand returned to clasp his. "Do you remember when I told you that your words had helped me find mine?"

How could he forget? The knowledge had given him courage to continue, had shown him he was on the right path.

"Now I know it's right for me to be the Ambassador for Brink."

"And stop hiding?"

"I hid because of my burn scars. I hid because I didn't want to be known only as Damaker's daughter." She gave a small chuckle. "Actually, my father didn't encourage me very much. He was so busy. At the beginning, there was the grief. Then came the responsibility. And then working night and day became habit. Always so much to do." Tears began to streak down her face.

He pulled her into his lap, wrapping her in his arms. She snuffled into his shoulder. In one brief minute, he felt like his past had met with the present, and then he wondered about the future. But that was tomorrow. For now...

"I'm exhausted," she said in a small voice.

"There's a bed..." He pulled back to looked her in the eye. "Is it okay to share it?"

She nodded. "But only for warmth, ok? I have nothing else to give right now."

That was all he wanted. And he told her so.

Stop 4 - Point Split

THE GROUP REACHED POINT SPLIT, growing ever closer to Eos. Even as short as the trip was, everyone had settled into a rhythm. Red had done a good job at providing accommodations. There had been some pairing up along the way, maybe quicker than normal? Not surprising, Woodard mused, considering that the trip had started with a crash.

Fyfe continued to keep both vehicles linked in tandem, expertly maneuvering the heavy mass through well-maintained roads. There could be no more off-road adventures, not if they were to meet their agreed upon arrival time window.

Woodard was sorry about that. He'd hoped for more exploration of Brink, but he'd signed up for this short trip and Red was delivering what had been advertised. He could always find other sources for more local history and stories to fill his documentary. Smith was full of Firster stories. And Moncada added flavoring about the Brotherhood and what it was like to be a Speaker. Demi's mission of recording Brink's vegetation added the scientific component. Really, what more could he ask for?

Coda.

After their night together following the Speaker Induction in Whistling Winds, it seemed natural for her to sit next to him in the brover. She had not asked him to keep silent about her offer for Brink's ambassadorship. But she hadn't told the group anything yet, so he'd kept quiet. But—did he owe CMG the news? It would be a worthy scoop. An important story like this could move him up the ladder of news consultants, which would mean more money for his family. The thought was very tempting.

"Smith, what happened at Point Split?" Woodard asked.

Red still sat in the front seat because of his arm. Moncada had protested, but gave in once Red agreed to keep his arm in the sling, stabilized by the safety restraints.

Smith sat in the middle tier of seats, facing inward so he could be heard throughout the vehicle. "Split is where the different factions, well, split." He looked down at his feet, as if he were trying to decide what to say. Smiling, he said, "Brink's known for calling things out. Not adding gloss. So—Point Split.

"After the flotilla landed, and Eos was built—okay, Eos as a name is a bit fanciful. But it was our new beginning, our Dawn. Others soon followed. Some were First Families looking for new markets. Others were groups escaping persecution." Pausing, he said, "I don't think I'm telling tales if I say Brink became a safe location for stowies finding homes and forming families."

Woodard replied, "That's true. I arrived as part of a stowie transport, picked up from one of the prison ships. My first family was conscript fodder and I had no choice but to join the stowies on the ship." He shuddered. Those painful memories would never leave him. "They told me to take a chance on the stowie transport, to find a new life." And a new family. He owed everything to those who had come before him, and those who were with him still.

Fyfe, looking at his passengers through the reflection in the rear view mirror, agreed. "I also arrived via stowie transport. It's why I damn the Finders. Too much glory attached to it. A new Find almost always means lives lost in securing the Find's value." He pounded his fist on the steering wheel with more emotion than normally seen from the stoic Fyfe.

Coda put in, "That's why the new Coalition ruling is so important —that there would be no Find registered for planets inhabited with intelligent life." She was leaning forward, both arms crisscrossed against the top of Demi's seat. "It's a start and means that First Families will no longer sweep worlds for conscripts to subdue and settle. There would still be lives at stake for other types of Finds, like medical testing, but the new ruling is a start."

Demi added, "We still need to consider the impact on the worlds themselves." She pointed at the glimmering globe to their left. "Can we find ways to integrate rather than subdue?"

There was silence within the brover.

Woodard finally spoke up. "Smith, who or what was split at Point Split?"

Gratitude flashed over the older man's face. "Ah yes. Back on track." He sighed. "Growing pains, I guess is one way to explain it. Expansion outside of Eos, with each group wanting to have things their way. Their own way to govern, their own laws, all based on customs from their home worlds. Or, more likely, the things they hated about their home worlds." He paused. "Brink became known for new beginnings. And everybody wanted their own. So, this became known as Point Split. We all split off into our own communities."

Moncada agreed, shadows from the brover's metal frame darkening his face. "Whistling Winds is such a place. The first group wanted to live in wide spaces, with freedom to live communally. They developed use of their moto bikes to build and retain their own sense of community."

Coda spoke up. "I remember those times. I don't think there was any big decision. Groups simply started to split apart. Damaker and his group decided to continue forward to what eventually became known as Point Decision." She hesitated. "But I was pretty young then. Maybe ten years old?"

Woodard considered what she'd said. It must have been a few years later when they had started their virtual friendship. He noticed Smith looking at her closely, but said nothing.

Red said, "Let's check into the inn, get settled. Shall we meet again in a couple of hours for the evening meal?"

The inn had overbooked the rooms and offered "luxurious tent accommodations including free breakfast" for the group. Red tried to hold the inn to the booked reservations, but to no avail.

When he rejoined them, he had a disgruntled look on his face, a departure from his normally cheery demeanor. "Sorry, all. I can't get us the rooms I reserved. This is what they've proposed." He gestured to the small lake and a cluster of three large tents.

"It's ok, Red, it's only for one night. Let's split up into the tents." Smith broke into a grin. "Point Split, get it?"

Red rolled his eyes heavenward. "I certainly don't want to dictate who sleeps with who. We're all adults." He looked around. "The tents are supposed to sleep at least three. There's seven of us. How about Coda and Demi take one, then Woodard and Smith? That leaves the last one for Moncada, Fyfe, and me." He paused, waiting for objections, but none came. "Ok, then. Fyfe, let's get the gear out."

Mobilized into action, Fyfe enlisted Moncada's assistance for the heavy lifting. Coda disappeared, carrying her case. Demi followed her. Red went back to the Inn, most likely confirming the meal options. Woodard sighed. What to do?

He decided to join Coda and Demi.

THE END of the trip was just a couple of stops away. Hefting her case, Coda was encouraged by its lightness.

And she felt lighter, too.

She and Demi walked in companionable silence for a time. Then Demi spoke. "Would you mind sharing a tent with Woodard? I think…I would like to share with Smith tonight."

Coda swiveled around to look at Demi. A slight tinge of red had spread over her face. "Demi! You and…Smith?" She shook her head. "I never guessed it." She sighed. What else had she not noticed on this trip, wrapped up in her own grief and the weight of difficult choices?

"Of course, it's ok," she replied.

"And that gives you a chance to spend more time with Woodard." Demi grinned at her.

Now Coda could feel the heat rushing up her own cheeks. She stumbled over the uneven ground. "Wha…"

"Coda. I saw you two leaving the same cabin at Whistling Winds. Hey, I'm happy for you."

Coda shrugged to cover her embarrassment. "It's complicated."

"Of course it is." Demi stopped and pointed to a nearby hill. "Let's go up there. It's high enough, and we should be able to see the road to Eos."

They stepped carefully over the small brush covering the hillside. "Or maybe it's not," Demi continued.

"Not what?"

"You and Woodard. Not complicated."

They had reached the top of the hill. Wetting a finger, Demi determined the wind's direction and pointed. "Let's face this way."

Coda crouched down to open her case and considered the remaining amount. Her father would always live in her heart. She didn't need to keep anything tangible anymore to remind her of his legacy. Should she let the rest of his ashes go now, right here?

No, she decided. Not yet.

Filling her little cup to overflowing, she stood, lifting her arms to the sky, and tossed the contents. The breeze caught the particles, the sunlight striking them golden. It seemed fitting, the golden color, considering the yellow dust storms. She refilled the cup. And tossed it again.

"That should be enough. There's still plenty left for Eos." She squinted at the balance. "No, on second thought, let's do it again tomorrow."

Demi agreed. "Up to you."

Coda clutched the brown case to her chest. "Thank you for doing this with me, Demi. I know you caught me at it, but I am thankful for your presence." Thankful for a witness.

They turned to retrace their steps to the inn.

"And Woodard?"

Oh. Coda realized she hadn't answered Demi about sharing the tent.

And suddenly, there he was. Following their path. Had he seen what they were doing? But then, did it really matter? She'd already made her decision.

"Look at that," said Demi. "Just showed up out of nowhere."

Coda wasn't sure if she should be happy or embarrassed that she still had the ability to blush. "Yeah, look at that."

Swinging the case by her side, she strode forward and met Woodard on the hillside.

He held out his hand to help steady her descent. How to begin what she wanted to say? But she decided to speak straight out. Just as she meant to go forward. Without fear.

"Demi suggested a slight adjustment to the sleeping arrangements."

Woodard's grip on her hand tightened. The terrain was rocky, so the three of them picked their way slowly down. He regarded Coda and Demi quizzically.

"Yes?"

Demi answered. "I'd like to share with Smith tonight. We enjoy each other's company, and the trip is ending soon…"

He was silent for a moment. "I guess I need to find another place to sleep, then. Oh—does that mean there's extra room in Coda's tent?"

Coda felt her chest tighten. There was fear there, for sure. But that was ok. Just like when they were younger, there were some things she couldn't control.

Leaning closer to him, she asked, "Would you share my tent tonight?"

He grinned at her. "Sure. Much better option than bunking with Red. Or staking out a space in the brover."

Demi announced, "Well, that's settled, then. I'm hungry. Let's go see what Red has managed for our evening meal."

Stop 5 – Point Commit

THE BARD'S essay for the day centered on committing. Committing to friends, committing to a new future, a forward path. What was he trying to say? It was getting ridiculous for him to leave her clues in his daily offering.

Stepping outside the shared tent, Coda carried her sleeping bag to the clothesline to allow it to air prior to packing. There was a whiff of coffee in the air, reminding her of the outside world. She felt at peace with her decision to accept the Ambassador position, at peace with the change in her relationship with Woodard, and the changes both would make to her future. It wasn't only her future, it was Woodard's, and it was also Brink's.

It was early still, the sun just beginning to tint the sky and hide the stars. Point Commit. The place where the Firsters had realized they could never return to their home worlds and would have to commit to making a new life on Brink.

The case she'd carried the ashes in was light, just as she felt. Where should she release them today? Her memories were so faded at this point, she couldn't remember where they had gathered all those years ago to make that difficult decision—to commit.

Perhaps it didn't matter.

A sudden warmth spread across her back as arms encircled her in a cradling embrace. Woodard's breath tickled her neck. She couldn't help it, she jumped. Just a little.

"Where do you go today?"

She pondered for a moment, still wrapped in his arms, luxuriating in the warmth.

"I'm not sure of the best place. Maybe it doesn't matter anymore." She looked at him over her shoulder. "You left early. To submit your essay?"

His arms tightened. "Have you finished your pilgrimage?"

"I think I've made my peace with Dad. Now I can leave with a good conscience."

He turned her around to face him. "I need to tell you something."

A breeze flickered by, gently ruffling the leaves at their feet. But the serious look on his face suddenly made her uncomfortable. What could be wrong? Last night had been wonderful. Perhaps she could lighten his mood again. But as she reached to tie up her hair, he caught her hand.

"No, let me finish." He took a deep breath. "I told CMG that you were approached for the Ambassador post. I had to."

She felt all the air whoosh out of her chest. Had she heard him correctly? In that moment, the world around her ceased to exist, narrowed to one point of pain in her pounding heart. She vaguely saw his face in front of her and the leaves ruffling over her feet. But none of that registered. Nothing but his deception. Had she meant nothing to him? Had she been simply the source of a juicy story for him to exploit?

Distance. She needed distance.

"*Had to?*" she managed to choke out.

"This is important news that impacts all of Brink. It's bigger than you, if you think about it."

"Think about it?" Coda took a step back. A raw sense of betrayal flooded her veins but was quickly displaced by anger. Once again, Brink had won. "If I thought about it? Fuck this. This was my decision to tell, not yours. Mine! Do you hear me? Not yours!" Her eyes narrowed as she spat out the deepest betrayal of all. "You took my words away from me."

Coda whirled and ran blindly through the encampment, heading towards the protected areas, barely realizing she still grasped the case in her hand. Tears blurred her eyes and she stumbled, falling to the ground.

Demi arrived and dropped down next to her, panting heavily after the race through the woods. Coda's throat constricted as she fought to control her tears and she shook her head, unable to speak.

Demi sat quietly next to her. She plucked a sprig of sage, twirled it between her fingers, then tucked it into her sample case. "Tell me about this place."

Coda pulled up a bit of her shirt and wiped her face.

"This is where Firsters realized that they had to commit to a life spent on Brink." She pushed herself to her feet and began to pace. "The flotilla was in a shambles..." This was the truth. But not the whole truth. "And we couldn't take off again to reach our intended destination." By this time, Smith had caught up with them, and he nodded his agreement. He glanced at Coda, eyebrow raised in question of her obvious distress, but Demi patted the ground next to her and shook her head in an unspoken signal for him to remain silent.

"We had pulled out everything we could salvage from the flotilla and buried our dead," he said.

Dead, *singular*, Coda silently corrected. Only her mother had perished in the landing. Others had suffered injuries, but they'd had enough medical equipment and knowledge to treat them.

Smith continued, "But what's not widely known is that we were actually escaping."

Escaping from what? Coda had long suspected that there was some reason the flotilla had changed direction from the original landing point, but she'd been too young to be included in the decision.

"Damaker had been given the commission to transport the flotilla to Grenpack." He shifted into a more comfortable position on the hard ground. "Do you remember hearing about Grenpack? It was a Find, supposedly. But it held sentient life."

The planet Grenpack turned out to be a decision point for the Coalition. The Grenpack Law was the first to recognize the rights of indigenous intelligent life. A primary tenet of Finds and Finder's Fees was the concept of first Finders. After the new Law was implemented, inhabitants always held Finder ownership and rights.

Smith shook his head as a serious expression played across his face, apparently reliving past days and past choices. "Damaker and the other flotilla leaders decided not to fulfill the terms of the commission because they didn't hold with the idea of taking over Grenpack for some major family, or Finder to exploit the passengers as expendable pawns to fulfill their own ambitions. So we Found Brink."

Actually, it had been her mother, Mary, who had Found Brink. Mary's Finder skills were not very acute but were always heightened when her family was in jeopardy. Coda remembered the discussions in the family quarters, poring over star maps, her mother's finger pointing at this tiny speck.

Smith continued, "No sentient life here, at least not at the time. And it was habitable. Barely. But we had enough smart, skilled and desperate folk in the flotilla to survive. The only Find in Brink was Brink itself. Alone, it wasn't special enough to be Found." Smith sat down and stretched out his legs next to Demi, taking her hand in his. The obvious tenderness in that clasp caught at Coda's throat. She searched for a dry spot on her shirt to wipe her eyes.

He pointed at Coda. "You have the look of your mother. You're Damaker's daughter, right?"

Coda heard a gasp from behind her. Moncada and Red had joined them.

"Say, what is it in that pack you're always carrying?" Red asked, horrified. "And what have you been doing every morning before we leave a site?" He shook his head in disbelief. "If that's what I think it is, how could you do that on one of MY TOURS? It's illegal!"

Moncada laid a steadying hand on Red's shoulder, gently but firmly pressing on the injured side. "Quiet, Red. Let Coda talk. But first, let me get Fyfe and Woodard. All of us should be here."

Red sank to his knees, wincing as his arm was jarred.

Coda felt dry, empty, full of ashes—as though she'd been cremated by Brink, just like her father. And her mother.

Moncada returned with Fyfe and Woodard. She turned her head away as a small shudder passed through her. How could she ever look Woodard in the eyes again? All she could see was his betrayal. How could someone who'd helped her regain her lost voice suddenly turn around and callously steal her words away? And how would she ever get through the remainder of the trip? The passengers were bound together until they reached Eos...Point New Beginning.

Perhaps it was fitting, here at Point Commit, to honor the commitment she wanted to make to Brink.

But how? What should she share with the others? She wavered, unsure how to begin. But all she knew was that she'd feel better once she was no longer hiding from the truth. It was time to finish breaking out of the protective bubble she had built around herself. Looking at Woodard, she realized with a start that she'd already begun that process with him.

"All," she stood up and faced the group, "if I might speak for a moment?" She took a steadying breath, gathering her courage, and plunged forward. "Some of you know, and some of you may have guessed, that I am Damaker's daughter, Aurora. Please, though, I'd prefer it if you continue to call me Coda."

She heard a surprised gasp from someone among her fellow travelers, but she pushed on and pointed to the case at her feet. "I embarked on this journey as a final pact with my father. He made no last wishes, leaving everything to me. I decided not to let Brink turn him into a martyr, worshipping his body in state. So I had him cremated. I thought to return him to Brink, scattering a portion of his ashes at historical points important to the history of our planet." She turned to Red. "I'm sorry. I know it's against the law, but it was only a cupful or two at each stop. And the cremation process left nothing organic behind."

Demi raised her hand. "I can attest to that. I checked them out with my bio scanner."

But Red's face was suffused with anger. "I can lose my transport license. You had no right to do such a thing without my knowledge."

"Yes. You're right, I'm sorry." Coda glanced at Woodard. He was watching her, face inscrutable.

She made up her mind in that moment. The full truth had to come out, and she wanted it to come from her own words.

"There's something else I want to share with you all. The Coalition and Brink's Council have both approached me to take the Ambassador position for Brink." She searched the faces of her fellow travelers, gauging their reactions. When she saw no signs of dismay, she continued, "We would not be a full Coalition member yet—there's work we still need to do to meet those requirements. But we would be able to join in policy making and have a voice." A voice. She smiled slightly as she said that.

She picked up the case containing her father's ashes. "Red, I know I haven't been the easiest passenger. But I need to be at Eos by a certain date to let the Coalition know my decision. The last shuttle before the council meeting is leaving in two days.

"I also came on this journey because I wanted to reconnect with the essence that is Brink. I couldn't represent Brink, still holding in the anger I felt at what my history with the planet cost me. I wondered, could I be the best person to serve our interests at the Coalition Council?"

Woodard was silent. So was everyone else. They were all waiting.

"Well, I may not be the best person to represent Brink," Coda said. "But this trip has shown me Brink has come a long way since we crash-landed. I think we're ready for the next...Brink."

Woodard stood up and stood by Coda's side. Facing the group, he said, "I guess I want to come clean, too. As some of you may have guessed, I'm the writer known as the Bard."

Smith slapped his hand on his thigh. "I knew it! Didn't I tell you so?" he said to Demi.

Woodard took up Coda's hand, and once again the warmth of his touch was surprising. "It turns out that Coda and I knew each other." He hesitated. "Well, sort of, several years ago." He glanced down at her, then squeezed her hand. "Coda had trusted me with her secret, with the knowledge of her true identity, and that she'd been approached about the Coalition position." He turned to face her and looked straight into her eyes. "I afraid I let my desire to keep Brink informed of important news override what was fair to her. Coda, I'm sorry. What I did was wrong, and I deeply apologize. Can you ever forgive me for betraying your secret?"

Coda's heart lurched. Could she forgive him? Woodard smiled at her, and she knew at once that his apology and regret were sincere. She nodded, and he beamed, pulling her to him in a hug.

Moncada stood and stretched with an exaggerated motion, breaking the moment. "Lots of apologies all around." He pointed at Coda's case. "How much of that is left?"

"Only a little." She disengaged from Woodard's embrace. "Red, if it's ok with you, I'd like to make another scattering here." Would he allow it? Did he understand?

Demi joined her. "She's right, Red. I wouldn't have let her do it if there was a risk of contamination."

Red's shoulders slumped. "I suppose so, at this point. But I still say it's not right to include us in something that could come back and implicate us all."

Moncada motioned Red and Fyfe to join them. "Did you plan the last distribution to be at Eos? At the beginning?"

She nodded mutely.

"Then, I say, let her scatter some of the ashes right now, and then we can be on our way to our final destination."

Fyfe joined in. "Yeah, we'll beat our schedule if we get on the road."

"What about it, Red? Is it ok with you?" Coda persisted. Whatever he decided, she would follow his wishes.

Red's face contorted with a look that clearly showed he felt he'd been pushed into a corner. "Yeah, I guess so. But if anyone comes after me, I deny everything. Or, I give them all *your* names."

A chuckle wound through them. "Ok, then." Coda reached down for her case, opened it, and retrieved her cup. "I would like to do this from the top of the dune."

Woodard took the case from her. "Let's go. Would the rest of you like to join us?"

One by one, the little band of travelers silently fell in behind the pair as they climbed up to the dune's crest. The sun was already halfway up in the sky, and a gentle breeze blew from the south.

Fyfe broke the solemn moment. "Let's not face into the wind, right?"

Coda reached into the case, filled her cup, and with the breeze at her back, threw the contents into the sky.

The sun lit the ashes, and the breeze carried them away. Coda glanced back at the group behind her and was surprised to see Smith's face shining wet with fallen tears. Demi, her constant companion, nodded in satisfaction. Red still scowled, but she thought she heard him give a sniffle or two.

Moncada stood with his arms upraised, shrouded within his Brotherhood robes. "And with this precious offering, dear ones, we all become one. The sun, the wind, the dune—all of us. Part of one united whole."

"Yeah, even I feel that." Fyfe shrugged and turned to go. "Okay, let's get on the road."

Today had been a turning point, Coda realized. Her fellow travelers had become her friends.

Stop 6 - Point Beginning

THE SPACESHIP STOOD BEFORE THEM, glistening in the morning sunlight. They looked at each other, recognizing that after today, they would no longer be members of the Scarlett Tour.

Red, his arm still in a sling, but much improved since the treatment at the med center, attempted to rub his hands together. "Group, I count success as all tour participants reaching the final stop." He looked around. "Agreed?"

They all looked at each other, smiling. He continued, "Let me help you get to whatever transport you need for your next destination."

It was like a mirror image of their first meeting, but with so much more meaning. Coda hefted the lightened case holding the remainder of the ashes. "I had thought to take these with me when I returned to Casilear, my home world. But now I think it's better to let them be used at the memorial. I have made my peace with Brink. My father's ashes are now part of the real world, the real history here."

Demi asked, "And what then?"

Coda said slowly, "I'm not sure. I started this trip knowing two things. One, I wanted to make my peace with this planet before I left it. And two, I wanted to leave Brink. But I leave now while working *for* it." She swung the bag carrying the ashes, showing how much lighter it was. "I've done the first. And I've also decided on where I'm headed." Tears flooded her eyes, and she wiped them away with a grimy finger. "Anyone else know what's next for them?"

Moncada stepped forward. "Like Coda, I started out knowing what my destination was going to be. But what I know now is not what I knew at the start." He tilted his head in the direction of the ship. "I'm heading that way. I'm going to use my medical training to secure a post on a First Family ship and serve in both a physical and spiritual way." A grin split his face. "And maybe even share some laughs along the way." He pointed to Smith. "You next?"

Smith looked like he was surprised at the question. "I guess I head back to Capital City. Is there some fast shuttle I can take?" He grimaced. "I mean, one that flies instead of a brover?"

Fyfe had finished unloading the gear and tossed the keys to Red. "I think I'm ready for something new. I checked with one of the scavenger companies docking here and they're always looking for fixers."

Red cuffed him on the shoulder. "I knew your future wasn't going to be a roadie. At least not with me. And yeah, they always need fixers. Not Finders, right?" Fyfe nodded.

"And you, Demi? Where are you headed?" Red continued.

"I thought I might travel with Smith for a while. I think the way we look at the world complements each other." Smith looked at her, a slow smile spreading over his face. Demi went to his side and tucked her hand in his.

Watching Smith holding that slender hand brought a tightness to Coda's throat.

Moncada said, "There's a rightness in that. I wish you well in your travels."

"Wait," said Red. "Woodard, what about you and your documentary?"

Smith said, "Yeah, Woodard, are we done?"

Coda had wondered the same. What would Woodard publish? He was still an unknown quantity, even with everything they had shared. She still didn't know what he might write. Which truth would he tell?

Woodard let out a deep breath and looked around at the group. "I've been wrestling with this." He held out both hands. Lifting one, he said, "There's this truth." Then, lifting the other, "there's also this truth."

Dropping his hands, he continued, "I started this trip positive that the Coalition was not the right solution for Brink's colonists and that Damaker had orchestrated the entire move to Guardianship. That he was planning for a new position for himself within the Coalition, as a reward for delivering Brink to the Coalition." He threw his hands up in the air. "Now? I'm not so sure. And I'm not so sure what good it would do to continue to pursue that."

Coda waited, holding her breath. What legacy would Woodard decide to provide for her father? She could not, would not sway him. She had to step back and let others make their own choices. She had done what she had set out to do—return her father to the planet her mother had Found and he had founded.

Woodard said, "But the one act he is most famous for, did he really do that? No, he did not." His body was tense as he seemed to wrestle with a final decision. Then Coda saw his muscles relax, and he continued, "And I don't think it would do anyone any good to know that."

He looked around at the faces of the Scarlett Brink Historical Tour group. "Do you all agree? I think we should let the legend stand."

There was a collective sigh. Everyone present now knew the entire truth. It hadn't been Damaker who had guided the flotilla to Brink, but his wife, who had Found a world just barely hospitable, but close enough and safe enough to support them on the brink of escaping certain death on Grenpack.

Coda looked over at the spaceport, her eyes searching out the scorched piece of land, still showing the effects of the initial landing on Brink. Even though her father hadn't Found Brink, it was true that he had named it and founded it. Now, she could accept the responsibility of representing Brink through the initial years of Coalition guardianship. She would learn to Speak for Brink. And learn diplomacy along the way.

Her own future? She turned to Woodard. "Once you've completed the documentary and the commission for CMG, what's next for you?"

Slowly, he said, "I have responsibilities here, to my adopted family." He took her hand in his, and as his fingers tightened around hers, he went on, "but I think I can help them up there." And with his other hand, he pointed to the ship standing tall at Eos. "May I travel with you?" Those words were said with hesitation—the former stowie to the founder's daughter.

She smiled at him and replied, "I suppose we can complete that documentary on Damaker together, right?"

Then she turned to Red. "Thank you for this cap. I'll keep it with me always." She carefully tucked it into her case. "It's time I started filling this case with new beginnings."

ABOUT THE AUTHOR

Julie Halperson has been enveloped in story universes ever since she read Dick and Jane as a child, and those universes just became bigger as she grew older. What else to do but to create her own to explore and discover? Currently living in the Washington DC metropolitan suburbs, she's enriched by her circles of family and friends. She also likes to explore the world and travels every chance she can – either by long road trips, tour groups, and pretty much anything in between.

Please look me up on Facebook for more news and pictures that help me explore the world.

Facebook: **https://www.facebook.com/julie.halperson/**
Instagram: **https://www.instagram.com/juliehalperson/**

BUTTERFLIES AND GOODBYES

SKYE KNIGHT

CHAPTER ONE

"Those fucking soul-suckers." Beatrix cursed fiercely for about the thousandth time while shoving a mouthful of shredded hash browns properly coated in ketchup into her mouth. Glaring at the latest news of their attacks on peaceful planets reported on a notification from her handheld device, she chewed forcefully, then stabbed the next bite from her plate with her fork, like the food itself was the culprit.

A snort erupted from her companion across the cold metal table.

Beatrix's eyes cut to her BFF, who sported bangs that fell almost into her bright green eyes and had a face framed by long, straight, black hair. Jett, while appropriately named when considering just the hair, had the most innocent of faces, fair skin, and sprinkles of freckles over her nose. It would be easy to think her friend would have the sweetest disposition. But Beatrix liked Jett's true personality —hard, bitter, real. Just like Beatrix perceived herself to be.

Jett reached over to trail her fingers along the inside of Bea's left forearm, tracing the winding tattoos from the inner elbow to the wrist. Giving her a sly look, Jett said, "You're one to talk," then arched her eyebrows and looked pointedly at the intricately inked art.

"Oh, burn." Beatrix rolled her eyes. "It's hardly the same."

"Yeah? How many men have you stolen tattoos from now?"

A smirk lifted one corner of Beatrix's full lips. "It's just to remember them by."

Jett squinted at her, the thick, dark liner surrounding her eyes almost obscuring their emerald depths. Black eyes were like the soul-suckers—and Beatrix didn't like that.

Jett said, "You don't think stealing their art for yourself is your way of saying F U to them?"

"I don't really bother digging into my motivations," Beatrix muttered, scraping the last hash browns from her plate before moving on to the actual reward—the bacon. She'd been down that road before, and she'd always found herself longing for who she could have been, for the past, for the people she'd lost. But there were no do-overs, so it wasn't worth looking back.

Her friend crossed her arms over her chest and waited. She could wait until the rebellion was won as far as Bea was concerned.

Jett eventually acquiesced. "I noticed you got another. I guess Liam is out now?" She had thought he was hot, but he'd been a bit too cheerful for Bea, like the golden retrievers on her old home planet, Rutheni. The memory made her sad.

Continuing, Jett added, "Listen, I get your weirdness, because I feel it in my very soul. I'm just trying to point out that the Morphos are on a mission to find happiness just like us."

Her fork clattered to the table. "Are you kidding me? You're comparing how my weird trauma manifests to those creepy black-eyed monsters? I don't steal other people's souls for my own happiness."

Jett's eyes shifted. "Of course not—" She shrugged. "But I deal with them daily on the job. They do attempt charm when they understand your function and respect you. And respect is so damn hard to come by here."

Dropping her forehead into her hands, Beatrix stared at her food in abject horror. There was no doubt all their lives were horrible, and there was little hope for anything good. She was doing what she could for the cause without physically putting her neck out there—too risky.

How had Jett's thinking warped so much that she thought the enemy was showing her respect? They clearly just wanted Jett's influence in her governmental employ.

Taking in a deep breath, then releasing it with a shudder, she lifted her eyes to meet her friend's and wrested her shoulders back into a strong and confident pose. Sometimes the right posture could help her feel more powerful in what was indeed a powerless place.

Jett gave her a soft smile. "I'm joking, Bea," she said, shaking her head. "You take everything so seriously, but what else is there to do? Of course, they're evil soul-suckers, but this is the life we're stuck living. We're just cogs in the wheel, but at least we're protected working here. They perceive us as little ants, keeping the universe running, and that's the only reason they won't touch us." Her dry laugh was harsh.

Beatrix's anger drained away. Directing it at her friend wouldn't do anything, wouldn't make the latest devastating news any better. Their world was on a path of destruction, and she dreaded to think they could all become Morphos or have their souls swallowed to power that insatiable black hole.

She stared listlessly at the bacon that she had been looking forward to enjoying, extra crispy just for her.

"How's your uncle?" Jett asked quietly, squeezing her fingers over Beatrix's uninked right hand.

"Oh, Tommy's all right. On bedrest for now after the hernia surgery. I told him he was pushing too hard here at the diner. But all he thinks of is providing and protecting us. I am indebted to him, but I have nothing to give back."

Her eyes teared up, surprising her.

"That's not true, babe—you give back to him by working here, helping him with his house, and providing him companionship. You both lost so much."

"No more than most, including you."

Their eyes met in understanding.

"Listen, we've all lost a lot of people," Jett said, then paused. "But it's a miracle you got off that dreadful planet you came from and are the strong bitch that you are."

Bea gave her a sad smile. "Rutheni was actually kinda special."

"Well, of course, you think that—it was your home. But it was perpetually under attack. I don't understand why your people were constantly taunting the Morphos by taking them on."

"Some of those people were my parents," Beatrix said softly. Now that they were gone, she was left with her secret paintings—her one gesture of hope, her one way of rebelling in honor of them that no one could know about.

"I'm sorry. You know I don't mean any offense—but we all know it's putting a target on your back. It's no way to live, constantly fighting." Jett widened her eyes.

"I don't want to live that way—but it's probably good that some people fight, that some people have hope," Beatrix said. She lifted her eyes to the ceiling. It was dirty. Gosh, the place was falling into disrepair—she would need to put in some extra hours to clean them when they weren't open for business, which, of course, was next to never. But French Toast & Roast was her and her uncle's sanctuary.

"You're joking?" Cynicism arched Jett's brows.

Beatrix let out a bitter chortle. "'Course I am. It's hopeless." She didn't want to be mocked or to tarnish her hard appearance by revealing the small flame of hope she hoarded deep inside.

"Good. At least you're still reasonable." Jett rose, grabbing her purse and slinging it on her shoulder. "I'm running late for my shift, but are there any imports you need me to intercept? The new tariff manager that started this week is likely to cause some hiccups and slow everything down."

Beatrix stood and started busing their table, realizing she didn't have long until her shift started either.

"Thanks, chica, but I'm good. Be careful around the damn soulsuckers, 'k?" She gave her only friend a quick side squeeze.

"Of course. They won't mess with me," Jett said confidently, then strode for the door and slipped the mandatory sunglasses on as she stepped outside.

"Don't be so sure," Beatrix couldn't help whispering after her. The fear of losing those she loved never went away.

Glancing down at her friend's plate as she went to stack it, she noticed Jett had drowned her French toast in syrup. Bea wasn't one for sweetness, but their diner's French toast was genuinely interstellar. However, it looked as though Jett had barely eaten a bite. The girl had to eat more. She was getting too skinny.

Bea looked nothing like the knobby-kneed, gangly preteen she'd been when she left home. Now solidly built while still sporting some womanly curves—she ate her protein and constantly worked—at least she felt physically strong.

Which was a good thing because it was 5 a.m. and there was work she could drown herself in. She always took solace that the Morphos had little interest in their tiny moon, fittingly called Odessa, or one who receives pain. The more joyful the planet, the happier the people, and the more powerful the souls. Their moon had little to offer in that way. Life here was desperate.

CHAPTER TWO

Deft hands chopped the vegetables with wicked precision. Sinewy forearms extended from the chef's shirt, one wrapped in winding tats, moving swiftly over the flat griddle. Her modern purple bob swung forward, her thick fringe of lashes cast downward as she focused on the task at hand. The woman's skill with the knives was scary and hot. And everything he needed and was looking for.

"Beatrix," he said, not wanting to startle her, disrupt her rhythm, and cause unnecessary harm. But he should have realized a woman working in a diner like this, with a diverse cast of alien races making up the three-piece ensemble jamming out to funk-inspired music in the corner and pulling in all sorts of clientele, would be unfazed by any kind of disturbance.

"What's up?" she asked, not even bothering to raise the iridescent blue eyes he remembered so well to meet his own. He wasn't going to admit to himself that he was disappointed she didn't recognize his voice. To be fair, it'd probably deepened since their preteen dalliance. Then he realized her name was sewn above her pocket, and anyone would have the ability to call her by name.

"I would like to request your time when you're free..." That might seem a proposition, so he qualified it with "To have a conversation."

When her eyes shot up to meet his, an ocean wave of intensity crashed over his head. And yet it was a look he imagined he might be happy to drown in at some point.

"Who are you, and what do you want?" she asked curtly, even as her eyes skirted along his form, appraising him.

Kendrick knew he stood out like a sore thumb. His hair was golden from the top of his head to the scruff on his face, and he wore light tan clothing while everyone else here was dressed darkly, from makeup and hair to tats and apparel. Surely, she must know exactly who he was and, at a minimum, what planet he was from.

"What do you mean you don't remember me? We were once betrothed," he said, a slow sardonic smile crooking one side of his mouth.

"By our parents!" She brushed her hands against her apron in exasperation, looking around her workspace like she was trying to remember what she was about to do.

Already, he liked getting under her skin.

"We weren't children still when you last laid—eyes—on me," he said gruffly, keeping their last kiss discreet, despite the memory being burned into his mind as a young man.

Eyeing him head to toe, she replied softly, "As good as." Was it longing he heard in her voice?

The girl he remembered invaded his memories, with soft honey brown hair that fell in waves to brush her shoulders, not this mod purple bob she rocked now. Rosy features, kind eyes, and those obnoxiously full lips she'd lifted to him as a simple offering, unaware of how that one moment would remain implanted in his memory. In their naivete, they'd only risked soft and warm pressure.

What he'd do to war with this woman's sharp tongue now.

The moment of that kiss was the last time he saw her. He'd been out on the young men's tribal training for a few weeks when he heard of the sordid killings of her parents. Shortly after, her uncle swept her from their home without a word of where they'd gone.

Apparently, her Uncle Tommy didn't put much stock in betrothals from infancy either.

"Well, since you remember me now"—he gave what he hoped was a cute smile—"I'd love to have a moment of your time to talk in private."

Her responding snort irked him. "As you can see, I'm working. Just like it's five o'clock somewhere, it's basically dawn all day here at our lovely breakfast diner."

It was hard to wait when he'd been searching for her, wishing for her partnership, for so long.

"Sounds horrible. Dawn should be the beginning of something, not something perpetual."

He suppressed a smile at her eye roll. Scanning the menu to have an excuse to wait, he blinked when he saw one item.

"Sitchy berry pie?" He was unable to veil the pain in his voice. "How do you get your hands on that fruit?"

Her movements stilled, as though she'd had a physical reaction to his suffering. "Helps when the moon you're on is a major trading hub. And home isn't the only place that grows them."

"Home doesn't—anymore," he uttered, closing his eyes briefly as visions of the desecration of the beloved place flashed through his thoughts.

"Oh," she said and resumed a flurry of actions.

The careless way the words slipped between those pretty lips caused anger to ripple through him. Could she honestly not give a damn? Not have kept track of what had happened to all of them, her people?

"I'll take a whole pie," he asserted.

"For right now?" She turned to him, eyebrows raising.

"Yes," he said with an affirming nod. "If I have to wait, I might as well savor a solid taste of home until you're available."

The brilliance of her blue eyes was shuttered as she squinted at him, trying to interpret the layers of his words. Probably she didn't like that he wasn't leaving and coming back later. But he'd been hunting her too long—no way was he going to provide her a chance to give him the slip again.

"Savor a taste of home via the pie until I'm available *to talk,*" she stated flatly.

"Yes, of course. What else?" He fervently hoped his face radiated innocence and not his thoughts of tasting her in memory of home.

"Pie will be up in ten, and I'll have a quick break in twenty. If you don't bug me until then, I'll consider giving you my precious moments of freedom in the hope that you will be on your way soon after."

He nodded that it was his intention, but knew it would never be that simple. Pulling out his device, he made clear he would leave Beatrix be.

Subtly, though, he watched her. Her knife skills seemed not to have waned. That was essential to his mission. To the rebellion. Their recent discovery of the Morphos' weakness made it necessary to find warriors with specific skills. She was trained from childhood.

And while he was sure her food was delicious, he had to believe that she felt the higher calling, like he did, to help save their world. To release all the souls that the Morphos so recklessly consumed.

He was lost, staring over the top of his device at her hands moving at lightspeed, chopping and preparing vegetables, so the sudden ruckus from the doorway caught him off guard. And that rarely happened.

A naked woman was falling, stumbling to the floor, filthy, with lost, foggy eyes.

Not another one. Not here.

Jumping to his feet, Kendrick raced to assist her, as others all around took steps away from her instead.

It was so different from Rutheni, where strangers rushed to assist, to help, to fight rather than turn away from others' troubles. What kind of place was this that Bea had fled to and why?

He held up the middle-aged woman, whose dark brown hair was messily falling out of a traditional worker's bun. He held one hand, gently applying pressure, trying to draw her darting eyes, fearful and unseeing, to meet his own.

"Ma'am?" No reply.

Kendrick led her to the closest table, empty only because it had yet to be bused, and lowered her onto the bench beside it. Hastily, he withdrew his large, heavy cloak to wrap around her. She folded into the warmth as naturally as an injured creature into a burrow.

And then the shivering started—the shiver of feeling one's soul mostly gone, body searching for its filling.

Odessa was supposed to be neutral territory. People were supposed to be safe here, as grounds for keeping the law, order, and trade—as unhappy a place as it was. And while it was transactional, this woman had somehow not been part of the deal.

"Do you have any family? Friends? Ma'am, who can I call?" She had nothing on her, no ID, and no scrap of clothing. The purpose of stripping her was hard to say when they'd already confiscated most of her soul. Perhaps the common criminal had their way with her first—evidence of how void of anything this place was. But this attack revealed the Morphos were escalating, growing more aggressive, and losing regard for the agreements that held Odessa as a place of relative truce.

The intergalactic peace force burst through the door. They were a joke—all they did was enforce the most fundamental laws to ensure there wasn't complete anarchy. There was no peace to be had, yet here they were.

Quickly, they surrounded the woman, interrogating her to no avail, and Kendrick slowly stepped out of the fray. After they realized their mission was futile, they turned to the crowd. "Whose cloak is this?" said the man who appeared to be the leader, with a few more bars indicating rank across his chest.

Kendrick thought it should be pretty obvious when he was the only person wearing light-colored clothing, but he didn't want to draw extra attention to himself, so he simply raised a hand and gave the man a small nod.

"May the lady keep it as we escort her to care? We can take your information to ensure its return?" The man offered his device to receive the signal from Kendrick's device for his contact.

"Unnecessary," he replied succinctly, sliding back into his seat at the bar to give the scene his shoulder now that he was no longer needed.

He saw the officer squint at him through his periphery and knew it was unusual for people not to cling to their possessions. Most here had so little. But he generally avoided giving out details about himself to anyone with his role in the larger rebellion.

The man apparently decided Kendrick wasn't an imminent threat and returned to the task at hand, leading the woman outside. His mother had been in the same situation once. He shuddered before dismissing the memory and wondered if the officers would pursue those who had dared break the peace on this sad little moon or just let it go. Who would hold the Morphos accountable?

His palms ached, and Kendrick realized he was clenching his fists. Slowly, he flexed his fingers and looked up to meet Bea's gaze.

Despite the time and distance, he believed she remained a kindred soul. So few had any intensity left in them, and she had it all shining out of her eyes as loud as the winter sun on this dry, cool planet.

She shoved the pie in front of him, the steam and smell grounding him immediately. He inhaled the fragrance deeply, feeling home in his bones, yet never breaking eye contact with Bea.

"Ten minutes," she mouthed before returning to her work.

Ravenous, he shoveled the goodness in his mouth, seeking to fill a place that might overcome him with emptiness one day. And as the sweet taste of the sitchy berries soothed him, he felt hope swell. Perhaps she'd become more receptive to him by seeing he cared for people. He prayed she did too.

After inhaling a third of the pie, he swiped at his mouth with a scratchy paper napkin. At least his hunger was sated. A hard tap on his shoulder almost made him jump. That was the second time he'd been caught in a moment here. Turning intentionally, he found himself face-to-face with Beatrix.

"Now," she said. "Come."

At least she was direct.

CHAPTER THREE

Rising, he obediently followed her, stepping through the swinging door behind the counter and another swinging door to the storage area. But she didn't stop there. She turned the back door handle, pushing her sunglasses on to protect her eyes, so he mimicked her.

Once they were through those doors, he saw an unending dry, dusty horizon. There was nothing this way. The back of the restaurant opened to flat, cold desert—the rest of the sparse town behind him. The sky was gray. Was it always gray here? He missed the sun that shone like hope back home.

She rounded on him.

"Why have you pursued me here?" she demanded, poking one aggressive finger into his chest.

He caught her hand in defense, and she jerked reflexively at his touch. But he wasn't letting go. Plus, she had assaulted him first.

So he took her hand into both of his, clasped but in a more treasuring manner—but a grasp he wouldn't be quick to release. The tension of Beatrix's body befitted that of a warrior, and he did not doubt that if he could see her eyes, they'd hold the same power. It was so attractive to see a woman with these capabilities. But he sensed she was on the verge of rearing back to plant one in his face.

"Because the rebellion needs you," he said before she could deliver on the promise in her stance.

She scoffed, her face inscrutable.

"For what?"

"We have new information. Knife skills like you have had since childhood are essential to our victory."

"What, you want me to stab the Morphos in their eyes?" Though the sunglasses that protected her from any rogue Morphos veiled it, he was sure she was rolling her eyes at him for the second time this morning.

"Their eyes actually aren't—" he started.

"Listen, I left Rutheni to escape this crazy fight. I am happy just to survive." But there was a waver in her voice that belied the words.

"You're happy here?" Anger pierced him, and he let it raise his voice. It was so selfish. Appalled, he almost released her hands, but then he clenched them tighter.

Her whole body squirmed in response.

"Of course not," she spat. "But I'm alive, aren't I?"

All he could do was shake his head in disbelief.

"Is that all you came for?" she asked.

The power scales had tipped, as he was no longer certain of his pursuit, his purpose with her.

A sneer spread across her face as she cocked one hip and placed her free hand on it.

Uncontrollably, his body naturally responded to her feminine pose.

"I had thought, with our betrothal and how both our parents had fought side-by-side, that bringing you back into the fold could provide important skills to the rebellion. And also that I might find the partner I've been lacking."

He hated the hopefulness in his voice because he knew this hard woman was not the same as the young girl he remembered.

Snorting, she asked, "You got a tattoo?"

What the fuck? Taken aback by the topic change after he'd just bared his heart, he said, "No. I haven't had time to think about body illustration." He frowned. What did that matter?

"Too bad—I don't sleep with men who don't have tattoos." She shrugged, her tone careless.

"*That's* not what I'm here for!"

"No, but I'm not here to partner with anyone and certainly not to join this futile rebellion. A little roll in the hay could have been fun, golden boy, but it seems that it's not meant to be. So why don't you let go of me and get lost, huh?"

He looked down at his own hands that clenched her calloused one. Her strong fingers revealed all the wear of the work she did, all the abuse she put on them, for such an utterly unfulfilling role. He didn't get her. Not at all.

She yanked her hand out of his, patted his face hard in an admonishing manner, and slipped back through the door, letting it slam behind her.

And as it did, the hope he always carried so strong in his heart flickered just a bit.

CHAPTER FOUR

Thud. Thud. Thud.

With each knife that sunk into the tree, Bea felt immense satisfaction. She knew it was an odd hobby, but she had her rebellion parents to blame for that. When you grew up trained for war, the physical repetition of drills was still a stress-buster, even if you no longer fought.

The dawn chill was seeping into her back porch through the black tarp that enclosed it, and she felt it all the more for the slight sweat coating her skin from exertion.

She loved this little private place—the way a tree grew into one of her walls, which allowed her to have target practice and a sense of nature in a space where she felt like she was outside but could safely take off her sunglasses. Not to mention it was one of the few trees in this part of Odessa.

Rubbing her hands on her biceps to warm them, she looked down at her black night slip. She might have chuckled if laughter hadn't become so foreign lately. When sleep had eluded her, she'd instinctually headed for the kitchen, where the knives were lined up on her counter. Her body had mindlessly swept them up and guided her out here. But now she was cold and needed some coffee.

The knives had impaled the tree in a perfect pattern. She walked closer and pressed her left palm to the tree, pulling hard with her right to yank the first one out. It was all Kendrick's fault. He who spoke of hope and, worse, looked like it.

If she were to paint the perfect portrait of hope, it would be him. But his amber eyes, golden hair, and light-colored clothing only put a target on his own back. He didn't belong here. And she had been trying to suppress her own hope since she arrived on Odessa—contain it to her expression in her paintings—but he was making it damn hard to ignore.

She didn't belong at his side, no matter what her parents had thought. No matter what her silly little girl dreams had yearned for. No matter if she'd felt like her soul had flamed in connection to him from the moment his light had come burning into her diner, so bright that she'd averted her eyes, hoping he wouldn't see her, hoping she could deny that feeling to herself.

But of course, he had seen her. And now here she was, trying to literally cut that feeling of connection out of her. Tugging, she got the second knife out.

She hadn't told Uncle Tommy that Kendrick had been to the diner. She didn't want anything to upset him in his state.

A rustle sounded behind her, and terror filled her. She didn't have eye protection out here. Her knives stood no chance if any connection was made, so body tense and ready to flee for the kitchen door—though she was unlikely to make it—she kept her back to the sound and called, "Who goes there?"

"Bea, sorry. I didn't mean to creep up on you."

The relief that rolled through her body at the warm tone was quickly followed by intense irritation. Yanking the last knife from the tree, she spun on her heel and paced toward the shadowy figure slipping onto her porch and lowering his shades. The golden glint in his eye halted her. It was like a sunbeam warming her when she was determined to stay cold.

"Yet creep you did," she said blandly, trying to convince herself she wasn't pleased to see him.

Kendrick moved lithely around the patio furniture, making his way closer, and she pivoted, keeping him in front of her. But he stopped before coming within reach. Perhaps it was the knives she was still wielding.

"Frankly, I just had to come because I was observing your friend Jett at the tax, tariff, and entry station, and I wasn't even thinking what time it was—"

"I'm sorry, what? How the hell do you even know who Jett is, and why are you creeping on my friend?"

"Well, after your kind send-off..."

She refrained from smirking at how she'd delivered what was essentially a light slap to his handsome face. Though truthfully, it was more of a reproach to herself because she'd wanted to touch him more.

"I felt I needed to understand you better. So maybe if I found the people you cared about—by the way, there are so few, it seems—"

"Oh, thanks for that. So you thought if you bugged my people *or* came up on me in my nightdress when it was still dark before dawn, one of those angles might be better?"

His eyes dropped to rove her body, and she instantly regretted mentioning her night slip. The top was primarily sheer and then fell to a short, black silk skirt. Her breath caught, and she felt her nipples harden as his gaze paused on them without humility. She was not going to give him the upper hand by hiding herself, so she stood proud, refusing to back down.

"As much as I like this angle, very much," he said, his voice husky, his eyes probing for some reaction from her own, "I very much did not like the former."

Her mind was a bit scattered, and she wasn't following. Kendrick must have seen the confusion on her face.

"Your friend Jett? She was basically flirting with the Morphos. And she appeared to be exchanging currency that looked more like bribes than legal transactions. If I'm being honest, it looked like some shady shit. No one seems to be watching what's going on there very closely."

"Well, thank heavens you are," she said caustically.

"This isn't a joke, Bea. This is dangerous."

"Jett is a flirt." But even as she defended her friend, she could picture it happening, and the idea repulsed her. "I can't fathom that she is doing anything other than taking a little off the top because we all lead shitty existences and are barely surviving. I can't fault her for that, especially if it's coming off those monsters."

"You don't flirt with the enemy! Jeez, Beatrix, I thought you would get it—they are killing people and taking everything from everyone!"

He was hollering, and she would not stand being shouted at. She did *not* like it when men used their size, strength, and volume for intimidation—on any matter.

Her knife whipped through the air and pinned the hood of his new, darker-colored cloak to the tree. He clearly hadn't been able to find one in his regular palette after giving his to the woman in the diner. Bea was happy to take responsibility for the hole slit into this new one.

But she was surprised at his quiet. He made no sound, and his body moved slowly as he turned to inspect his entrapment. And then he turned back to her with a look of awe and shame. He knew he had pressed her too far.

When he spoke again, she had to lean closer to hear him.

"Don't you see how bad we need you? You're too good," he said urgently.

She had so many mixed emotions right now—rage swirling with lust and tinged with regret. Truly, she hadn't been with a good man, especially one who was also strong, in a long time. Generally, she searched out the wimpy bad boys she could manipulate. They were no threat to her.

Kendrick was a threat. He represented what she used to be, what she wanted. No, correction—what she *used* to want. But it still made her heart clench and her body feel edgy. She dropped one knife to the table but kept the other.

"I don't need your stupid rebellion," she said. But she was enjoying the power of having her childhood first love—probably the only love she'd ever had—stuck to her tree, pleading with her.

With the knife clenched in one hand, she strode closer to him, so close that her nipples grazed his firm chest. She looked up at him, liking that he might be taller, but she was still the one in control.

But was she?

She stared at his soft lips, strong chin, and angular nose and then up into those eyes. "And I don't need you."

They stood there, and his warm breath caressed her face. He breathed deeply, holding himself rigid, but she would not fold.

"Don't fuck with me." Her voice wavered, so she took a deep breath. "And stop fucking with my life," she said firmly.

An annoying, cocky grin split his face, under his very straight nose, too perfect for a man who'd been fighting in a freaking rebellion. What the hell did he use, a shield?

"You look like you want to fuck me," he whispered. "You even feel like you want to," he added, glancing down to where her nipples were tracing lines up and down his chest with her exhalations.

Needing a little space to keep from jumping him right there, she took a step back.

"I told you, I don't fuck men without tattoos," she said, casting her eyes to the risers above her, trying to gather her composure and rebalance.

"Yeah, I thought you said that the other day. What kind of fucked up shit is that?"

It was like he had a dagger of his own he'd stabbed her with.

"Who are you to judge me and my choices? You don't know what I've been through."

Glaring at him, she feared she had revealed too much. His expression was stunned, as if it had never occurred to him that she might have been through anything more than what he already knew and could see.

Before he could dig into what she'd said, she pressed the tip of her knife to his jugular notch. He kept his face lifted, not trying to restrain her in any way. His Adam's apple bobbed up and down once.

Unable to help herself, she hissed at him, "Is there anyone left from home, anyone at all, who would miss you if I took you out right now? What does it all matter?"

"Actually, there is," he said. "If you would—" He gestured with one hand that she should lower her weapon.

When she did, he continued, "There are a lot of people fighting for the cause—who believe lives, souls, matter."

She reached over his shoulder, freeing the knife that pinned his hood to the tree without looking at him. Backing slowly to the table, she gathered her third knife from where she'd left it. Then she shook her head and turned for her kitchen door.

"I think you do too," he said, his voice brimming with this belief in her. She wanted it to be misplaced—it'd be so much easier than caring. That's what she had been trying for and failing—apathy.

Diner confrontations she could do all day. But this was too much for Bea. She didn't like questioning herself and the path she had chosen. And this man, in particular, made her far too uncomfortable.

Pulling the sliding glass door open, she tossed over her shoulder, "At our last meeting, I slapped your face. At this one, I held a knife to your throat. I recommend you do not pursue a third."

And then, once again, she slammed a door, leaving him in the cold. She prayed he'd take the hint and not realize that she, on the other hand, was burning for him.

CHAPTER FIVE

It was good to have a distraction from thinking about Bea. It'd been two days since he'd found her, and she was nothing like he'd remembered. She was gorgeous and skilled more than he'd ever dreamed, but she was also stubborn and, sadly, bitter. None of his tactics were working, so it was time to refocus on the other mission that had brought him to this forlorn moon.

He had to find old man Andres, whose work had been crucial to the rebellion for the past twelve years, passing hidden messages for the rebels in plain sight. Kendrick had only heard of these infamous paintings, so he was excited to see them for himself. Unfortunately, the time for the paintings was coming to an end.

Pushing through the thin metal door of the bar, he paused once inside to remove his sunglasses and let his eyes adjust to the darkness. It was super early morning and dark, just a few hours past midnight, but the place was far from empty. Eye See You Girl was a place for women who loved women.

He was immediately aware that he was one of the few men in the space, as many more heads turned to inspect him than had at the French Toast & Roast diner next door, and he'd already stood out like a sore thumb there with his light-colored clothing.

Probably he should buy some stuff to blend in better, but who had time for that? He had hoped this was going to be a short mission. And the color of his clothes wouldn't have helped him to stand out less here anyhow. He was acutely aware of his manhood, and not in a proud way, as eyes squinted in his direction, evaluating his threat level.

Ignoring the calculating looks upon him, he searched the room. As dark as it was, he could still make out tacky, jewel-toned leather seats on swiveling silver stools, which were posted around the oblong central bar. Along the walls were many nooks, booths covered in the same worn-out leather as the bar stools, with heavy drapes that could be pulled for privacy or to stem the draft. Above each table were astounding paintings of haunted eyes that reflected images out of their depths of trees, oceans, butterflies, hands holding one another, crossing swords, and so much more.

Kendrick yearned to study the encrypted messages hidden in the depths of the artwork, but he didn't want to draw attention to them and reveal their secret purpose. Furthermore, he needed to find the old man, but not a single head sported gray hair.

It was the purple hair that caught his attention. And her bright blue eyes that shocked Kendrick into stillness.

Damn that woman. Quickly, he evaluated her company—it was the tricky Jett. This would be interesting. Unable to evade Bea's magnetic pull on him, he gravitated toward her like a planet in the unrelenting hold of a star.

"Ah, so you're a lesbian," he said, wriggling his eyebrows to imply teasingly that this was why she wouldn't have him.

"I never knew you were," she said innocently, eyes wide and eyebrows arched. Her elbows were planted on the table, and she gestured around the room with her large, strong hands.

Chuckling, he said, "Well, I do love women. However, I take your point. I'm not sure I belong here."

"This is a safe space for women, and we welcome all who pose no problems." She gave him a smirk, her implication that he posed quite a few abundantly clear.

Jett jumped in. "Yeah, I'm not sure why you're here." She sucked from her straw while glowering at him.

"Kendrick, have you had the pleasure of meeting my friend Jett?"

"I haven't—any friend of Bea's is a friend of mine." He extended his hand to shake hers.

Archly, she said, "Bea?" and looked at her friend.

Beatrix shrugged. "Flash from my past."

At that, Jett cackled. "Oh? Where's his tattoo on there?" She flipped Bea's tattooed forearm around.

Kendrick dropped his hand. "What does that mean?"

Color flooded Bea's pale features.

"Not like that!" She snatched her arm back from Jett and crossed hers in front of herself defensively. "From my *childhood*."

"Oh." Jett looked him up and down more slowly. "Clearly, you're new here. What's your business?" She paused only a second. "Wait, I think I may have glimpsed you at my station."

"Yeah, well, we all have to pass through there at some point or another when we arrive to Odessa, right?" he replied, evading the primary question but noting that she had called it "my."

And then, the dark bar exploded in blinding color for a second before everything went black.

KENDRICK'S EARS rang and yet felt fuzzy, muted. He opened his eyes, orienting himself, and realized he was lying flat on his back.

An explosion. He'd been speaking with Jett and Bea when the bar exploded.

Beatrix.

Hopping to his feet, hand palming his sword, he searched the room. She was knocked out cold on the shambles of the booth she'd been sitting in.

As his ears cleared, yelling became more pronounced. He turned to look at the front entrance. Morphos were swarming the space, confronting the clientele but also wearing their sunglasses, so their mission was apparently not souls at the moment.

No sign of the Intergalactic Peace Force, damn it.

He moved toward Bea. Jett was sitting up, touching a gash on her head and looking at the blood on her fingers.

"You all right?" he asked while he felt the pulse at Bea's throat.

"I'm fine," she snapped at him. Looking down at her friend, she asked, "Her?"

Bea's heart rate was strong under his fingertips. "She's alive," he replied.

"Good. They're setting fire—get her out of here. I've got to run." And Jett sprang to her feet, slid along the dark wall, and slipped out the front door.

Some friend.

But it was the right move. The Morphos were torching everything —they must have heard that this place was used to house secret codes. It was best he and Bea blow the joint too—and at least the old man who created the paintings didn't seem to be in the vicinity. Kendrick would have to find him later, after he got this stubborn woman who was born to be a fighter into a condition to actually do so.

CHAPTER SIX

Once out on the street, it was oddly quiet in comparison, other than the raging fire that was now taking over French Toast & Roast as well. Kendrick headed toward his rental street glider. The gliders were the most common mode of transport on Odessa and hovered over streets much like a car but wouldn't aid them in escaping into space, as they couldn't gain much altitude.

He laid Beatrix gently in the passenger seat before sliding into the driver's seat and engaging the tint for the windows. They needed to get away in case Morphos were pursuing the bar's clientele into the streets.

As his engine roared to life, Bea jolted, sitting upright.

"Whoa, take it slow," he said. "You don't want to pass out again."

The daggers in her eyes were enough to silence him as he watched her take in the damage. And then, she crumpled, head in hands, curling into a ball, moaning, "Nooo, nooo, nooo, this can't be happening."

"I'm so sorry. I know it must be devastating. But we gotta get away from here—"

She managed a quick nod of assent as her whole body convulsed, ejecting sounds that jumped between whimpers and outright sobs. It wrenched at Kendrick's heart. This woman had played so tough with him, but the barriers she'd erected between them had been destroyed.

She wouldn't like that he had seen this raw devastation in her. If only she understood that with his empathy, she could not hurt him worse than by showing her vulnerability.

Once he pulled onto a quiet neighborhood street, a random one with a rare few sparse old-growth trees and apartments to help provide more cover in a generally barren place, he killed the engine and turned to her.

Hiccuping, she looked at him, eyes watery, the red in her eyes turning the irises almost teal. She spoke more clearly. "It's just it's my way—" Another hiccup interrupted her.

"Your way of life, your income and stability, I get it," he said, then started to pat her back as her crying took on a more hysterical quality at his words. "Shhh—"

"God, you're dense," she said, shaking her head, swiping madly at her tears and laughing.

Offended, he pulled his hand back into his lap and looked at her.

She composed herself before turning to face him. "No, it was *my way* of fighting."

What did she mean? His brain was jumping through everything she'd said to him and the moments they'd been together, but all the puzzle pieces wouldn't fit together.

"Okay, I'm dense. Break it down for me."

"You're a rebel, and surely you knew that was a place of some import for your movement."

He looked at her. He'd wanted her to fight on his side, and trusting her now was imperative. Plus, she seemed to know already. He nodded.

She took a deep breath. "They're mine."

Frowning at her, he said, "What are?"

Bea rolled her eyes and shouted, "The paintings!"

"The eyes? The secret messages we've been passing—have been through you? You are old man Andres?"

"Seemed a safer identity," she muttered.

Shocked, it took a moment for his mind to process what she'd said. He grabbed her hands, squeezing them, hope swelling in his heart.

"You mean you've been working for our side all along?"

"Don't get your knickers in a twist. Yes." She sighed. "But I'm still not fighting with my knives. I—I can't do it, Kendrick. It's not in me anymore, no matter how good I am. Something happened, and I can't face combat. I'm sorry."

Looking at her, he wanted to know it all, take all the pain away, and soothe her. But she had to learn how at risk now she was of the very thing that she feared.

"I was here—besides looking for you—to warn Andres that the supply chain on the paints had been corrupted, that there was an informant who knew something of what was happening here to help the rebellion, that the paintings were involved and the Morphos would seek him out and destroy him."

Unable to help himself, he raised the back of his hand to the side of her face and gently ran it down her soft skin. "I don't think they'll stop at burning the place down, Bea. They will hunt you."

She bit her lip and, like a kitten, rubbed her face against his hand as though trying to erase the thought. It was all he could do not to groan. For once, she received his touch and was not the aggressor.

Looking down, trying to distract himself from the growing arousal and tightness in his loins, he took in the tattoos winding up her arm. And there, he saw the Morphos butterfly.

Dropping his hand to trace the outline, he raised his eyes to meet hers. "These butterflies—do you know about them?"

Wrinkling her forehead in perplexity, she shook her head. "Know what? They...each of my tattoos are replicas of those worn by men I slept with. This one, well, he was part of the rebellion, and that was part of why I left him."

So many questions.

"Why are you tattooing yourself with art that is significant to other people rather than yourself?"

She stared out the window for a moment before turning to meet

203

his gaze. He saw a mixture of shame and righteousness in her expression.

"I always took pictures of my lovers' tattoos. When they inevitably disappointed me, I'd have one of theirs put on my left forearm and send a pic of it to them to break up with them, saying it was to remember them."

Silence fell between them. He wasn't sure how to respond to that.

She popped the knuckles of one hand. The movement seemed like habit rather than her intentionally avoiding him. Finally, she said, "But truthfully it was to hurt them back. I liked that tattooed people were so blatant with what they cared about, partially because it made it easier to wound them in return. I stole the symbols of what they loved, and there was no way for them to take it back from me."

"Wow. So none of your tattoos represent what you care about?"

A snort. "I wouldn't be so dumb as to declare how someone can hurt me for everyone to see."

It was becoming more apparent to him that Bea had suffered trauma, likely more than her parents' deaths. But he knew better than to pry right now. She was raw and still sharing, but he didn't think she'd take it kindly if he were to dig into what motivated her to act so cruelly. It was clearly a protection mechanism.

"So the rebel, the one that the butterfly came from—his name, please," he asked softly.

Her face turned pink at the personal question, but she replied boldly nonetheless. "Justin."

Releasing a deep breath of sadness tinged with a little jealousy that his former friend and comrade had been with her, Kendrick replied, "Yes, he's dead now. I'm sorry. But he had learned the key to our success—to defeating the Morphos."

Her eyes showed the first real glimmer of hope he'd seen on her face, and while his spirits were lifted to see that she wasn't holding back, he knew explaining all this to her would be heavy.

"Justin was on the mission where we discovered their weakness. Bullets don't work—they are too small. Complete decapitation by sword can do the job, but takes great strength. Knives thrown just so, vertically penetrating the jugular notch, releases all the souls they've consumed. Sadly, they don't return to their initial owner, but it kills the Morphos since that was what sustained them, and the souls are no longer trapped in such an evil container. The souls exit—as beautiful morpho butterflies. That's the form the soul takes after consumption by a Morphos. Thus the name. Have you ever seen one?"

"A butterfly? Not that I recall," she said, slowly shaking her head, the information clearly still sinking in.

"Well, I actually meant the specific kind, the morpho. They're quite large and the color of your eyes. Stunning." His voice trembled a little in memory of the times he'd seen them.

Her eyes were on him now, reflecting her beautiful soul. He didn't want to reiterate right at the moment why her skills were so essential. Hopefully, it was apparent.

His stomach fluttered with the belief that her soul was reaching out to him, yearning to tap the hope he always carried with him that this terrible war could be won. He prayed she would actually touch him, and while he feared pushing her too much, he couldn't help telling her what he saw in her despite the rigid outer shell she adorned like a chrysalis.

"Stunning like you," he said softly, leaning toward her, not touching but showing his utter desire to lose himself with her and forget this terrible dark start to the day.

She seemed to wish for the same as those devastating eyes flickered shut behind her dark curtain of lashes. She inched toward him, then he heard her breath catch.

Frozen, eyes still firmly closed, she whispered, "You, tattooless man, saved me. I can't give you my all, as you're still a risk to me. But I desire you, now as a woman, though I wanted you even as a girl." Then she leaned forward as if guided by a heat-seeking device and pressed her lips to his.

It was all he could do not to grab her and pull her into his arms. But he knew this had to be slow. And that he dare not ask questions like why she considered him a risk. So he brushed them aside and, this time, framed her face with two hands like she was the sweetest treasure he would ever be lucky enough to sample.

But then that sharp tongue came out again, this time not to wound. Beatrix invaded his mouth aggressively. She moved, coming at him like the warrior he knew she was at heart, ready to take control and assault. And how he was prepared to receive her. Settling herself in a straddle across his lap, she ground against him, slowly asserting her demand.

The swelling pain took over him, and he couldn't help but buck under her, to press his length to the hot center he could feel driving this rhythm. Groaning, he accepted all she wanted to take and let her have the reins, showing that he wanted her and was willing to do it however she pleased.

That purple hair swung forward to tickle his shoulder as she pressed hot kisses to his ear and down his neck. Her touch made him utterly weak.

He was confident that his stubble was scraping her face, but when she rubbed her cheek against his jaw like a kitten again, he guessed she liked it. He wanted her to enjoy it all. However he could please her, he would.

Pivoting to turn her back on him, she leaned down and pulled the lever under the seat to push it all the way back. He hadn't realized how flat it could go.

Then, she stood as much as she could in the space, unbuttoned her dark jeans, and shimmied them and her scrap of panties down along the curve of her ass. When she leaned forward to hang her hands on the bottom of the wheel and raise her beautiful core to his face, he understood that this was the only way she would let him have her.

And it was everything. Bea's taste was sweet lava, a volcano on the verge, and he gave her all the love she could want there. The world was literally going up in flames around them, but this flickering flame symbolized the center of his hope that together they would find completion and live to fight another day.

When she howled her release, body jerking in her openness to allow him to take her there, he prayed that this was the step, and this physical representation was the sign that she would open the rest to him.

And when she lowered back down into his lap, after swiftly slipping her clothes back into place, she curled up against him, laid her head on his chest, and nuzzled in. He felt the trust, the warmth, the friendliness. This was what she was hiding under that hard exterior.

Her breath slowed until he was sure she was asleep. Despite all that had gone wrong, all she had lost in the past few hours, he hoped that her momentary contentment meant that he could help her find the way to it in the long term. Fulfilling at last their parents' betrothal wishes for them. Heck, maybe he'd even get a tattoo for her.

CHAPTER SEVEN

Her fingers clenched and dug into his chest, the first sign
Beatrix had awakened. Only hours had passed since they'd
made their escape, from the fire, from the chains holding them back
from one another, and the morning dark was just subsiding to reveal
the light of early dawn. Kendrick hadn't slept a wink but had felt
fulfilled, considering everything had blown up around them, and that
he should have been planning their next steps.

But this quiet moment with his first love in his arms, the only girl
he'd ever really considered, had felt like a respite for his brain to
pause, for his heart to feel, to regather himself before the inevitable
fight he knew they had ahead.

"Shhh . . ." he breathed into her hair. "You're safe here." His hand
caressed the top of her head, wishing he could induce her to purr like
a kitten, but knowing he would be lucky if he just avoided being
scratched.

She sat up and pulled out of his arms. He relinquished his hold on
her with regret as her spine stiffened with awareness.

"My uncle . . ." she whispered. "He owns both those joints. He's not
there due to health issues, but you don't think—"

"Tommy," he said, remembering him as a tattooed, generally warm yet gruff man. But he was also the person who had taken Bea away from him. "We should check on him. They may think he is the fabled Andres."

"Nooo," she breathed, and he knew she was blaming herself.

As she directed him to her uncle's abode, Kendrick tried to be inconspicuous while making the best possible time.

He stopped the street glider in front of the minimalist home. It looked like it was built as an afterthought, like many of the dwellings on Odessa did. His breath caught when he saw the door had been busted in. Not a good sign.

Their eyes met, hers dim with fear. Tommy was important to her, and he knew she probably did not want to see what was inside.

As she started to open the door and slide out, he halted her with a firm hand on her shoulder.

"No. Let me. Please stay here," Kendrick insisted.

She squinted at him, and he could nearly see her mind working. She had to know that whatever was inside might not be pretty and possibly more than she could take after all she'd already lost.

Bea consented with a nod.

It took him less than ten minutes to gauge the situation and return to the car. She had lost so much already, and he was asking her to fight, but surely she would understand now why this mission was so important. Why they needed her.

"I'm sorry, Bea. He's been vacated. Nothing left."

"They took his soul?" she shrieked in a fury.

Nodding, he reached for her, but she jerked away from him, pressing against the door.

"They probably felt that was the only way to stop him if he was Andres. And sadly, as you know, every soul is a win for them, even if they're taking a risk breaking these rules on Odessa."

She pressed her fingers to the inner corners of her eyes, likely trying to keep more tears from falling. Trying to pack all the wrought emotions back into their container, trying to mute them.

"Bea . . . I think that by consuming his soul, they'll know it was you. Not to mention, I saw that paintings of yours cover his walls. Same style. They will hunt you now."

Nothing. She didn't move, didn't make a sound, didn't look at him.

"You have to fight. It's time. What will life be like when there are no more souls to take?"

At that, she raised wet eyes to meet his, but looked resolute.

"My uncle got me off Rutheni so I wouldn't have to fight. To protect me. That is what he wished for me."

"You have to let that go! Your parents died to stop the Morphos from taking souls, and so did mine," he argued.

"How did yours go?" she asked, resigned and without surprise.

"Rutheni is gone. The Morphos essentially imploded it when they failed at flattening the rebellion and figured they should take out the home base. We knew the missiles were coming and evac'd, but my father was literally tossing the last people onto the airship as it departed, and he didn't make it. My ma, well, she got soul-sucked on a separate mission. She didn't lose it all. They got her out, but there were always pieces of her missing after—she wasn't fully present in her heart and soul anymore. When our airships were later invaded, we all had to fight to survive, and she just didn't have enough fight left in her anymore."

Looking down and shaking his head, he pressed his fists into his thighs to suppress his anger, his sorrow. He hoped she'd comfort him as he had her, as he'd tried to again a moment ago, but she remained sitting erect beside him like she was steeling her spine against all the pain and suffering.

She had to understand.

Imploring her, he put his hand on her leg and squeezed. "On the mission where they took some of my mom, that's when we discovered their weakness at the jugular notch. And did you know a video was captured on your parents' devices after their bodies were recovered? There is a black hole surging and swirling with the Morphos butterflies."

He swallowed, trying not to plead but desperate for her to understand the importance of the discoveries. How vital her parents' sacrifice had been.

"We believe if you were to enter it, you would be suctioned back to the Morphos world. And they are delivering much of the soul light they are capturing into this hole to be swallowed and funneled back to their world to lighten it and to give their nonfighting population hope in their hopeless world."

Wearing no emotion, she asked, "So what's the plan to defeat them?"

"Well, besides taking out their fighters individually with skills like yours, we need to find a way to reverse the direction of the black hole, make it so that it doesn't suction all the hope into their world, but instead release all the hope and light back into our universe. It sounds crazy, but we are thinking if we can create a massive net, like a butterfly net, and ensnare it, and then use the strength of a fleet of our mightiest airships, pivot it ninety degrees, that maybe it could reverse the effect. Worth a shot at least, right? But finding the materials to make a net that large, strong enough to contain it without being sucked in itself, and getting enough allies willing to use their airships for the mission, is proving difficult."

A skeptical snort issued from her.

Desperation overcame Kendrick. After she'd opened herself to him, shown where she could be soft, exposed her hope, he knew that what he'd always envisioned was meant to be.

"You and I are twin flames! Don't you feel it? We're meant to fight side by side, to complete this mission for our parents once and for all. That's why they betrothed us. That's why they trained us together from childhood."

He might have squeezed her muscular thigh too hard, but it was better than trying to shake the sense into her. He couldn't figure out how to break through.

"Are you fucking kidding me?" she said scornfully. "I can't believe you just said twin flames. I have no flames of hope in my heart. And here is why. I was assaulted horribly by a man, a man with no tattoos. He seemed kind enough and harmless, but he hid what he wanted, what was important to him. And he had no problem taking what he wanted, which was me barely crossing from childhood to womanhood."

She took a deep breath in and out, but he dared not move or draw her attention while she had a blank-eyed stare and explained what had happened.

"He was one of the trainers on Rutheni."

Kendrick couldn't help but lean toward her as rage fired through him. "Who?"

"Ian!" she spat. "And maybe while my parents were alive, he was too scared to do anything, but right after they died, he cornered me when I was all alone. The only reason he was unsuccessful in his horrid attempt was because my tattooed, pacifist hero, Uncle Tommy, came upon us, whupped his ass, and decided it was time for us to pursue a different kind of life. A peaceful life in a place of neutrality. There may not be much hope here, but we don't take sides, and we don't have to risk our lives."

Kendrick couldn't help but push.

"But the paintings?"

"Were a dumb idea! I wanted to give back without fighting. But look where it got me? Now my uncle is dead, and I'm on the run, and what for? I forfeited our sanctuary."

Now she was twiddling her thumbs anxiously and tapping her foot, and he sensed that her body was tensed for action.

"Can we just go? I'm getting nervous sitting here," she said.

Still in shock from the story she'd shared, he realized she was right. This was the most unsafe place they could be. He started the engine and drove, racking his brain for where he could take her, where they'd be safe until he got her in a solid mental state to be able to fight.

As he took a corner pretty fast, her door opened, and Bea rolled out of the vehicle, hightailing it down a narrow pedestrian alley. He slammed on the brakes, threw the glider in park, and hopped out to pursue her, but when he reached the alley, it was empty.

He had no idea where she would have gone, and she had the advantage of knowing Odessa intimately while he'd been here for only days. She'd successfully given him the slip. Once again, a decade-plus later.

CHAPTER EIGHT

"Jett? Jett, where'd you go?" Bea tried to suppress the panic in her voice as she spoke through her wristwatch device while everything in her mind was swirling. Her sight was blurring, and all she could do was follow her feet, which seemed to know where they were going.

"Bea! I'm so glad you're okay. Kendrick said he'd take care of you, so I ran for safety—but I've been second-guessing making that call over and over."

"Oh, of course, he did take care of me. I mean, he saved me." Bea swallowed, thinking just how well he'd taken care of her. But he still didn't get her. He still wanted her to be a fighter when all she wanted to do was crawl into a hole and not come out for years.

She'd wanted him since his glow had reentered her life, and she'd fought against it. Then, in a moment of weakness, she'd kept her boundaries and only let him orally please her, but she feared she'd still let him into her heart.

And then after he'd saved her, to find that her original savior—her Uncle Tommy—had been killed and the Morphos were likely hunting her was too much. She just wanted to go back into hiding and avoid the looming fight.

Terror consumed her, and Jett was the only friend she'd had the past few years, who was still alive and who would understand why she didn't want to engage.

"Where are you now?" Jett asked. "Can I come get you?"

"I'm headed toward your apartment." But normal work hours were commencing, and she was more likely to be spotted with the growing traffic on the streets. She had to make haste.

A large exhale came through the line. "Good—how soon will you be here?"

"Like five minutes, I think," she answered, wanting to get there as urgently as it sounded like Jett wanted her to arrive.

"Okay. I'll watch the exterior camera and buzz the door as soon as I see you. Just come straight up."

"Okay, yes." A hiccup escaped as Bea tried to smother the tears attempting to erupt again.

"Where's Kendrick?" Jett asked in an urgent tone.

"Oh, I lost him a while back." She was surprised Jett cared. Though he was so present in her own mind that she knew he'd come up eventually. "He wants me to fight in the rebellion, but I just can't!"

"Oh, babes. Of course not. That guy has a death wish clearly. I'm sorry I left you with him. I shouldn't have. A stranger doesn't know what's right for you."

Bea huffed a watery laugh. "Kendrick's not a stranger—I've known him longer than anybody"—she thought of her uncle, gone now—"still alive."

Jett didn't react to that statement. "Let's just keep you alive and away from this mess. Hurry up and get to me, girl. I'll keep you safe."

Safety. It was all she wanted. And Kendrick, while he'd saved her, wanted her to fight.

"I'm hustling—almost there. See you soon."

She clicked the device off, needing a few more moments to absorb everything that had happened. The bar, her paintings, her mission—gone. The diner, her place of work and income, and hiding—gone. Her uncle, the man who helped her find a safe place—gone.

She hadn't had much, and now she had nothing. Except for an

antiquated betrothal to a very hot man who put her on a pedestal, who thought they should live out their parents' lives—but that hadn't ended so well.

He didn't accept her trauma, her fears. But things burned hot between them regardless. The connection was undeniable.

At least, even though he had no tattoos, she was pretty confident about what he wanted and what was important to him. But she couldn't be that—even if a part of her wanted to be. Her little girl crush had evolved into a full-on womanly strong desire and appreciation. She loved the hope he wore like a shield around him—but she didn't trust it to save either of them.

As she approached the glass doors to the building, the click of the doors unlocking sounded. At least her friend seemed to have her front of mind and was eagerly awaiting her.

Maybe together, the two of them could find a route out of this, hide away and survive somewhere. If anyone might know a way out of here, Jett should. After all, she worked at the tax, tariff, and entry station. Which also meant exit.

Bea stepped into the elevator, then turned to push the button for Jett's floor. The doors were closing when she met Kendrick's lionlike brown eyes. He raced to catch the doors before they closed, but he wasn't fast enough.

He must have had more success catching the exterior doors before they shut. Bea was conflicted about whether she wished he'd been as successful in this case. Would he take the stairs? How'd he know she'd go here?

It was probably pretty predictable, which meant Kendrick wasn't the only one to whom it would have occurred. Oh God—might she have brought the Morphos to Jett's door? Would she cause the death of yet another person she loved?

She ran for her best friend's place. They would have to plan an exit quickly as Kendrick and the Morphos would be banging down the door soon enough.

Jett stood in the doorway with her sunglasses on, holding the door open. Did she already realize what they were facing? But Jett didn't know that Bea was responsible for the paintings or about her uncle.

Halting her sprint in front of the door, she told Jett, "Kendrick's here. Probably going to try to convince me to go back with him."

And with perfect timing, he exploded off the elevator and pounded to her side. "Don't look at her, Bea—she's one of them!"

What was he talking about? Who was one of what?

"That's absurd," Jett retorted, but her body was tense, unsure.

"Poor thing," he said, shaking his head, eyes veiled behind his own sunglasses. "They made you one of them, but haven't trained you to fight to survive. They're using you for your ability to trick your own friend. You will never get the happiness, the light back. If they had cared for you, they would have put you on their planet with their other non-warrior types who are bathing in and consuming our light."

The fact that he was talking to her friend, feeling pity for her, not just attacking, made Bea question whether he had learned something he hadn't shared. But why hadn't he? She had to remain calm and process. It was no time to be a victim. She wouldn't be anyone's victim ever again.

"Don't believe him, Bea. They haven't changed me. It's not true!"

Bea looked back and forth between them, her flight instincts over-whelming her. She didn't know who to trust, and her self-preservation was shouting the loudest.

As she hesitated, Jett shouted, "Let me take off my sunglasses and show you!"

Her friend whipped her glasses off, and with horror, Bea realized the bright, sardonic green eyes had been replaced with coal black ones. They were the worst she'd ever seen.

"I won't let you have any piece of her!" A sword sliced through the air, and her friend's head popped off like a doll's.

All Beatrix could do was stare in shock. Enormous blue butterflies erupted from Jett's neck, floating in the air, flying toward the windows and the stairwell, trying to escape.

The body toppled to the ground.

Bea felt like she was outside of herself, watching as this person who looked like her slowly crumpled to the floor. She wanted to curl into a ball and try to rock the horror away, but strong arms wrapped her into an embrace, bringing her back to the present. Those arms suddenly felt like they were restraining her from her desire to self-protect.

"No! No way! I will not go with you! You just *killed* my best friend, you lunatic!"

She was shouting, hitting, and even attempting to bite him. She did not want to seek comfort in his arms. He had taken the life of the last person she had on this godforsaken moon.

"Is that what you saw?" Kendrick asked. "Not proof that I was right? She was about to kill you—to take your soul. You saw it. She removed her sunglasses, her eyes had gone black, and she had every intention of doing the same to you."

When she stilled, he added, "I'm sorry, but I reached the rebel base on my device while searching for you. They confirmed that she had been turned and that the Morphos were going to use her to end your threat to them. You need to make some decisions, and I insist that you come with me. We can find a safe place to hide and plan to leave Odessa. There's nothing left for us here."

Was that fear in his voice? It sounded like he was choked up when he talked about Jett ending her. Regardless, what choice did she have?

"So it's the rebellion and you—or staying here with no protection on my own? Thanks, that's not really a choice," she said bitterly, wondering why tears were not yet erupting. She must have run dry, or the horror had frozen them.

"Let's start with finding hiding, and then we can talk options. We can't stop here. The Morphos are probably closing in on us even now." He handed her a knife, and she accepted it reluctantly. She still didn't want to fight proactively, but she would defend herself.

Behind Kendrick, a man flew through the hallway window, feet first and rolling. When he popped to his feet, crouched in a ready position, sunglasses still veiling his eyes, Bea reacted without thinking. She flung the knife with flawless aim right at the jugular notch.

The incision was the perfect size to release more gigantic butterflies before his body collapsed to the floor.

Frozen in a silent gasp, she covered her mouth with one hand. She couldn't believe she had done it.

"All right, you're ready," Kendrick stated matter-of-factly, striding forward to remove the knife from the man's neck and swiping it on his tan leather pants before handing it back to her.

"Come on, we gotta get out of here. Now!"

He grabbed her hand and tugged, and she followed him at a jog for the stairwell, knowing now was not a time for thinking or questioning. Her heart said that despite all she'd just seen, despite being unsure whether all her hope had been abolished, following Kendrick was the only option.

CHAPTER NINE

Having made her hands sore by mashing herbs, flowers, dirt, clay, and water, Bea finally had enough colors to start. Like a child, she painted the thistle tree trunk using only her fingers. She wasn't cold—thankfully, Kendrick had plenty of layers in the street glider—but she was dressed in the lightest colors she had worn since she was a child on Rutheni.

The feeling of home wasn't quite comforting, more a little eerie, but it was an escape from Odessa, as was this strange forest where they'd slept on the far side of the moon. The Morphos never came here because there were no inhabitants.

The ground was so hard it made building difficult, but these short trees seemed to have been made to root here despite the desert climate. While they didn't provide much cover, it was remote enough to feel safe for the time being. It was morning yet again, and they'd have to figure out their next step soon, before the desert sun rose too high and compromised their position.

She sought comfort in painting. After seeing all her hopes eviscerated when Eye See You Girl had gone up in flames, she hadn't known if she would be driven to paint again. But now she knew it was an essential part of her. When she couldn't cry and felt dead inside, this would be how she would emote.

Her fingers moved swiftly, stroking the bark, quickly shaping the form of many eyes, tears in every corner, a complete migration of butterflies swarming about them. It was all the tears she couldn't cry for all the souls that had been lost.

Strangely, though, losing Jett, her last bastion of her bitter, survival-oriented lifestyle, seemed to have purged her of relying on that crutch. There was no safety, only risk, and accepting that was oddly freeing. The hope in her heart built from a smolder into small flames the way the paint had flowed from her fingers.

She heard the slow, quiet crunch of the prickly leaves on Kendrick's approach behind her. Staying loose as she continued to release her feelings into the art, she acknowledged to herself that he was her protector now. She ached with all the space between them. Running from him had been unwise—and running to her former best friend even more so—but her fear had driven her beyond logic.

His voice slipped through the quiet. "I wish you could just be an artist."

Turning to meet his gentle eyes, she saw the longing there and found herself wishing that the longing was for more than that.

He reached one hand out, cautious, hopeful. Beatrix placed her colorfully stained one in his with a small smile.

"I'm sorry. It wasn't fair of me to push you. I see you now," Kendrick said. "I understand your fears, your boundaries, and your why. I want you to know we will do everything we can to protect you."

He shook his head and looked down. "I was blinded by the part I saw you playing in this rebellion, the part I saw you playing by my side." He raised his eyes to meet hers. "My vision is clear now."

Immense emotion swelled in her chest, and she struggled to define it. Was it just this growing hope she'd been feeling, or was it something crazier? Could it be something as risky as love? He looked at her like no other man ever had.

This wasn't the flutter she'd felt as a young girl when she had looked at him. He was no longer an adorable adolescent boy, but a robust and broad warrior—one who was finally able to take her off the pedestal.

But did he see her as weak now? It wasn't that she didn't want to be by his side—it was that she couldn't. Sure, she had killed that one Morphos in defense. She had the physical capability. But the trauma she still carried was only exacerbated by all that had happened in the past few days.

However, the light and hope in his eyes made her feel strange, affirming there were things worth fighting for again, even if not physically. This man had put everything on the line for her, and now he seemed to understand her too.

The dark cloud she'd always let sit on her was lifting, and she was ready to accept some rays from the sun. Perhaps they did have enough information to somehow win this war.

"Bea. Are you okay?" he asked after she had let the silence run far too long.

Swallowing, she nodded and gently pulled his hand to her lips to kiss his knuckles.

"I accept your apology, and I'm sorry I ran. I'm a coward. Thank you for saving me. I just don't know what to do with myself now," she muttered, embarrassed.

He drew her into his arms and squeezed her tightly.

"You are anything but a coward. You were still painting those paintings even when the only thing you wanted to do was escape it all. Your heart wanted to fight even when you were too afraid to take this big thing on yourself—which is completely understandable! You have suffered more than many I know. Many would have given in to the darkness, but instead, you mocked it. The tattoos"—his mouth tipped up a bit in the corner—"may be a bit much, but it's just part of your armor."

Smiling in return, she realized he saw her tough exterior but also recognized how soft she was on the inside. Yet he still seemed to honor her.

"When the rebel team arrives to get us out of here, let me take you to our secret hideout. It's an asteroid called Port Haven in the asteroid belt Eos. Eos was the goddess of the dawn, according to the ancient Greeks. I hope it can be a new start for you."

For you, he'd said. Not *us*.

"And you? Where will you go?" She hoped he'd be staying with her, as it wasn't only her paints that provided comfort.

His look was soft as he brushed her hair behind her ear. "Oh, well, I'll refuel and check in with the base. Be given my next mission. Off to fight another day."

Those words sank a stone in her gut. Kendrick saw her, he understood her, was probably even fond of her, but she wasn't what he wanted. Not really.

Bea had lost everything and everyone in this last assault by the Morphos, and yet through it all, Kendrick had remained a bright spot, a solace. It'd made her realize that living a life of fear and hiding wouldn't protect her, so she might as well fan the flames of hope and let them grow.

She was optimistic about joining a new group of people with a different vision for their universe and future. But as he was the one who had brought her to this path, she had thought they might find some way to partner in it—even if she couldn't—wouldn't—fight. Apparently, it still wasn't enough for him.

"I see," she said, pulling away to swipe her hands against her still-dark jeans under the tan poncho. But she didn't really see at all.

"Bea, I have to fight. It's what I was raised to do, trained to do. I can't give up. And I'm so glad you're not giving up. But I see now that you can't go fight alongside me. I look forward to seeing you find your new place in the rebellion."

She supposed it was as simple as that to him. And frankly, she didn't want to be the one to dim his light because that, she was coming to understand but would never say aloud, was what she loved about him.

So Bea put on her brave face and said, "All right, let's do this. Show me the dawn."

She didn't exactly look forward to what the new dawn might be without him, but maybe he just needed to see that she was done trying to stay in the dark.

CHAPTER TEN

A s Kendrick approached the small cement building, its walls and windows painted in winding, colorful murals, the déjà vu struck. He was confident Beatrix had a hand in brightening up the place, as it reflected the style of how the exterior of the Eye See You Girl pub had once looked, and pride inflated his heart.

He'd heard that she'd served as a true sensei in the art of knife-throwing, training the next gen of rebels and giving hope to them all that they would have the skills to take down the Morphos fighters.

And on the flip side, she'd also transferred her artistry into tattoos, making them a gesture of love instead of revenge. For the past few months, she'd been gifting all races of people coming to Port Haven with inspirational markings and memories that brought joy to each person.

Did she realize that the amount of hope and light she'd brought to this one little asteroid might shine and brighten the whole damn universe? Time and space had shown him two things—that he didn't have the spark anymore without her around to fuel his fire, and that she was not going to run away again, that she was committed to the new dawn.

Kendrick understood that she had new, additional wounds that needed to heal, but he hoped that she was willing to take the risk of loving him, and potentially losing him, now that she had hope again.

When he pulled the glass front door open, a brass bell chimed, announcing his arrival. It was quaint but made nerves shoot down to his toes. Luckily it was morning, shortly after dawn, and he might be the first customer.

A young front desk assistant with a septum piercing and the happiest of smiles beamed a welcome at him. The greeting felt like a lifetime from the frontlines, but he knew every person on this asteroid lived and breathed their rebellion.

"How may I help you, sir?"

The crumpled paper from his pocket needed straightening, so he stretched it across the glass display case of piercings, running his calloused and scarred hand across it to flatten it. Reluctant to release it, he slid it slowly toward the young man.

"I need this," Kendrick said, knowing his word choice revealed far too much. The man would immediately recognize his sketch, as shoddy a job as he had done. It was unmistakable, and it was the essence of her, no matter how she might have changed her appearance since her arrival on Eos.

The young man's eyebrows rose, but if possible, his grin spread wider, positively mirthful.

"Oh, she's gonna love this." He chortled. "Be right back!"

Kendrick was unsure whether he should feel insulted, embarrassed, or fearful, but he doubted that true enthusiasm was implied. Likely just amusement.

He felt like a young boy again and shuffled his feet as he waited. How could he take out the most lethal creatures in the universe and still fear how this woman would receive his token gesture of love?

But he knew how. Bea might be soft on the inside, but that tough exterior was nearly impossible to penetrate. Would she let him in?

At the back of the store, the teenage boy gently rapped on something that sounded more like a table than a door.

"'Scuse me. This is what the next guest wanted—seemed only you could do it best?"

The volume of the gasp almost shook him. Again, he was on pins and needles—was it a good gasp, a bad gasp? Was she crying, or should he apologize?

Unable to wait any longer, he pushed around the desk and through multiple sets of curtains, using his instincts to locate the sound.

The young man slid out swiftly when Kendrick pushed back the last set of curtains.

Bea's hand was still pressed to her mouth, the other one trembling as it held the paper. She dropped it to her side when she looked at him. The tears he saw glimmering in those beautiful blue eyes, as brilliant as the souls represented by the Morphos butterflies, tore through his own desperate soul.

He wanted nothing more than to hold her, to comfort her, but he knew he should let her make the first move.

"I wanted a piece of you with me," he explained roughly, "the most beautiful, full-of-life eyes I've ever seen—wherever I go, wherever I fight. I know you can't fight by my side, but I still want you right with me."

A slow smile spread across her face.

"You know eyes are the windows to the soul. So you might be no better than a Morphos if you want mine."

And then she had the audacity to wink at him, and all felt right.

Striding to her, he pulled her into his arms, and she fit in, filling his heart and soul when he'd been walking around with a gaping hole. Gently holding her left forearm, he stroked his fingers along the ink there, and she tipped her face up to his. But it couldn't be this simple. He couldn't just kiss her—she had to understand what he'd learned in their time apart.

"Why are these all on your left arm? I was never able to ask."

"Because I intended to wear them and never a wedding band—"

"Despite having already been betrothed to me?"

"I never anticipated seeing you again. And also just no."

Dropping his forehead to meet hers, he breathed that answer in. It wasn't the vision he'd always had, but he'd also thought they'd fight together. He realized none of that was important to him anymore.

What was important was that she had hope again and he wanted to be there for her in whatever capacity she would have him.

"I'll never leave you, Bea. I'll always be right by your side, in soul, in heart. Please emblazon your eyes on my right forearm as my symbol to you of that. That I'm always right here for you. Will you take a risk on me?"

She placed her hands on either side of his chin and pulled him in for a kiss. A long, sweet, teasing kiss, darting her tongue between his lips, licking lightly, playfully, before she pulled away to look up at him, eyes shining with hope and happiness. It took his breath away.

"Are you sure you're not just trying to get to finally fuck me?"

"Well, that would be a solid bonus," he replied, grinning mischievously.

"You know, now that I know what's important to you, you don't need a tattoo for that to happen anymore?" she asked, smiling archly.

"I still want it," he stated stubbornly.

Pushing him against the tattoo chair until the backs of his thighs hit it and he was forced to sit, she breathed, "Let's get on with it then."

He wasn't sure which he would get first, a tattoo or a fucking, but all that mattered was that he had his girl, they both had hope, and together they would fight in their own way, even if it was risky, for their own souls, and for others.

ABOUT THE AUTHOR

Skye Knight writes stories about scrappy heroines fighting falling in love. Before achieving her dream of being a full-time writer, she worked for 15 years as a cable TV executive. She lives in Washington DC with her husband (and college sweetheart), her two spunky elementary school-aged daughters, and her dogs: mini sheepadoodle Huxley and labradoodle rescue Sasha. She hails from South Carolina y'all (but was born in New Hampshire) and escapes to her happy place in Kiawah Island, SC, as much as possible. To stress bust, she plays tennis and takes pilates reformer classes. She also has been known to pick up a paintbrush and creates in watercolor, acrylic, and oil.

Please visit Skye's website and subscribe to her newsletter at:
http://www.skyeknightwriter.com/

To help support Skye's work please **leave a review** on your favorite book-selling site or share on social media! Your support is appreciated!

Also, you can follow Skye at any of the following social media sites:

Instagram: **https://www.instagram.com/skyeknightwriter/**
Facebook: **https://www.facebook.com/skyeknightwriter/**
Twitter: **https://twitter.com/skyeknightwrite/**
TikTok: **https://www.tiktok.com/@skyeknightwriter**
BookBub: **https://www.bookbub.com/profile/skye-knight**
GoodReads: **https://www.goodreads.com/skyeknight**

A REALLY BIG DAWN

J. KEELY THRALL

CHAPTER ONE

E *lyria*

AT THE FOOT of a dune on Lake Michigan, I pitch a softball to my little sister. Ravenna catches it in her mitt then swipes the two through the sand, as though tagging a base, with an exaggerated, "Youuu're out!"

Her dance of triumph turns into a race toward me, hands flailing. "Escape, escape! Black fly!"

Sun baking the sand griddle hot, we giggle-shriek down the shore, an exuberant, innocent 7- and 12-year-old sister act trying to outrace the sting of our summertime nemesis.

We dive into the water. When I come up for air, my dream from a long ago childhood vacation recedes as adult me faces the burned out wreck of a small two-story commercial building.

A new vision. Another puzzle to solve. I take a deep breath and set my shoulders.

Time to go to work.

Roof gone, second floor windows creepy black holes framed by soot. A temporary fence laced with crime scene tape warns folks away from the structure.

It's night. A stiff breeze and clouds play keep away with the full moon, and a lonely street lamp shines its orange glow about twenty feet away. No street signs. I examine the flora, trying to piece out a clue about my location. Maples, oaks, and beeches in full leaf, gossiping with the wind about the coming storm. Ornamental grasses and pansies that survived the blaze line the wide sidewalk leading to the building's entry. I could probably rule out Alaska, Hawaii and a large swath of the western United States. But from first look, there's nothing to anchor this vision to a time, a when, besides the season.

Is this a fire that has already occurred or one I need to prevent?

My nape prickles. Someone's watching me.

That's…new. Unsettling.

I pivot in a slow circle, searching the shadows, breathing too hard for all that I'm standing still.

My visions are always solitary. Even when they plunk me down in the middle of a crowd, nobody sees me and that's just the way I like it.

Who the hell is crashing my party?

A rustle off to my left rises over the constant, low pitched crackling in my ears and the chatty trees. The darkness splits to reveal a big dog. My heart kicks. A really big, really beautiful, definitely male, really, really big dog. RBD pads closer, moving with a muscular grace, his toothy dog smile revealing really big teeth and a hint of pink tongue.

The only props missing to make his look complete are a pair of granny glasses and a mob cap.

I stand frozen as he sniffs my sneakers, nosing up my jeans.

"Don't you dare," I warn as he hesitates near my crotch.

I could swear RBD winks at me, but he skips sticking his snout into my privates and continues up, stretching only a little to snuffle at my neck.

"Hey, stop, that tickles," I squeak, raising my shoulder to my ear, a heated loft of goosebumps arcing over my skin.

RBD sits back on his haunches, one pointed ear standing alert, the other flopped down, disarming and adorable. Eyes filled with intelligence, humor, and appreciation seem to laugh at me. We stare at each other, long enough for the humor to die and awareness to spark.

For some reason, I want to sink my hands into his silky black and silvercoat, maybe feel up his muscles. See if I can get him to growl. Or howl.

OMG. I'm horny for a dog.

That's just—nope. I might be lonely, but I have lines. Standards.

I take another look, trying to puzzle out why a really big dog with flippin' sex appeal is appearing in my vision. He cocks his head, inquisitive and patient and still smiling, waiting for my next move.

"Oh, for crying out loud," I say as logic finally punches through my hormones. "You're not a dog, are you?"

RBD shakes his head no.

The relief washing through me is short lived, because if he's not a dog...

"Werewolf?"

A soft huff yes.

Okay, okay. No need to freak. Or stare more than I have already.

Werewolves might have a reputation as being all jaws and claws, brawn over brains, but this one seems disinclined toward disembowelment. At least at the moment. He's simply another kind of parahuman, like me. It's all good. It's cool. Nothing to worry about here.

Plus, hello, this is a vision, not real life. If he tries any funny business, I'll snap out of the vision, no harm, no foul.

I wipe clammy hands down my hips and choose to ignore how he tracks the movement. How his attention is intimate and focused, like he's calculating when he could try something similar.

Stop. This vision isn't going to last forever, and I need answers before it dissipates.

Less perving, more sleuthing.

"Any idea why you're in my vision?"

Shake.

He had to be there for a reason. Even if said reason is my subcon-

scious telling me it's been way too long since my last hook up. But…
werewolves are hunters. Hunters with really big noses.

Was there something to smell in the burned out husk of a
building?

"Want to help me search for clues?"

Huff.

Surprisingly, we settle into an easy rhythm, making quick work
slipping into a chink in the fence and scouting the exterior of the
scene. Evidence of the incident management team dots the narrow
strip of land surrounding the building. Puddles of water, torn sod,
muddy boot tracks.

Fighting fires always leaves a soggy, chaotic trail.

A sharp gust of wind wafts the stale, acrid scent of harsh chemicals
our way. RBD coughs and sneezes as he snuffles at the back corner of
the building. Giving him a sympathetic ear scritch, I squat beside him
to examine his find. He leans into me, his warm weight oddly
comforting.

One of the weird truths about fire is how items migrate. That hair-
brush from the upstairs bathroom? Winds up in the neighbor's yard.
Clothes decorate shrubs and trees. Your kid's favorite stuffed animal
hides partially singed under the tomato plant in the vegetable garden.

So the aluminum baseball bat half submerged in the mud and ash
of a trampled flower bed isn't that surprising. But the lack of other
debris is.

"Maybe the building owner is a baseball fan," I say, wiping away
the muck as a light rain begins to fall. There's a worn image of a
rampant tiger on the once shiny blue shaft and faded text underneath
it in a pseudo-medieval font that's impossible to read but could be
three words. A clue? "Sometimes I wish I could snap a pic in my
visions and have it manifest in the real world. It would make research
on this sucker go so much faster."

RBD offers a huff of compassion. I toss the bat down, scoop
dampish hair behind my ears, and head to the rear entrance. The top
left corner of a Do Not Cross taped X droops over his partner strip of
yellow caution, as if exhausted by his sentry duty. The used-to-be-

glass doors are now metal frames with a few jagged shards sticking up from the bottom. The glass side panel sports a huge spider web of cracks radiating from a tight circle of three head-of-a-baseball-bat sized dents.

"One guess what made those dents, eh?"

Huff.

"So did the building owner set the fire and try to help it along by opening up some air passages? Why not just wedge the door open? Do we have a dissatisfied customer with an ax to grind? A scorned lover? And what kind of business operated out of here? Are we talking dental practice? Accounting firm? Something retail?"

A clap of thunder, not close, but not far enough away, makes me jump.

Okay, elements. Hold off just a little while longer, pretty please. I cross my fingers, adding weight to my plea. The drizzle increases in the next second because of course it does. My ever-present tinnitus decides it doesn't want to be upstaged, turning up the volume to make sure I can hear its ruckus over the weather.

Little bitch. I yank at my earlobe, a move as useless as ever. It'd be great if I could wrap up my search before the noise in my inner ear reaches the point of true pain, but so far I have beans to go on.

No signage to inform me what the building was used for. No diaspora of junk on the lawn to pick through. That leaves a bat–and maybe the werewolf–to provide a trail to follow in the waking world. I need more.

I step toward the entrance and RBD body-blocks me. "Woof."

"Don't you woof me. Checking out the interior is the next logical step."

RBD sneers at my rationale, black muzzle crinkling to reveal a glint of white fang. Drizzle turns to downpour. The wind kicks up, blowing sideways.

I try a second time. RBD blocks me again, his furry side instantly warming me from the waist down. Rather than damp dog, he smells of woods and wild freedom.

"Listen. I don't have enough information yet to determine whether this is a vision of a past or future fire. If it's a fire that hasn't yet happened, it's on me to prevent it. I don't have the luxury of stopping just because you want to play the role of chivalrous he-wolf. Also–" I twirl my index finger in the air–"this is a vision. Nothing I find in there is going to hurt me."

Not physically anyway.

He woofs again, this time nudging me with enough oomph so that I trip backwards a few steps.

"What the hell–"

Lightning splits the sky in a blinding strike. Thunder booms on its heels. I hit the ground, squelching into the mud, breath squeezed out by a metric ton of werewolf landing on my chest.

The world freezes a bright purple white for the space of a heartbeat before the back half of the building collapses.

CHAPTER TWO

E *lyria*

MIMI'S KITCHEN lightens as dawn stretches her arms and blinks open her eyes. Hunkered over my laptop, tired from the interrupted sleep caused by the vision I walked last night, I apply pressure to the hollows behind my ears and listen to the sounds of the farmhouse waking up.

Thumps and bumps, water rushing, cranky near-tantrums soothed with soft murmurs. The twins of the household tumble downstairs after their dad, the three of them pausing to stomp into boots before heading to do their pre-breakfast chores in the barn.

Sassy the cow will be happy.

Mimi swings into the kitchen, humming and moving at her usual lightspeed. Earth mother crofter elf, unexpected friend, landlady. Stubborn mini-tyrant who generously loves everyone who enters her circle of influence into seeing things her way. Even this lonely vision walker who'd been all set to do my normal slink away after solving the case that brought me to Green Haven, Tennessee. If she hadn't good-naturedly strong-armed me into moving to her farm, I'd still be roaming the country, untethered and alone.

Eight months on, and the everyday normalcy of this family's morning routine has finally stopped spiking my veins with a toxic mix of grief and dread.

I release a breath. Progress.

"You're looking rough, sweetie. Catch a vision last night?" She unhooks the cast iron skillet from above the island and sets it on a burner before heading to the fridge.

"Yeah." Fighting a yawn, I hit go on the alerts I set up and close the laptop. My research on the tiger baseball bat has come up empty so far. I'd let my snooper program do some of the heavy lifting while I take a refueling break. "This one was a little different."

"Tell me."

I fill her in on the hot werewolf, the baseball bat, the storm, the anonymous building and paucity of good clues while I help chop veggies for the egg scramble.

"Hot werewolf, eh?" She hip bumps me. "Sounds promising."

"Out of everything I said, my tiny, little, passing, barely there, kinda crush on a werewolf is what you glom on to? What is it with married people wanting to pair off all the singles in their orbit?"

"Share the bliss, that's my motto."

"He could be ugly in human form, you know."

"Who cares? He's already shown you he's a protector at heart."

But had he? Or had he prevented me from learning valuable intel? I didn't know enough to make a conclusion.

I screw up my face to underline my skepticism.

"I say go for it." Meems flips the bacon, the sizzle competing with the crackle in my ears, the scent waking up my stomach. "You can't let that fiasco of a date a month ago dictate the rest of your life. Ditto what happened to your parents and sister five years ago. As tragic as that was, you deserve to live fully. No, abundantly. In fact, to help move you along, I hereby challenge you. You ask the hot werewolf out for coffee before your birthday next week, and I'll order that new kiln you've been drooling after."

"Oh, low blow, sinking to that level of bribery. And anyway, I should have the money saved for the kiln in another month. The pieces I placed with the gallery over in Knoxville are selling better than I expected so your little venture into extortion won't work. Plus, honestly, go for what? He was part of a vision. There's no guarantee he'll appear in another. To tell the truth," I transfer mushrooms into a bowl, "I'm more unsettled he was in the vision than by my fleeting attraction to someone furry and four-legged. How did he show up? Why did he show up? Is he a real person or did my unconscious conjure him into being?"

"You think it might be another change in your magic?"

"I don't know." I move on to setting the table while Mimi fries up potatoes in the bacon grease. "It's not like I have a mentor to show me the ropes, so maybe?" I shrug and fold a cloth napkin.

Five years ago, I lost my parents and sister to a house fire that might have killed me, too, if Ravenna and I hadn't had a knock-down drag-out fight about her dating a guy too old for her. She accused me of being a dried up nun at the ripe age of twenty-two.

Furious, I spun out of the drive in Old Blue, Dad's mint condition, powder blue, 1980 Ford F-100, kicking up a rooster tail behind me filled with gravel and attitude, and headed to an art gallery two states away with a delivery of our family studio's newest ceramic pieces a day earlier than scheduled.

One phone call at dawn changed everything.

One phone call, and an arsonist the authorities never caught.

I'd lived a refrain of if only ever since.

If only I'd stayed. If only I had been calmer, more understanding with Ravenna.

If only I'd ratted my sister out to our parents.

If only any of our family's constellation of visionary powers–even mine as weak as they were–had kicked in to give us a hint of impending disaster.

Three months later, my life upended again when the balance of my visionary powers manifested. My abilities until that point had been more gut feelings telling me when to turn to avoid bad traffic or which fruit would ripen first. Piddly stuff compared to Ravenna's vision walking or our parents' more common clear-seeing.

I ignored the first vision, too caught up in my grief to care about its content or what it had to do with me. I ignored everything, sleeping, eating, showering, until the tinnitus started screaming in my ears, so loud, I finally had to pay attention.

And so my life changed a third time, and I became an amateur arson investigator, parahuman-style.

That first vision helped prevent the death of another family a couple of towns over, a family like mine, only they were machinist elves, not visionaries. Thankfully there'd been a parahuman high enough up in local law enforcement that they could persuade the sheriff, a norm equally as suspicious of other norms as she was of paras, not to arrest me for being a pushy nuisance, or the arsonist, before I could help.

The next day, I walked through a vision calling me to New England. Alone, without family to keep me anchored to our hometown, I sold our studio, packed up Old Blue, and became a rolling stone.

If it hadn't been for Meems deciding I needed to have a base of operations and a friend, I'd still be living out of the truck, traveling the length and breadth of the country. Learning more about my evolving powers. Searching for the arsonist who killed my family. Helping to prevent some fires and investigate the causes of others.

And I'd still be alone.

Setting the last fork in place, I shake my head and drift back to the kitchen island. Some days alone sounds peachy. Especially when Mimi sets her sights on some improvement I could make in my life. But...it's damned hard to fight an earth mother crofter elf on a mission of love.

They just feed and cuddle you into submission.

"I guess we'll see what's what when the next vision comes." I snitch a strip of bacon. "In the meantime, I'll keep trying to find more about the tiger emblem. Someone designed it. Had it printed on a bat. Finding that out will hopefully help me narrow in on a location."

"Which will then help you figure out whether the fire is past or future tense."

"Hey, look who's been paying attention in class."

"Smart ass." She flicks a teatowel at my butt. "Don't make me give you extra chores."

CHAPTER THREE

D*eclan*

"EARTH TO DEC. COME IN, Dec. It's your turn," Major Logan Greenway, my alpha, commander of my U.S. Army Special Forces parahuman team—we put the para back in paramilitary—and oldest friend says, amusement and impatience at war in his tone.

I go through the motions of checking my cards. It's no use. The red and black pips dance around on their white background, refusing to resolve into any discernible pattern. With a self-directed snort, I fold. "I'm out."

"What's the matter? Girl trouble?" Nessa asks with her usual friendly nosiness. The communication specialist on our team, my cousin has a thirst for being first when it comes to sussing out the inside scoop on team romances.

All action in the room stops as a dozen curious werewolves zero in, waiting on my answer. It's rare that the pack's communal dining room at Hearthstone goes completely quiet, but we have our moments when potentially juicy gossip flavors the air.

Bunch of busybodies, the lot of us.

I suppress a smile. Since I couldn't very well have fun trouble with a dream apparition, I'd have a different kind of fun with my pack-mates. Leaning back in my chair until it balances on its hind legs, I fold my hands behind my head.

"If you call having a smart, sexy, good-smelling lady coax you into being her clue-sniffing helper as she investigates an arson girl trouble, then yeah, I guess you could say I have a problem."

"When did this happen?" Logan's frown stamps a vee between his eyes.

"Yeah, you haven't left packhome since you stepped on the grounds two days ago," Nessa says. "Your chip hasn't beeped."

"Around 4:30 a.m." I pause as they lean in closer. "Never had such a vivid morning dream in my damn life."

Everyone moans. Berkeley pelts me with a pretzel. Nessa crosses her eyes at me.

Only Logan refrains from expressing mock disappointment, his frown carving a deeper vee. I'd have to take him for a run soon. Get him to let loose. All work and no play make alphas volatile, grumpy SOBs and ain't nobody got time for that.

Red Smitty slides into my spot as I leave the table and the game continues.

Wandering to the window, I let the new round of smack talk become background noise as I try to peer past the reflection of the room through the glass, though who knows what I'm hoping to glimpse. Ghost Girl, maybe. I chug down the rest of my Wolverine IPL, trying to wash away the remnants of my hyper-realistic early morning dream.

Ghost Girl, with her red hair, slim build, sweet butt, and wry wit, resists my efforts.

Would I dream of her again?

I set my empty in the collection bucket of the busboy station to my right, suddenly ready to return to my cabin.

"Dream threw you for a loop." Logan passes me a replacement brew.

"Yeah." As it's in my hand, and one doesn't squander a Wolverine lager, I twist off the bottle top, flipping the lid into the bucket. "If I had even an ounce of artistic talent, I swear I could draw her face down to the last freckle on her nose, it was that real."

"You say the two of you were sniffing around an arson scene?"

"That's right. What about it?"

"Probably nothing." He shrugs a shoulder. "Have anything lined up for your leave beyond spending the next month four-footed, chasing rabbits?"

"Might help Leon pound a few nails on the library edition. Might add skinny dipping to the rabbit hunting."

"The life of Riley."

"You said it."

I add daydreaming to my heavy agenda of pounding and dipping and hunting.

Ghost girl might not make a repeat visit to my sleeping hours, but nothing says I can't edit my dream and give it a more interesting outcome.

CHAPTER FOUR

E *lyria*

THROUGHOUT THE WEEK following the first *Vision with Hot Werewolf*, as Mimi calls it, RBD and I meet up in different versions of the same set up. Once it rains so hard, I can't see and he can't smell. Another time, the building has already been hit by the lightning strike. In yet another, we barely have time to greet each other before the vision dissipates and I come to with a misshapen pot on my wheel and twenty minutes missing from my afternoon. In each rendition, something keeps us from entering the building, though by the tenth time, even RBD is growly and frustrated by our lack of progress.

But tonight's vision is different. The building is intact, no fence, no tape, windows reflect the afternoon sunlight. As he's done since the third vision, RBD shows up wearing a body harness. As I've done since the fourth vision, I croon and make a big deal out of scratching under the straps. My reward is a satisfied groan and a quick neck lick that sends shivers to wake up my boobs.

Part of me rolls my eyes. This isn't a dog. Talking baby talk and giving snoot smoochies is probably giving the guy beneath the fur the wrong impression. Like I'm flirting or something. But the other part of me can't stop. Can't stop petting the hot werewolf.

Damn it, I need a shrink.

At least it's just a vision, not waking life. I don't have to worry this will develop into something I can't handle.

I rise from my squat and face the building, RBD on my left. Magic pulses through the air, rippling through my veins. I glance over and quickly squeeze my eyes shut.

"What are you doing?" It's a dumb question.

"Getting dressed," RBD says. His voice, matter of fact yet somehow filled with laughter, paints a line of heat down my spine. "You can look now. I'm decent."

Cracking one eye open, I'm hit by a wall of bronzed abs. He's huge. Six foot four, at least, lean and muscled. His sweatpants cling a little too lovingly to his upper thighs and hips, giving a coy hint of how much firepower he's packing. He pulls on a loose tee shirt, and I mourn the loss of the washboard.

I give myself a discreet, but ouchy pinch. Girl, focus.

"Gonna let me explore inside the building this time, slugger?" I begin down the sidewalk toward the building.

"We'll have to see." RBD falls in beside me.

I should probably ask his name. Ask what he's doing in my vision. I don't. No, instead I ride the pingpong of awareness and nerves bubbling away in my belly and struggle to keep from skipping. I poke my stomach. Quit it. This is not a date. And despite Mimi's hopes, he is not a potential boyfriend.

We get to the front entry. Doors locked. The lobby is dingy with bare white walls and scuffed light gray linoleum. No artwork, no furniture. Nothing to give us a clue what business or businesses work out of the building.

"Bland," RBD judges.

As we round the building, he stops at the corner where he found the tiger bat. Nothing appears out of the ordinary, but it was smart to check the area out. His initiative floods me with more puzzle pieces about this mystery man. Why is he showing up in my visions? What's his background that he's so patient and thorough with the tedious parts of investigation?

Why does it feel like I can trust him when he's a stranger whose second form has really big, really sharp, teeth?

I stow my questions in favor of speed...and a disinclination to study that last question too closely. We have favorable, pre-fire conditions to search for clues. I'm not going to waste them with a round of twenty questions.

The back entrance serves us better luck. RBD swings one door open and ushers me inside with a bow.

"Is it just me or is it odd that there's no signage on the doors? No street address, phone number, business name, logo?" I ask, checking out the interior. Hallways to the left and right. There's a door marked bathroom, another marked stairs. More dingy gray linoleum and drab white walls.

"Maybe whoever owns the place wants to keep a low profile?" He ducks his head into the bathroom. "Clear."

"How can you tell so fast? You didn't even duck to check under the stalls."

He points to his nose, but holds the door open for me to inspect. Empty. The room is bare but for pipes pushing out of the walls and floor. No toilets, sinks, mirrors. Nothing but some demo dust in the corners.

"Curiouser and curiouser," I murmur.

"Maybe the owners are planning to renovate," he says in a low, rough voice that prickles over my skin.

I turn to exit, and we're chest to chest in the doorway. Or front to front at least. At five foot eight, I'm no shrimp, but we don't exactly line up square. If I take a deep breath, my breasts will brush against him. Funny, I've never hated clothes before. Slowly, I tilt my head up, up, up until our gazes lock.

Almost unreal blue eyes steal the air from my lungs until I couldn't take a deep breath if I tried. The lack of oxygen makes me dizzy, and I place my hand on his waist to steady myself, my palm burning from his body heat.

I lick my too dry lips and somehow he gets bigger, hotter, his full attention on my mouth. Greatly daring, I yank on the werewolf's tail, darting my tongue out to tease the bottom lip. Kiss me. Do it.

A dull thump sounds over our heads, breaking the spell.

"Stay behind me," he says, moving swiftly and silently to the door leading to the stairs.

We creep up the staircase, RBD deftly avoiding all the treads that squeak, me hitting about half of them, damn it. He opens the second floor door a crack and waits. And waits and waits. I poke him to see if he's sleeping with his eyes open. He captures my hand, threading our fingers together and rests the knit job on his thigh.

His warm thigh that's inches away from his really big firepower.

I bonk my head against the wall. Repeatedly. Why? I've gone months, heck, years, not thinking about sex, not wanting it, not missing it. Now I can't stop? This is balls. Tugging, I try to regain custody of my hand and my dignity. RBD keeps the first, giving a light squeeze.

"Shh. Settle."

I let my head drop to my chest, defeated. Shushed in my own vision.

Could things get any worse?

At some signal only tall, dark, and maddening senses, the tension in his body loosens and he opens the door, leading us into a single wide, hallway. I manage to disentangle our hands and womanfully ignore his wink.

We clear each room, empty and as lacking in personality as the public spaces, making our way toward the front of the building. RBD hesitates outside the last room.

"How about I do this one on my own then we'll head downstairs?" He places his back to the entry and shoots me a brilliant, *trust me*, smile.

One I immediately don't trust.

The door is slightly ajar, but reveals nothing special, no visible reason for him to put me off.

"What do you smell?"

He grimaces and pushes the door farther open with his back. Oh. Dead body alert.

Sprawled on the floor like a doughy starfish near a junk-stuffed built-in bookcase and a stack of flat packing boxes, the DB is fresh, the bright red pool of blood around his head not yet congealed. No time for animal predation, insect egg laying, or rigor mortis to occur. No time to rot, but now that I'm in the room, the rank odor of death is unmistakable and impossible to ignore.

Male, mid-forties, white, blond, wearing a decent suit, no tie, and newish shoes. Maybe six foot, six-one, and carrying a few extra pounds. Ignoring the way my stomach roils, I crouch by the dead guy to rifle his pockets, searching for ID, and get a better look at what killed him. Small caliber gunshot wound to the temple.

"No gun, so probably not suicide." I gingerly reach into the inside jacket pocket of his suit. "This didn't happen while we were in the building. We would have heard the shot or the killer fleeing or something. So what made the noise?"

"Plain old gravity?" RBD points at a baseball hiding behind the door. "Could have dropped from one of the shelves."

Finding nothing but a roll of antacids, I give up and stand, accepting the ball he holds out. White with red stitching and a stylized dark blue D imprinted on the leather.

"The Detroit Tigers," he says.

"My sister's favorite team when we were growing up," I say, my voice crunchy and crowded. I follow the curves of the D with my fingertip, heart squeezed in an unexpected vice.

"Hard memory?" he asks, a world of understanding in his gaze. Not as sticky as sympathy, more like he has his own hard thoughts that mug him out of nowhere, so he gets it. My acknowledgement is more grimace than smile, fleeting and flat lipped.

"She and my parents died in a fire a while back. Still smacks me in the face sometimes." I clear my throat. "So, do we think this is a clue to our location or is this simply the dead guy's sports tribe of choice?"

"Presuming it belongs to the dead guy."

"Right."

Like a sentimental hot potato I'm too stupid or stubborn to set down, I toss the ball from hand to hand and turn to inspect the crammed bookcases. In contrast to the blank nothingness we've encountered so far, the shelves are chock-full of noisy color, heavy on the orange and black. Sports memorabilia is stuffed cheek by jowl with other collectibles, mostly toys and old advertisements.

"That's a lot of tigers," he says.

Tony the cereal king, Hobbes the cartoon sage. Various versions of the Esso/Exxon tiger decanting fossil fuels into the tanks of cars from bygone decades. Magazine cutouts of tigers in zoos. Framed photos of Tiger Woods selling a luxury watch and the Tiger King hugging one of his menagerie. Pooh's pal Tigger. A fencing club from south London. Another based in the Georgetown neighborhood of D.C. Dozens of similarly lesser known logos.

All tigers.

"Someone has a fetish," I mutter.

"One might say a tiger by the tail."

I snort, and we share a grin.

While RBD uses his greater height to check out the top shelves, I find the shelf the baseball escaped from at waist height. A thick half circle of dust near the edge suggests the ball had probably been dancing with gravity for a while. Reluctantly, I return the ball to its spot, freeing up my hands to paw through the rest of the flotsam on that shelf. I discover a business card under a Hobbes bobblehead. White linen cardstock with black text. A man's name, Logan Greenway, and a phone number with a 202 area code.

The ever-present crackle in my ears flares up, hissing and popping like a strungout campfire with a shiny new log to smoke.

Like I needed a hissy fit to tell me the card is a big fat clue. I give my ear a discreet pinch, achieving exactly nothing.

"Found something." His arm brushes against mine. The tinnitus recedes back to its customary dull roar. Goosebumps shout along my skin, demanding more touch, more sensation.

"Me too." Smoke from that campfire must have found a way inside me because I sound throaty, almost spicy.

As if I have seduction on the brain.

I blink and somehow he's standing closer, somehow we're no longer side by side, but face to face. His blue eyes are dark, primal. Intent on me. I blink again, and his hand rests on my butt, anchoring me to him. My hands lie flat against his chest, not to push him away, no, but to soak up his heat.

"You first," he urges in a guttural demand. He lowers his head, breathing in my scent, nosing behind my ear. He places a barely there kiss on my neck that calls forth a flood of need. I give him my weight, my legs no longer functioning. Under my hands, he vibrates with a rumble of approval.

Planting succulent little kisses along my jaw, he pulls back an inch when he reaches my mouth.

"Okay?"

"I'll wallop you if you don't."

The man's a werewolf. An apex predator.

I expect power, force, wild roughness.

Instead I get sweet.

Teasing and tempting, his tongue is a velvet, playful, frisky delight, luring me into a game of hide and seek. Call and response. Give and take.

Stamping down the inner voice insisting I'm in a vision and I have no business getting distracted by kisses, I give myself up to fun.

To the way my body slowly wakes up from its five-year-plus hibernation. The dazzling simplicity of wanting another person—I rub up against his erection, the blood in my veins oozy and triumphant when he shudders—and knowing he wants me back. The dizzying trust that this hunky stranger won't hurt me. I climb him until I can wrap my legs around his waist, holding on like a limpet. He pulls me tight, until my tender breasts are smashed flat, and I'm wondering why our clothes haven't incinerated from the heat.

A loud thwack on the linoleum flooring makes me startle and break the kiss

The Tigers baseball rolls until it rests beside his foot. Glaring at it, he hefts me a little higher, seemingly disinclined to set me beside the poor, innocent ball. I tap his shoulder. His glare softens to grumpy when I release my ankles. By the time I slide down his body, we're both steamy and out of breath again.

"Buddy, you should come with a warning label," I say, stepping away from temptation, lest I be, ah, tempted.

"Pot, kettle." With a wince, he adjusts his erection before crossing his arms and shoving his hands in his pits. To keep from reaching for me again?

I'm not swooning, you are.

With a sigh, he reaches for the top shelf and pulls down a gimme cap, dark blue with a red bill and a stylish white W logo. The chaos in my ears jumps another level, a radio shock jock spewing angry static.

"Not a tiger," I observe, like a genius, curling my hands into fists, repressing the urge to scratch my ears off. "The Washington Nationals keeps with the sports theme, at least. So now we have three possible settings. Detroit. D.C. And whatever geography the 202 area code covers."

"202? That's D.C. What have you got?"

I hand over the card. His body goes solid as he reads, the kind of solid that's bulging with energy and ready to explode.

"Recognize the name?"

"Yep." He stuffs the card in the pocket of his sweats, a worried frown marring his brow.

"Gonna share any deets?"

"Nope."

"Why not?" I ask calmly rather than reminding him that he can't take the card with him when the vision dissolves. Or sharing that I have a lot of experience memorizing the shit I come across when I'm walking in dreamland.

Or taking a swing at him for being stingy with his info.

"Too dangerous."

"Dangerous how?"

"I don't know yet. But you can leave any further investigation to me. I'll handle it."

A dead body, a soul stealing kiss, and an overprotective werewolf with no name who wants to take my investigation away from me.

Well this answers my earlier question. Things could indeed get worse.

CHAPTER FIVE

D *eclan*

"FUUUUCK ME." I kick free from the bedsheet, morning wood pressed tight to my belly.

It's one thing to wake up with a boner. Shows I'm alive and healthy, right? Lots of red blood cells lining up for the big salute like soldiers ready for inspection.

Nothing wrong with a strong, long dong in the a.m.

"But shit, could we stop with the weird dreams that keep leaving me het up and hanging?" I stalk to the shower. "Dreams, visions, whatever the hell they are."

With soapy hands, I take care of the first issue. Try to figure out what, if anything, to do about the second.

Ghost Girl and her dream hauntings have been an intriguing diversion the past week as I adjust to the slower pace of my leave. She smells fucking fantastic, her scrupulous care and attention to detail in examining the crime scene each night is a thing of beauty, and her sad smile makes me want to slay all her dragons.

Before jumping her bones.

But are the nighttime visits based in real life or my fantasies running amok?

I have a champion imagination, yet these are different, more solid, more...substantive than my usual overnight entertainment. More... real life.

After drying off, I take a sniff of yesterday's jeans–not too awful–and dress.

Okay. We'll use real life as our working assumption.

Which begs the question, what the hell is Logan doing, showing up as a clue at a murder scene?

I stuff my feet into a pair of running shoes and head to my cabin's kitchenette.

I'd provided enough details of the building and surrounding area when he last asked for an update about the dreams, he should have recognized the location if he'd ever visited.

So if he doesn't have first hand knowledge of the place, what's his connection to a dead man with two bullets in his head?

And does the connection explain why I'm an active participant in someone's vision? Who *is* the dead man? How is Ghost Girl returning to the scene of the crime over and over at different points in time? Why is she doing it?

And what the hell is her name?

Too many questions and–I peek into my tea caddy for confirmation–no Morning Breakfast to compensate. I drum my fingers on the counter. I'd give the visions one more night, see if I can gather some more practical intel–and a name–then tag Logan for another convo.

Before anything though, tea.

Dawn is a hint in the east as I mosey toward Hearthstone's mess hall, drinking in the sharp scents of the forest. Maybe a post breakfast run through the wilds of the pack's rural territory will ease the itchy sensation of foreboding between my shoulder blades.

The snap of a branch downwind raises the hair on the back of my neck. I halt and wait with patient stillness, all senses on alert.

Logan materializes out of the gloom wearing his *I have bad news* Grim Alpha Face™.

"There goes my run." I shake the mini adrenaline hit out of my arms. "Killjoy. Lucky you're so cute."

"Cute killjoy, huh? I'll have to update my profile on ParaMatch," he says, not cracking a smile. "Walk with me."

I fall in with the route he sets, and we climb to a narrow lookout above the bank of the stream. Young sunlight torches the leaves of the treetops until they glow a vibrant green. Almost worth missing tea for this view deep in the wilds of Virginia's Blue Ridge mountains.

"S'up?" I ask after we've had a moment to soak up a dose of nature's tonic.

"We have ourselves a firebug. An accomplished one. Ten fires set overnight in D.C., a combination of residential and commercial properties. Details are still coming in, but it looks like six para families sustained various amounts of damage to their homes and three para-owned businesses are now more charcoal than brick. The only norm property involved is a townhouse in Georgetown that belonged until recently to entrepreneur and pro para advocate Enzo Costa. No deaths, thank fuck, but one dad and his teen had to be treated for smoke inhalation and second degree burns."

"So we have a dude with a fiery hard-on for parahumans and allies. Special." I kick a pinecone over the ledge, wishing it were something bigger.

Like an arsonist.

"Got a call from the chair of the Mid-Atlantic Para Council asking me to help with the investigation, liaise with regular law enforcement." He claps a hand on my shoulder. "Which means I'm going to need my best tracker."

"First you tank my run, now my leave? Keep this up and I'm gonna get a complex."

"Sorry not sorry."

We condense a lifetime of duty, trust, understanding, razzing, and friendship down to an exchange of manly grunts.

"Fire, fire, everywhere," I say after a beat to let any residual squishy emotions evaporate. "Had another dream last night. A doozy."

"Tell me."

"Pre-fire this time." I fill him in on the latest installment of *As the Building Burns*, including his business card, the tiger fetish, and the body, but leaving out the kiss. A guy reaches a certain age, he doesn't dream kiss-and-tell.

"You get Ghost Girl's name this time?"

My hot cheeks answer for me, and he rolls his eyes.

"No, you were probably figuring out how to convince her to swap spit. Damn it, Declan."

When caught dead to rights, admit nothing, deny everything, make counter-accusations.

"How was I supposed to realize these dream visiony things would lead anywhere but a semi-persistent state of frustrated arousal? Besides, we still don't know for sure if they're anything more than my subconscious at work. And what the hell was your personal business card doing at a crime scene anyway?"

"We'll figure that out, count on it. In the meantime, I put Nessa on tracing your woman. There may be a lot of variety in the Visionary line–pre-cog, oneiromancer, dream weaver, telepath, who knows how many other subgroups–but they make up a sliver of a slice of the para population."

"And you're betting the number that investigates arson is–"

"One."

"Can't fault that logic."

"Nobody targets my people, not even in dreams." Grim Alpha Face™ reappears, cool and flinty.

"She's not–" I shut up when he raises his brow. Yeah, okay, I don't know enough about Ghost Girl to jump to her defense. Yet every atom inside me stands ready to lead with tooth and claw if my oldest friend blinks funny.

Spiky as a cactus, I take his long inspection, his head cocked to the side like I'm an unexpected puzzle. At last, his mouth quirks into a brief, barely there smile, one that says *aaah, got it.* I frown daggers. What? What exactly has he *got?*

"Stand down," he says in a soothing, amused *there, there* tone that only manages to irritate the fuck out of me. "It's my job to be suspicious as hell, remember? Goes with the whole alpha thing."

His phone buzzes, letting us both off the hook from having to acknowledge I'm not exactly leaping to comply with his suggestion slash order.

"Greenway."

"Logan Greenway?" a smoky, feminine, *familiar* alto asks.

No. No she did not. Ghost Girl did not go against my express direction and call Logan when I told her to leave him to me.

I try to grab the phone, and he wrestles me into a half-Nelson face down on the ground, inches away from the edge of the cliff.

"Speaking. And you are?"

I stop struggling and listen for her answer, more grateful that I've ever been for werewolf hearing.

"My name is Elyria Naismith. I'm a vision walker, and I'm calling to see if you could provide information leading to the identification of a murdered man–or possibly soon to be murdered man–I saw in a recent vision."

Wriggling like a latter day Harry Houdini, I free myself and pop the phone out of Logan's hands, rolling toward the treeline.

"You gave him your real name and para designation? Are you high? You have no idea if he's the bad guy. Do you have zero sense of self-preservation, woman?" I ask, though maybe, possibly, it comes out more bark than a polite request for input. "I said I'd handle it."

"Don't you talk to Lyri in that tone of voice," a second woman says. "You are not the boss of her, RBD, or whatever your name is."

"RBD?" Logan asks.

Hints of a scuffle issue from the phone's speaker. Logan takes advantage of my distraction to repatriate his phone. With a look that says *try me,* he sits beside me, leaning back against the trunk of a white oak, and flips the cell to speaker mode.

Prudence has me directing my glare toward the piercing blue of the sky while the women wrap up their skirmish.

"RBD stands for–" the second woman says.

"Mimi, no, don't–"

"Really Big Dog," Mimi says. "Are you a werewolf, too, Mr. Greenway?"

The official term for Logan's reaction is bust a gut. He laughs so hard, tears run down his face.

"You thought I was a dog?" I ask over his guffaws.

"At first?" Elyria says. "It was night when we met, remember? And who expects a werewolf? Seriously, no one. What I want to know is, how could you possibly guess I gave my real name and talent? And why did you try to scare me off following up with Mr. Greenway when you clearly know the man?"

Admitting nothing, denying everything, making counter-accusations. A guy could fall in love. I grin dopily at the sky.

"It's Major Greenway," Logan picks up the conversation as I keep smiling, "I'm an alpha in the Greater National Area Werewolf Pack and the leader of a U.S. Army Special Forces team. For my sins, your RBD serves as my second in both capacities."

"Oh. So, probably you're not the murderer," Elyria says.

"Not in this case at least." Logan sounds almost sorry to disappoint her.

"I can't believe you called him." My complaint holds the merest hint of a whine. Barely noticeable.

"If you'd explained yourself instead of trying to usurp the investigation because you don't think I'm capable of handling a little danger, I might have."

"He pulled the 'don't-worry-your-pretty-little-head' card?" Elyria's friend asks. "The nerve."

Logan and I share an eye roll. Civilians.

"No ma'am," I reply. "I pulled the 'I-have-a-better-chance-of-going-up-against-an-alpha-werewolf-who-also-happens-to-be-my-best-friend' card."

"That's a compelling argument," Mimi concedes.

"It is not," Elyria says. "He should have come clean about his close relationship with our only lead."

Our.

She thinks of the investigation as a joint venture.

Contentment settles in my gut.

CHAPTER SIX

E *lyria*

"YOU TWO CAN CONTINUE DEBATING this at a later point." Major Logan Greenway's firm tone echoes off the walls of Mimi's kitchen where I've once again set up to do my research at the long farm table. "Ms. Naismith, you implied the man you saw in your vision may not be dead yet. Can we save him?"

"Honestly, I don't know. My visions are always fire-based. If they're arson, they've usually already occurred, and I'm investigating post conflagration. When the fires are accidental in nature, I can intervene, stop the fire from happening. But–" I slow down to let my tongue catch up with my thoughts, "–all indications point to this fire being set by a seasoned pro. If that's the case, it's possible the fire was set to cover up the dead man."

Greenway crawls us inch by inch back over the details of each vision. Mimi, sitting beside me on the bench, asks a few clarifying questions of her own. By the time we get through reexamining our impressions of the dead man and the memorabilia collection, my head aches. The scratchy ringing in my ears is near deafening, but my respect for both men's dogged–ha, ha–pursuit of clues joins my respect for Mimi's practicality to hover somewhere in the stratosphere. If only the three could be part of all my investigations.

Sans RBD's over-protectiveness.

At some point Meems slips away to fuss at the island, making reassuring kitcheny noises. While the werewolves argue about the various smells of the visions, I prop my elbows on the kitchen table and rub my temples. Mimi returns to switch out my cold coffee with a mug of peppermint tea. She plops down in a seat across from me. My unlikely, unlooked for, but cherished chaperone.

I smile my thanks. If you're going to live with an earth mother-level elf as your landlord bestie, you have to accept certain things. Like she's going to cut off your caffeine supply when she deems you've had enough. Or horn in on a business call if she senses you need the support. I soak up the comfort of her care and drift as the steam and the scent work their mellowing mojo, and the werewolves squabble over some technical something to do with scent trails.

The 202 area code for the phone number of an alpha of the Greater National Area Werewolf Pack. The Washington Nationals. The fencing club in Georgetown. A photo of two tigers in the National Zoo. A tiger mascot from one of the middle schools in the Northeast section of D.C. In the sea of orange and black fur, only these had a secondary connection.

Location.

"It's D.C. We need to look for the crime scene in or around D.C." I lay out my reasoning.

"I'll buy it," RBD says. "It's a more substantial angle to work than anything else we've come up with. But does this mean we have an eleventh arson? One that hasn't been reported yet? Or are the cases separate?"

"Eleventh arson?" I ask.

RBD fills me in on what happened in D.C overnight.

"I take it you haven't had any visions of the other fires?" Major Greenway asks.

"No. I can't say why some fires capture my visions and others don't. But once I start walking, I'm locked into a single one until the investigation is over. No channel hopping to see if there's a more interesting arson out there to examine."

"Frustrating." RBD manages to pack a wealth of sympathy and understanding into his single word response.

"Extremely." Reflexively, I tug on my earlobe. Damn, I really need to learn his name. "Let me add this. The lack of a vision doesn't indicate an absence of connection. It is possible I'll catch a vision of one of the other fires in the course of investigating this one."

"There's one more link we haven't explored," Greenway says. "Why one of my wolves is showing up in your visions."

A connection and an oddity I'd clocked in those first visions. Before having a werewolf companion beside me became a dependable routine instead of a suspicious thread to follow.

"Good question. I wish I had an answer." Too much about this situation is off, my own performance included. But I can indulge in a round of self-recrimination later. Right now, I needed to step up my game and find a murderer. "I don't always have to travel to the site of an arson for my investigations, but there's a lot about this case that's out of the norm. I think I should head to D.C."

"Agreed," Major Greenway says.

"Wait, wait, wait. Hold the phone," RBD says. "You do not need to head into possible danger. Keep dreaming safe in your own bed. I'll run your legwork."

"I agree with your RBD." Mimi stretches across the kitchen table to lay a hand on my wrist. "Those trips shred you. After one, it takes all my cooking wiles to lure you back to family dinners and fatten you back up to your fighting weight. Why go through that if it's not necessary this time?"

Without warning, the noise in my ears goes haywire, the static hissing and spiky, desperate, almost violent. Panting, I squeeze my eyes shut against the stabbing discomfort.

Mimi jumps from her seat, her chair falling adding to the crash in my ears, and rushes to my side. I hold my arms up to ward her off, unable to handle any physical stimulus.

The pitch rises to a level so high, so intense, I'm afraid my ears will start to bleed, the staccato frequency sounding like wordless shouts. But rather than a message, all that hits me is excruciating pain.

"Elyria? Lyri? What can we do to help? Are you under attack? Can you lock down your location? What do you have close to hand that you can turn into a weapon?" RBD's whiskey-rich voice pours into my ears, a soothing, mellow relief even if his advice leans toward the combative. "Mimi, ma'am, tell me what's going on."

"Nothing," I say. "Just a little headache. If I leave in the next hour, I can make D.C. by 8:00 or 9:00 tonight, traffic willing."

With my recommitment to the case, the pain disappears as suddenly as it descended, the tinnitus retreating to a low ebb. I shush Meems with a finger against my lips before she can protest.

"If you suggest a hotel, I'll book a room and let you know once I've arrived and checked in."

"We'll get your lodging squared away," Greenway says. "You drive safe. It's supposed to start storming this evening."

"I'd like to go on record as stating this is a bad idea." RBD says. "You should stay home."

"Your lack of confidence in my competency is duly noted." Stung by his rejection, my reply drips with frost.

"Wait, that isn't what–"

"Text me where to go–and any details on the other fires you have. See you later." I press the end button, wishing my cell was an old fashioned princess phone, the kind that lets the other person know without a doubt they've been hung up on in mid-argument.

If only I could linger in my snit, build it into something of enduring distraction.

Boo-hooing over RBD's desire to cut me out of the investigation wouldn't be productive, but it would keep me from having to face the evidence that the ringing in my ears I developed in tandem with the increase in my visionary power is getting worse.

A lot worse.

"What happened?" Mimi asks, hovering but not touching.

"The tinnitus staged a coup. Clobbered me good this time," I say with a chipper grin to cover my unease. She doesn't buy the grin.

"That's it. As much as I want you to connect with your Hottie McWerewolf in person, you are definitely not driving to D.C."

"Ah, Meems. What did I ever do to earn your friendship?" I give her a squeezy hug. "You know I have to go. The ear thing will only get worse if I don't. Besides, this is my job."

"No, honey," she says with rare sadness, returning my hug. "It's your hairshirt."

CHAPTER SEVEN

D*eclan*

LOGAN HAS me check out each of the arson sites to see if my keen nose and sorta kinda apprenticeship with Elyria help pop any clues that a shedload of highly trained emergency response personnel didn't pick up. Other than the obvious–our firebug likes to use himself some gasoline as an accelerant–I get nada más from the scenes, beyond a desire to skip the next few bonfires out at Hearthstone.

Some materials just shouldn't catch fire. They stink.

Bad.

Elyria's updated arrival time comes and goes while I'm at the ninth site, diligently abusing my olfactory system in the name of justice instead of heading to see if she's okay.

If we're okay.

She's settled in for the night. What's your ETA on 10? Logan texts.

She's safe. That's good. I tell myself I can ride herd on my urge to get eyes on her until morning. Myself snorts his doubt. I tell myself not to be such a weirdo proto stalker. Myself shakes his head at my choice of priorities. I stop dialoging with myself. He's impossible to deal with when he's in that mood.

Thunder rumbles in the distance as I climb into my vehicle. I put the SUV in gear and call Logan.

"Anything?" he asks.

"Nary a dropped cigarette butt nor a one of a kind shoe tread. Firebug is 9 for 10 on choice and lavish overuse of accelerant. Headed to see if it bumps up to an even 10 now. How'd she seem?"

"Tired."

"That's it?"

"If I say beautiful, are you going to try to rip my throat out next time you see me?"

"Maybe."

"Then yeah, that's it." Before I can call him a smart ass, he adds, "Nessa reported on Ms. Naismith's background. Seems the woman entered the arson investigation after her family died in a suspicious house fire. The person responsible remains unknown. Presumably at large. One fire chief who's worked with her on a couple of cases believes Naismith's motivation lies in a hope she'll find the killer during one of her investigations."

"Understandable goal, even if the method seems akin to trying to find a needle in a haystack." I loosen my grip before I break the leather covered steering wheel.

There's so much missing in Logan's bare bones recitation. Horror. Grief. Courage. It takes everything in me to keep from beating a path straight to her hotel.

She might not need a hug at near one o'clock in the morning, but damned if I don't.

"She doesn't accept money, she doesn't play politics, and she's not chummy, but her clearance rate has earned her respect even from folks who aren't normally fans of parahumans."

"How does she earn a living if she doesn't charge for her investigative work?"

"Apparently your vision walker's day job is ceramic artist. Makes a decent living at it."

"Does this mean we can cross her off your watch list?" I make a note to see if I can find her work online.

"Provisionally. Hold on, Nessa's calling. Let me conference her in."

"Enzo Costa is the linchpin," my cousin says without waiting for hellos. "He has a connection to each of the buildings and or the affected owners and renters. In some cases multiple points of connection. And he has a guess about our probable bad guy. An engineering elf named Larry Featheringham. Brother of Travis Featheringham, the alchemist elf who ended up in the hospital with his son after trying to keep their house from becoming burnt toast. Costa provided the seed money for their research and development startup ten years ago. What were they trying to develop, you ask? A portable gas chromatography unit intended to speed up identification of accelerants in the field."

I whistle. "That's an in your face clue."

"Anything else?" Logan asks.

"Lots. The company imploded–flaky science and bad money management. The brothers went in opposite directions. A few years later, Larry landed in prison for check kiting–do people really still write checks?–and related fraud charges, nothing to do with Costa. He was let out on parole about six months ago, overcrowding issues, and promptly disappeared. Travis kicked around the country, working a series of third-rate postdocs before applying for a job at another of Costa's startups about two years ago. Costa, apparently big on second chances, okayed the hire. By all accounts, Travis has kept his head down and produced solid, if not innovative, work."

"Guess it's time to track down Brother Larry," I say.

While we toss around possible next steps, I navigate from Georgetown along the Tidal Basin of the National Mall, enjoying the pomp of monuments lighted up against the gloomy night sky. At this time of night, traffic is nearly nonexistent, hallelujah. I hit 295 South and head to a tired business district just inside the border between D.C. and Maryland.

As I roll to a stop at the curb outside the tenth arson site, an independent self-storage business, I take a moment to admire the vintage

Ford truck parked across the street, its light blue paint glowing under a street light. Someone had a suh-weet ride.

"I'm here." I turn off the SUV and climb out to assess the big picture. Yellow crime tape flutters in the wind, reminding me of the visions and our mysterious eleventh fire.

"Right. Nessa, keep searching for Larry's bolthole. Dec, I don't hold out a lot of hope this last site will give you any more than the others, but check it out then get some sleep. We'll regroup in the morning, see if Ms. Naismith, and by extension you, have had a vision that gives us any better leads."

"What, you're not gonna tell me to be careful?" I ask.

"Who am I, your mother? Sniff, report, sleep. That's it. Do not pass go on the way to a certain stranger's hotel."

"Killjoy."

"That's Major Cute Killjoy to you."

CHAPTER EIGHT

E *lyria*

DONE STEALTHING around the perimeter of the self-storage company to ensure I'm alone, the hum in my ears more drowsy bee than angry hornet, I adjust my go bag to a less annoying position across my chest and straighten from my semi-crouch, a tiny, little, smidgeon of hope unfurling in my chest.

The structure facing the street may be a blackened shell, but its two untouched companion buildings give me a two out of three chance that my hunch didn't go up in smoke between my hotel and here.

The static in my ears gives a happy bounce of agreement.

I circle back to the darkest corner of the second building and yank on the nearest door.

Locked. No surprise, really, but easy would be nice for a change. I sidle along the building toward the next entrance.

"You don't text, you don't call. And now you're sneaking around on me?" RBD asks at my back, his husky voice warming me from the inside out like that first sip of bourbon after Dry January. "I see how it is."

"How what is?" I aim for cool and suave, aloof, even. The Jill Bond of arson investigators. Until I catch first sight of him and my heart revs into fifth gear. Damn, his brand of bourbon is even more potent IRL than the visions.

"Our relationship."

"What relationship?" My pulse spikes again, more leery of the R word than at being surprised by an almost stranger in a mostly strange place. A stranger who didn't want me traveling to his turf in the first place. I scowl. "We don't have a relationship."

"Couples therapy, identifying our love languages–I like words of affirmation, but I especially dig physical touch. Partner yoga." He nods. "Yeah, we have a lot of tools to help nip this issue in the bud before it derails us."

"Issue?"

"Our communication skills. Or lack thereof. We need an intervention."

"I don't even know your name."

"You're only proving my point." As he comes closer I back up until I'm the tomato filling in an RBD-door sandwich.

"Hi. I'm Captain Robert Bruce Declan McDowell, U.S. Army Special Forces. Call me Dec. Why are you here? Should I be flattered you're in that big a hurry to meet me in the flesh you'd forgo your beauty sleep, or is something else going on? And so there's no confusion in the future–see, I'm working on those comms skills already–you could have just shot me a text. I don't usually make house calls, but in your case, I absolutely will. May I kiss you?"

"You...What...I...No." I plant my hands on his chest to push him away, but they don't cooperate. Instead, they slide down to his waist, taking their sweet time, before my index fingers find the loops on his jeans and tug him closer. Heat from his body seeps into me. His scent, richer, earthier, than in the visions, seduces my nose. It takes a greater act of will than I've ever willed before to lay down what's what. "No kissing. No interventions. No house calls. I'm here because I'm following a long shot."

"Not to see me?" He looks bummed. Forlorn. Dejected. Crestfallen.

Possibly in need of a kiss to soothe his disappointment.

I stay firm in my resolve. He's likely dangled that lure out to a hundred women. I don't need to be number 101. Especially not with a guy who wanted me to stay home.

"You ought to go on the stage. You're a natural ham."

He chuckles. I shiver. He inches closer, encasing me in the protection of his body.

"Seriously now," he says, dipping his head to speak directly into my ear. "What was so compelling that you left the safety and comfort of your bed in the dark of night instead of waiting until morning?"

"During one of my early cases, I liaised with a small town volunteer fire department. One of the crew was a guy named Goose. Goose Featheringham."

"Featheringham?"

"Not a name you run across every day, right? When I ran across it in the materials Logan shared, I ran a search to see if it's the same man whose house got torched last night."

"What'd you find? And what's the connection to this place?" His lips tickle my ear, jiggling the tinnitus into a muted peel of delighted bells.

Weird.

"Zip on the VFD records. Seems they had a glitch in their system backup, lost a couple of years' worth of personnel files. We'll need to follow up, see if we can locate someone who actually worked with the guy, maybe has a photo from the time. As for this place...it could be nothing."

I fiddle with one of the loops on his jeans, a wash of shyness stinging my cheeks. It's one thing to investigate an arson scene with a hairy, friendly, helpful werewolf. Another to share an unplanned, unwise–if *ah-may-zing*–kiss with said werewolf in his two-legged form while vision walking.

Both kept RBD, *Dec*, at a handleable distance.

It's something else altogether when the only thing keeping me from melting into a puddle of desire is Dec's heated, hard weight pinning me to the cool, metal door.

Even my lingering hurt from his initial lack of enthusiasm for my traveling to DC is a weak block against my totally unprofessional, unprecedented attraction. But worse, the attraction is interfering with my brain, urging me to investigate whether he tastes as good in real life as he did in our vision.

The hell with that. I haven't spent five years building up my talents to chuck them aside for a pretty man.

I let go of the loops. After a bare moment of hesitation, he takes my cue and a medium step back.

"But you don't think it's nothing," Dec says.

"No. I channeled my frustration at getting stuck toward plowing through the rest of the info, which included a manifest of customers for the self-storage company. Two more names caught my attention. F. Duck. and G. Down."

"More riffing on the last name?"

"That's my working theory."

He fills me in on the brothers Featheringham, Travis and Larry.

"Larry's been in and out of prison for the last ten or so years. I'll get Nessa to cross check his stints inside, see if there's a gap that falls at the right time."

"Nessa...?"

"Our communications officer." Even in this dark corner, his really big teeth gleam as he grins. "Also, my cousin."

"Kissing cousin?" Did that just come out of my mouth? The sting factor in my cheeks zooms past mild pink to *please-let-the-earth-swallow-me-right-now* red.

"Not that kind of cousin." He cups my cheek, brushing his thumb over the heat. There goes using the shadows to keep my embarrassment to myself. He runs his hand over my shoulder and down my arm before lacing our hands together. "Besides, there's only one person I'm interested in kissing these days. My partner."

"Partner?"

"Yeah. She's smart, cute, and sexy as hell. Also prickly, quick-witted, and possibly a little too used to going it alone in situations where she could use some muscle for back up." He twists the door-knob with his free hand. There's a scrunch and pop of metal, and the solid presence of the door behind me disappears. "Well, would you look at that? Door's open."

"Partners?" I ask, a slight variation on the theme. How did we get to partners when a minute ago I was ready to pull a Joe Friday imper-sonation and be all just the facts for the rest of the investigation?

"Don't tax yourself about it right now. We have work to do."

I take a big breath to argue, inflating my lungs to full capacity. The air sighs out of me when I can't quite get my thoughts to line up.

Politely ignoring my inner drama, Dec leads the way into the building.

"You have storage unit numbers to go with these aliases?"

CHAPTER NINE

D *eclan*

"WAIT." Elyria knocks my hand aside and brushes in front of me when we find the first storage unit, and I attempt round two of impressing her with my manly muscles.

Grabbing a flashlight from her well-worn messenger bag, she starts high before squatting, running the beam around the door jamb. Careful, meticulous, she measures each crack and discoloration, each speck of dust.

It would probably be bad timing to tell her how the squat pulls her jeans just right over her ass. How much I appreciate the view. How turned on it makes me to watch her singular focus. Her...not just competency, but expertise.

"I worked a case where the bad guy liked to boobytrap his hidy-holes," she says, standing straight. "Made me paranoid ever after. This looks clear. And in case this is some poor innocent F. Duck, how about we not do more property damage?"

"Spoilsport."

She rolls her eyes at my grin, but can't hide the small twitch of her lips. Unzipping a flat brown leather case, she chooses a couple of picks and has at the padlock.

"I'd like the story on what case taught you those skills. Can't imagine anyone in law enforcement being eager."

"My dad," she says with a wistfulness that whispers through my soul. "He liked solving puzzles. I never thought about it, but I guess maybe I get that from him. Let's see what we have here."

Pressing the door wide, she runs the flashlight in a grid around an empty unit.

"That's not looking promising." To the left of the door, I flick the switch for the overhead light, a single low wattage bulb. More nothing. Not even dust. We enter the unit, and the door swings shut behind us with a whisper.

The scent of pine spikes in my nose. Pine cleanser, followed by a fake fir air freshener chaser. Not my fave combo. Worse than the gas I've been sniffing all day. I stifle a sneeze.

"Hold up." She rustles in her bag again and clips a filter onto the flashlight. "Turn the light off a sec."

Complying, I follow the beam of the flashlight as she paints another grid, this time on the wall of the entrance. Like the other three walls, the cinder blocks on this one are a mess of scratches and divots. But in this case, the results lean less toward the random accumulation of pockmarks over time and more toward someone having a sustained hissy fit with a screwdriver.

"What's that?" I ask when the light hits a faint, somewhat more cohesive, collection of lines at the base of the wall near the doorframe.

"The Detroit Tigers' D." Reaching out, she stops shy of touching the elaborate capital D before curling her fingers into a fist. "Even with the shallowness of the etching, it had to take a significant amount of time to create something this intricate."

"Time, attention to detail. If you were to keep the door propped open, you'd never see it, but even with the door closed and the regular light on," I turn on the overhead again, "it blends, hiding in plain sight. Clever."

"But why's it there? A message between conspirators? A bored teenager? Cosmic coincidence?" She stumbles, clutching at the sides of her head.

I swoop in to keep her from crashing to her knees. "What's wrong?"

"Tinnitus flare up. It'll pass, just give me a sec."

She presses her forehead into my chest. Supporting her weight, muscles tense and twitchy, I scowl at each corner of the unit with utter futility. It's not like her inner ear problem has a body whose ass I can kick. After too long a time of listening to her pant in the *it hurts* way and not the much preferred *you're making me hot* way, I force my hands to loosen their grip when she shrugs free.

"Better?" I probe her gaze, not bothering to hide my concern. Partners are supposed to be concerned about each other. Her short-lived, thin-lipped smile doesn't reassure me, but I guess now is not the time to sweep her off her feet to cradle in my arms.

Probably something in the partner code of conduct that frowns on shit like that.

"Yeah, better. Mostly, at least. The noise is always there, but sometimes instead of a constant low key tide, the static boils up like a tsunami. Throws me off my stride for a few." She tugs at her ear lobe, seems to realize what she's doing and drops her hand, turning away. "So, reason for its existence, to be determined. But I think it's safe to say, the etching connects the two cases."

"'Tyger tyger, burning bright, in the forests of the night,'" I murmur, complying with her conversational pivot. I could wait to thoroughly debrief her about the tinnitus once we identified our murder-minded arsonist.

"'What immortal hand or eye, could frame thy fearful symmetry?'" she finishes. "You a William Blake fan?"

"That poem at least. Though to be honest, I think he missed an opportunity. Poem would have been more compelling with a were-wolf as the subject."

"Color me unsurprised by your hot take." The last, lingering line between her brow relaxes as she chuckles.

We painstakingly comb every inch of the walls, searching for more tiger tracks but find nothing. Elyria suggests we hit the next unit.

"Fine by me. That damn pine cleanser has royally fucked my sense of smell." I massage my nose, trying to wake it back up as she dutifully relocks the empty unit.

"Does that happen often?" she asks as we head toward the stairs. "Getting overwhelmed by a powerful scent?"

"Thankfully no. But some scents are stealthy buggers. They build in the sinuses until that's all you can smell. Then you stop smelling altogether. That's a dangerous place for a werewolf. Or any shifter, really. We rely on our noses like an early warning system or a bat's echolocation. I've heard olfactory fatigue compared to a seeing person going suddenly full on blind."

"Not fun."

"Not especially." I thread our fingers together as we walk and give a soft pump of support. For a few steps her hand lies inert, like it's lost all animation, but then she's holding my hand. Tentatively and like she'll drop it at the least possible cause, but still, it's reciprocal.

I take it as great progress on the partner front.

We go through the same deal with the second unit's door, and this time she finds a tripwire. We disarm it, me belatedly developing a case of the sweats.

This isn't one of Elyria's visions. If something blows up in our face, she could be harmed. I angle in front of her when we open the door so I can take the brunt of any attack.

"Jackpot."

"This is crazy." She squirrels her way past me and turns in a slow circle just shy of a square folding table piled with papers planted in the middle of the room. "It's like a revenge-minded stalker threw up in here."

"And used his puke to paint the walls."

Scattered among tacked-up schematics of incendiary devices, architectural blueprints, and handwritten notes, hundreds of photos of Enzo Costa paper two of the walls: full color, black and white, some with the eyes exed out, others with doodles in red ink displaying a variety of bloody demises. Costa at work, on dates, speaking at press conferences. The ones of him asleep in his bed rake shivers down my spine. To the right, another corkboard dominates the wall with push-pins connected by colored twine making a macabre timeline, dating right back to when the Featheringham brothers first worked for Costa Industries.

My partner bellies up to the timeline for a closer inspection so I inch along the montage. Near the corner where the two photo walls meet, I hit on something.

Three somethings.

"Hey, check this out." I wave her over and point at the Blueprint of Interest. "Look familiar?"

"Our mystery building. With address. Score."

"How about this?" I flick my forefinger at a drawing below the blueprint.

"The tiger emblem from the baseball bat we found in the first vision." She takes a photo and frowns. "Still doesn't tell us what the heck it represents."

"No, but the two together tell us definitively the fires, the Featheringhams, and the vision are wrapped up together." I pivot to the second wall and tap the first of dozens in a series of 8 x 10 glossy full color photos. "It's a leap, but this may explain how Logan's business card wound up in the building from the visions. Could be the card was scooped up as a souvenir."

The series tells a story. Logan and Costa, in tuxedos amid a sea of similarly clad men and women in finery all the colors of the rainbow, shake hands and exchange cards. A stunning young woman with purple hair and purple eyes and a smile to rival the sun jostles Costa and the card misses his pocket, fluttering unnoticed to the floor as Costa reassures her all is well with a solar powered grin of his own. The crowd starts moving toward an entrance one way, while the purple haired looker heads the other direction. In the final shot, Costa glances over his shoulder at the woman, but she faces the camera, ignorant of his interest, her face robbed of all animation.

Quiet pools in the room, building into something solid as Elyria's attention remains riveted to the final photo. She reaches toward the image before letting her hand fall, closing her eyes as if she's hurt.

"What?"

"The woman reminds me of my sister. What Ravenna might have looked like if she'd lived long enough to grow into the promise of her cheekbones." She tugs on her ear lobe, a lone frustrated, grief-tinged yank, before spinning away from the display, jerking her head toward the timeline. "I have something to share, too."

She leads us to the end of the timeline and taps her finger on the final cluster of data. Three colored push pins hold up various sizes of paper with writing. Addresses, names, the order of when the fires ignited, how much accelerant to use at each location. Wait.

"That's our mystery building."

"Bingo. Check the date and time."

"5:00 a.m. today."

"We may be able to stop the murder, Dec."

CHAPTER TEN

E*lyria*

AFTER DEC FINISHES DROOLING over Old Blue–"What a beauty. Ford F100, what, late 70s, early 80s? All original parts? Never mind, let me pretend for a while"–he calls Logan, and we hash out an approach as I pilot Dad's old truck along deserted roads. Rain just light enough to foil the intermittent wiper setting catches the yellowy glare of my headlights.

"I have a team headed to the storage place, and we're thirty minutes behind you," Logan says. "Stay safe."

"Aw, see? You care. That's so sweet." Dec chuckles when Logan ends the call without a goodbye.

"What do you think we'll find?"

"I could ask you the same question. You're the one who has visions. I'm just the lucky son of a gun who gets invited to the party."

"I wouldn't call that luck. And I'm still not sure how it's happening. Ravenna used to be able to pull me into her visions on purpose. Frustrated the hell out of me as a teenager and into my early twenties, like, girl, stop dragging me into your beeswax, I have enough of my own. Never would have guessed how much I miss it. Her. My parents."

"I'm sorry for your loss."

I nod in acceptance, his simple words triggering a lump to grow at the base of my throat and cutting off any words I might say. Breathing through the wash of guilt, the constant companion to my grief, I focus on turning off of the two-lane highway.

Flick on the turn signal, slow down, accelerate out of the curve.

"My power changed after they died. I went from being mad good at games of chance and guessing what my parents would get me for my birthday surprise to"–I wave a hand–"all this. It can be a little extra sometimes."

"I can imagine. I was born and raised in a pack, but I've met a few people whose shifter genetics didn't activate until well into adulthood. If they're not a part of a pack or somehow don't know they have shifter roots, things can get dicey."

"I wish visionaries had a pack. Growing up, it was just the four of us. Our small town wasn't particularly para-friendly, so we didn't advertise our abilities, you know? Tried not to draw attention. Become a target. Fat lot of good that did."

"The authorities never found the one responsible for the fire?"

"Did some research on me, huh?"

"Logan's a worrywart." Dec offers a rueful grimace.

"I get it. Better safe than sorry. By the time local law enforcement stopped trying to pin it on me, they'd lost too much of the evidence trail. They finally called in the staties, but the two departments seemed more interested in conducting a turf war than an investigation." I check the GPS read out and waggle my jaw, trying to relieve old tension. "It's still considered active, but it might as well be a cold case, given the lack of progress. We're about two miles out."

"Right. I'll change. But we're not done with this conversation."

Threat or promise? The fluttery roil in my chest can't decide.

He tugs off his black tee shirt. I only ogle his muscled chest for a brief second before wrenching my gaze back to the road. The rain picks up, and I flip the wipers to a steady swipe, hyper aware of the rasping slide on his zipper.

How did I wind up with a hunk getting naked in my truck? And why do we have to be on our way to visit a crime scene?

His seatbelt clicks open, and I slow down, unsure of what will come next. His shift had been fast and unannounced in the vision. Would anything be different this time?

Ten percent of the population. That's all we are. Ten percent. And most of us don't wave semaphores around announcing to the world the little something extra lurking in our genes. Has any of the edutainment depictions of shifters changing come close to capturing the real thing?

Warmth engulfs my body as an unseen shimmer musses the air in the truck's enclosed cabin. The scent of old growth forest fills my nose, beckoning with secrets. A moment later, a subsonic burst of power makes my heart skip, my ears pop. I hold on to the wheel, eyes wide, desperate not to crash. After a second, two, three, the sound of a furry body shaking itself fluffy returns the cab to normal.

"No poking holes in the bench leather with your really big claws, buster."

He licks my cheek and settles his head on my thigh with a wolfy sigh of contentment. It takes gargantuan effort not to sink my hand into the silky fur around his ear.

Who is this guy, this friendly werewolf, who calls himself my partner and whom I let crowd my personal space?

Mimi could explain this peculiar thing between us. But she's not here. And we're headed into a potentially fraught situation. And, well, *this* mystery is just going to have to wait.

Despite trying to stomp on it, the stubborn grain of hope that cracked open at the storage place sends out a tendril. Enough details changed during each of the visions that I can't predict what we'll find, but what if we're not too late?

I kill the headlights and coast to a stop down the street from the stand-alone building. Yellow glows in each window, enticing us onward. Looping my go kit across my body, I open the door and Dec jumps over me, no hesitation, no by your leave, and becomes instantly drenched.

"Excuse you." He woofs, soft and unrepentant, tail wagging. I take a deep breath and plunge into the storm. Getting vision wet way outranks getting real life soaked.

Dec leads the way behind the building. For once it isn't the Geiger counter in my ears but the talent I was born with that alerts as we get to the corner where we found the baseball bat. On instinct, I stir through the wet dirt, not really expecting a return on my action. The bat had only been there the one time. But my fingers brush against a round object. Hiding the glare of the flashlight against my belly, a certain someone's interested snout nudging into the way, I inspect my discovery.

"The Tigers' baseball." I heft it into the air a couple of times before wiping the ball clean and tucking the familiar weight into my bag. "When we were kids Ravenna and I lived, breathed, and slept baseball, you know? I even pitched on the softball team in high school. My sister ended up cheering, but she never lost her love for Detroit." Odd, though, that it's another object altogether, for all that it fits into a baseball theme.

Of course, nothing about this investigation has been standard. Why should this be any different?

We peer around the corner of the building. A small moving van is parked at the rear entrance, doors open and halfway filled with boxes but empty of people.

We stick to the shadows to reach the back entrance. I test the glass door, ready with my lockpicks, but it swings open. Dec makes a beeline for the door to the staircase, looking over his shoulder as if to say hurry up. I open that door too, and we inch our way to the second floor.

Even on four feet and sopping, he moves with a stealth I can't match, blast it.

Voices, raised but muffled, reverberate down the long hall from the tiger junk office, one angry, the other pleading.

My heart revs into overdrive, and I race toward the room, trying to match the speed of a werewolf.

That stubborn hope pushes through the earth, stretching for sunlight.

Until Dec bounds into the middle of the argument, the middle of danger. Hope shrivels.

Reckless man.

Doesn't he know he's not bullet proof? Not flame retardant?

He could die. Die like my parents. Like my sister.

I freeze in the doorway, all but my hands, which shake with an uncontrollable palsy. My breath backs up in my lungs. My ears shriek.

Two blond men, presumably the Featheringham brothers, both still very much alive, stand on opposite sides of a large desk. They stare at four-footed Dec as though he's a genie popping out of a bottle.

The one on the nearside of the desk, the one with the gun, redirects his aim toward Dec, but addresses his brother, "You promised to see this through. That means you don't turn chicken livered at the last second because of a sudden attack of conscience. And that this monster, wherever you found him"–he waggles the gun to indicate Dec–"isn't stopping the show either."

Crouched low, Dec snarls, the sound vibrating deep in my bones. He circles away from the door and the gunman follows, aim keeping pace with each step Dec takes. Breaking eye contact with the guy, Dec jerks his head at me as if to say scram.

No.

No, I'm not leaving someone else to die, not when I can do something to prevent it this time. The hell with that.

Dipping my knees, I find my center and pull air deep into my belly. The baseball nestles in my hand like an old friend.

"Dodge," I say. "Now."

Trusting my partner to comply, I don't hesitate.

In one fluid move, I wind up and bean the gunman in the side of the head. He collapses, his gun clattering across the wood floor.

I secure the weapon first then check the gunman.

Out, but not dead

I pull a pair of handcuffs from my go kit and fasten his wrists behind his back, leaving him on his side in case he barfs while unconscious.

"Little help here." The voice sounds wheezy and faint.

I round the desk to find Dec standing with his front paws on the second man's prone body, tongue hanging out in a happy grin. Despite the man's protests, I cuff him too. Someone else could sort out the dude's role.

In the meantime, I'd choose prudence over trust.

Giving in to need finally, I seek out Dec's silky ear.

He leans into me as I scratch, a solid, damp, warm weight groaning with pleasure.

We'd done it. Prevented a murder, at least one more arson, and what looked like conspiracy to commit industrial sabotage with a side helping of vendetta.

Not bad for a rainy night's work. Not bad at all.

"I am so mad at you, I could spit," I say with one last scritch, and walk away as a dozen uniformed men and women burst into the room.

CHAPTER ELEVEN

D*eclan*

DRY, dressed, and back on two feet, I approach Logan at the center of the chaos spreading out from the building's back entrance. He raises his chin to acknowledge my presence but continues issuing orders to the men and women clustered around him with earnest faces.

"Got it? Good. Go."

"Yes, sir." They scurry away to do his bidding.

"Were we ever that young?"

"You still are."

"Hey, is that any way to talk to the guy who delivered not one but two bad actors into your grabby hands? And managed not to blow himself or his woman up in the process?"

"Your woman, huh?"

"If she'll have me."

A big if.

She accepted my help on this whirlwind of an investigation, but it's clear she's used to working alone. And that I did something to piss her off.

What if she's not feeling the same spark of connection? Or my mistake, whatever it was, is a deal killer?

I kick a clump of mud. "This sucks."

"What, having to work at wooing a woman? It'll do you good. Put hair on your chest." His amusement makes me scowl. Logan answers another raft of questions from a new batch of eager beavers before barking an order that cuts through the noise and has Berkeley picking up his pace. Turning back to me, he clamps a hand on my shoulder. "Dec. You won't know if you don't ask. And I'm sure as shit not going to put up with you moping from here to eternity about the one who got away all because you had an attack of cold feet."

"If she says yes, it'll mean me traveling with her on investigations." I hold my breath, braced for no.

"You're three steps behind, my friend. I started the paperwork to extend your leave another thirty days about ten minutes after we hung up the phone yesterday morning. If things work as you hope, we can discuss a more permanent solution."

"What?"

"You were ready to tear out my throat trying to get to Ms. Naismith when she called. Believe we call that a really big clue. Now, how about you let me handle the logistics and you go rustle up a yes?"

"Yes, sir."

CHAPTER TWELVE

E *lyria*

"WE STILL DON'T UNDERSTAND what's up with the tigers." I tug on the ear not covered in phone, trying to dislodge the itchy sensation of a task left undone as I fill Meems in. My tinnitus isn't grouchy so much as insistent, like a motormouth striving to make their point before they run out of air. "But the authorities have mounds of papers to go through at the storage place, so it has to be only a matter of time before someone figures out the connection to the Featheringhams' plot-o-mayhem."

"Way to go, Lyri! Two baddies for the toil of one. That's working smarter, not harder."

"Have you been reading those self-help blogs again?"

"Don't you heckle me. My addiction is purely benign. Besides, much more interesting is whether you're going to follow my suggestion about RBD."

"I don't know, Meems." I swing in a one eighty to retrace my steps, pacing at the edge of the building's parking lot. Out of the way of the response team. Not hiding exactly, not from a raft of Special Ops shifters, but not underfoot. "I'm not sure I'm cut out for–"

"Whatever you're about to say, stop. You've spent five years making grief your priority and forcing yourself into a straightjacket of practicality. You've done amazing things and without question, you'll continue. But the world is a bountiful place. Opening yourself up to experiencing the breadth of it doesn't mean you'll forget your family. You can still honor them and take a damn chance. Trust that the universe will provide."

"Trust, huh?"

"Trust," she says with a sharp click on the second T. "Plus, girl, it's only coffee."

But is it? Only coffee?

The panic and outrage I felt when he put himself in harm's way would beg to differ.

Could I stomach opening the door even to something as low stakes as coffee with a man whose job requires him to make life or death sacrifices on the regular?

The tinnitus gets louder, more loquacious, more insistent, as though it, too, is on Team Declan.

Team Take a Damn Chance.

"I'll think about it. I need to get back," I say, trying to end the call.

But by the time we hang up, she manages to prod me from thinking to promising.

Damn, sneaky earth mother bestie.

Belly jumping with anxious–excited?–pop rocks, I turn toward the building. Dec sits on the trunk of a sedan, eyes closed, face angled toward the lightening sky.

As if he can sense the weight of my attention, his intent blue eyes meet mine, making my heart stutter.

Shoving my phone into my bag, I walk toward him, maintaining eye contact, until I stand before him, not quite between his legs. I open my mouth and close it without speaking. I try again. No dice. I wipe my damp palms on my thighs then wonder what to do with them.

What made coffee so hard?

He captures one of my hands and squeezes a dash of courage into my veins. I clear my throat.

"I'm still mad."

"So I gathered. Care to tell me why? I'll fix it if I can."

"I don't think it's on you." My gaze dances from object to object, knee, bumper, tail light until I settle on his face again. "I think I'm mad because you scared me. You rushed in like you were wearing Kevlar instead of black and silver fur. That man could have shot you. You could have died."

His face goes soft. He loops a strand of hair behind my ear. "You know I train for these scenarios."

"Doesn't make it easier to witness. But, Mimi says I can't continue through life alone in an attempt to protect myself from more hurt. Mostly because she'll kick my butt if I try. So I'll work on my knee jerk response."

"I could lead you through some training exercises. Knowledge is power, they say."

"Sounds like you read the same self-help blogs as Meems."

We smile for a second before my eyes flitter away again. Tail light, knee, sexy collar bone I wouldn't mind examining closer.

"What else? Your partner is all ears." Another squeeze sends a new dash of comfort from my fingers to my heart. I clear my throat once more. I could do this.

"Do you w–"

"Yes."

"You didn't let me finish." I give him a narrow-eyed stare. It bounces right off him.

"Answer is still yes."

"Would you–"

"Yes."

"Robert Bruce Declan."

"That's my name."

"Stop being an asshat and let me ask you out."

"Okay, I'll go out with you."

"I haven't asked yet." I try to retrieve my hand. Grinning, he foils my plan, tugging me closer.

"But now you don't have to worry about my answer."

"Insufferable."

"Eminently sufferable. I mean, you only have to think of my really big–"

"Enough. Robert Bruce Declan McDowell. Will you have coffee with me?"

"I'd rather have tea." He settles his really big hands at my waist. Goosebumps shiver awake along every square inch of my skin. "Should we kiss to make it official?"

Nodding, I rise onto my toes to meet him halfway, giddy and light and bold with success.

Tiger. Lyri. Detroit. Sis. Listen. Listentome. Help. Me. Help. Detroit. Tiger. Please please please. Please work. Please work. Lyrihelpme.

Stumbling, I crash into him, my forehead cracking against his jaw. He catches me as my knees give out, reversing our positions so that I'm the one sitting on the trunk.

Surrounded by his heat, his scent, his body, I tremble as the message repeats once more before cutting out.

I gasp as the pain and static in my ears, my most constant companions of the last five years, disappear with a snap.

Poof, gone.

I blink at the loudness of the silence. Echoey and vast and somehow, some way...lonely.

"Talk to me. What do you need? How can I help?"

"I got a message." I point to my ear, scrunching my face in confusion. "From my sister?"

"Your sister Ravenna. Who died in the house fire."

"The one and only." I rub my sternum but it doesn't dislodge my sudden onset case of the willies. "I think...I think she's in danger."

"So let's go rescue her." He wipes a tear from my cheek with his thumb.

"Just like that?"

"Just like that."

He kisses the spot he cleared, a gentle buss. I wrap a hand around his nape and redirect his aim. Our lips fuse, and I let myself sink into this really big moment.

There are worse ways to spend a dawn than planning to save your sister and kissing a hot werewolf.

ABOUT THE AUTHOR

J. Keely Thrall writes thrilling, enthralling paranormal and contemporary romance. A proud member of the Stays Up Too Late Society of Book Addicts (our motto: just one more page, I swear!), she's super excited to share a story with the world that will keep others turning the pages all night long. Or at least some of the night. It is a short story, after all.

You can discover more about Keely's writing at her website **www. jkeelythrall.com** (while you're there, sign up for her newsletter!) Follow her on Facebook (**www.facebook.com/jkeelythrall**), Insta-gram (**https://www.instagram.com/jkeelythrall/**), Bookbub (**https://www.bookbub.com/profile/j-keely-thrall**), and Goodreads (**https://www.goodreads.com/jkeelythrall**).

Oh, and hey, help a debut author out and leave a review on your favorite book selling site!

FALLING INTO PLACE

LAUREL WANROW

CHAPTER ONE

S pring 1867
　　Peaks District, England

A HAND REACHED into the mixing bowl as Mary Clare Pemberton folded in the dried apples. In a practiced move, she blocked her youngest sister with her elbow.

"Why can't I taste it?" howled Mary Grace.

"Do you see that recipe? Where does it say, 'Mix in germs liberally'? Go away."

With a flounce, Mary Grace ran from their family's farm kitchen, probably for the weaving room. But Ma wouldn't object to her disciplining the six-year-old.

Mary Clare began spooning batter into the buttered tin cups. Her sister Mary Ellen arrived to refill Ma's tea, complained the kettle wasn't hot, then accidently turned off the gas. Mary Clare relit the tricky burner, but the almost-teenager stomped out instead of waiting. Mary Clare sighed.

She'd finished dropping dollops when Granny hobbled in. "Did I tell you raspberry? It's the birthday girl's favorite."

Mary Clare had discussed the order with Granny's friend. "I reminded Mrs. Silvie no one has raspberries this early in the spring. She agreed cinnamon apple was fine." Mary Clare scraped the bowl while Granny harumphed, checked the kettle and settled at the table to wait.

"In the old days, we'd have plenty of dried on hand," Granny said. "Right up to the next season."

"You had only three children, Granny. Seven means—"

Returning, Mary Ellen chimed in with Mary Clare on the oft-repeated family mantra, "You make do."

While Mary Ellen refilled Ma's mug and Granny's—thank the Creator—Mary Clare spooned cinnamon and sugar over the muffin batter. Only five of the girls still lived at home on their parents' sheep farm, but that meant the summer fruits Ma and Granny put up lasted merely a month longer. The vegetables, of course, lasted forever. Mary Clare should be out of the house already, like her two oldest sisters, but patching together part-time cook's assistant jobs in Chapel Hollow didn't cover living expenses. And…her Knack was an issue.

If only she had a Knack for growing plants, the most in-demand skill in the rural Farmlands shire. Her Knack wasn't the kind one mentioned in conversation, polite or otherwise. Folks outside the family assumed she wasn't a Knack-bearer. The magical Knacks weren't everything. Without one, her oldest sister, Mary Alice, had secured a job at Wellspring Collective, a cooperative farm at the edge of town, managing their canning inventory and shipping. She and their second-oldest sister, Mary Beth, who had a grower Knack, shared a room in Wellspring's bunkhouse.

As Mary Clare slid the tins into the oven, Mary Grace darted in and swiped the batter spoon.

"Soon I'll have a job with no little sisters underfoot!" called Mary Clare, with a glance at the clock. She hardly needed to. Daily baking had ingrained an automatic thirty-minute reminder into her head.

During the baking, she washed up to be ready to deliver the muffins while they were still warm, so a customer wouldn't hesitate to hand over the payment. Now if only she had that spoon to finish up—

The back door burst open, and Mary Alice rushed in. "You're here!" she said breathlessly as she grasped Mary Clare's shoulders, her eyes gleaming. "I volunteered to fetch you as soon as I heard. Come on!"

"Heard what?" Granny asked before Mary Clare could. "Not trouble?"

No, it wasn't trouble. Mary Clare could sense that through her Knack. Excitement and joy rolled off of Mary Alice, and Mary Clare forgot her lecture about kitchen cleanliness and reached up on tippy-toes to hug her taller sister. Mary Clare bounced twice on the spot. "You're thrilled for me? Why?"

Mary Alice lifted a finger, and trepidation flowed forth. "Ah-ah. You can't! Not now."

Mary Clare's Knack shifted again to match her sister's emotion. "Darn it all, I had *no* warning." Frowning, she backed away, batting the air between them as Mary Alice moved her hands in the boxing motion Ma always made to indicate Mary Clare should ward her Knack.

She pressed her forehead, bringing up barriers to block incoming feelings. "I don't need reminders," she huffed. "I secure it when I'm anywhere else." Because if she didn't, and swayed the wrong stranger's emotions, she'd be labeled a Basin witch and banned from the magical Blighted Basin valley forever.

Thus, she'd lived at home longer than most young women, perfecting her warding. But seeing her sisters' freedom swelled her urge for independence and spurred her goal of living outside their tight-knit family.

The risk would be worth it. "Ugh. I'm so *tired* of family interfering," she muttered.

Mary Alice sighed. "Consider it for your own good. Get changed and come."

"What exactly is the news?" asked Granny.

"Wellspring's kitchen assistant has up and left with no notice," squealed Mary Alice. "Rumor is, she either got a job at the new station diner up at Cross Corners, or she's run off with an animacambire, but our cook isn't saying. The best news is, Mrs. Betsy came to ask me if Mary Clare might be available."

"To replace her?" Mary Clare asked breathlessly. This was the answer to her dreams.

Mary Alice shook her head. "That wasn't mentioned. She needs kitchen help *now*. With the new growers who came on, and planting season in full swing, Mrs. Betsy is beside herself. You're every bit as proficient as that girl was, and I think you and Mrs. Betsy would suit, if only you keep…"

Mary Clare didn't wait for the rest. She spun for the stairs. In her room, she changed into her newest bib and brace and a clean flannel shirt. As for what to do with her braided hair, she hesitated. Curly hair never behaved. With no time for more, she found a pressed kerchief, brushed back the wayward red strands from her face and covered the lot. Perfect. She pounded down the stairs, and the sweet scent of browning sugar met her.

"No," she cried. "The muffins for Mrs. Silvie!"

But Granny already had the tins out of the oven. Breathing her thanks, Mary Clare grabbed one tray and lifted each muffin onto the cooling rack.

"Is she expecting them now?" An edge of worry seeped into Mary Alice's question.

Oh, dear. "Yes." Mary Clare pressed a hand to her forehead and re-warded her Knack. This was all too exciting, and she'd best do that immediately. Forming a plan, she arranged the muffins in the flat basket she used for delivering baked goods, already lined with a fresh cloth. "Mary Ellen?" she called. "Would you deliver the muffins to Mrs. Silvie?"

Mary Ellen appeared in the doorway with a thoughtful expression, like she had no idea what the errand involved, when she'd tagged along numerous times. "For half your fee."

"One-tenth," snapped Mary Clare. "Otherwise, I deliver them myself and am late to Wellspring." She leveled a raised-brow-stare at the twelve-year-old.

"Now, Mary Ellen, be a dear and help your sister," cooed Mary

Alice. "Think on it a minute. If she makes a good impression and is offered this position, Mary Delia will surely move into her empty room, leaving you a room to yourself."

Her sister's excited gasp as she ran to the coat closet said she hadn't thought that far ahead. Mary Clare rolled her eyes and followed to don her own woolen jacket.

The trio left the house and crossed under the cherry trees to the gate. She took a deep breath. The blossoms hadn't opened yet, but white buds capped the branches, and the promise of their sweet fragrance was in the air. Mary Alice held open the gate, and Mary Clare handed Mary Ellen the basket. "Thank you for your help."

Mary Ellen nodded. "One-tenth." With the basket held carefully in both hands, she set off, then called over her shoulder, "Go, get that job."

"I certainly plan to." She checked her Knack wards once more.

KNEELING on the concrete floor of Wellspring's workshop, Rivley Slipwing pecked a screwdriver at the dirt wedged between the gears of a machine's leg joint. How had a grower ruined a perfectly fine clockwork spider after only two days in the field? Gravel showered down, but didn't clear the mechanism. Rivley pressed his lips tight and got to his feet. At the workbench, he found an ice pick, started back, then fetched a canvas drop cloth.

He lifted the spider applicator onto the spread canvas and brought in another. Both new growers had complained the clockwork legs weren't agile enough to walk the planting rows on the sloped hillsides. They were.

Under his questioning, one fellow confessed his machine had rolled down the slope planted in spinach and into a gully. Rivley knew that field quite well, since until a month ago he'd been one of the raptor shifters patrolling the new plantings from the air and picking off mice and other farm vermin. In a year of flights, he'd never seen a machine *roll*.

The ice pick fit perfectly between the small sprockets, dislodging sprinkles of powder. He pulled over a crate and settled into the work, flicking out grit before dousing the joint with oil to flush the remaining dirt. He bent the joint to expose a different section of the gears and wiggled the pointed tool into those spaces.

The rear legs weren't as tightly compacted as the front two. He tried to imagine the fall. Forward, like onto its knees?

A *thump* interrupted his thoughts. Outside the shop, Master Brightwell had dropped his leather travel case into a waiting cart. The older dark-skinned man with springy white hair strode in with a smaller case.

Wellspring's head mechanic—and Rivley's mentor—shook his head at the debris under the machine. "Good morning, Mr. Slipwing. Any hope of returning that equipment to Mr. Hortens' workers this morning?"

"Well, no gears appear out of alignment."

"Several hours, then, a morning's annoyance. Don't let our spiders go out again until you've instructed the growers and watched them practice here in the farmyard."

"Didn't they have training with Mr. Hortens?"

Master Brightwell nodded as he unfolded wire-rimmed glasses and put them on. "Most assuredly, they did. However, that doesn't mean the new hires paid enough mind." He went to the workbench. "Taking a few of my own tools so I can inspect any potential purchase as I wish. Duplicates here of everything, so I won't leave you short." Master Brightwell sounded excited as he dropped the tools into his case.

Who wouldn't be? The farm sale might be a day's travel across Blighted Basin, but the poster listed all sorts of machines. Master Brightwell had his eye on a steam lift, a machine purported to lift a worker to a tree's upper branches to aid in picking fruit. If it worked well, they hoped to reproduce another before the cherries ripened a month from now.

Master Brightwell came to the opposite side of the spider machine, making a cursory check of its oil before he returned his glasses to their pocket and tucked the tool case under one arm. "I leave the workshop operations in your capable hands, Mr. Slipwing. I wouldn't feel as comfortable traveling without you here. Address the inventory as you can between Mr. Hortens' needs for the growers."

Rivley rose and wiped his hands on a rag he kept in his leather apron. "With any luck, this is the worst that will come through, sir. I plan to have those stalls sorted and organized before your return. I'll be anxious to inspect everything you find."

Master Brightwell smiled. "Perhaps next year, Wellspring will have resources to bring on a second apprentice, allowing us to attend sales together. You have a mind for mechanics, Mr. Slipwing, aided by your sharp eyesight and hearing."

"Thank you, sir. Have a good trip." Rivley extended his hand, and the inventor shook it.

A year ago, he never would have dreamed the inner workings of a machine could make sense to an animacambire raised to protect the safety of their hidden valley. Everything about the Farmlands was so different than his shapeshifter home in the rugged Black Mountains lining the southern edge of Blighted Basin. He'd never seen a mechanical device until he and his best friend, Daeryn Darkcoat, escaped the aftermath of a tragic accident down those rocky slopes. Finding the advertisement seeking 'cambire guards for Wellspring Collective had opened their eyes to a different life—one with a new and exciting future, in his case. If he learned enough during his apprenticeship with Master Brightwell, one day he could study at a mechanics' institute and run his own shop. First, he had an obligation to resolve with Daeryn.

CHAPTER TWO

Mary Clare dashed into Wellspring's kitchen and grabbed another dish to ferry to the dining room.

"It's noon," Mrs. Betsy Campbell called, her short, white hair waving in time to her vigorous mashing of baked squash. "Please ring the bell, duck. Then this squash will be ready to serve."

Hustling, Mary Clare pivoted and headed for the kitchen's outer door. Her prior work at Wellspring had taught her it was far quicker to go outside to the bell than navigate the big farmhouse.

Unfamiliar workers were queued, and many smiled at her. When she reached the bell pole, she figured out why—she still held a giant wooden bowl of rolls. Grasping the rope with one hand, she managed a low *thunk*, not the usual loud peal.

Ach. She couldn't put them on the ground—what if Mrs. Betsy saw?—and she needed both hands to pull the rope. She turned toward the kitchen—but no, she was already here, so she turned back, face heating as a twitter of laughter rose behind her. *Land's—*

"Let me help," said a quiet voice. His freckled hands reached from a neatly tucked flannel shirt covering broad shoulders. The clean-shaven fellow smiled, from his freckled cheeks to the prettiest hazel eyes glinting with orange.

Oh, my lands. An animacambire. Animal changers weren't rare in the Farmlands, but she'd never met one this handsome or with such a musical accent. From his lean, muscular body and tawny hair glinting blue-gray, he had to be a bird. He was a head taller than she was—although most folks were, so he wasn't especially tall.

"Then you can ring the lunch bell?" He cupped one hand to the bowl, his warm fingers overlapping hers.

A shiver shot through her. Mary Clare pushed the bowl to him when what she really wanted was to open her Knack to learn if he was genuinely as nice as he appeared. She couldn't, and with her head muddled, she must be staring like a townie going into the Wildlands.

"Uh, thank you." She forced herself to turn and grasp the rope, cringing as hoots accompanied the peals. The ten rings for lunch gave her nerves time to settle. Those bloody farmhands acted like a herd of toddlers. She was new and had to take it until she had a position secured here. Then they'd get a piece of her mind.

When she turned back to collect her rolls, the fellow had carried the bowl to the back door.

Blocking the entrance, he faced the line of workers. "We'd heard the kitchen was short-staffed today, so you lot will count to one hundred, *slowly*, before you put on your best manners and *walk* into the dining room and collect your plates in a manner befitting Wellspring. Because if you're hungry now, think how much hungrier you'll be when dinner is late because you've flustered this new staffer and she's decided to throw in her apron and leave our overworked cook with no help."

Folks shuffled, and someone called, "Sorry, miss." Others echoed the apology.

That's all it took? Then standing up to these workers would be the same as putting Pa's hired hands in place. Times fifteen, but she could do it. Mary Clare raised her chin and surveyed the growing line. She said, "Accepted," and gave them a firm nod before striding to the 'cambire fellow and taking back her bowl with a grateful smile.

He opened the door for her. Mary Clare marched inside, and he easily caught up, their footsteps echoing down the dim back hallway. Was all that just an excuse to be first in line?

When they turned left into the quiet dining room, he asked, "You must be a sister to Mary Beth."

Everyone could tell the freckled, strawberry-blondes were sisters, even when they weren't side by side. "Mary Clare," she answered as she slid the bowl onto the sideboard with the other food. "I've helped out before. Usually during the harvest."

"Mary Clare," he repeated. "Then I would've been far too tired to notice. I was a day guard until a month ago."

"And now?"

"Mary Clare?" Mrs. Betsy called, startling her. The stout cook stood in the kitchen doorway, a bowl of orange mash held against her flowered apron. "This food does not deliver itself, duck."

Mary Clare darted over and took the warm bowl. *Land's sake, I canna make the cook angry, or this won't become permanent.* She dared not risk talking more, but she didn't even know his name!

"Sorry for the delay, ma'am," the fellow said to Mrs. Betsy. "Some of the new hires forgot Wellspring operates on manners. They're pausing outside to remember. Can I help?"

Mrs. Betsy *tsked.* "Please take these..." Her voice muffled as she turned to the table they used for staging the serving dishes. "You're a good lad, Rivley."

Rivley. His name was Rivley.

AFTER COLLECTING HIS FOOD, Rivley scanned for a place at the long dining room table. The cook's assistant wouldn't be sitting down to lunch. Only at dinner, which was served family style, did the kitchen staff sit. Not that he would sit with her then—they always sat at the end closest to the kitchen. But he could be early and select a nearby chair to overhear anything she said, even if he didn't speak with her again. He rubbed his growling stomach.

His fingers grazed the metal talisman underneath his waistband.

What was he thinking? He was in the same situation he'd been in since leaving Rockbridge—the situation *they* were in. A clicking rose in Rivley's throat, and he quickly squelched his irritation. He and his best friend, Daeryn Darkcoat, shared the blame for the accident in which a teammate had died. The gildan enchantment the Elders had imposed bound them together and limited their social privileges—like the taking of life mates. Yet, a year and a half later, Daeryn still refused to address the lessons to learn what they'd done wrong so they could resolve the bond. Rivley was starting to question when Dae would learn to live with the grief.

So what was the point in courting someone?

Chairs scraped across the slate floor as the hungry growers seated themselves. Rivley carried his meal to a spot with a view of the kitchen door and sat. He didn't know Mary Clare at all. Why push Daeryn when it might be for naught and cause a rift?

Within seconds, Mary Clare emerged, said, "Excuse me," and added rolls to the bowl, as if shoving aside men twice her size was a daily occurrence.

"Can you sneak me out some cake?" a bloke asked her.

Mary Clare laughed and walked away, leaving the grumbly worker to stalk back to his chair.

Rivley found himself grinning at the redhead's alpha manner.

"What has you smiling for once?" asked Famil, who led the day guard team. She scooted into the next chair and began eating.

Neck heating, Rivley ducked his chin and spooned up squash. "I smile," he muttered.

Famil laughed softly. "You are the most solemn person I know. Good for a guard. Well, if we were guarding people. Half the staff are afraid to approach you." When he didn't respond, she added, "Fancy a mating dance with that little Knack-bearer?"

Heck, secrets didn't last long in this community. Even when there wasn't anything to keep secret. Famil, twice his twenty years, probably had a better sense than he would. "You think she's a Knack-bearer?"

"Hmm? Let me take another look." When Mary Clare re-entered,

Famil narrowed her eyes. Their shape changed slightly, bringing her 'cambire's golden eagle sight into play.

He should learn this trick.

"Not a 'cambire, that's for sure. She's sisters with the other redheads who work here, right?"

There were more than one?

"Like them, could be a grower Knack or a human," Famil continued. "It doesn't always pass down."

Rivley nodded. He couldn't be interested. Not until he and Daeryn resolved their gildan.

Famil said goodbye, carried her dishes to the serving tray and intercepted Mr. Hortens. They had a word, then the head grower walked in Rivley's direction. He hurriedly chased his last beans before the man arrived.

"Will those spiders be done soon?"

Rivley wiped his mouth and rose. "They're done now, sir. However, I'd like to review operations with their operators. Could they stop by?"

Mr. Hortens eyed him.

By the Creator, had he made a mistake only hours into his responsibility? He started to add Master Brightwell had requested it when Mr. Hortens spoke.

"Five of the new hires continue to have operations issues with their spiders. All would benefit from another review, and perhaps coming from a mechanic, it will make a stronger point. Rather than carting in the three other machines, are you willing to ride out and conduct the training on the hillsides?"

"Sure. If you have an available wagon, I'll load the spiders and head over."

That pleased Mr. Hortens, which pleased Rivley. In another hour, he could start that inventory.

Out in the field, a grower rushed to catch a machine at the end of a tilled row, and Rivley spotted the problem: They weren't guiding the machines far enough onto the roadbeds to make their turns before heading into the next row.

As he instructed Mr. Hortens' five growers, several others collected at the edges. Fine, training for more growers meant fewer repairs. After each executed proper turns, Rivley suggested they switch to walking on the downhill side to avoid bumping the machine.

Mr. Hortens clapped his hands for attention. "We have four hours to finish the fertilization before planting the peas. If he has the time, perhaps Mr. Slipwing can circulate and check each machine *while it is in operation.*"

Many scattered, but two young women approached and asked him to inspect their machines' joints, but then asked for his shop hours... unnecessary information.

Now, if it'd been Mary Clare asking...

CHAPTER THREE

A knock came at the workshop door, followed by the squeal of metal wheels rolling on their track.

What now? A brisk draft circled Rivley's body, but he didn't turn from tightening the housing screws on his fifth repair of the day. "If your machine is even halfway operating, please return it to the equipment shed and take it out in the morning. The *repairs*"—he spat the word—"ahead of yours will take until afternoon."

A chuckle answered his order—a familiar one. Rivley leaned his head to the machine's cool metal. "Thank the Creator," he muttered, then louder, "Quick, close the door."

It squeaked again, and Daeryn Darkcoat tread over, flannel shirt barely tucked into his trousers, but his unruly dark hair was brushed and brown cheeks freshly shaved for his night's work. "I don't even have to ask. At dinner, the female growers were all a-twitter at having the opportunity to have a word with you."

"Argh!" Rivley threw down his grease rag. "They claim *something* is wrong with their spiders. Several had dirt in the joints, but not compacted like the fallen ones. Two had lost screws on the housing. One had a leg disconnected."

"You have to tell Hortens the damage was intentional."

314

Rivley rose. "And sound like I canna handle the workshop?"

"Then call out to them what you said to me."

"I have. Turned away the last three."

Daeryn swept his hand toward the five machines in line and laughed. "Does appear you should have caught on sooner. Just thought I'd pass on the chatter. Do yourself a favor and get dinner before it's cold."

"I want these two done before I head to bed."

Daeryn walked to the door. "You're taking this too seriously. Don't you think of anything besides mechanics these days?"

"Not if I want my own shop…" Well, there was something. "Did that new kitchen helper survive the day?"

"The redhead? Yep, she was eating with her sister. Cute—oh no." Daeryn waved his hands. "Please don't say it."

Rivley crossed his arms. "Haven't said a thing."

Daeryn narrowed his eyes. "You haven't asked after a female since we left Rockbridge. But unlike those girls, this one isn't 'cambire."

"That matters because?"

Daeryn frowned, going all alpha…except for the telltale slide of his hand over his gildan talisman.

Rivley eyed him. "We're not returning to Rockbridge any time soon."

"Maybe not ever," Daeryn said quietly.

"Maybe not ever," Rivley repeated. "No decision yet."

"Unless you fall for a human."

Or a Knack-bearer, but neither would fit into life in the Black Mountains. Rivley tapped his belly. "We *won't* have a life waiting for us there. Unless you'll start work on this gildan."

Daeryn huffed. "Don't have time to argue. I have to begin my guard rotation, or Owen will be on my tail." He shoved open the door, letting in the cold. "At dinner, Hortens announced smudge duty, whatever that is. In particular, he called on the growers whose machines are in repair. And the mechanic's assistant." Then Daeryn banged the door closed, cutting off the draft.

Smudge duty?

Following dinner, Mary Clare cleaned the dishware and platters, then started on the roasting pan. Mrs. Betsy was ferrying leftovers to the icebox off the screened-in porch and speaking with someone.

Dinner had gone well…except Rivley never turned up. Good, because she hadn't been distracted by him. Bad, because she was dying to check if his hair was as blue as she'd thought. She sighed and scrubbed at the stubborn edge of browned grease.

Chilly air whooshed into the kitchen before Mrs. Betsy firmly closed the door. "Land's sake, I swear we've retreated to February." She *tsked* and set down the crock of butter and a bowl of eggs. "This isn't good." She took a large mixing bowl from where Mary Clare had stored it in the cupboard and retrieved the farm's bread pans.

"What's wrong?" Even as she asked, Mary Clare's thoughts raced back to breakfast and her family's concern about how cool it'd been overnight. Pa had said if the temperature dropped further, they'd need to put out the smudge pots for—

"The cherry blossoms," Mrs. Betsy said.

"Oh, dear. What is the temperature?" The smoking smudge pots would warm the undersides of the cherry trees to protect the blossoms from freezing.

"Down to five degrees Celsius already. Mr. Hortens will give it another hour before he decides."

A snort escaped Mary Clare before she thought to hold back her opinion.

Mrs. Betsy raised her white brows.

Darn it, now she'd ruined a perfectly good workday. Face warming, she said, "I…uh, my pa will have the pots filled and my sisters setting them out. At five degrees, he wants to be prepared. But we only have six trees for family use. I'm sure it's a bigger decision on a large collective."

Mrs. Betsy's frown cleared. "Ach, true. Eight rows, Mistress Gere has—eighty trees. You're from a farming family, so you understand." Mrs. Betsy peered at her speculatively. "While you finish up, duck, I'll start an extra batch of bran breads. If tonight's temperatures plummet, it'll be as busy as daytime out there."

Right, just like at home when she and her sisters would bundle up and check the pots and fan the smoke with Pa. Coming in to Granny's sweet biscuits and hot chocolate always felt good. It'd been a few years since they'd had a freeze during blossom time, so now even Mary Frances was old enough to pitch in. She didn't need to rush home. "Can I help with anything?" she offered.

The back door creaked, and Rivley stepped in.

Mary Clare's heart began thumping. He closed the door, glanced at her and ran his fingers through tufted bluish hair. Her breath caught.

"Yes, duck?" Mrs. Betsy asked him.

"I, uh, Mr. Hortens sent me in. I missed dinner, and we're to work tonight."

"He's decided, then, has he? Of course you need food. Everyone will need food. Mary Clare, get this boy some food, whatever he wants." Mrs. Betsy plucked a plate from the stack and pointed toward the porch.

Mary Clare took it and cast a smile at Rivley. But he wasn't smiling, and she quickly looked down. What was wrong? Had she done... no, of course not. She hadn't even been around him. Had he heard something about her? Only her sisters knew her here. She approached the door, but he leaned forward, opened it and gestured her out. She all but brushed him, not intending to be that close, but they had no extra room, what with Mrs. Betsy's rocking chair at the woodstove.

Then a thread of doubt wafted off him.

No! Her Knack wards had come down! It'd been a long day, and she was tired... Understandable to her family, but forbidden to everyone else.

On the screened porch, she darted into the outdoor pantry. Plenty of time to reinforce her wards while he waited in the kitchen... Footsteps sounded behind her, and his pang of hunger gripped at her own gut and twisted.

"Shall I hold the plate?" He shifted from foot to foot.

"Uh, thanks." With a shiver—only half from the darned cold—

Mary Clare pushed the plate to him. "Wait there," she ordered and moved two blessed steps away. His feelings dissipated. Opening the icebox door, she gripped the handle and pretended to look over the contents. She pulled at the magic in her. *Come on.* It moved sluggishly, like it knew she only half wanted it to. Yep, she'd love to know what this fellow felt about her, but he was a stranger, and no matter how nice he was, she couldn't pry.

After a moment, the magic wrapped completely around her, sealing off the outside. Her breath rushed out. *Thank the Creator.*

"I'm not particular," he said. "Those beans will be fine."

"Mrs. Betsy would have my head if you came in with just a plate of beans." Setting out several containers on the adjacent table, Mary Clare found the leftover chicken. She reached for a piece, then stopped. This wasn't family. She needed a serving fork and hadn't brought one, nor a spoon for vegetables. "I shouldn't be touching your food. I'll fetch a fork—"

His stomach growled. "Excuse me. Can I just take one while you…" When she offered, he plucked out a leg and immediately took a bite, closing his eyes to chew.

Mary Clare set down the dish and skirted around him. "Be right back."

By the time she returned, he'd eaten that piece and started on another. With the fork stuck in the meat in case he wanted more, she heaped beans and potatoes onto the plate he'd put on the table. "So, they're setting out the smudge pots soon?"

"Mr. Hortens is sending them 'round on a wagon for me to fill with Basin coal." He took another bite of chicken.

The way he said it… Something wasn't sitting right with him, which she could tell even without her Knack. "Surely there's enough?"

His alluring orange eyes darted aside. "Likely? Down in the Black Mountains, we don't use coal. I hope one of the growers knows how much it'll take."

Mary Clare nodded. "My sister knows…" What was she doing, volunteering Mary Beth? "*I* can show you how to fill the pots. Certain tools help so the goo doesn't get all over everything."

He frowned. "Goo?"

"*Basin* coal is unpredictable." She tilted a spoonful of squash. As it oozed onto his plate, she explained, "If you're lucky, it never gets looser than this and will stay on the shovel. But sometimes it turns with no warning and lands on the floor or, worse, your trousers and boots."

Grimacing, he shook his head. "I can't ask you to come out. It's dirty work."

She grinned. "It sure is. We heat with Basin coal at my family's place, so I've moved it lots. I know how to keep it from my clothes." Whether or not it dribbled over her best bib and brace, she'd get to spend more time with this polite fellow.

He nodded solemnly. "I'd appreciate the help, if Mrs. Betsy gives her permission. Give me five minutes?"

He carried his food into the kitchen, and Mary Clare thumped her forehead. Argh, this wasn't the Pemberton farm where everyone was expected to help.

Minutes later, Rivley strode across the farmyard with Mary Clare, his belly now full and his head clearer. With her help, he wouldn't have to admit he couldn't deliver what Mr. Hortens wanted. He eyed the short female with a new appreciation. Never had she said to Mrs. Betsy he didn't know anything about Basin coal. Instead, she'd offered to help in the kitchen for the evening and asked for a ten-minute break, "For a bit of fresh air and physical movement helping Rivley fetch coal for the smudge pots."

Mrs. Betsy had *tutted* and proclaimed it a blessing not having the nasty stuff in the house any longer. As soon as he'd eaten, she'd shooed them out.

He led the way to the stall in the back of the workshop. There, on hooks above the coal, hung several buckets, a shovel and long-handled scoops made from metal cans, all stained with a tar-like substance

Mary Clare banged together two larger scoops over a bucket.

Pieces of coal pattered down, leaving the scoops clean. "The coal from last use rehardened. Let's see how the rest reacts tonight." She set the bucket close to the pile of black hunks and gestured for him to use the shovel he'd taken down.

He tried to push the shovel into the pile, but the metal *thunked* like he'd hit a rock. "It's a single lump."

She laughed. "For now. Hit it again from the top."

He did, and miraculously, a chunk broke off.

"Quick, shovel it into the bucket." She leaned forward and held a scoop between the pile and the bucket.

Not the easiest shoveling, but he'd try it her way before suggesting she move back.

The shovel slid under the lump, but as he swung, it melted like he'd lit a fire beneath it. "Whoa." He hesitated, and she caught the trail of liquid running off the blade.

"Go on," she ordered, startling him into action.

He dumped the mush into the bucket. "This will burn?"

She poured her liquid onto the top, and lumps formed again, like the crystallization of sugar candy. "It will. Smoke, too. It's tricky filling the smudge pots. An ice pick is handy."

"We've got those."

They filled a bucket, and Mary Clare straightened. "The growers will need more than these four buckets to keep the smudge pots smoking all night."

Mr. Hortens had explained that. Apparently, Master Brightwell always helped monitor the smoking, and Hortens wanted Rivley to fill in. It seemed expected rather than a request. "Why don't they use deeper pots if they don't last all night?"

"A low level of lit coal produces more smoke when you get the vent adjusted just so." She indicated the first joint of her pointer finger. "About this much in the bottom. More, and they flame and waste coal."

Her small hands made a different measure than his, so he automatically put his palm to hers, lining up their fingers. His first joint extended beyond hers. Three-quarters? Half? As he held her hand, trying to determine a precise measure, her skin turned from warm to clammy. *Oh. I made her nervous? Was it a good nervous?*

"It's, uh, approximate," she mumbled, pulling away her hand. "Checking them overnight is an event for sure, but saving the blossoms is worth it for the cherries."

His mouth watered. "Last year was my first taste of these sweet Farmlands cherries. They let us day guards eat the topmost ones the growers missed." Would she know what he meant? How would she react?

Her nose wrinkled. "How did you get them if...*oh.*"

"On the wing," he confirmed. "They're easy to spot from the air."

She laughed. "You should come around my family place to clean up. I've always hated that we canna get every last one."

Grinning, he eyed her. She *sounded* comfortable with the animal shifters, but how comfortable? "I might just do that."

"Is your bird form light enough not to break the branches?" she asked as they filled the buckets.

He'd brought up the subject of 'cambires, and the query flowed naturally, but he detected the real question: *What are you?*

"Yes." He let that sit for a moment, and she bit her lip. The "don't ask what you aren't told" policy was ingrained into Basin residents as fledglings, kits and toddlers. You didn't pry into others' Knacks.

"I'm a Eurasian sparrowhawk," he said quietly. "From the Black Mountains."

"Ah. Pretty plumage."

He wasn't sure how she knew, since sparrowhawks didn't frequent the Farmlands. He waited for her to volunteer her heritage, but Mary Clare busied herself with the buckets, moving the empty ones closer to the pile. Soon, they'd filled them, their opportunity for private conversation disappointingly over.

They carried the buckets outside. The wagon had arrived, with two of the grower females who'd brought in their spiders. They didn't look happy to see Mary Clare. But then, she wasn't happy to see them.

Rivley suppressed a grimace. This game had played out so many times in Rockbridge, usually with him enjoying it. Tonight, he wanted to shoo it away. He remembered his manners and introduced Mary Clare while she set her buckets on the wagon.

Mary Clare pulled over a smudge pot, dug a scoop into a bucket and showed him the now-liquid coal. "Get out several scoopfuls real quick. If it hardens—and it probably will—whack it with the ice pick or jostle the buckets again."

The growers watched as she filled five pots and he managed two before the coal solidified. She lowered her bucket, kicked it twice and filled three more before it hardened again. "Weren't there more scoops? Folks could help if you fetch them, Rivley."

She handed her scoop to the nearest grower. "I have to get back to the kitchen, but let me know if you need help later."

He watched her walk off.

One of the growers harrumphed. "She's bossy for kitchen help."

"She knows more than we do." The other grower banged the closest bucket and poured a measure of liquid into a smudge pot. "Come on, or Mr. Hortens will be here before we're done."

Each of those things was true, and somehow warmed Rivley's belly. He handed off his scoop. "I'll fetch more." What excuse could he use to call upon Mary Clare later?

CHAPTER FOUR

Rivley placed a smudge pot where Mr. Hortens directed, beneath cherry limbs laced high above their heads, each twig bearing white buds glowing in the setting sun. Then the head grower demonstrated how to light the coal and adjust the vent once it caught. Lighting the pots fell to Rivley and a team of three—all but one new at this—while the wagon moved on.

Rivley positioned the flint scraper so the sparks would fall onto the coal. The porridge-like substance caught, but the next pot held solid hunks and required more strikes. The third, a pot of liquid coal, flared a foot high, singeing the hairs on the back of Rivley's hand.

"Too much in that one," yelled Sticks. "Shut the vent, quick!"

He put it out, and Sticks came to inspect it. The wiry, midthirties grower grumbled. As Mary Clare had said, overfilled ones burned too hot.

With the coal presenting differently in every smudge pot, Rivley couldn't get a rhythm. But he learned to judge the state of the coal and how close to place his flint scraper. By the third flash of flames, he easily rolled away. Rising to his knees, he raked fingers through his hair, feeling feathers poking through. At least in the fading light, the others couldn't see how much this rattled him.

The youngest grower howled and fell back, shaking her hand.

"Iris, are you all right?" yelled another grower as three of them ran over.

"No," the teen cried. "I'm burned, and I canna tell how badly."

"This is horrible!" the other female groused. "The experienced staff should be out here, but instead, they get the night off so they'll be fresh for the morning planting."

"You will have the day to sleep," Sticks said. "This is how you gain experience, and if we have another freezing night, it'll go all the faster."

"I'll accompany her in," Rivley said, "and fetch a bucket for extra coal." He clasped Iris' elbow and walked her to the wagon road between the trees. She didn't protest as she cradled her hand.

A four-legged silhouette bounded toward them—Daeryn had heard Iris' cry.

"She needs to see the healer," Rivley called to the polecat. "Can you lead us down the quickest path?"

With a yip, the weasel-like figure leaped toward the trees and trotted forward, checking they were following. Rivley increased their pace, weaving between the branches behind Dae. Within minutes, he ushered Iris into the back hall of the farmhouse, called for the healer and delivered Iris to her.

He could collect the refuse bucket near the workshop door, but Mary Clare's offer of help echoed in his head. She knew what to do, if only Mrs. Betsy would agree.

The dining room glowed with light. Hot kettles lined the sideboard, and the tray of butter and jams sat at the ready. The scents of cinnamon and sugar wafted from the kitchen, followed by the sweet aroma of berries as he approached the doorway. Mouth watering, he was blocked by a serving table lined with rows of muffins, the pink ones reminding him of the cherry trees he had to get back to.

"Rivley, hello," Mary Clare called, quickening his heartbeats. She held a muffin tin filled with batter. Opening the oven, she bent to put in the tray.

Oh, drat. She was busy.

"What can we get you, duck?" Mrs. Betsy approached the opposite side of the table. "We have meats, too, and cheese with bread if you need to keep moving." She gestured to the stacked napkins.

"Thank you." He took a pink muffin, which was indeed studded with canned cherries. "Actually, Iris was burned in a flare—"

"No!" exclaimed Mary Clare, coming up behind the cook.

"—which wouldn't have happened if more growers knew what to do. Mary Clare knows. Could you spare her to help us light the pots? An hour, maybe?"

Mary Clare opened her mouth, then closed it again and looked over at the cook.

Rivley held his lips in a firm line, not cracking a smile or daring to glance her way again. Great Creator, this female was used to doing things her way, but was adapting quickly to Wellspring's ways.

"Poor little Iris." Mrs. Betsy shook her head. "Of course." She turned Mary Clare by the shoulders, like she wouldn't have gone on her own. "Fetch your jacket, duck. I can manage on my own for an hour."

While Mary Clare put on her coat and scarf, he bit into his muffin. It was good, a new flavor that had to be Mary Clare's recipe.

Outside, he asked her, "Have you been baking long?"

"All my life. I love it, especially experimenting with flavors and seasonings for vegetables and meats. Most places have their signature tastes already established, but I've created some 'specials' at the hotel in Chapel Hollow."

They'd crossed the farmyard and passed the bunkhouse, her shorter legs keeping up with his pace. Should he take her elbow to guide her on the shortcut through the fruit trees? Her hand? Or would the confident female think he viewed her as weak? Rivley had inter-acted with alpha females in Rockbridge who would scoff at such a gesture, but with a human, this could go either way.

Beyond the greenhouse, Daeryn, in his polecat form, cleared the orchard grass in a leap.

With a hiss of breath, Mary Clare stumbled and pressed against Rivley. "What—*who*... Is that a guard?"

Automatically, his arm went around her shoulders. "That's Daeryn Darkcoat, a friend of mine. A European polecat."

"He's also from the Black Mountains?" She leaned into Rivley's side.

His breath hitched. "Ah—*yes*. A common 'cambire."

Daeryn paused before them, a cock of his head pinging awareness in Rivley.

He dropped his arm so only his fingers pressed the small of Mary Clare's back, a touch Daeryn wouldn't see. "He'll lead us on the quickest path to the teams. Thanks, Dae," he added.

Daeryn pivoted and leaped.

As they walked, Mary Clare's shoulder bumped Rivley while crossing the rough ground, so he clasped her elbow. She didn't pull away.

IT TOOK every ounce of strength Mary Clare had not to lean into Rivley again. He smelled like a breeze on an autumn day, reminding her of crinkling leaves. And he was nicely warm. She'd heard 'cambires had a higher body heat than Knacks or humans, but hadn't thought of bird shifters as being especially warm, compared to furry ones, like wolves.

She wished he'd hold her hand, rather than her elbow in such a formal posture. But he was polite, much more polite than some of her past suitors.

Rivley's friend kept looking back. She knew enough to know 'cambire hearing was sharp, and she couldn't ask, not while the polecat led them. Surely Daeryn heard their feet rustling the dried grass, so his curiosity gave her the feeling her sisters did when they were inspecting a boy. Had Rivley said something about her to him?

The scent of coal smoke grew stronger, then in the next orchard row, a fire flared, and voices rose.

"Land's sake!" She ran forward, following...er, the *growing* figure.

The polecat rose on two legs as he shifted. Rivley sprinted past her, and they raced toward a patch of flaming grass.

Someone was scooping dirt onto the flames, and Daeryn, naked, joined him. Rivley whipped off his leather apron and dropped it over the high flames. He jumped onto it, stomping with his boots. A few flames licked at the edges, which a grower squelched with her boots, but the tilted smudge pot still flamed, its liquid coal streaming out.

Mary Clare darted to the pot, cursing she didn't have the metal poker Pa insisted they carry. She hitched up her trouser leg and kicked the thing over until it was upside down. Most of the flames extinguished when the opening hit the ground, then Rivley threw his apron over it.

The reek of charred grass surrounded them. Coughing, they moved away. Rivley pulled his shirt over his head and gave it to Daeryn, who yanked it on. The tails barely covered his nakedness.

Mary Clare's breathing, ragged from running and the excitement, had evened out but accelerated again. Rivley's chest—*wow*. His beautifully sculpted muscles begged to be explored—argh, what was she thinking? Looking around, she asked, "What happened?"

The grower shook her head. "One flamed when I lit it. I jumped back and knocked over another."

"Are you all right?" Rivley asked, and she nodded.

Was he this nice to everyone? If so, then it probably meant nothing when he'd held her arm. Disappointment flooding her, Mary Clare flipped over Rivley's apron and righted the pot with her boot toe.

Sticks shone his lantern over it. The remaining coal had solidified into a cake and stuck out of the vent.

She broke it off using Rivley's flint sparker and prodded it into the hot metal pot.

"With the fire out, I'll return to my rounds," Daeryn said.

Rivley followed him a few steps, their voices a murmur. Trying to ignore them, Mary Clare showed the growers where the coal level should be and checked the other pots with them. By the time she demonstrated lighting one, Rivley returned—his shirt on, darn it—with the bucket he'd dropped.

After adjusting the coal levels and lighting these, the team moved to the next tree. Mary Clare stayed with the grower who'd started the fire until her hands no longer shook, then hung back while she lit the next.

Rivley came up beside her. "How's she doing?"

"Much better. How are you?"

He hefted the bucket. "Half are too full. Those growers helping me didn't follow your instruction, and I didn't check their work. Sticks said once the workers on the wagon finish putting out the pots, they'll start lighting from the other end."

The steam tractor chugged along several orchard rows away. "Ohhh, someone should tell them."

He nodded. "Would you come with me?" When she nodded, he called to Sticks, and they set off.

As they hurried, avoiding the low-hanging limbs was difficult. One snagged her hat, and another jabbed her shoulder. "Oof!"

Rivley waited for her, holding up a limb before the grassy road. When they entered another row, she reached for the bucket.

"Let me carry it while you save our heads."

He handed it over and held out a curved arm. "If you're right beside me, we can move faster. May I?"

Put his arm around her? She grinned. "Yes." That might have come out too enthusiastically, but who cared?

They wove between the limbs, Mary Clare tucked against his warm chest, the scent of fall leaves filling her nose. He seemed to grab branches from nowhere and lift them aside with one long arm.

"Do all 'cambires have good night eyesight?" she asked.

He made a sound that sounded like a squelched laugh. "Sorry, just thinking how Daeryn would howl over that one. My eyesight is terrible at night, likely no better than yours."

"Then how are you...?"

He shrugged against her. "I feel a branch coming and know how to avoid it."

They emerged onto the road and ducked into the last row. Across it, the tractor rumbled loudly, the moving lantern lights outlining the folks carrying them. "It's a bird thing?"

His hold on her loosened. "I suppose, from flying between trees. I hadn't thought of it before." One tree away, the workers hadn't seen them yet. Rivley dropped his arm. "'Cambires are different in many ways from...humans.'"

From you. Land's sake, this was going downhill, as Granny would say. Mary Clare didn't want it to.

He reached for the bucket.

Instead of releasing it, she stepped closer and looked up at him. "I come from a family of Knack-bearers. Most of us. We embrace different, because we are, too. You can't live in a longtime market town like Chapel Hollow and not. Your differences are good."

Slowly, his cheeks lifted in a smile, and she smiled back. He leaned toward her, head tilting as if he was moving in for a kiss. Then his gaze shifted toward the tractor.

A wince of disappointment froze her. The growers couldn't see. Or was he worried what *she* thought? One way to solve that.

She tugged the bucket handle. He followed it, and she clutched his jacket collar to lower his head while she went onto tiptoes. Her lips brushed his cheek, not really where she was aiming, but that should relay the message.

She parted, but he didn't move...her hand still held his collar. Oh. She released him, but his head descended again, and this time, his lips met hers.

Rivley tasted sweet—her muffins, she realized—and the wind, if that had a taste. Also, like trees in the breeze and faraway mountaintops and...wild mint.

Mary Clare shivered, and Rivley lifted his head from the kiss, his gaze fixed on her, his hand cupping her elbow as she lowered onto her heels.

"All right?" he whispered in his endearing accent.

"Oh, yes," she gushed, and her cheeks heated at how giddy she must sound. Yet, she couldn't stop grinning.

He flashed a crooked grin and nodded toward a small commotion she hadn't noticed. "We best..."

Someone cursed, and in unison Mary Clare and Rivley paced toward the growers. While he asked what'd happened, she checked the smudge pot, emptied a third of it into the bucket Rivley held and demonstrated how to light the proper amount. She said nothing, letting him give the instructions and answer questions.

Just kissing Rivley had been like an adventure. So different than her previous short-time beau she couldn't even compare. With this gentle 'cambire, she could just erase that memory and renew her dreams. She loved her family and routine at home, but she'd always wanted to meet someone who would be a partner in adventure.

RIVLEY FORCED himself to pay attention to the growers. He wasn't angry when they admitted they'd added more coal to avoid having to do refills. Their friend's burn topped any punishment his words could dole out, so he took their apology and mindful attention to Mary Clare's demonstrations as a lesson learned.

The kiss with Mary Clare had felt like flying, that lifting mindlessness of just sensing the currents and letting them take him. He glanced at the short redhead bundled in her woolen jacket. Why was she so quiet now? Not a bad quiet. She'd liked their kiss. She'd started it after all, but that little peck had only made him curious. Yes, she knew how to kiss...and maybe more.

They worked through additional pots to verify these growers knew the correct coal levels. But he wanted to walk into the dark with Mary Clare. Every time he came close to her, his excitement built. Finally, she murmured apologetically that she should return to the kitchen. Yet, she slipped her hand into his as they walked the long way down the row to the farm road.

They stopped in the shadows of the bunkhouse, out of sight of the farmhouse and a few workers crossing the yard. He put his arms around her, and in seconds, their lips met. Opened. His tongue teased over hers, which traced his lips before returning to his. Like the burst of a tail wind, their lips and tongues worked in a frenzy, and he clung to her like the drop would kill him.

At last, he parted for a breath. "It's so...exciting," he murmured. "I haven't felt this way in a long time." He should tell her why he hadn't courted anyone in two years, about the gildan. Why this could go only so far... *What am I thinking? It's a kiss, not a life-mate commitment.*

Mary Clare looked up at him with unfocused eyes. "What? Oh—" She bit her lip and pressed fingers to her forehead.

Something was wrong. He could see it in her face, how her manner had changed... She felt stiff against him now. He should let her go, but he didn't want to. She wasn't pulling away. "Change your mind about kissing?" he asked, trying to do so lightly.

"Not that." She stroked his shoulder. "That was the most wonderful kiss. I'd love to continue, but I'm on trial for this job, and Mrs. Betsy must expect me. I can't bungle this."

"Can I see you later?" he blurted, surprising himself. "If you want to..."

"I do," she said quickly.

"I'd like to tell you...uh, trade more about ourselves. In the past, I grew up in the same shire as those I've courted." Great Creator, did he just say *courted*?

Stepping back, she tossed him a wry smile and ran her hands down her trousers. "I never have—known the fellow well, I mean. I've courted. Talking would be good, but..." She looked around. "I wouldn't know where to find you."

CHAPTER FIVE

Mary Clare hedged her wording, giving Rivley a chance to back out. She'd let her Knack sway him. That was as dangerous as telling him about it.

She pressed her hand to her head again, assuring herself her wards were up. These last minutes, he'd been free from her sway. Seeing her again was his idea. She was sure...she thought. With a Knack like hers, she didn't have a lot of practice reading facial expressions.

"I'll come by the kitchen," Rivley said.

She stopped a flurry of words from rushing out. *I must calm down and focus on doing my job well.* "Sorry if I can't leave. I don't know Mrs. Betsy's plans for tonight."

The sooner she walked across the farmyard and into the kitchen, the sooner she would be to finishing work and seeing Rivley again. And—darn it—she needed the time alone to reconstruct *solid* walls for their next kiss. *Exciting*, he'd said. Well, she'd certainly felt excited.

He twined his slender fingers with hers and squeezed as they walked.

She squeezed back. *I promise, I won't let that happen again.* She had to let him have his feelings alone to know what he truly felt about her, not her projected feelings...unlike her last beau.

At the door, she climbed the steps so she wouldn't hug him again and, with a last squeeze of his hand, said good-bye. He smiled and hurried off.

Mrs. Betsy, at the far end of the warm kitchen speaking with several growers, hadn't heard her enter. Mary Clare hung her outer things and began washing dishes.

The last time she hadn't been careful—with a fellow she'd met at Market Day. He was her age and cute, and as Granny said, she'd pinned her feelings on her sleeve. *Her Knack.* For weeks, he'd bought sweets while she worked at Mrs. Ruby's, and on her breaks, they'd kiss and such in the alley. Then he'd go back to his farm, hours distant from Chapel Hollow.

Her older sisters had told her all about the next level of a relationship, which she'd already known from growing up on a farm. She'd thought she was ready, but that first time, her Knack had run rampant, and so had his excitement. He'd been too rough, they'd fought, and when she'd returned, weepy, her sisters had gotten the secret out without much prodding. They'd told Ma, who'd insisted her Knack be warded, which Mary Clare had already realized. Thereafter, the fellow hadn't been interested, proving how dangerous her *talent* could be.

An hour later, Mary Clare was washing dishes again. Farmworkers came and went, none of them Rivley, so she stopped looking up until a familiar voice asked for milk. Mary Clare whirled around, and Mary Beth grinned at her across the room.

"Will you be ready to go soon? I could walk you home before my shift starts." She lowered her voice. "And hear why you're still here on your first day."

Mary Clare glanced at the clock. Its hands pointed nearly straight up.

Also seeing the time, Mrs. Betsy *tsked.* "You should go, duck. Though your help has made my evening easy. One of the night guards will walk you two."

Or Rivley could walk her out...though the path to their family farm led opposite the cherry trees and his work. Which must be

333

busy, because he hadn't been in again. She stopped a sigh from slipping out. There would be time to see him and make a connection, even if she didn't get the position here. She eyed her sister. "Or I could sleep in your bed since you'll be working, and I would be early to help at breakfast before I leave for the hotel." She'd already told Mrs. Betsy about her standing Wednesday lunch special. The meal had been announced, so Mrs. Betsy said Mary Delia could fill in.

Mary Beth and Mrs. Betsy both eyed her, then each other.

"All right," Mary Beth said. "I'll let you in our entrance."

Complex Knack protections permitted only those her sisters chose into their room. But if she left the kitchen, and Rivley came... Mary Clare chewed on her lip.

"I'd be happy for your help in the morning, duck," Mrs. Betsy said. "It'll be an off-schedule day with many arriving late for breakfast."

"I'd love to help," Mary Clare said automatically, and she meant it. She fetched her coat. As soon as they were outside, she pulled her sister beneath the shadows of a walnut tree in the farmyard's circular drive. "Do you know a fellow named Rivley?"

The porch light lit Mary Beth's wicked grin. "Sooo? You've met Rivley?"

"Just tell me what you know about him."

She crossed her arms. "You saw him in the dining room? Or you tried talking to him?"

"We've chatted." Mary Clare didn't want to say she *liked him* until she'd learned more.

"Wait. He *talked* to you?"

Mary Clare started to huff, then stopped. The way Mary Beth said that... Rivley didn't talk to anyone? She shivered at the news. *Maybe he does really like me.*

Her sister unfolded her arms and patted her shoulder. "After the last fellow, I don't blame you for asking. He was—"

"Please!" Mary Clare pressed her temples. "Don't mention that louse."

Mary Beth sighed sympathetically. "None of the female staff have gotten to know Rivley, but everyone wants to. He fixed my spider machine weeks ago, and I was considering him—"

"No." Mary Clare gripped her arm. "You're not, or you'd already have tried."

Mary Beth blew out a breath. "I did try and got nowhere. He's quiet, though I wouldn't say shy. Really quiet. I can tell he's gentle by the way he cares for the machines."

Mary Clare frowned. "Are you saying he'll treat me like a machine?"

"Yes. No. I mean, he's careful with his tools, never says a mean word even when you've missed an oil change. Sheesh, if you can get him to talk to you, you're lucky."

A smile crawled over Mary Clare's face before she could stop it.

Mary Beth squeaked and shook her shoulder. "Ah, that's wonderful. Now if we could get you hired here full time..."

"Exactly. Take me to your room."

Minutes later, Mary Beth had shared the magical warding, and the sisters parted. Too restless and not wanting to wake Mary Alice, Mary Clare went to the bunkhouse's outer door. She checked her wards while scanning the farmyard. *Rivley has to be out there still. If I find him, we could have that talk...or something.*

She'd make enemies if she waltzed in and snatched up a sought-after fellow. Her experience with males was limited, but with six sisters, she knew all about jealousy. Especially having an emotional Knack. Rivley was handsome and nice. And so serious.

A low whistle sounded.

She looked around, gripping the door handle. A figure hurried across the farmyard. She released the latch along with a breath as an apron flapped around his long legs. Rivley.

"Was that whistle you?" she asked as he approached.

He nodded, and a nervous laugh escaped her.

"Do you need help?" she asked.

"The early team is training the new shift. I'd like you to make sure they have things correct."

Well, with Mary Beth working, they would have them correct, but she didn't need to tell Rivley that. Mary Clare smiled. They'd get in that talk.

He led the way to the mechanic's workshop, where four buckets waited. "If you don't mind, we can take these along."

Now, smoke hung underneath the trees in a thick fog, the air warm. Out of habit, Mary Clare took Rivley's lantern and checked the level of a pot cranking out smoke.

"Three-quarters of an hour left before it needs refilling."

He looked into it. "Seriously? You can tell to that precise a time?"

She shrugged. "To an hour, but you don't want them going out, so best to be early. Were these the first put out?"

"From this end, yes." They left two buckets at the tree.

She heard Mary Beth directing folks before they reached the group's lantern glows. "My sister will keep these folks on track." Mary Clare clasped Rivley's elbow. "Let's find the other team."

With a nod, Rivley pivoted in the roadway, put an arm around her shoulders and led them between trees.

His arm is only to guide me. They wove through rows, spied lanterns and met with the new team, some only barely awake.

She went over lighting and refilling the pots and helped this team, while Rivley ferried coal. In an hour, he found her again. A warm fuzziness filled her as they surveyed the smoke wafting through the branches and the bobbing lanterns' blurry glows.

"Mr. Hortens is pleased this is running so smoothly. I told him you've been advising us."

"You did? He doesn't even know me."

Rivley laughed. "He knows Mary Beth and wishes she'd been on the first shift. Your sister set him straight that you're more than capable."

"That's Mary Beth," she said. "Always ready to speak her mind." Land's sake, Mary Beth wouldn't have said anything to Rivley about Mary Clare's interest, would she?

"He'd like to sleep a few hours and return when it'll be the coldest. I told him I could manage the coal ferrying and refilling if you and your sister were available for troubleshooting." Rivley's eyebrows rose.

It'd mean she'd be awake all night before working breakfast here, Mrs. Ruby's for lunch and then returning in the late afternoon. Mary Clare bit her lip. Missing sleep sounded awful, but Rivley looked so hopeful...

"I know it's a lot to ask when you aren't even on staff—"

"I can do it," she said quickly. The meal at Mrs. Ruby's was planned, a dish she could cook in her sleep, or without any.

Once they'd refilled the buckets, both leaned in to pick them up at the same time, cheeks brushing.

Mary Clare froze. *Will he kiss me?* Desire swelled in her...

In a split second, Rivley ducked. His lips molded smoothly to hers, and her heart leaped.

That taste of the wild wind again—*oh, my!* She nibbled his bottom lip and kissed him back. They straightened, buckets forgotten, hands on each other instead. Her head muddled.

He was so perfect. To fall for a fellow so quickly—

Her Knack—she caught it just as the wards slipped.

RIVLEY'S HEARTBEATS SPED. She was smart and fun. Easy to talk to. At Mary Clare's willingness, he deepened the kiss. They kissed until they were as breathless as racing on the wing between tree branches and broke apart.

Panting, she touched her head.

He'd asked before, and she'd brushed it off, so he simply put an arm around her and nudged her closer. She hugged him. A chucking rose in his chest, an involuntary avian show of satisfaction. He squelched it. Fine, she made him happy, but Great Creator, what would she think of his bird habits?

To cover it, he stroked her chin and lifted it to kiss her again, which she returned eagerly. All right, she'd said she didn't mind 'cambires, so he'd continue being friendly.

337

They were later getting back to the cherry rows than he'd planned. No one noticed, because he'd been hiking all through the trees in the dark. They refilled pots, checked with team leaders, then returned to the workshop to reload the coal buckets. And kiss again.

This time with more touching.

After dropping off two buckets, they strolled across the rows with their fingers entwined, a haze of pleasure filling his head...until they crossed paths with a certain polecat guard. They dropped hands immediately—as much her idea as his, it seemed.

Daeryn went on his way, but heck, the mere sight of his best friend rocked Rivley back on his heels. He hadn't talked to Mary Clare like he'd promised himself he would. She'd hinted she was a Knack-bearer, so kissing wasn't too serious. Not enough to confess his gildan bond.

Mary Clare stiffened when he clasped her hand again. "I like you, Rivley, but I'm not ready to let anyone else know we're...this." She raised their linked hands.

"Agreed. I don't care for gossip, and"—he sighed—"there will be gossip. Are you ready for that?"

She grinned. "I can take it. Six sisters. But I need to secure the kitchen position. If I don't, then we can..."

His belly dropped. *Not* go their separate ways. "Decide then? You don't need to live here for us to see each other."

"I want this position."

He nodded. "It's only been a year and a half since Daeryn and I arrived in the Farmlands looking for work, and I recall the feeling."

A team's lanterns came into sight, and they stopped in the dark. "You don't feel this is only my idea?" she asked.

"What? No, I returned to fetch you, hoping."

"*Before* you whistled?"

What was she getting at? Should he admit it? "Definitely before."

She broke into a broad smile. "Good." The smile faded, and she pressed her head again. "I sometimes want things so much I convince others it's the thing to do."

They'd just met, but she clearly felt the same about not keeping secrets. "I like you, too, but I have to tell you—"

Her bucket clunked to the ground, her arms wrapped him, and her lips demanded he kiss her. His bucket followed, and they clung together, tongues feverishly exploring.

He parted from her to whisper, "Don't worry. I want this, too. Maybe more."

She laughed. "Really?" Her hand slid to his rear and pulled him closer.

His breath caught. "Yes," he rasped.

"Hello?" someone called. "Rivley, are you there? We've a smudge pot out."

"Oh, lands!" Mary Clare flung herself back. "My sister."

He snatched up the buckets and strode forward, breathing deeply to clear his head. Mary Clare followed a few paces behind. After they refilled the pot, someone reported another sputtering.

Mary Clare returned from checking around the next tree. "A number of these are low and should be filled now."

She and Mary Beth frowned at each other, then at two growers. One female kicked at the ground. "We didn't want to be burned like Iris, so we kept the coal level low."

"Eyeball the measure," Mary Beth said. "The depth you'd plant squash seed."

The growers eyed Rivley instead. The same looks as when the females brought in their purposefully damaged spider machines. Sheepish. *Great Creator.* He knew what this was about. But accusing them aloud of doing this to get his attention sounded like putting on airs.

Mary Beth looked between them and him, then snapped her fingers. "See here. We are *not* compromising the cherry crop so new workers can get a closer look at the cute mechanic's assistant. These trees are our responsibility, not his."

Rivley's ears burned while the females scampered to fill their smudge pots.

"Mary Clare, check the other team's pots." Mary Beth jabbed a finger. "Tell them I sent you. I'll survey my rows, then talk to the other leader about this...situation." For the first time, she glanced at Rivley.

"Sorry to call them out in front of you, but I promise I'll put a stop to these antics. Could you bring more coal?"

"I'll bring the wheelbarrow." He handed the lantern to Mary Clare.

Mary Beth took the bucket from him, but as she marched away, Mary Clare caught her arm and leaned in to whisper.

Rivley turned and walked off. They'd agreed to keep things secret. So what could she be telling her sister?

CHAPTER SIX

Mary Clare didn't want to cross Mary Beth while she was this far up on her high horse. But she had to start out at Wellspring like she'd be here permanently, and that meant working *alongside* her sister. Mary Clare hissed, "Don't boss me around like we're at home."

"I-I'm sorry," Mary Beth whispered, her hands fisted as they walked on. "I forgot. I was just so angry to see them gawking at Rivley."

Anger wasn't what Mary Clare had felt, but she held her tongue. Thank goodness her sister had said what she couldn't, but now that she and Rivley had an agreement, she was sticking to it. She smacked Mary Beth's arm. "You sounded like Pa back there. No nonsense."

Mary Beth grunted. "I don't want this crop lost on my watch."

"Nope, and I'll help." She cut beneath the trees to find the other team.

Two growers had skimped on coal, causing four pots to go out. When Mary Clare's coal was gone, Sticks sent those folks back with her to fetch additional buckets from the greenhouse and shovel more coal. To her amusement, when they met Rivley returning with the wheelbarrow, they didn't meet his gaze.

Once back in the orchard, Mary Beth wasn't around, so Mary Clare answered questions, moving from smoky tree to smoky tree. The air brushing her cheeks felt warm, definitely above freezing.

Rivley found her with a team. "Mary Beth and Sticks have decided the growers will ferry coal and asked us to check the pot levels. Will you?"

Mary Beth is handing me time alone with Rivley? Then...she wasn't pursuing him. "Where should we start?"

Rivley smiled, and her head muddled with happiness. He'd meant it earlier when he said he'd hoped she'd come out with him.

Now, she needed to keep her wits about her—and her Knack warded.

RIVLEY LED THE WAY TO STICKS' rows in the smoky half darkness. After they'd walked out of earshot, he clasped Mary Clare's elbow. With no more than that, they were in each other's arms. The kiss was long and thorough. He was ready for more, but at a rustling of footsteps, he lay a finger across her lips.

"Someone is coming."

She cocked her head. "I don't hear anyone."

"Trust me. I do." He tapped his ear.

They strode beneath the tree and separated to check the pots, just before two growers ducked in from the other side.

After a brief conversation, they started down the row.

"My eyesight's excellent, but not in the dark." He held his breath.

"That's why you were a day guard," she said matter-of-factly.

His heart raced as he slid his hand into hers. This was going well. He'd tell her more about guarding at Rockbridge and lead up to the gildan. Yet, when they escaped into darkness, Mary Clare cuddled into him. Sneaking kisses between trees grew only more exciting. Even dropping hands when anyone approached, they became more familiar over the cold hours. When Mr. Hortens joined them for the coldest hour before dawn, Rivley had to bite his tongue. *Why now?* he wanted to scream. A good moment to tell her had never arrived.

Apart from him, Mary Clare stood with her arms crossed, a slight frown on her face. Weariness?

Of course it is. He probably looked ragged, as did everyone who'd been awake twenty hours. With no sleep, she'd work in the kitchen—an hour from now. Likely, she was regretting her decision to stay out versus focus on the kitchen position.

"You could go," he whispered when Mr. Hortens started rounds.

She shook her head and paced alongside him. While Hortens checked the buds with the team leaders, Rivley and Mary Clare showed the growers pots that needed to be topped off to burn until the temperature rose above freezing.

Under the last tree, Mr. Hortens turned to them. "Thank you for your assistance overnight. I'll put in a word with Mistress Gere, especially regarding you, Miss Pemberton," he said to Mary Clare. "You aren't on staff, according to Mary Beth, so I'm even more appreciative you shared your smudging skills."

"I was glad to," murmured Mary Clare.

"My growers can handle the remaining hours. If they can't, they won't be with us much longer. Find your beds and rest." Mr. Hortens returned to his growers.

Rivley eyed Mary Clare. "Shall I walk you home?" He didn't dare suggest going to his room. A 'cambire would think nothing of the invitation, but who knew how a Knack-bearer would react?

She sighed. "Mary Beth said I could nap in her room."

"To the bunkhouse, then." He offered her his arm, and she rested her hand on it.

With a pale orange glow painting the sky in calmness, he didn't want to part from Mary Clare. He nudged them toward the workshop, hoping they could have a private word in warmth.

Once he closed the doors, Mary Clare wrapped her arms around his neck and kissed him.

Better than talking.

They took up where they'd left off in the orchard. Again, her hands found their way inside his coat, then *she* was inside his coat and unfastening her coat buttons. He helped. It *was* getting warm. He let her take the lead. She'd proven herself alpha several times, and he didn't want to mess this up by assuming 'cambire norms.

Sweaters dropped, leaving flannel shirts, his trousers and her bib and brace encumbering them. Her forwardness surprised him, then it became right. As she pressed ever closer, the sweet taste of her lips sent him soaring.

"Rivley?" she breathed.

Huh? Talking now was the last thing he wanted to do, but he pulled himself back to ground. "Mary Clare, you're so sweet, and...*this* is wonderful."

Her palm pressed to his chest, as if she was putting a stop to their activities. "I really like you. Like we're meant to be together."

"I like you, too. It's been a while since I've said that to anyone. I feel myself with you, so...natural with you."

FEEL. The word shook Mary Clare from her happy cloud. While returning to the farmyard, she'd been careful and kept her Knack locked away. She checked it again. Walls still up. She grinned up at Rivley. This wasn't only her feeling this way. This was Rivley himself feeling he liked her.

His head dipped, and she answered with a kiss.

The kiss returned her to that lovely cloud. Her feelings enveloped her and carried her to *that* urge. It'd come and gone all night, and now it wouldn't go away.

Parting from his lips, she panted, "I want to... It's been a while, but I want to. So badly."

His lips came down on hers again, hard and pushing. She pushed back, and he returned with more, finally moving his hands where she wanted them to be.

Abruptly, he pulled away. "Are you sure?"

Her body was nearly erupting. "I...*yes*. Is there somewhere..."

With dawn shining through the shop windows, Rivley led her to the stack of canvas drop cloths and laid his coat across them. She dropped her coat beside his and unfastened the hooks on her bib and brace before sliding her hands around his waist and under his shirt again. *Ohhh—his muscular chest!* Smooth and sculpted, as fine as any she'd seen. She tugged his braces off his shoulders and laughed when he gasped as he noticed her bib and brace had puddled around her ankles.

On the makeshift bed, she giggled at his soft clicks. "What's this?" she asked, and when he stopped, she stroked his face. "Come on, it's sweet."

"It's avian." He shrugged. "It's a thing."

"A good thing?"

"Yep." He rolled them over and into a deep kiss. The clicking resounded through his chest, and she let the rhythm carry her, let his touch carry her.

"I love it," she gasped when she could, and then… "More. *Please.*"

Mary Clare woke, warm and content…and happy. Very happy. The fog in her head cleared at the same time she realized someone was breathing against her shoulder. Her eyes flashed open. Rivley.

He was watching her, lit in the pink of sunrays bursting across the sky as if sharing their celebration.

"You're not late," he whispered. "I would have woken you."

"I, uh, thanks."

His lips twitched into a shy smile. Beneath that, he felt happier than he was letting on. *Very happy.* She'd been asleep, so… Her breath rushed out. Of course her Knack was open.

"How long?"

"That you slept, or until Mrs. Betsy arrives in the kitchen?"

She rubbed her head, trying to bring up her Knack walls. The darned things stalled—because she didn't want to push away this feeling, though it was the right thing to do. "Both?"

He caught her hand. "Don't worry, please. You slept about fifteen minutes, and we have a half hour." A wave of doubt wafted off him. "Are you... Is everything all right?"

If I haven't ruined it by not telling him. She was fairly sure the walls hadn't gone down until they'd...so that made it fine. She took his face in her hands and kissed him. "Everything was perfect. I feel"—oh, why did she say that?—"lovely. You?"

He brushed her hair from her forehead. "I would say I'm perfect as well. Er, I mean...*feel* perfectly." He returned the kiss.

A half hour. They had time.

As soon as she had the thought, *the desire*, he pressed against her. Argh, she couldn't. Not now, not swaying him. Not without telling him. The brush of cold metal reminded her of something she hadn't stopped to question earlier. She tapped the odd jewelry on his belly. "What's this?"

He stilled, but the real tell was his abrupt loss of wanting. This was...something.

"It's from back home. A talisman of an obligation I carry."

She sat up. "You're mated to someone?"

"No." Feathers broke out through his hair, raising it as he also sat up. And apart. "I'd like to tell you more, but when we have time."

In the growing light of dawn, she glanced at the silver spiral, and... er... *Look at the silver spiral.* He made no attempt to hide himself or it. A dark stone graced the center, and the metal twisted *through* his skin. A piercing.

She reached for her coat. "I hope its story is as fascinating as that talisman."

RIVLEY RAKED fingers through his hair. She needed to understand why he couldn't have a life mate. In fact, the gildan laid down opposite rules. He touched her shoulder, now covered in her woolen coat. "I want to explain."

"We need to talk, but I should wash up and go to work," she muttered and pressed her head again.

"You can use our spray washroom. Daeryn won't return until after sunrise." He dragged on his trousers, pulled up his braces and helped gather her clothes. Mary Clare followed him upstairs, quickly showered, and he showed her out again. He watched her cross the farmyard from the workshop.

Once she disappeared inside, Rivley returned to his room. He couldn't stay here, not with Daeryn returning, sniffing and knowing what he'd been up to. Instead, Rivley dropped his trousers and shifted.

Why didn't I tell her beforehand?

AS THEY FIXED BREAKFAST, Mrs. Betsy asked about the night's work, and Mary Clare answered her questions and reassured her the cherry crop would be fine.

"That's wonderful, duck! I canna imagine spring without cherry pie." She exclaimed over jelly and other cherry recipes, blessing the workers and Mary Clare for pitching in.

Mrs. Betsy's talk became task directions, giving Mary Clare time to speculate on Rivley's mysterious obligation. Would it have been better to have known about it before they... Would knowing have changed anything?

Ha. Not after kissing him. By then, she'd known how much she liked him. She still liked him. She'd listen to his story and hope he'd listen to hers.

She swallowed. *And accept my Knack.*

CHAPTER SEVEN

S oaring over the farm fields didn't ease Rivley's worry, but he caught two mice, so he didn't need to go inside for breakfast. By lunch, he'd worked up the nerve, but Mary Clare wasn't there.

He reviewed everything they'd said, every action he'd taken and her responses. Had she decided not to pursue the position here?

After an anxious afternoon of addressing the inventory—repeatedly losing focus and dropping things—he didn't want to attend dinner. In his present state, he'd make a fool of himself staring at her. But worse, what if she still wasn't there?

He lingered in the workshop until finally he had to know.

Mary Clare was clearing the platters when he arrived. Their gazes met. Shadows surrounded her tired eyes. She set down several dishes and nodded to a nearby chair. Then she disappeared. Not speaking—was she angry? The clink of dishes echoed around him. The room emptied. Each time she returned to collect the dirty dish tray, he scanned her face for clues, but she didn't meet his gaze again.

She was making sure he ate, leaving the food platters. That meant something, right?

The *thump* of boots approached, Wellspring's owner entering from her office across the hall. The tall woman still wore her split trouser-skirt and wellies, brown hair pinned in a roll.

"Still awake?" Mistress Gere asked gently. "I hope you had a nap after your work last night."

Holding his tea, Rivley nodded, though sleep hadn't come to his busy mind.

Smiling, she perched on an adjacent chair. "Mr. Hortens reviewed the night with his team leaders. They agreed the effort wouldn't have been successful without your hard work. I'll let Master Brightwell know he has a fine apprentice, and we'll increase your wages."

"You don't need to, ma'am."

"You have more responsibility than you did under Famil with the guards. We also discussed the...*workload* while Master Brightwell is away. You have the authority to decide which machines need to be in the shop."

Well, that was a relief. "Thank you, ma'am. And for the raise."

Saying good night, Mistress Gere continued to the kitchen. The clink of dishes stopped. A murmured conversation reached him. Then a squeal erupted, cut off quickly, but he recognized Mary Clare's excited voice.

He stood. He should leave. Talk to her later. Instead, he stepped closer to the fire so he wouldn't hear the conversation. Minutes later, Mistress Gere returned to her office.

Mary Clare rushed in. "Rivley. I'll be done in thirty minutes. See you then?"

He'd barely nodded when she picked up two platters and whirled away. She seemed more excited than upset. Had Mistress Gere paid her for last night's hours? They'd promised to talk, but a bad feeling about revealing his gildan swirled in his gut.

———

MARY CLARE WASHED DISHES, with Mrs. Betsy clucking beside her.

"Go home, duck. You need sleep."

But she wasn't going straight home, so it wasn't right to leave the dishes. Afterward, she hurried into her coat, said a quick good-bye and rushed out the door.

A few workers crossed the dusky farmyard, and a tall figure separated himself from the spreading tree in the center. She veered toward Rivley, with his pretty hair, freckled cheeks and broad shoulders. *Such a looker!* She pinched herself and gave a come-on wave. They needed somewhere private to talk.

He paced beside her, following along the southeast field. A stone wall separated the Collective from a neighboring pasture, mounted with wooden steps that she and her sisters used to go back and forth.

Arriving, she checked her wards again. All up. She'd had a momentary falter when Mistress Gere had given her the news, but she'd recovered. Facing Rivley, she leaned against the stile and clasped her hands. She'd never given the dangerous truth about her Knack to anyone outside the family.

"I have to—*want to*—tell you something about me that cannot be repeated to anyone."

He cocked his head, his eyes darting. "No one is nearby. Your secrets are safe with me, but you don't need to tell me anything you don't want to."

"That's the problem. If I want to continue seeing you, you need to know. And I'd like to see you more, Rivley."

He nodded.

Right, good. So now to tell him. She'd practiced the wording while mixing sauces and scraping bowls. *I have a Knack that sways people's emotions, and I likely swayed yours.* Yet, now those words wouldn't come out. "How are you feeling about us?" she blurted. "Honestly."

He rolled his eyes skyward, searching. "It's as if I've seen a mouse, and I'm hungry, but perhaps it's not my mouse. And if I catch the mouse, I still can't have it right now and maybe not for a long time. I'm not sure if I should dive down or not."

What? She stared at him.

He shrugged. "Well, you asked. The human response is probably 'unsure.' I'd like to court you, but I'm not certain you'll want to when I tell you my...situation."

She nodded knowingly. "I had the same thought about *my* situation. You may not wish to continue seeing me, because asking how someone is feeling is unnecessary for me." *It's now or never.* "I must lock away my Knack whenever I'm in public. Otherwise, it tells me folks' emotions. But when I sleep, or at private times"—she sideglanced to judge if he was catching on—"my wards can slip."

His gaze narrowed, his eyebrows becoming more pronounced. "So...you knew I had an interest in you before we even talked?"

"No, I was working. I had my wards up. But after we'd talked more and when we kissed the first time, they slipped." She shrugged. "Folks only kiss someone they like, so that wasn't secret, but...my Knack sends the feelings both ways. You might have noticed I was excited."

"I was excited," he said slowly. "Was that because of you?"

She swallowed. "That's why I asked if you'd hoped I'd join you *before* you came close to me. I wanted to make sure you liked me because it was your idea, not because I liked you."

He frowned.

"I don't do it intentionally," she said. "Most of the time, I can keep it in check, but your kiss was...rather nice. *Everything* was rather nice."

"I could tell. A fellow likes to have his *everything* appreciated." He grinned shyly.

Mary Clare wrung her hands. "I don't think you understand." She took a breath. "My Knack likely swayed your emotions."

"I understand."

So... He didn't *seem* angry. "You're still willing to see me?"

He crossed his arms. "How would I know you're influencing me?"

"It only happens if you're near me, three feet or less. I feel you and you feel me." She gestured between them. "The stronger emotion overwhelms the other. You'll come to know it's not you, and when you're away from me, the feeling disappears." She swallowed. "You learn to assess it. I had to."

His eyes turned a deep amber, and he stared into the distance, his features a mask.

Aw, damn it. He was upset. "I'm sorry," she whispered. "I-I'd appreciate it if you keep your word and not tell anyone." She mounted the steps to leave.

He caught her elbow. "Not all of the excitement came from you. I felt it away from you. Although I've never heard of such a thing."

She shrugged. "Who would tell anyone?"

"In Blighted Basin, no one is certain what Knacks are possible." He sighed. "I need to think about it, and you should hear my situation." His mouth crooked into a wry smile.

A bit of weight lifted from her shoulders. Nothing could be as bad as her Knack.

———

RIVLEY SWIPED his hand over his hair, flattening the feathers sticking through. Being with Mary Clare meant he'd have to be on his guard. His gaze roved over her clear green eyes, sweet lips and farther down. He suppressed a sigh. Yesterday had been the first he'd felt any connection to anyone since the accident.

Yet, had those been *his* feelings?

Itchy shifting feathers crowned his scalp. He pressed them again, weighing his choices. He didn't have any choice if he stopped now.

"Some of the gildan isn't my tale to tell, but my part is clear. Daeryn and I share the obligation, lessons to resolve what went wrong on our team when a teammate died. As the alpha and beta of the team, we were responsible."

"I'm sorry for your loss."

He sighed. "Thank you. The point is, until the gildan is satisfied, we're banned from partaking in our traditional ceremonies."

"Some remote shires hold to old Basin traditions more than folks in the Farmland villages. I respect your beliefs," she said gently, "but you aren't in Rockbridge, so does it still matter?"

Rivley tapped his belly. "It's a blood-bound obligation. I can't take a life mate."

"Are you talking about us?" Her voice was low, incredulous.

"Because I've known you a mere day. I'm interested in *courting*. Any future will be based on that."

The twitching urge to shift fell away. She wanted to...but what exactly did courting entail here and for a human? "Right, I'm interested in courting. But it's fair you know where I stand." He cleared his throat. "Daeryn may take years to address the lessons."

Mary Clare crossed her arms and frowned.

He fought the beta instinct to step back. But he was no longer a beta. He scoffed at himself—unfortunately aloud.

"What?" she huffed. "You can't start when *you* decide to resolve this bond?"

His shoulders stiffened. He couldn't back down from this alpha female. If they were to have balance in this relationship, he had to make his priorities clear. "That is between Daeryn and me. Do you seriously want to insert yourself? Because he doesn't favor *courting* humans."

Her gaze dropped to the ground. After a moment, she whispered, "You're right. It's not my business. You have to do what you feel is right for you."

He took a step closer. "Exactly. I left my home shire. I've taken a position folks back home have never heard of. I want to court a human when I'd never met one before coming to the Farmlands. Like me, you go after what you want. You're confident and skilled and not afraid to show it. I think we could get along if we have an understanding...about your situation and mine. What do you say? Should we give this a try?"

Mary Clare looked up at him, her hands now clasped behind her back. "I've gone after what I wanted. I learned to control my Knack so I could work outside the family, and now I've achieved that independence. Mistress Gere and Mrs. Betsy offered me the kitchen assistant position."

"Ho!" He grasped her shoulder, about to hug her...then realized they hadn't come to an agreement. But at her smile, he didn't draw back his hand.

"It was thanks to you asking me to help. They liked how I pitched in when I wasn't officially staff. Mrs. Betsy and I work well together, so Mistress Gere saw no reason to wait."

Her eyes were sparkling, but Rivley felt no excitement drifting from her.

"Tomorrow, I'll move into the bunkhouse, and I want you as a part of my new life."

Yes!

She put up a finger. "Yet, I can tell that if we're together, I'll immediately be shunned by jealous growers."

"You won't..." he started. "Ah, perhaps."

"You *are* quite the looker," she whispered.

"You're beautiful." He brushed a curl from her forehead.

"Maybe we could quietly court while we get to know each other?"

"Do you mean step back from"—he waved his hand between them—"activities like this morning's?"

She laughed. "Land's sake, you're so discreet! Not have sex? I don't want to stop—unless you want to?"

"Furthest thing from my mind." He gave a wry grin and tugged her closer.

Mary Clare looped her arms around his neck and met his kiss with a gentleness that lasted a wingbeat before it turned hungry.

Once again, Rivley felt the soaring sensation of being carried into the clouds. "I could get used to knowing how excited you are."

"Oops," she whispered against his lips. "Let me know if you spot your mouse."

Because the feeling was just right, he whispered back, "I think I have."

MARY CLARE, Rivley and other characters living at Wellspring Collective are part of *The Luminated Threads* series. Read more in *The Unraveling, Volume One.*

ABOUT THE AUTHOR

Passionate about nature since she was young, Laurel Wanrow writes stories about living close to the land, falling in love, and the magic in both. She's the author of *The Luminated Threads* series, a Victorian historical fantasy mixing witches and shapeshifters, and *The Windborne*, a nature-focused YA cozy fantasy series. When not writing, she loves to camp, hike, garden with native plants and dream about building out a camper van to explore North America. Join her newsletter at **http://laurelwanrow.com/NewsSignup** or connect through her website: **www.laurelwanrow.com**

THANK YOU

We hope you have enjoyed this collection of love stories. As writers, we seek to entertain, spark curiosity, arouse passion, and perhaps send you scurrying to find more of our work, and we hope our individual stories in this collection have done that and more. Through this particular book, however, we are also working to raise money to support the continuing efforts of <u>World Central Kitchen</u>, an organization that is feeding the hungry and displaced throughout the world. Your purchase of *Love At Dawn* has helped in that goal, and we thank you.

Made in the USA
Middletown, DE
28 March 2023